True Colours

Mandy Lee

Copyright

Acknowledgements

Huge thanks to Jackie Bates for her wonderful editing skills, and to my Beta readers.

I'd like to dedicate this book to my sister, Sarah, who's never been vile to me in her entire life!

Chapter One

Southwark is darkening. Clouds thicken. The waters of the Thames deepen in colour: charcoal grey, indigo, raw umber, olive green, black. Definition disappears from the cathedral, the Shard, the office blocks. Consumed by the storm, the buildings are barely recognisable now, and I'm spellbound by the colours, the shapes, the light and the shadows. Caught in a trance, I'm not thinking, just painting.

For the first time in hours, I stand back from the canvas and take it all in: the stormy skies, the snarling mass of water, and there, right in the middle of it all, fifteen storeys of darkened glass reflecting the seething weather: the headquarters of Fosters Construction. Exhausted, I slump onto the end of the bed, sitting perfectly still, clutching the paintbrush, and survey the end result. It's not my usual style; no simple landscape. Instead, this is a landscape of pure emotion. Perhaps I should send it to him as a gift, a message. This is what you've done to me with your secrets and lies, Mr Foster. You see, if there's one thing I don't put up with, it's deception. I don't stomach it and I don't tolerate it. I simply defend myself against it. Lowering my head, I tear my gaze away from the scene and I feel it again: an ache deep in my chest. It's been with me all night and no matter what I do, no matter how I distract myself, it just won't go away.

'Hey.'

I turn and find Lucy in the doorway.

'How are you this morning?'

If she wants an honest answer to that, she doesn't have to look far. It's right in front of her, propped up on the easel.

'Fine.'

'Oh, come off it.'

1

Irritation snaps into life.

'What do you want to hear?' I demand, as if there's any need to ask. I know exactly what Lucy wants to hear. She wants me to break down in front of her, to sob, release the anger and admit that I've made the wrong decision. Well, she's getting none of that, because I'm a fortress. Unbreakable.

'You haven't said anything,' she forges on, apparently oblivious to my resolve. 'You haven't cried. It's not normal.'

'It's normal for me.'

'It's not healthy.'

Dropping the paintbrush onto the palette, I run my fingers through my hair, remembering too late that my hands are smeared with oil paint.

'What time is it?' I ask.

'Just after seven. You've been at it all night.'

I flex my shoulders. My muscles seem to have stiffened. 'And what time did we get back here?'

'I don't know.' She shrugs, and then inches her way into the room, carefully. 'Ten o'clock, maybe. You've been painting ever since.'

She inches further. Glancing uncertainly at me, and then at the picture, she comes to a halt. Her eyes widen, her lips part company, and I'm curious about what's going on inside that brain of hers. Perhaps it's shock. After all, I've never painted anything like this before.

'I'm worried about you,' she remarks absently.

'Don't be.' I wipe my hands on my shorts. 'I just needed to finish it.'

'It's different. Not your usual style.'

'You don't like it?'

'I ...' She falters. 'It's very ... angry.'

'I wonder why.' I stand up. 'You *don't* like it then?'

She sidles round the bed, positions herself in front of the easel and examines the canvas.

'I do,' she murmurs at last. 'It's ... brilliant.'

I glare at her, wondering if I should inform her that just because I've been shat on by a man, there's really no need to mollycoddle me.

'You don't mean that.'

'Actually, I do. We should exhibit this at Slaters.'

She waves a hand at the storm clouds and I shake my head. That's a definite no-no. Seeing my work displayed in the gallery was certainly a buzz, only to be topped by discovering my painting had been sold, even when I found out that Dan was the buyer. I could get

2

used to that kind of thrill, but not with this picture. This one is far too personal.

'It's not for sale.'

I roll my head to one side and then the other, let out a huge yawn and stare at my paint-smothered hands. I really should clean up now and maybe try to get some sleep, but I already know that won't be easy. Painting kept the thoughts at bay and now that I've finished, I know exactly what I'm in for: an onslaught of emotions. For the past nine hours, they've been lurking in the gloom, waiting to take their chance. It's only a matter of time before they bring me to my knees.

'I'm making breakfast,' Lucy announces. 'Clean up and join me. That's an order.'

Backing out of the room, she closes the door, leaving me alone with the shadows ... and they're already beginning to stir. Keep busy, I tell myself. Just keep busy and they won't bother you. Stripping out of my shorts and T-shirt, I throw them into a corner, take myself off to the bathroom and fill the tub.

As soon as I slip into the water, my muscles relax. Listening to the sound of raindrops against the window pane, I close my eyes. And then it begins. The shadows move and I'm ambushed by memories, sensations rather than images: the softness of his lips, the feel of his hands on my skin, his taste, his smell. Trying to drown it all out, I dunk my head under the water.

'Shit,' I grumble, coming back to the surface and reaching the conclusion that I've been an idiot. I've lowered my defences just long enough to let a man get to me, and I should never have done that because right from the word 'go', I always suspected he'd break my heart. I just never thought it would happen like this. Staring at the soap, I do my best to empty my brain, but now it seems intent on reminding me of yesterday: the time spent curled up in a ball on my parents' bed, Lucy sitting by my side while the storm passed overhead; my refusal to move, even when the thunder had receded; the concerned voices finally coaxing me downstairs, out into Clive's car; the silent journey home to Camden.

'Shit, shit, shit.'

This is no good. No good at all. Time for more action. Once I'm out of the bath, I put on a fresh T-shirt, a pair of combats and examine myself in the mirror. God, I look awful, what with the bags under my eyes and the pallid skin and the hair that's sticking out in all directions like a pile of straw. Tugging a brush through it, I curse my locks, deciding that a visit to the hairdressers is well overdue. And then I remember that I'm practically broke. Okay, so there'll be a payout for my stint at Fosters, but three weeks as a sort-of-secretary doesn't amount to much. And then there's the money for the painting of the woods: three thousand pounds which I'll never accept. As soon as I get the cheque, I'll rip it up ... and he can keep the bloody picture.

I'm about to put my hair into a pony tail when I falter. Quite inevitably, one thought has slammed into another. And now his words are nudging into my brain. *It's too important. One day you'll understand:* his explanation for why he couldn't let the painting go to anyone else. So, was he always planning to tell me in his own time? Did events simply overtake him? I'm wavering now, and that's not good. Fortress Scotton must stay intact. Keep those memories at bay, woman, because if you don't, they'll be breaking down the walls, brick by brick, and then you'll be showing up on his doorstep filled to the brim with forgiveness and desperate for a good seeing to.

Still gazing into the mirror, I catch sight of the necklace, a Tiffany one-off owned by his mother. I touch it, sensing that ache again. My brain's saying one thing, my body another, but I need to listen to my brain. Logic tells me to cut and run because the man I fell in love with was nothing but an illusion. He's deceived me once, and he'll do it again. Reaching up, I unclasp the necklace and pull it away, slowly, carefully, reminding myself that it's a priceless work of art. Holding it in my palm, I set about searching for something to hide it away in. I open a drawer in the dressing table, choose an old earring box, empty out the earrings and store the necklace safely inside. I'll hand it over to Clive. And he can deliver it back to Dan.

With a renewed sense of resolve and a building headache, I make my way to the kitchen and find Lucy sitting at the rickety table, gazing at a huge plateful of toast.

'I've made this for both of us. You need to eat.'

'I'm not hungry. I'll just have tea.'

She picks up a slice of toast, takes a bite and chews thoughtfully.

'Clivey's coming over later.'

Wonderful. That's all I need.

'I don't want to talk to him.'

'You don't have to. He wants to take me out, and he's bringing your handbag back.'

I gaze around the kitchen, stunned that I haven't noticed before, but strangely enough, my handbag and all its contents have been the last thing on my mind.

'You left it in Dan's car yesterday.'

4

At the mention of his name, my mouth dries up and my heartbeat doubles in pace.

'Oh.'

'It's got your mobile in it. Your mum's been trying to contact you all morning. I texted her, told her not to worry. Do you want to call her from my phone?'

'Not right now. She'll only tell me to get back on my bike.'

'Good advice.'

'Did Clive stay the night?' I ask, opening a random cupboard for no apparent reason. I'm not exactly sure what I'm looking for.

'No. He stayed at Dan's.'

I pick up the kettle, decide there's enough water, and flick it on.

'He's in pieces.'

She's staring at me now, as if I'm some sort of dangerous dog. Her eyebrows climb a little, then settle into a frown. Without taking her eyes off me, she dives in for another mouthful of toast.

'Dan, that is.' Watching me closely, she waits for a reaction, but I'm being tough this morning. I'm giving her nothing.

'Aren't you bothered?' she asks.

I don't answer because I can't. Right now, I'm sleep-deprived and nothing sensible is going to come out of my mouth. The contents of my head are like the contents of my drawers: everything slung in together, with no rhyme and definitely no reason. Instead, I simply shrug.

'Maya, say something.'

I shrug again. Turning away, I grip the worktop and look down at a gathering of dirty mugs in the sink.

'You should talk about it,' she insists.

'No I shouldn't.'

Silence lingers in the room, broken only by the clinking of mugs as I remove them from the bowl and lay them out on the counter top. Turning on the tap, I squeeze too much washing up liquid into the mix and wonder what the hell I'm doing.

'It might help,' Lucy says at last, her voice barely making an imprint on the sound of running water.

I send her a look of death. She's doing exactly the wrong thing here, blundering into all the wrong places, pressing all the wrong buttons, and now I'm beginning to seethe.

'How can it help?' I demand. 'Can it change the facts?'

'No. But ...'

Jesus, she's not giving up, is she? Seriously, the woman must have a death wish. After all these years, she should know by now that you never, ever push it with a sleep-deprived Maya Scotton.

'But what, Lucy?' I snarl. 'These are the facts. He grew up on the same road as me, walked the same streets, went to the same school. He knew my sister and he never mentioned any of this, not once.'

For a second or two, Lucy seems to shrivel under the weight of my vitriol, but she recovers quickly.

'Is that any surprise, considering what Sara did to him?'

'Are you on his side now? You're supposed to be my friend.'

'I am your friend.' She grimaces. 'Although at the minute, I'm not entirely sure why. And there are no sides. I'm trying to make you see sense.'

'I am seeing sense.'

'You're seeing red.'

We exchange glares: long, evil, bitch-slapping glares.

'He deceived me. He let me believe he was someone else. And worse than that, the only reason he ever wanted to meet me in the first place was because of my sister.'

'It didn't last.'

'Oh, fuck off.'

'Bubbles.'

'What?'

'Bubbles.'

She motions towards the sink. I look back to find the bowl overflowing, a mountain of soap suds rising upwards and outwards, almost level with my chest.

'Shit.' I scrabble to turn off the tap, and survey the suds. I'm useless. I can't even wash the pots without some sort of foam disaster. Whatever made me think a relationship could go smoothly? Opening the window, I scoop up a handful of bubbles and waft them outside.

'You know what you're doing, don't you?' Lucy asks.

'Throwing fucking soap bubbles out of the fucking window.' I gather another mound.

'No. You're doing what you always do. You're blocking it all out.'

'Whatever.' I blow the suds into the rain. I'm about to dig in for a third handful when I feel a touch against my arm.

'Sit down.'

Drawing me away from the sink, she gently encourages me to take a seat.

'You need tea. Tea makes everything better. And then you need sleep.'

In a grump, I watch as Lucy sets about washing the mugs and making tea.

'Denial isn't a good thing.' Placing two mugs on the table, she lowers herself onto a chair. 'You need to work things through, talk about them, get them out of your system. If you don't, you'll only end up with constipation.'

I let out a sigh.

'Emotional constipation,' she explains seriously.

Oh great, she's about to give me a dose of magazine psychobabble.

'You did exactly the same thing with Boyd. You never talked about him.'

I take a sip of tea, wondering why on Earth she's bringing that up now. Just thinking about that man brings up the bile in my throat, never mind talking about him. Putting my mug down, I close my eyes, fighting off the flashbacks to the basement at Slaters: the breath stinking of alcohol, the lecherous eyes, the hands on me, the mouth smothering mine.

'And Tom.'

I bristle.

'He dumped me. That's it. Neither of them deserve to be talked about.'

'Right. So Boyd abuses you and you deal with it by running straight into Tom's arms, convinced that he's going to make everything alright, only Tom doesn't make it all alright at all. He dumps you. And how do you deal with that? By shagging anything with a pulse.'

'Stop it.'

'And how did all that work for you then?'

'Just fine.'

'Really?' Her face rumples with disbelief. 'And then you find this one amazing man, the most amazing man you're ever likely to meet in your entire life, a man who falls for you hook, line and sinker.' She pauses, and I know that she's about to deliver her punchline. 'And then you run at the first hurdle.'

I'd like to remind my flatmate that this isn't exactly the first hurdle. In fact, according to my fuddled calculations, it's probably about the third.

'And why is that?' Lucy demands, pointing a finger at me. 'I'll tell you,' she goes on before I can even register the question. 'It's

7

because you're screwed up, that's why. Because you never deal with anything. You just run away and hide.'

I stare out of the window. Lucy's words scratch at the outside of my skull, begging to be let in, pleading to be acknowledged, but I'm having none of it.

'You're emotionally constipated, Maya. You never talk about the things that really matter.'

'That's my decision, and it would be great if my best friend could honour it.'

'You're making a huge mistake.'

I glance at the doorway. Perhaps I should just slink off back to my bedroom, simply close the door on the rest of the day. And perhaps I should do it quickly because I can hear Lucy breathing now, big deep breaths, in and out, and I know she's building up to something else.

'Clive says he's in love with you.'

My heartbeat accelerates, blood pumps and suddenly, I'm feeling dizzy. I close my eyes and I'm back outside my parents' house in Limmingham, and Dan's in front of me, his face twisted with anguish. She knows exactly where to hit me. She's got me cracking now … and I can't crack.

'He's not in love with me, Lucy. He doesn't know the meaning of the word.'

'Well, perhaps he's learning.'

I open my eyes again. I seem to be looking straight at Lucy's face, only she's a blur, and that can only mean one thing. I'm crying.

'You've had a shock,' she says quietly. 'I understand that. And now you're dealing with it the same way you deal with everything: sling up the defences and avoid the issues.'

'Just leave it, please.'

'He deceived you, and I get why you're angry, but that's not the real problem, is it?'

'As far as I'm concerned, it is.'

She shakes her head. 'Wrong.'

'So what is the real problem, Luce? Get on with it. I'm sure you're dying to tell me.'

'You're acting like you're determined to move on but …'

'But what?'

She takes in a breath before she flings her answer at me.

'You're deceiving yourself.'

Chapter Two

I'm dreaming. This isn't real. I'm back in Limmingham, back in my place of sanctuary. These are my woods ... and yet they're not. For a start, the branches are too bulky, knotting overhead like giant fists, almost blocking out the light. I blink, once, twice, aware that there's something in the shadows. Something or someone, hovering, watching and waiting. Sensing a prickle, I know that whatever or whoever it is, they're determined to destroy me. My mouth dries up as I realise this is no sanctuary at all. I need to get out of here. I need to run. I try to move but my legs are weighted by fear. I force out a scream, a silent, choking scream for help, but there's no one here to save me. And then I call a name. It comes out mangled, but I know who I'm calling.

I'm calling for Dan.

The tree trunks disintegrate, darkness scatters and with a shiver, I open my eyes. I'm back in reality, lying on top of crumpled sheets, listening to the steady hush of raindrops and staring at a cobweb on the ceiling. I will my body to relax. Slow it down, I tell myself. Control the breathing, control the heartbeat. There's no need to panic. It was just a dream. It meant nothing.

At last, I raise my head and glance at the clock. It's nearly six and my stomach's rumbling. Finally, I'm hungry. On my way to the kitchen, I stop off at the lounge door. It's open: so that Lucy can keep an eye on me, I'm sure. Poking my head around the door, I find her splayed out on the sofa, watching a film.

'I'm making fish finger sandwiches,' I inform her. 'Want any?'

She shakes her head. 'I've had beans on toast.'

'What's on?'

'*Pretty Woman.*'

I stare at the screen: Richard Gere and Julia Roberts on a piano, shagging their way towards a perfect, romantic ending.

'Oh, I'm sorry, Maya.' Lucy sits up quickly, her face plastered with worry. 'I didn't think.'

I shrug, determined to be apathetic about the whole thing.

'That's fine. Just because I've been shafted, it doesn't mean you can't watch slushy films.'

Before she can argue that I didn't get shafted, I close the door. I'm not in the mood for further discussion and anyway, in spite of all my bravado, I'm not entirely sure I can deal with romantic slush at the minute. Back in the kitchen, I take a box of fish fingers out of the freezer and lay a handful under the grill, buttering a couple of slices of bread while they brown, and discovering a cheap bottle of white wine on the top shelf of the fridge. I notice two glasses laid ready on the table, and even though the wine's probably part of Lucy's preparations for Clive's visit, I'm sure she won't mind if I help myself. Pouring a glassful, I turn the fish fingers and set about musing over the dream, replaying each and every part of it. I must be on the third repeat when the smell of burning tickles my nose.

'Bugger.'

Rescuing the fish fingers before they're thoroughly singed, I lay them out on the bread.

'You need a proper meal,' Lucy announces from the doorway. She's changed into one of her flowery summer dresses. There's no make-up yet and her hair's a mess.

'This is a proper meal.' I pick up a sandwich and take a bite, cursing myself for diving straight in: the fish fingers are superheated. 'When's Clive getting here?'

'Any minute now.'

'With my handbag?'

'Of course.'

Right on cue, the doorbell chimes. While Lucy gets on with the business of letting Clive in, I open up the bread, squirt ketchup all over my fish fingers, and close the sandwich again.

'That looks interesting.'

And that's not Clive's voice. My eyes travel up from my gourmet meal and meet the perfectly made-up face of Lily Babbage. What's she doing here? That's the first question that springs to mind, shortly before I start wondering why she's got a pair of Ray-Bans resting on top of her perfectly sleek brunette hair-do. It's still raining, and I'm pretty sure the sun hasn't shown itself all day. There's just no need for it. I take in the rest of her outfit: a pair of designer jeans matched with some Boho Chic flouncy white top, and

I'm betting that's a Louis Vuitton handbag dangling from her skinny arm.

'Can you spare me a few minutes?' The perfectly made-up face gives me a smile.

Can I? Should I?

'I ... er ...'

I watch in disbelief as without waiting for an answer, she draws out the spare chair, lowers herself gracefully, positions her ridiculously expensive handbag on the floor and eyes up my plate.

'What on Earth are you eating?'

'Fish finger sandwiches.'

'Oooh.' She purses her lips. 'Don't let me stop you.'

'You won't.'

And how dare you look down your nose at my completely adequate evening meal, I'd like to add. I bet you've never once touched a fish finger sandwich in your charmed little life ... maybe a caviar sandwich at a push.

'You've been painting.'

'How do you know?'

'Paint in your hair. Dan said you're a messy pup. He's not wrong.'

'Why are you here?'

She scans the table top, taking in the bottle of ketchup, the cheap wine, the spare glass.

'May I?'

She points at the bottle. I nod.

'Clive told me what happened.' She pours herself a glassful of our local supermarket's finest plonk. 'I must say, I was shocked Dan hadn't told you the truth. I went over to see him this afternoon.'

'Good for you.' I'm bristling now, premium blue ribbon bristling. If he thinks he can send in his friends to smooth the way, then he's got another think coming. 'And I suppose he's asked you to talk to me.'

She takes a sip of wine. Leaving a print of deep red lipstick around the rim of the glass, she swallows, recoils.

'He doesn't know I'm here. And if he did, he'd go mad.' Another uncertain sip. She pulls an I-think-I've-just-swallowed-drain-cleaner type of face, and places the glass back on the table. 'He doesn't like people meddling.'

'Well, don't meddle then. How did you find out where I live?'

I pick up a sandwich, take a huge bite and set about chewing my way through a mouthful of overcooked fish.

'Clive.'

She stares at me, focussing on my mouth, and I begin to feel uneasy. Shit. She's currently into women. Please don't tell me she's moving in on me.

'You don't like me, do you, Maya?'

I swallow a lump of bread. 'No,' I admit. 'Not really.'

'And why's that?'

I hazard a guess. 'Women's intuition?'

'I hope you don't mind me saying this, but I think your women's intuition might be malfunctioning.'

'It's in perfect working order, thank you.'

'But you've got me all wrong.' She holds me with her gaze. 'Gut reaction isn't always the right way to go.'

Okay, so she might have a point. After all, the first time I ever laid eyes on the woman, I jumped to the massively wrong conclusion that she was a madam, or a kinky dominatrix, or both.

'You were jealous of me.' A smile creeps across her crimson lips. 'When we last met, I could smell it. Jealousy.'

'Why would I be jealous of you?'

'Oh, I don't know. Maybe it's because you thought I was fucking Dan.'

'Don't be ridiculous.'

I shrug, feigning indifference, and take another bite of my sandwich, but the truth is she's got it right. When I first saw her in Dan's office, the green-eyed monster went on the rampage. But who could blame me?

'Go on, Maya.'

'Go on what?'

'Ask the question.'

'What question?'

'You know. The one you want to ask.' She leans forwards, her tiny breasts forming the slightest hint of a cleavage. 'You want to know if I've ever fucked him.'

My mouth opens. I clamp it shut again, just in time to prevent a lump of fish from falling onto the table. What the hell is she playing at now?

'Have you?' I whisper.

And what the hell is my brain playing at? That shouldn't have happened. I've opted for the whole nonchalant bitch routine, and that was definitely the wrong way to go about it.

She watches me a little, and then she answers.

'Yes.'

And that does it. My face launches into chaos. Mouth. Eyes. Eyebrows. They're all over the place.

'But ...'

'Ha! You didn't expect that, did you?' She waves a finger, triumphantly.

No, I certainly didn't. And now I'm wondering why she felt the need to land this on my plate. After all, it's of no concern to me: I'm done with the man.

'We were sixteen,' she explains, obviously determined to give me the details. 'I popped his cherry. We might as well get it all out into the open.' She picks up the glass again, slugs back the remainder of the wine and cringes. 'One time only. Drunk as a skunk at a party. Teenage fumbling. Very embarrassing. We never bothered again.' She slips the glass back onto the table. 'Now,' she goes on, 'the very fact that you needed to know tells me a lot.'

'Does it?'

'Oh yes. And your reaction just told me a whole lot more.'

'Really?'

She laughs. 'Really. It tells me that you're still jealous. You're not finished with him, are you? Not by a long stretch.'

Picking up the bottle, she pours another glass of wine.

'And you're deluded.' I put down my sandwich. Suddenly, I'm not hungry any more. 'Like I said, it's over.'

'I don't think so.'

I examine her for a while, this woman who looks for all the world like a high class prostitute.

'Why are you so keen for us to get back together?' I demand.

Her eyes gleam.

'Because he's changed, and I like it. I like the new Dan. He's more like the old Dan I used to know.'

The old Dan? I thought he'd been an arrogant, womanising shit for most of his life. I'm looking confused now. I'm pretty sure of it. And I'm absolutely certain that Lily's noticed. Her smile has widened.

'You know, when he first appeared in my world, he was only twelve,' she explains. 'A lovely boy. Very sweet, very kind ... a little lost.' She points at the second sandwich. 'May I?'

'Go ahead.'

Picking up the sandwich, she turns it in her hands, narrowing her eyes at a blob of ketchup as it oozes from the side. At last, she seems to make a decision, possibly to take her life into her own hands, and takes a dainty bite. Rolling her perfectly oval eyes, she chews.

'Mmm. This is really good. Where did you get the fish?'

'Local supermarket. Freezer aisle.'

She chews some more, probably for a good minute or so before she finally swallows. No wonder she looks like a stick insect, eating like that. It must take at least three hours to down a regular meal.

'Aren't you going to say any more?' I demand.

'Do you want to know more?'

I'm fighting the urge and not doing a very good job of it. I nod, meekly, and still holding the sandwich, she begins her story.

'My parents knew John and Lydia Foster. When I was younger, we were always at their house. Clive's family too. That's where we all met.' The blob of ketchup falls from the sandwich onto the table top. 'Dan wouldn't say boo to a goose to begin with, but I liked him. We used to play in the orchard, climb trees, go exploring in the fields, that sort of thing.' She leans forwards, lowering her voice to a conspiratorial whisper. 'His first kiss.' She puckers her lips and grins mischievously. 'He started at the same school as me and Clive. They hit it off straight away. Thick as thieves.' She takes another tiny mouthful of the sandwich, swallowing quickly before she proceeds. 'The older Dan got, the better looking he became, but he never seemed to understand that. By the time we were in sixth form, he was already a stunner.'

She inspects the sandwich again, eyeing up the next place for a bite, but I'm not prepared to wait.

'Just leave the bloody sandwich,' I grumble. 'Get on with your story.'

'Okay, so all the girls were after him, including me. Hardly anybody had any luck.'

You did though, my brain fires out.

'He had a couple of girlfriends. Nothing major. He was more focussed on his studies than anything else. He worked hard and he was incredibly bright, and still very sweet. I think that was what was so charming about him.'

'So what changed?'

She places the half-eaten sandwich back down onto the place. Suddenly, she's serious.

'When he was eighteen, he went up to Cambridge. Clive got in at the same time. They shared a flat. Dan was doing really well until the Fosters were killed. That was in his third year. He went off the rails, drank too much, did no work. Eventually, he was thrown out.'

'Thrown out?'

'Oh, he didn't tell you that?' An eyebrow curves upwards. 'He raided his bank account and disappeared off the face of the Earth. We didn't see him for two years. Nobody knew where he was and he's never talked about it. All I know is that when he came back he was a totally different man: self-controlled, shut off from emotion, pretty much the man you met. He took over at the company, learned the ropes and transformed it into a huge success. And in the meantime, he had no desire for relationships, no wish to connect with anyone.' She pauses, fixing me with her hazel eyes, waiting for the right moment to drop her bomb. 'Until he met you.'

She gives a broad smile and I'm floored.

'But why me?'

'There's a saying, isn't there? You don't choose love; love chooses you.' She winks and then returns to the serious face. 'He's lived behind a mask for years, and you've pulled it back. He's changing into himself again, and I like that. Long may it continue.'

While she draws in a breath and lets it go, I drum my fingers on the table. The ache is back, and it's weakening my resolve. Lily Babbage has turned up on my doorstep, nicked my dinner and dangled a juicy piece of bait in front of me. And now, whether I like it or not, I seriously want to bite. Oh yes, Fortress Scotton is in deep trouble.

'I'm finished with him.' I whisper, my words nothing more than brittle shells, easily broken. 'I told you ...'

She holds up a graceful hand.

'And I told you, appearances can be deceptive. Try to look beneath the surface, try to think about where he's coming from. Go and see him. Hear him out.' She pauses, dragging out the seconds for emphasis. 'And give him another chance.'

I stare at skinny Lily and she stares right back at me.

'And drop your own mask,' she adds. 'The one you're wearing right now. It's not good for you.' She rubs her hands together and glances at the remnants of my meal. 'Fish finger sandwiches and Pinot Grigio. I'll have to try that little combo at home.' She stands up, smooths down her outfit and rearranges the sunglasses on top of her head. 'I look forward to meeting again, Maya.' She picks up her handbag. 'And we will meet again because you're not over him at all. In fact, I think you need him.'

With that, she takes her skinny backside out of the kitchen. I listen out for the click of the front door before I pick up my glass and take another glug of wine. Her final words are still echoing round my head and I do my best to brush them away. In the history of jumping to conclusions, that little leap has to be a record breaker. The woman barely knows me. How dare she tell me how I'm feeling? On top of Lucy's pronouncement that I'm up to my eyeballs in self-deception, I've just about had enough. It's time to gather the forces, assess the damage and plan the way ahead.

I stare at my half-finished glass of wine, my thoughts slipping further into a muddle, the ache returning to my chest. And before I know it, I'm no longer focussed on the glass because, already half-forgotten, the dream reassembles itself in my mind. And now I'm thinking of thick branches, broad trunks and movements in the shadows ... and the name I called.

Chapter Three

I don't know how long I spend staring at two half-eaten fish finger sandwiches. It could be five minutes. It could be an hour. Exhaustion seems to have washed right through me, wiping out everything in its path, including time, leaving nothing but a thick murk of confusion in its wake. I need more sleep. That'll sort me out. But before that, a little more wine. I've just about lifted the glass to my mouth when the doorbell rings again. This time, it can only be Clive and like Lily, he'll be batting for Team Dan. I should get up now and beat a hasty retreat to my bedroom, but they'll only catch me on the way. Listening to the thud of the door, the murmur of conversation and a lull that can only indicate a quick snog in the hallway, I grit my teeth and wait for the next onslaught. It's not long in coming.

'Mind if I sit with you for a minute?'

In an attempt to look cool and unruffled, I lean back, glance at Clive and wave towards the empty chair. 'Why not?'

'Lucy's changing her outfit ... doing her make-up ... all that stuff.' He circles a finger around his face, as if to indicate where 'all that stuff' should go, and takes a seat. 'How are you doing?' he asks briskly.

'Fine.'

'Seriously?'

'Seriously. I'm eating fish finger sandwiches and drinking cheap wine. What's not fine about that?'

He half-smiles, half-frowns, and then the next attack begins.

'Look ...'

I cut it short. 'Don't bother. Lucy's already had a go and Lily Stupid Surname's tried her best. I'm not changing my mind.'

Clive's eyebrows seem to wiggle, and then his lips twitch: a sure fire sign of guilt.

'Fair enough,' he mutters.

'And that's the end of it,' I mutter back, riled by the fact that the world and its dog seem determined to break down my defences today. It's nothing less than a bombardment. But is it an organised manoeuvre? And is Dan behind it all? Sensing a flutter between my legs and another in my stomach, I press my thighs firmly together. I wouldn't put it past him.

'This is him, isn't it?' I demand. 'He's sending you in one at a time.'

'I don't know what you're talking about.'

'Dan. This is his plan of attack.'

'There is no plan of attack.' He sits back. 'Nobody's sent any of us. Whatever Lucy's said, that's her business. As for Lily Stupid Surname, well she was at Dan's earlier. She's worried about him. She asked me where you lived and I told her. I'm sorry if she put you out. Nobody asked her to come round here. And as for me, I'm just the idiot who's going out with your flatmate. I can't stop seeing Lucy just because you and Dan aren't together. And I'm sorry if it bothers you, but that's a fact you're going to have to deal with.'

Clamping his lips together, he widens his eyes, as if to say 'so there' … and I feel like a fool. I've been put firmly in my place by an accountant. Hardly knowing what to say next, I venture a quick 'sorry' and then set about staring at the fridge, the window, the toaster, anything to avoid making eye contact.

'I'm not going to harangue you about this.' He stands up and straightens his suit. 'You'll make up your own mind.'

Of course I will. In fact, I already have.

'Now, do you need Lucy's company tonight, or would you like me to take her off your hands?'

'Please take her off my hands,' I reply quickly. 'And the sooner, the better.' Because just like Marlene Dietrich, I want to be alone.

Right on cue, Lucy skitters into the kitchen, sporting another trademark flowery dress and a heavily made-up face.

'Did you bring the bag, Clivey?'

'Shit.' He scratches his forehead.

'What do you mean shit?'

'I forgot. Sorry. I left it on the counter in his kitchen.'

Plonking her hands on her hips, Lucy scowls at him.

'Clive, you need to go back and get it for her.'

'I haven't got time to go down to Lambeth and then come back up here. The traffic's appalling. I'll bring it over tomorrow.'

'She needs it today.' She turns to me. 'Maya, you need it today, don't you?'

'I can cope without it.'

'No, you can't. What about your pills?'

I wince. Does she really have to mention that in front of Clive?

'I've only got two more to take. Besides, I don't need them any more.'

'You might do.' She gives me a knowing look. 'Clive, she needs her pills. You don't want her up the duff, do you?'

Before I can hold it back, a full-blown shout erupts from my mouth. 'I don't bloody care about the bloody pill!' Swigging back another mouthful of wine, I decide that while it was certainly enjoyable, another full-blown shout just isn't the way ahead. Instead, I take the deepest breath possible and resolve to keep calm.

'Ah,' Lucy drawls. 'That's why you're being the bitch from hell.' She mouths the word 'period' at Clive. He blushes slightly in return. 'So, what about your mobile? You need your mobile.'

'I can wait for it.'

'No you can't.'

'Oh, just go and get on with your bloody life, Lucy.'

Refilling the wine glass, I look up just in time to see her mouth the word 'menstruation.' Clive blushes again.

'I'm not on my sodding period,' I snarl. 'Not yet. So just shut up about it.'

'I'm not leaving you alone while ... you know ...'

'While what? I'm on my period?'

'No. While ... while he's around.'

Referring to Ian Boyd just once in twenty-four hours is more than enough. And now she's gone and done it again.

'He's gone.'

'I wouldn't be so sure of that.' She narrows her eyes. At least I think she does. She's been at it again with the 'smoky-eyed' look and it's nigh on impossible to make out what's going on. 'I'm not leaving you unless I can contact you.'

'I'm perfectly capable of looking after myself.'

'Lucy,' Clive interjects, tapping his watch. 'We need to get to the Tate.'

'The Tate?'

'The Tate,' he confirms. 'I'm taking you to a party. It's a big deal. Lots of movers and shakers in the art world. It's your chance to do a bit of networking, but we need to be there for seven. A friend's meeting us at the door. He's got the tickets.'

'Oh, Clivey.' She clasps her hands to her chest. 'Have you done this for me?'

'Of course.'

While Clive touches Lucy's cheek, and she gives him a sickly sweet smile, I wrestle with the compulsion to tell the pair of them to pack it in and show more respect for a woman who's recently been dumped on by Cupid. In the end, I simply slump across the table.

'Just bring it over later,' I groan.

'No,' Lucy insists. 'You need your mobile. If that Scottish psychopath's back on the scene, I want to stay in touch.'

'He's not back on the scene.' I think back to Friday night, to Ian Boyd's unexpected reappearance in my life and his fight with Dan, and I shudder. After that little set-to, there's no way he's ever going to come near me again. 'Just go the bloody party, Lucy, and pick up my handbag on the way home.'

'No,' she states emphatically.

'We've got a front door. I can lock it, you know.'

She shakes her head.

'So give me your phone,' I press on. 'I can call Clive if I need rescuing.'

'No. You can't work my ruddy phone. And besides, I might need it.'

'Oh, for fuck's sake,' Clive growls, suddenly irritated. 'I wangle tickets for the most prestigious art event of the year, and you're pissing about? Lucy, come on.'

'I'm not going.'

'Okay, maybe Maya can come with us?'

Now this is getting out of hand. I'd like to launch myself at Lucy and man-handle her out of the front door. Instead, I stare at the cold fish finger sandwiches and moan: 'Don't be ridiculous.'

'I'm not being ridiculous,' Clive insists. 'I'm pretty sure we can get you in, and we can swing by Dan's on the way.'

My heart skips a whole gaggle of beats and I sit up straight, holding out a hand. 'No. That's not happening.' Strangely, I'm just not in a party mood, even if it the most prestigious art event of the year. And besides, somewhere at the back of my over-tired and fuddled head, I've got more than just a sneaking suspicion that this is all part of some evil plot. 'I'm not going anywhere near Dan.'

Because if I do, that'll be the end of me.

'You don't have to,' Clive explains. 'When I left, he was just off to the house for a couple of days. I've got a spare key. I can nip in and fetch the handbag. It won't take me five minutes.'

'I don't know.' Taking in a few deep gulps of air, I will my pulse to behave.

'It's the only way.' Lucy folds her arms and taps her foot. 'Otherwise, I'm staying here.'

'No, don't do that,' I snap, dreading a night of Lucy's fussing. I'm being ground into submission, and I know it. The trouble is I just haven't got the energy to deal with it. I'm through with thinking and arguing and fighting my corner. My brain's on the verge of throwing in the towel.

I switch my attention to Clive. 'He's definitely gone down to Surrey?'

'Yes.'

So maybe I should just get on with it, go with them, collect my handbag and beat the hastiest retreat ever. I'm reaching out for the wine, determined to finish it off when it's snatched away from me.

'You're coming with us,' Lucy snarls into my face. 'And that's that.'

I'm grabbed by the arm, yanked upwards and dragged out of the kitchen into Lucy's bedroom. Clearly, I'm getting no choice in the matter, but it's hardly a problem. I've already made my decision. I'm going nowhere near The Tate. After Clive's rescued my bag from the apartment of doom, I'll simply get a taxi home. Letting Lucy kit me out in a flowery dress, I beat off an attack with the make-up bag and pull a brush through my hair. At the last minute, remembering the necklace, I manage to escape Lucy's clutches for just long enough to rescue the tiny black box from my room. I'm ready to go through the motions, and nothing more.

***

Outside, it's a miserable evening. Summer seems to have washed its hands of London. Instead of pure blue skies, a mess of filthy grey clouds lurk above our heads and a constant drizzle fills the air.

'Don't worry.' Lucy guides me towards Clive's BMW. 'No storms. Just pissy showers.'

I'm vaguely aware of a door being opened, of sliding onto the back seat of the car. It's only when the door slams shut that I start to panic. What the hell am I doing, letting this pair drag me half way across London on a quest for handbag? And why the hell am I going anywhere near Dan's apartment? This is a gigantic mistake. In fact, it's the mother of all mistakes. I don't know whether it's the sleep deprivation, or the lack of food, or the two glasses of cheap plonk I've downed: but I don't seem to be able to make any decisions today. By the time I finally make one, to get back out of the car, Lucy and Clive are fully installed in the front and the engine's sparked into life.

Hearing the whir of the central locking mechanism, I fiddle with the handle.

'You've locked me in,' I gasp.

Lucy looks back at me. 'Are you thinking of getting out?'

'Yes.'

'It's not going to happen. Drive Clive!'

Perhaps I should scream, or lie across the back seat and kick at the door. Or maybe both. Yes, I really should make a scene, but I'm exhausted and seeing as Lucy's determined to reunite me with my mobile, I'm pretty sure none of it would make a blind bit of difference. Besides, the car's already moving. As we pull out onto the High Street, I scowl at the back of Lucy's head, deciding that there's just no way out of this. The further we push into Central London, the slower we move, snagged up in one traffic jam after another, halted by just about every set of lights along the way. And the further we crawl, the more colour I seem to register: the flash of a cyclist's yellow jacket, the red, amber and green of the traffic lights, a rainbow flashing to life in an oil slick.

I close my eyes against the onslaught, opening them again as we finally reach Whitehall. Before long, we're picking up speed, moving past the Houses of Parliament, swinging out onto Lambeth Bridge and crossing the broad, choppy waters of the Thames. By this point, my stomach has begun to churn, just like the river below. I have a distinctly strange feeling about all of this. Taking a right at the south end of the bridge, Clive swerves by the roundabout and turns in to the left. I'm at Lambeth House again. And suddenly, I'm hearing Dan's words in my head. 'Make a mental note. You'll be coming here a lot.'

Well not any more, Mr Foster. This is my very last visit.

When we come to a halt, I stay exactly where I am, listening to the rain as it patters against the roof of the car, waiting for Clive to make a move. But he doesn't budge. Instead, he simply grunts, takes his mobile out of his jacket pocket, opens up a text and stares at it.

'Oh shit.' He waves the phone at Lucy. 'It's my mum. I just need to call her. Something's going on with my brother.' Entering a number, he opens the car door and steps out into the damp air. 'Mum, what's up?' The door slams shut behind him.

I'm about to tap Lucy on the shoulder and ask her to give Clive the necklace when she unfastens her seatbelt and gets out, leaving me alone in the car. Feeling like an idiot, I turn the little black box in my hands. Someone's got to take it up to the penthouse and dump it there, and it's certainly not going to be me. Unfastening my own seatbelt, I open the door and stand on the forecourt. While Clive wanders off towards the road, listening to the call, and Lucy folds her arms impatiently, I just can't help myself. Tipping my head back, I look up at the top floor, taking in the penthouse windows and the wall that surrounds his rooftop patio: the place where he watches the sun come up every day in the summer.

'Right,' Clive sighs, pulling a key fob out of his pocket, the mobile still clamped to his ear. 'You're going to have to do this, Lucy.'

'Me?' she squeaks.

'Yes, you. It's the top floor. You can't miss it.'

'Clive.'

'Just do it, Luce.' He holds out the fob. 'It's the gold one. I need to ring my brother and I need to do it now. He's about to do something very stupid.'

'But ...'

'Seriously, Lucy. This is urgent.'

Taking the keys, Lucy turns to me, her face splattered with panic. 'I'm not going up there on my own.'

I glance across at Clive. He's already back on his mobile, head down, staring at a puddle.

'I'm not going up there with you.'

'But it's breaking and entering.'

'Technically, it's just entering.' I look back up at the apartment. No way am I going up there. No way. No how.

'Lucy!' Clive calls out. 'Now. It's quarter to seven. And Maya, you'll have to go with her. The concierge knows about you. He won't let Lucy in on her own.' His attention flips back to his phone. 'Brian, what the hell's going on?' And with that, he walks off again, listening intently to his mobile.

'Brian,' Lucy gasps, watching him go. 'Brian and Clive? What on Earth was their mother thinking?'

'Who cares? Just go and fetch my bloody handbag.'

'You heard what he said. The concierge won't let me in without you.'

'Then I'll come into the lobby, but that's it.'

Grabbing Lucy by the arm, I drag her through the main door.

'No,' Lucy snaps, stumbling to a halt. 'We've gone to all this bloody trouble to get your bloody handbag back, the least you can do is just come up in the bloody lift with me.'

'No,' I snap back.

'Then I'm not bloody going up.'

'Jesus Christ.'

'Good evening, Miss Scotton.'

A stranger's voice cuts across our argument. In unison, we turn to face the concierge. I've only ever seen him once before, and I'm wondering how the hell he knows my name.

'See.' Lucy jabs me with a finger. 'He knows who you are. We've come to collect her bloody handbag,' she announces. 'You won't let me go up on my own, will you?'

'To Mr Foster's apartment?' He shakes his head. 'Miss Scotton, of course, has full access.'

Obviously, he hasn't been informed by Mr Foster that the former piece of skirt is out of the picture.

'I've over-ridden the code,' he goes on. 'The lift will take you straight up.'

'There.' Lucy prods me again. She gives the concierge a smile. 'And is Mr Foster in?'

The concierge shakes his Brylcreemed head. 'He left a couple of hours ago.'

'There.' Her eyes flicker with determination. 'So, what's the bloody problem? Come on.'

I'm tugged across the lobby and watch helplessly as Lucy punches the call button for the lift. The door opens immediately and I step inside. It doesn't take long for us to reach the top floor, but all the way Lucy huffs and puffs like a steam engine. When the door slides open again, revealing the white marble of the entrance hall, I feel the hackles rise on the back of my neck. Stepping out into the hall, I'm half-expecting the lift to close behind me, to be trapped. But it stays open.

'I'll wait out here,' I tell Lucy.

'Fair enough.'

She fiddles with the key, slips it into the lock and disappears inside the flat. And I wait, listening to the jittering of my breath.

'Maya, you've got to see this.' Her voice is distant now. Muted.

'What?' I call back.

She reappears in the doorway, her face bright with excitement.

'He's hung your painting. It looks amazing.'

I shake my head and swallow hard. The picture of Limmingham. I didn't get a chance to get a last look on Friday night. Ian Boyd's arrival saw to that.

'There's nobody here,' she grins.

And what harm could it do, my brain niggles. Go on. Take a quick peek, say goodbye and draw a line under everything. And while you're at it, drop off the necklace. That's called closure.

'Come on.' Grabbing me by the arm, Lucy hauls me into the apartment and my stomach lurches. On full alert, I edge my way through the kitchen. It's eerily silent but Lucy was right: there's no one here. He really has gone to Surrey. Either that or he's lurking at the Tate, waiting to take a chance that I'm not about to give. Inching further, I notice the handbag, perched on the counter top, the very place where Dan first kissed me and lured me into his world. I touch the bag, place the little black box on the counter, open it up and take out the necklace. Watching the tiny sweet pea flicker in the light, I think of the jar of sweet pea flowers, of sitting in the kitchen garden with Dan by my side, and my ridiculous vision of a happy ever after. Tears prick at the corners of my eyes and I blink them back. No crying, I tell myself. Not now. Not here. You've made a decision and now you're going to stick to it. After all, it's the only way to keep your sanity. Holding the necklace in my hand, I say a quiet goodbye and lay it gently on the worktop.

'There it is.' Lucy's voice snatches me out of my dream world. Unusually serious, she waves a hand towards the living area.

Following the direction of her wave, I turn and catch sight of it: hanging above the fireplace, the colours shimmering with life, it's my painting of the woods in Limmingham. It looks so different to when it was propped up in my bedroom, or on display at Slaters. I take another step forwards, amazed by the way the light catches the branches. I'm about to take another step when I hear the door slam. Swivelling round on my heels, I find myself alone.

'Lucy?'

No answer.

'Lucy!'

Nothing.

A whirlwind of panic spirals into life. I stumble back to the kitchen, my eyes raking pointlessly across the cupboards, the counter, the sink. And then some tiny, still fully functioning region of my brain registers what's just happened. That was Lucy slamming the front door.

Racing over to it, I tug at the handle, but nothing moves.

'Lucy!' I'd lean down and call through the letterbox but there is no letterbox, just a solid mass of wood. I run a hand over it. 'What the fuck's going on?' I shout. 'I can't open the door.'

'I know.' Lucy's muffled voice comes from the other side. 'I've locked you in.'

I gape at the door, my thoughts reeling. Locked me in? But why has she locked me in? And then my brain lands on the only possible answer.

Shit.

Resting my forehead against the wood, I close my eyes, desperately reminding myself to breathe. The stupid bloody woman. She's come up with a last-minute, hair-brained plan to get me back with Dan. Of all the ridiculous ideas she's ever had, this has to take the biscuit.

'Lucy, for fuck's sake! Let me out!'

'Sorry, Maya.'

I give a start. That certainly wasn't just Lucy's voice. In fact, it was Clive's voice, muffled too. He's here? Blood pounds through my brain. I'm in full-on flight-or-fight mode and I know it.

'What are you doing?' I plead.

'It's an intervention,' Clive calls back.

An intervention? A bloody intervention? Has the world gone mad? I'm starting to shake now, furious at the interference.

'Let me out,' I shout. 'I'm perfectly capable of making my own mistakes, thank you very much. I don't need your help.'

'No!' Lucy shouts back. 'Sometimes, drastic actions are called for.'

'If this is your stupid fucking idea of how to get me back with Dan, you can take a fucking hike.'

'It's not my idea,' Lucy shouts. 'And it's not Clive's either.' She pauses before she springs the next surprise on me. 'It's Dan's.'

Dan's idea? How can it be Dan's idea?

'Shit.' I've been a complete idiot.

'And if you don't like it,' Lucy goes on, 'you can tell him yourself.'

'What?'

I stare at the door, somehow knowing what I'm about to hear.

'He's in there with you.'

'Shit,' I breathe. 'Shit, shit, shit, shit, shit.'

This is a trap.

And I've walked right into it.

Chapter Four

I hold my breath as I turn. Don't ask me how I already know he's close by. I just do. And sure enough, there he is, right in front of me, wearing faded jeans that hang loosely from his hips and a white T-shirt. In an instant, I register it all: the ruffled blond hair, the perfect face, the soft lips, the glimmer in those bright blue eyes. With his hands in his pockets, he stares at me, all mean and hot and moody. And it hits me immediately: the full-on Daniel Foster effect. It's like standing in the path of a freight train and watching a beautiful sunrise and launching into a bungee jump, all rolled into one. I freeze, shortly before I gasp, and then the adrenalin takes effect. My stomach goes into a spin, my heart beat triples and all manner of sensations kick off between my legs. I curse my body to hell and back. I might have decided to get this man out of my life, but Jesus, he still manages to set off the sex fairy. And dear Lord, don't let him come anywhere near me because if he does, I'll be half way to oblivion.

He takes a step forwards and I flinch.

'You took your time,' he murmurs.

The first words he ever spoke in my presence, on my very first day at Fosters. All part of the evil plan, I'm sure, to remind me of where we started. But I'm not playing his game. Oh no. In fact, I'm going to scupper it. And bearing that in mind, I'd better come up with something pithy and intelligent in return. I scramble through my head for something fitting. Finding nothing, I opt for the easiest route.

'Piss off.'

'You know ...' His lips curl upwards. 'You don't have to swear like a builder.'

And that sets me off.

27

'Really? I'd say I've got every right to be swearing like a builder. What the fuck's going on?' I wince at my own foul mouth. Making a mental note to cut back on the cursing, I fold my arms and squeeze my legs together. I'm going to get through this in one, unsweary, respectable piece if it kills me.

'Isn't it obvious?' He gives me a classic Daniel Foster eyebrow arch.

'Of course it's fucking obvious.' Damn it. So, I'm not doing too well on the swearing front, but never mind. 'Open this door.'

He tilts his head to one side, ever so slightly. 'I can't.'

Seriously?

'Yes you can. Just get the fucking key.'

He shrugs dismissively and walks over to the fridge. And I can't help myself. In amongst all the anger and confusion, there's a distinct ground-swell of lust. I take a second or two to take in his sexy backside and his even more sexy walk before I give myself a quick mental slap. No, no, no. Don't get sucked in by all that again. Firm buttocks should be the last thing on your mind right now, woman.

'I don't have the fucking key.' As if nothing particularly interesting is going on at all, he opens the fridge and helps himself to a bottle of water before sauntering over to the counter and sitting down. 'Clive's got the fucking key.' He unscrews the bottle top and takes a swig. '*And* he's got the spares.'

My mind sifts through this new information. In the lift at his office, in the garage, even in my own bed: he's trapped me plenty of times before. But locking me into his apartment, well that really is going that extra mile. As if it's going to make the slightest bit of difference, I glance at the door again.

'You've locked us in?'

'Yup.' He takes another swig of water.

'For how long?'

'Until Tuesday morning.'

'Tuesday?' My bottom lip takes a dive.

'I think that should do it.'

He may still be turning me on, but his arrogance is nothing less than a spark in a tinder box. I sense a flare in my gut, a rush of blood, a sudden urge to lash out.

'That's false imprisonment,' I seethe. 'I could have you done for this.'

He shakes his head. 'I don't think so, seeing as it was Lucy who locked us in ... with Clive's help.' He takes another swig of water, places the bottle on the counter top, folds his arms and leans forwards. 'Now, I'm sure you don't want to land our friends in trouble, do you?'

No, I don't, Mr Foster, but this was your idea and they're simply accomplices. And if you think you can wriggle out of it that easily, you're very much mistaken. That would be the best thing to say, the only sensible thing, but when I open my mouth, I hear nothing more than another dose of profanity.

'Bollocks.'

'And can I get arrested for falsely imprisoning myself?'

Another rush of blood. Another urge to scream and shout.

'This isn't funny.'

'I know.'

I'm about to turn and kick the door when I make the mistake of locking eyes with him. Firm and determined, those whorls of blue are totally fixed on me, drawing me in like a ruddy tractor beam. I'm already half-mesmerised when I finally manage to snap myself into action. Looking round the room, I fix my attention on the floor-to-ceiling windows.

'I'll go out there and yell. Somebody's going to hear me.' Running over to the windows, I tug at a handle. Nothing moves. 'Open this,' I growl, wheeling round.

'I can't. Clive's got the ...'

'Yes, I know,' I cut in, losing it now. 'Clive's got the bloody keys. Fuck it, Dan. I'm sick of this.'

'So am I.' He pushes the bottle away and rubs his hands. 'And that's why nobody's running any more.' Placing his hands on his thighs, he watches as I slink back over to the front door. 'Neither of us.'

Okay, so it's time for a glare. And I give him one: a top-of-the-range, you're a total bastard glare. Unwavering and unbothered, he stares right back at me and try as I might, I can't detect a trace of weakness in him. No nervousness. Nothing apart from sheer determination and a good dose of lust. His eyes are hooded, his lips parted slightly, and I know exactly what he's after. A delicious shimmer of want pulsates between my thighs. Fuck it, no! Determined to get through this in one piece, I squeeze my legs together.

'Why would *you* run?' I demand.

'I've got my reasons.'

He gets up and I shiver. Whatever happens next, I need to avoid contact at all costs. I'll cave in at the first touch. History has taught me that.

'So, I cooked this up.' He takes a step forwards. 'Lock the pair of us in, and no one backs away.'

'You deceived me. It's over. Just accept it. Locking us in here is going to achieve nothing.'

'Three things.' Giving me a slow, languid smile, he runs his eyes up and down my body. He's back to being the cocky bastard I first met. And why wouldn't he be? After all, over the last few years, it's been his way of getting exactly what he wants.

'Number one.' Holding up an index finger, he takes another step. 'I didn't mean to deceive you.' Another step, and now there are two fingers in the air. 'Number two. I'm not going to accept that it's over. Ever.' Another step. A third finger. I flinch again, sense another twinge. 'And number three, locking us in here is going to achieve everything.'

He's close now, so close I could reach out and touch him. Instead, I stare at his face, flabbergasted. The corners of his lips curl up a little further, setting off a thousand tiny electrical charges in my groin. I close my eyes and shut him out. There's only one way to go about this.

'Coffee,' I mutter. My eyes flip open.

He stares at me blankly for a second or two, processing the words, obviously deciding on the next move.

'Fair enough.'

With a shrug, he strolls over to the coffee machine and begins to fiddle with the jug. At first, I'm relieved. He's backed off and I've been given a few precious moments to gather my senses. But then again, why the hell is he making me a cup of coffee? Does he actually think this is funny? If he does, I'm determined to put him in his place.

'I don't want a fucking cup of coffee, Dan. I'm using my safe word.'

'Why?' I watch as he takes the jug out of its holder and makes his way over to the sink. And yes, bugger it, the way he moves is still causing my lady parts to do a special dance. Just the sight of his pert backside threatens to have me slavering within the next few seconds.

'Because I want out of here.'

'Oh.' He turns on the tap.

'Coffee,' I repeat. 'Let me out.'

'Didn't you hear me, cloth ears? Clive's got the keys.'

30

When the jug's filled, he saunters back to the coffee machine, pouring the water into the top. Taking his time, looking all cool, calm and collected, he sets about making me a cup of coffee that I don't even want. I sense a knot of anger in my gut.

'Right,' I growl, realising that there must be some sort of intercom. 'I'll call the concierge.'

I find it almost immediately, right next to the door. But the small silver box has clearly been tampered with. Dangling at an angle, it's attached with a single loose screw. I pull it away from the wall and hold it in my hand. The wires have been cut.

'What have you done?' I demand. 'You've ripped it out.'

He opens a cupboard and produces a couple of mugs.

'I had a little accident.'

'An accident?' I let go of the ruined intercom and leave it to bash against the wall. 'You're a conniving shit.'

He smiles at that and I'm fuming and panicking and, yes, bloody turned on. 'Fine, I'll just call Lucy.' But seeing as she's the one who lured me here, she's hardly likely to let me out. 'Or the Steves,' I add, knowing that I'm sounding ridiculous now. Stomping over to the counter, I rummage through the contents of my bag: tissues, receipts, my purse, more receipts. 'Where's my mobile?'

'Downstairs.' He pauses, leaning back against the counter. 'In my car.' He pauses again. 'Along with my mobile, and my iPad. I'm afraid you're non-contactable. There's no escape.'

My brain struggles to process this new piece of information. Every single time he's ever trapped me before, he's always offered me a way out. But not this time. This time, I'm a prisoner.

'So, all of this ...'

'I think it's called an elaborate ruse.'

'You were behind all of it? Everything?'

'Pretty much. I sent Lily over to soften you up. Did it work?'

'Did it work?' Suddenly, my fingernails seem to be digging into my palms. 'Did you tell her what to say?'

'No, but she was more than willing to help. And as for Lucy and Clive, I left them to come up with their own ideas.' He reaches into a cupboard for a packet of coffee. 'How did they do?'

I stare at him, dumbfounded by his attitude. For all the world, he sounds like he's having a harmless little chat.

'I'm guessing it was an Oscar-winning performance.' He spoons the coffee into the top of the machine. 'After all, they got you here.'

'This is ridiculous. I'm going.'

In a frenzy, I grab hold of the door handle, tugging at it for dear life. Suddenly, a hand appears to either side of me, palms flat against the wood. I feel the warmth of his body against my back. And while my brain fires up in anger, just about everything from the neck down fizzles with lust: muscles, veins, sinews, nerves. Shit, shit, shit. I'm in trouble.

'Let me out!'

'I can't.'

'I want to get out.'

'No you don't.'

And that does it. Hasn't he learned anything over the past few days?

'Stop!' I swing round to find myself caged in by his arms. 'Just stop telling me what I want.'

'Why?' His eyes bore into me. 'I've been right so far.'

'Arrogant fucking arse.'

This seems just about the perfect time to give him a good hammering. Balling my fists, I hit him hard on the chest, over and over again, growling like a mad dog. Keeping his hands in place and bracing himself, he simply takes it. No gritting of teeth. No wincing in pain. I barely make an impact. I don't seem to be making much progress here so I move on to his face, slapping it once before he grabs both of my hands, pinning them above my head. With his face close to mine, breathing unevenly, he fixes his attention on my lips.

'Don't you dare ...'

Before I manage to push out the final words or turn away, his mouth is on mine. And now that he's kissing me, I should resist. But I don't. In fact, I can't. His lips are as smooth and warm as ever, and I cave in straight away. Kissing him back with a passion, I let his tongue twist and turn against mine, lapping up the taste of him, listening to my brain as it nags me to get a ruddy grip. Enjoying the absolute perfection of a Daniel Foster kiss, I waft it away. As ever, physical contact reduces me to a wanton hussy. A hand slides around my back, pulling me in tight as he practically devours me. At last, when he's finally had his fill, he pulls back, waiting for me to open my eyes before he speaks.

'Feel that, Maya? That's attraction. The strongest fucking attraction I've ever felt in my life. And you feel it too.' Releasing my hands, he runs a finger across my neck. 'That's why you'll be wearing the necklace again before you step out of this door. You and me are made for each other.' He presses his crotch against mine. 'Capiche?'

'No,' I squeak.

'Never mind. You will.' He takes a step back. 'So, if you don't mind, I'd like to get started.'

'Started?' I gasp, still struggling to get my lungs back under control. 'On what?'

'My agenda. We're going to talk things through. And then we're going to sort things out. And then I'm going to fuck the living daylights out of you.'

'I wouldn't be so sure of that.' I straighten my dress.

'I would.' He withdraws another step. 'Now, why don't I make you that coffee?'

I glare at his self-assured smile for a good ten seconds before I push past him, huffing my way over to a sofa, muttering obscenities under my breath. While he sets about making me an unwanted cup of coffee, I take off my shoes, tuck my legs under my bottom and fold my arms across my lap. Watching the rain lash against the windows, I listen to the sound of water gurgling, the chink of a teaspoon. At last, he appears in front of me and offers me a mug. Reluctantly, I take it, holding it in both hands and curling my fingers around the sides.

'Well?' I probe.

'Well what?' With a mug of his own, he positions himself on the coffee table, right in front of me.

'Item number one. Talking things through.'

'You're going to listen?'

'What choice do I have?'

Resigned to the fact that I've just got to grit my teeth and get on with it, the sensible half of my brain finally seems to have calmed down. And if the idiot half wasn't currently wavering, swamping itself with visions of sweaty bodies thrashing about on a bed, I'd definitely have the upper hand.

He chews at his bottom lip and stares at the floor. The show's clearly over for now. He's locked me in, whacked me with a good dose of the arrogant, womanising arse and kissed my face off. And fair play to him. He's done pretty well with the shock and awe, but now that we're down to the nitty gritty, he doesn't seem quite so sure of himself. And I'm beginning to melt.

'Would you like to get started?' I ask, breaking the silence.

He shakes his head. 'I don't know where to start.'

'How about with the deception thing?'

'I told you. I didn't mean to.'

'Not good enough.'

'Maya, when I realised who you were, I lost all reason ...'

'That's not making me feel any better.'

'I know you hate me at the moment.'

'I don't hate you.' His head flicks up, his features softened by a look of hope. 'I pity you.'

His forehead creases. 'I don't want pity.'

'Not for the way you grew up. I pity you because you wanted revenge. That's pathetic.'

He stares at me, his eyes suddenly cold. 'Can you honestly tell me you've never wanted it?'

I think of Sara. Oh God, I've wanted it so many times. In fact, if memory serves me right, only last week I paraded Dan in front of her while she was at her lowest ebb.

'I should never have told you,' he mutters.

'But you did.'

He stares at me some more.

'I'm no angel. I have faults.' He places his mug on the table. 'It was a few moments of madness.'

Now, that's not quite right.

'A few moments? When did you first find out about me?'

'Friday,' he answers quietly. 'I saw your file on Friday.'

'And you had me moved to Norman's office?'

'Yes.'

'And then you called me on Monday, and then you ordered me up to that meeting. I'd say that's more than just a few moments of madness.' My voice is rising now. 'That's four fucking days' worth of it.'

'Okay,' he snaps, sending a jolt right through my body and coffee spilling all over the plush cream sofa. 'Maybe it was more than that.' Glaring into my eyes, he struggles to calm himself. 'Happy now?'

'You used me.'

'Oh, get real.' He grimaces. 'That's not true.'

'You used me to get back at Sara.'

'Think about it, Maya. I did not use you.'

Pushing himself up from the table, he prowls to the window. With his back to me, he folds his arms and stares out at the Thames.

'Whatever happened, I wouldn't have gone through with it. I'm not that sort of man ... not deep down. I've never done anything like that in my life.' His head dips. 'I would have come to my senses sooner or later. I don't even know what made me think like that in the first place.'

34

He drifts off into silence and I wish I could see his face. Both of us know what made him think like that: my sister's relentless bullying, a miserable childhood, the past we share. I'm about to tell him as much when he begins to speak again, more quickly this time, as if he's trying to force out the words before he loses the strength to do it.

'I found out who you were on Friday afternoon. I organised the swap because I wanted you near me. And then I spent the weekend ...'

He pauses and I wonder what on Earth he's going to say next. Plotting how to use you? Planning how to destroy you? When his answer finally comes, it throws me.

'Pissed out of my head. Trying not to think at all. It was a fucking miracle I sobered up by Monday morning.' I hear him blow out a breath. 'I walked in that day. I knew you'd be in the lobby at nine. I timed it so that I could see you but you had your back to me. You were filling in a form. I don't know what I expected to happen when I saw you, but I certainly didn't expect ...'

'What?'

He turns. 'You were wearing a tiny strip of material that could barely pass as a skirt. I rode the lift up to my office with the biggest hard-on of my life.'

I feel my lips begin to curve upwards. No, no, no. This isn't good at all. They're breaking ranks. This is a serious conversation, and I'm smiling at his crassness.

'I called you because I wanted to hear your voice. I had you come to the meeting because I wanted to see you properly.' He pauses, weighing up his next words. 'You took my breath away as soon as I laid eyes on you.'

I'm thinking back to that meeting now, to his cold greeting. Good God, if that's taking someone's breath away, then I'm a monkey's aunt.

'You covered it up well.'

'I'm good at that sort of thing.'

As he moves back towards me, my body prickles with anticipation. He comes to a halt in front of the sofa, reaching down, taking the mug from me and placing it next to his own before he positions himself back on the edge of the coffee table. He leans forwards and rests his elbows on his knees.

'Right from the start, I knew I was in trouble. I was a complete fucking mess.' He pauses, watching for my reaction. 'You do that to me, Maya. You turn me inside out. You're in here.' He touches his head. 'Every single minute of the day. I need to fix this.'

I'm already captivated by the flecks of copper dancing around his pupils, the layers of dark blue that permeate his irises. They're pleading with me now, those eyes, and I just want to fall into his arms. Reaching out, he takes my hand in his, triggering the same electrical charge that pulsates through me every single time we're in contact. Logic won't last long. I know that. I need to drop in a weak and pointless protest, and I need to do it fast.

'I don't know if I can trust you.'

'You can trust me more than anyone else in the world.'

'How can I trust a man who keeps secrets from me?'

'I tried to tell you, more than once. It was never the right time.'

I stare at his long fingers, saying nothing. I'm crumbling steadily.

'And I'm not the only one who kept secrets. You didn't tell me about Boyd.'

It's an instinct. At the mention of his name, I pull my hand away.

'That's different.'

'How is it?' he demands, his voice still gentle.

'That's nothing to do with who I am.'

'Of course it is.'

And he's so bloody right. Boyd, my sister, Tom: the whole lot of them have left me riddled with self-doubt and fear.

'I never talk about him. I don't even like to think about him. I block him out. That's the way I cope.'

'And how do you think I deal with my past?'

He falls silent. Taking both of my hands now, he gently encourages me to my feet, pulling me in to his chest and enclosing me in his arms. I feel a hand at the back of my head, another at the base of my spine, and I can smell him now, that fresh signature scent of his. A familiar spark of energy flutters through my body, concentrating in my chest and in my loins. And then the tears begin to flow. Maybe it's because of Boyd, because Dan's just scratched a wound that's never really healed, or maybe I'm crying for Dan, suddenly overwhelmed by the awfulness of his past. I have no idea, but a gentle trickle soon grows in force.

'Maya, don't.' He moves back, wiping away the tears away with a thumb. 'I hate to see you cry.'

I can't resist any more and anyway, I just don't want to. Instead, I lean in to him, every last bit of tension ebbing away. And finally, I admit the truth: I've been the queen of self-deception. I want him, I need him and in spite of everything, I was never going to let him go.

I hear him let out a quiet sigh of relief. He kisses the top of my head and places his palms against my cheeks. My head is angled upwards, so that I'm looking straight into his face.

'You'll never cry again,' he whispers. 'Not if I can help it. This is your sanctuary, remember? Right here, with me.' He wipes away more tears, slowly, carefully, watching my face for any sign of a reaction. 'And it's mine too,' he adds. 'You've saved me.'

'From what?'

He blinks.

'From being nothing.' He shakes his head, struggling to find the right words. 'When I'm with you ...' A smile spreads across his face. 'You make me remember who I am.'

Lily's words return to me. He's becoming his old self again, the real Dan. I've pulled back the mask.

'Give me another chance. I won't let you down, Maya. I promise. I need you in my life.'

Still holding my face, he waits patiently for an answer, and I have no problem in giving it. Swallowing back another sob, I nod.

'I need you too.'

He gazes at me for a moment, before lowering his lips to mine and delivering another perfect kiss. While he holds me tight, I soak up the softness of his lips, the way his mouth shapes itself around mine as our tongues intertwine. It goes on for an age.

'Does this mean I'm forgiven?' he asks, finally releasing me.

'Possibly.'

'How can I make that a definitely?'

'For a start you could fuck the living daylights out of me.'

I give him a cheeky grin.

He shakes his head.

'I don't think I'm going to do that, after all.'

'So what are you going to do then?'

He runs a finger down the side of my cheek.

'I think it's generally referred to as making love. But before we do ...'

Making his way over to the counter, he picks up the necklace. I follow, turn, gather up my hair and wait. The sweet pea appears in front of my face. He threads the chain around my neck, back where it belongs, and closes the clasp.

Chapter Five

A nd then he leads me back up to the bedroom. As we come to a halt in the middle of the room, I'm tingling. He lets go of my hand and stands in front of me. While the seconds draw themselves out into an eternity, I see nothing but his eyes, hear nothing but the quivering of my breath, feel nothing but the ache inside. And now I know exactly what it is: I'm consumed by a need for him, on every possible level.

I'm half expecting him to say something, but as he lifts my dress over my head and drops it to the floor, he remains soundless. Taking his time, he surveys my body, smiling his appreciation before he leans in and unfastens my bra. For a few seconds, I feel his breath against my cheek, and I silently will him to kiss me, but he's in no rush. Instead, he trails the bra away from my shoulders, watching the slow progress of the straps across my skin before he lets it go. And then he touches my face, lightly running an index finger down my cheek, my neck, across my sternum, tracing his way over each breast, circling my nipples again and again. My skin comes alive at his touch. Suddenly, I'm trembling. Anticipation surges through every nerve and fibre ... and I just can't wait any longer.

Taking hold of his T-shirt, I push it over his head, ruffling his hair in the process. And then I drink in the definition of his form. This man is physical perfection, absolute and complete. I'll never cease to be awestruck by the sight of him, just like I'll never get used to the fact that he's all mine. Reaching up, I brush my palms across his broad shoulders, his biceps, his firm pecs, his taut stomach. He gives me a minute or so to admire him before he guides me back in to his embrace and while he nuzzles his head against my neck, I curl my arms around his back, loving the feel of his body: the warmth, the smell, the softness of his skin. It feels like home.

At last, he releases me, cupping my face in his hands.

'This is for keeps. Understand?'

I nod mutely and it's all I can do because, true to form, he's already rendered me speechless. In a stupor, I watch him sink to his knees. He strokes a big hand across my stomach, setting off a spark of lust at my clitoris. And then he leans in, kissing my crotch through the fabric of my knickers. The effect is immediate: the spark seems to catch, forming a ball of warmth that travels inwards through my muscles, almost causing me to orgasm on the spot. I dig my hands into his hair, close my eyes and let out a groan. I hear him chuckle, feel him tuck a finger into the waistband, running it slowly from left to right before he draws my knickers downwards.

With my knickers removed, he returns to my crotch, curls an arm around my buttocks and gently encourages my legs apart. Holding me in place, he touches his tongue against my labia, stroking me, exploring the folds of my flesh and homing in on my g-spot. And now I'm a mess, a shambolic, sexed-up, brainless disaster area. Soaking up the warmth of his mouth and the ripples of pleasure that course through me with every flick of his tongue, I moan shamelessly.

I'm pretty certain that my legs are about to give way when he finally comes to a halt. Rising to his feet, he slips one arm around my back, the other beneath my buttocks, and lifts me. He carries me to the bed, lays me down and straightens up. Studying my body, his line of vision climbs from my crotch to my breasts and finally to my face. And I feel no shame, no embarrassment. I simply watch as he unbuttons his jeans and removes them. The pants quickly follow and now I just can't help it. At the sight of his cock, all hard and ready to go, a grin spreads across my face.

'Hands above your head,' he says quietly, fighting back a grin of his own.

I reach up towards the wooden slats, automatically following the order, silently hoping he's about to fetch the cuffs. But he doesn't. Instead he climbs onto the bed, props himself on his left elbow, manoeuvres his right leg over me and pins me into position.

'Now I've got you.' He leans down to land a kiss on my lips. 'Are we ready for some serious pleasure?'

I'd like to ask him exactly what he means by 'serious pleasure', but he's already made a start on delivering it. Using a palm here and a finger there, he strokes my arms, my breasts, my stomach, leaving a trail of goose bumps in his wake. Still taking his time, he retraces his path over and over again. And while my skin becomes super-sensitive, ripples of warmth undulate throughout my groin, every last one of them converging in my vagina. I'm soon wet, and before long I'm desperate too, craving his touch further down.

'Turn over.'

'What?'

'Do as you're told.'

I roll onto my stomach and immediately, I'm straddled. Lowering himself onto my backside, he presses his hard balls against my buttocks. And that sets me off. In a futile attempt to spur him on, I grind my buttocks against him, but he's clearly working to his own agenda and a full-on fucking seems to be a little further down the line. In a whirlwind of desperation, I bury my hands beneath the pillow and wait.

'Are we in need of a good fuck, Miss Scotton?' he asks, his voice light with amusement.

'You know I am.'

'Patience.' He moves my hair to one side, carefully. 'Everything comes to she who waits.'

His lips land on my neck, right at the nape, drawing themselves slowly across my skin, stopping here and there for a kiss. I sense another movement. Adjusting his position, he takes the kisses lower, repeatedly trailing goose pimples down my spine and before long, I'm shuddering under his touch. His hands come to my sides, holding me firmly. And then he moves lower again, covering both sides of my body with his mouth, smoothing its warmth across me. At last, I feel his breath against my skin, right at the base of my spine ... and somehow it causes me to jolt.

His grip tightens. 'You like?'

'God, yes.'

'This is what you get when you're with me. No more running.'

'No.' I gasp. 'Definitely not.'

Another movement and his palms touch against my thighs, gently urging me up onto my haunches and guiding my legs apart. A finger runs from the base of my spine, down along the space between my buttocks, and then it disappears. I feel his tongue in its place, licking its way along the same route. Oh, good God, he's going straight in for that again. While half of me is quaking at the thought of it, the other half is currently sitting on the edge of its seat, quietly begging for him to get on with it. He circles his tongue slowly around the edge of my anus, and then back up to my spine. The last few kisses are planted right there, just above my coccyx, where he always gets me with his touch.

'I thought you were going to ...'

A hand comes into position over my backside.

'Not now. Just reacquainting myself with an old friend.'

He moves again, kneeling by my side and encouraging me over onto my back. As if I've been thoroughly drugged, I move like a rag doll under his touch. There are no two ways about it: he's got me totally in his control. I'd do anything for him.

'I don't mind a bit of back door action,' I offer.

'Later, maybe.' He brushes a finger across my stomach. 'When I've got my kink on.'

An exquisite contraction erupts out of nowhere, a flood of heat deep in my core. He's breathing fast now, obviously just as aroused as me, but instead of getting on with it, he seems determined to kiss me to death. Straddling me again, he leans down, sweeping his lips across my neck. I turn my head to one side, allowing him more access, and he makes the most of it, skimming his mouth from the bottom of my ear down to my shoulders.

'A hundred years,' he murmurs, *'should go to praise thine eyes and on thy forehead gaze.'* He lifts his head, watching for my reaction, but I have no idea what sort of reaction to give. What the hell's he going on about?

'Pardon?'

'Poetry.'

'Oh.'

I suppose that's what you get for going out with a man who studied literature at university, and then got thrown out ... and then spent two years in the wilderness. You have no idea what he got up to, my brain reminds me. And you're letting him do this to you? My thoughts must have spilled out onto my face, and he seems to have noticed.

'What's wrong?'

'Nothing.'

'Relax then. Where was I?'

I groan as his mouth travels further, down to my breasts, setting me alight with new sensations. His lips latch onto my right nipple and he sucks gently. And while my pulse soars, I gaze at the mop of blond hair that's right in front of me. It's far too tempting. I dig my fingers into it.

'Behave, Maya.' Raising his head, he smiles at me. 'Hands up.'

'Or what?'

He grabs hold of my wrists, manoeuvres my arms back into place. 'I'll think of something.'

41

Pushing out an exasperated sigh, I resign myself to my fate. It's all I can do. Seeing as I've already given him my complete submission, there's really no point in arguing. His lips are already back on my skin, batting any logical thoughts to one side. Moving to my left nipple, he sucks and releases, slowly, over and over again. When he's finally finished, his eyes meet mine.

'*Two hundred to adore each breast.* Are we in a tizzy, Miss Scotton?'

'Yes. Get on with it. Go there.'

'Where?'

'You know. There.'

'But I'm in no rush. *Thirty thousand to the rest.*'

'No,' I groan.

'*An age at least to every part.*'

He lowers his head again, running his mouth between my breasts, across my stomach, smelling me, tasting me with lazy, unhurried movements. I'm a gargantuan, sweaty mess by the time he returns to my crotch. Breaking contact, he looks up at me, his eyes glinting.

'*And the last age should show your heart,*' he whispers, his voice deep and smooth.

I raise my head from the pillow. 'You ... you already have my heart,' I manage to stammer.

'I know that, Maya. I'm reciting a poem. Go with it.'

I smile and let my head fall back.

'*For lady, you deserve this state.*' He runs a hand across my pubic hair. '*Nor would I love at lower rate.*'

I quiver inside. 'Love?'

'Did I say you could talk?'

'No. Sorry.'

'Bloody woman, ruining my poem.'

'It's not your poem.' I'm betting on that.

'Correct, it's Andrew Marvell's poem and he was a dirty bugger, I can tell you. Now, spread these legs.'

Yes! At last! And about time too! Don't get me wrong. I'm in seventh heaven here, on top of the world, drunk on ecstasy, but now I need the release. He takes a while to run his fingers across my clitoris, sweeping further down to my vagina. And then he leans in, his warm tongue lapping at my labia while a finger enters me, finding just the right spot and massaging me from the inside. Gripping the pillow, I moan and groan, drowning in a floodtide of delicious warmth, wanting nothing more than to run my hands across the muscles of his broad shoulders, but I'm under orders. I must resist.

I'm teetering on the edge when he finally comes to a halt.

'And now for some real poetry.' Slowly, he lowers himself onto me.

I feel his cock at my opening, sliding its way in, filling me perfectly like it always does. He pauses, wraps a hand under my buttocks and smiles into my eyes before he begins. Withdrawing to the hilt, he eases back in again, over and over, with the same controlled, unhurried movements, keeping it up until my insides become super-charged.

'Oh Jesus, fuck! Go quicker.'

'I'm taking this slowly,' he retorts, barely out of breath. 'I've put in the groundwork, laid the footings if you like.'

'Oh.' I swallow back a grunt. 'Builders' talk.'

'Exactly. Now when you've spent all that time on the foundations, you don't want to rush the erection, do you?'

With a devilish grin, he drives into me again, sending me to the edge of sanity, and I just can't resist any more. My hands fly up to him, fingers clutching at his hair, pulling frantically. I move on to his shoulders, digging in as the pressure intensifies.

'I'll come,' I gasp. 'I can't hold it. I'll come.'

'Come all you like.' He brushes his lips against mine. 'I could do this forever.'

'Shit, no.'

'Shit, yes. Tantric sex.'

And then the joking stops. Our eyes connect. Secured by his gaze and helpless beneath him, I let it all go as, moaning as my muscles seem to implode. A deep, long orgasm undulates inside me, rippling outwards and clutching at his cock. Soaking it all up, I'm lost in a Never-Never land of ecstasy. And through it all, he keeps up the same steady rhythm, holding me tight.

Time backs out of the room, leaving us in oblivion, and at first I hear nothing apart from the sound of my own breathing, my heartbeat pounding inside my head. But then it filters through. His breathing has picked up pace too, and it's coming to pieces. He's struggling to control himself. His hands tighten against my skin as the pressure begins to build again. Forcing his head in towards me, I press my lips against his, kissing him with a feverish passion. And he kisses me right back, his tongue probing my mouth while his muscles stiffen. For all his trash talk, he won't be able to hold on for much longer.

'Fuck it,' he growls.

Finally reaching breaking point, he ratchets up the tempo. With his eyes fixed on mine, his pupils dilated and his lips open, he drives into me relentlessly, and spurred on by the intensity of his pounding, a second climax builds in my core. Sensing the tension in his back, I hold my breath, feel him jolt as I come to the boil. Knowing that it's time, I release myself again, tripping over the edge into pure bliss while he empties himself inside me.

'Jesus!' he cries out, continuing to thrust.

For a minute or so, he slows the rhythm, bringing us both down from an intense high. Steadying me in his grip, he kisses me tenderly, riding through the aftershocks until we both begin to slide into a post-coital fug. At last he flops on top of me, digging his head into my neck. I run my fingers up and down his back, through his hair, and I feel it again, that incredible attachment between us. At times like this, we're one.

'You're rubbish at tantric sex,' I grin.

He lifts his head. 'It's you. You make me want to go hell for leather.'

He nudges his face back into my neck.

'I love you, Dan. You're the most infuriating man I've ever met, but I bloody love you.'

I feel his smile against my skin and I wait for the words to be returned. Surely, this is the moment. But nothing comes. When he finally pushes himself up, balancing on his elbows, he's already super serious.

'Remember what I said on Friday?'

I flick through the memories but thanks to Boyd's involvement, it's all a blur.

He helps me out. 'I want you to move in. Here. With me.'

I'm flummoxed, again.

'And I want you to slow down,' I counter. 'It's too soon. Three weeks.'

'I'm sure other people do it in three weeks.'

'But ...'

'Listen.' He shifts slightly, moving his weight onto his left elbow and sliding his right hand onto my chest, just above my heart. 'In here, does it feel like the right thing to do?'

'Yes, but I hardly know you.'

Because you're a puzzle, Mr Foster. And I want every last part of it in place before we go any further with this.

'You know me better than anyone else. You didn't say no on Friday.'

44

'That was before ...' I trail off into silence, spotting the concern on his face. That was before Limmingham. I watch the shadows settle in his eyes. 'It's not that,' I add quickly. 'It's not because of where you came from.'

'Then what is it?'

'I just want to know more before I commit to something like that. I just wonder how many more Dan bombshells you've got to drop on me.'

'Bombshells?'

I gaze up into his eyes, but I just can't work out what I'm seeing there now.

'I want you to open up to me. I don't want any more surprises.'

The seconds tick by as he watches me, and God knows what he's thinking about. In all probability, he's rifling his way through all the secrets he's keeping, wondering which bombshells he can drop and which ones to keep stored away. Finally, he pecks me on the lips and withdraws.

'I understand.' Reaching into a bedside cabinet drawer, he takes out a tissue and cleans me up. When he's happy with his work, he flops back onto the pillow and holds out an arm, inviting me into his embrace. I snuggle up to him, wondering how he can still smell this good, even after breaking into a full-blown sweat.

'So, how do we do this?' he asks.

'How do we do what?'

'Get to the point where you say yes?'

I stare at him, incredulous, and then I remember. He's never done anything like this before. He really doesn't have a clue.

'It's very simple,' I explain. 'We spend time with each other and we talk. Small talk. Big talk. That sort of thing.'

He grimaces, bites his lip and claps me on the arm before edging his way out of bed. 'Fair enough.' He bends down and grabs his jeans. 'I'll give you the small talk and the big talk, but you can do it my way.'

'Which is?'

'Ever heard of fast-tracking?'

'You can't fast-track a relationship.'

'Think outside the box, Miss Scotton.'

'Think inside the box, Mr Foster.'

He ruffles his hair. 'Never.'

While he searches for his T-shirt and pulls it on, I chuckle to myself and close my eyes. I let out a yawn, content to be back in his bed and back in his life. The world is locked out and we're locked in.

And right now I just don't care. Feeling the bed dip, I open my eyes to find him sitting next to me. He draws a finger down my cheek.

'You're tired.'

'I didn't sleep last night.'

'I know.'

'How? Have you got Lucy spying on me?'

The same finger runs lightly across my bottom lip. He watches its progress. 'I asked Lucy how you were. That's not spying.' Rain drops patter against the skylight. It's an age before he lifts his eyes to mine. 'I was worried about you yesterday. When the storm broke, I just wanted to hold you.'

'I wish you'd been with me.'

'I'm with you now.' He leans down and lands a gentle kiss on my mouth. 'Take a nap. I'll go and rustle up some dinner.'

I'm smiling like a village idiot as I close my eyes again, brim-full with contentment, and before I know it, I'm back in a world of dreams. But this time, there are no nightmares. Instead, I'm in a kitchen garden, sitting on a bench beneath a shower of sweet peas.

And Dan is by my side.

Chapter Six

When I wake up, I find a crisp white shirt laid out on the bed next to me. Taking the hint, I put it on, stumble into the bathroom and retrieve my toothbrush from the space age cabinet. I'm half way through brushing my teeth when I notice a host of toiletries arranged next to the sink. Swilling out my mouth, I leave the toothbrush on the side and the cabinet door wide open while I set about sorting through the bottles and tubes of shower crème, face wash, moisturiser and God knows what else. It's all brand new, distinctly expensive and definitely female. And all part of the dastardly plan to move me in. Grinning to myself, I survey the bathroom: the marbled floor, the vanity unit that stretches along the length of one wall, the sleek mirrors hanging above it and the huge walk-in shower that I've already experienced, Dan style. But no bath, and that will never do. Making a mental note to add it to my list of requirements, I wander back into the bedroom and take a look out of the window, watching as a cruiser makes its way downriver, an oasis of light against the black glass of the water. The Houses of Parliament are glowing now against the darkness and according to Big Ben's illuminated face, it's just after eleven. A strange time for dinner ... but never mind, I'm ravenous.

I find him in the living area. With his back to me and his shoulders hunched, he's looking out over the river, talking quietly. For a split second, I wonder if he's talking to himself, and then I quickly come to my senses. That's a mobile clasped to his ear. A bloody mobile. I'd love to ambush him, grab the mobile out of his hand and demand to know why he lied to me, but he's listening intently to someone at the other end of the line, and I want to hear what he says next.

47

'So, where is he now?' He pauses. 'You don't know?' Another pause. 'Bank accounts. Withdrawals. Come on, you can get access to all that.' He listens again. 'How can I be patient?' Finally, he turns and spots me. 'Dig some more,' he says coldly. 'Everything. I need to go.' He hangs up and throws the mobile onto a sofa.

'So, I see you've got your phone.'

'Oh, that.' He prowls towards me. The closer he gets, the more my body seems to sparkle. 'Yes, I forgot. It wasn't in my car after all.' He reaches out and skims a finger down my arm, sending a rush of adrenalin right through me. Fight it, my brain calls out. He's bloody well distracting you.

'You lied to me.'

'It got the job done.' Slipping a hand round my waist, he guides me into his chest and holds me firm. Shit, he's smelling good. Clearly, while I was in the land of nod, he managed to fit in a quick shower.

'And who were you talking to?'

'A private investigator. The best in the business.'

'But why?'

'Why do you think?' He watches me for a moment, his face impassive. 'I need to know about Boyd. After Friday night, I want to know everything about him.'

'You scared him off.'

'And I want to make sure he doesn't come back.'

'He won't come back.'

I'm pretty sure of that. Boyd might have more than just a slight touch of the psychopath about him, but he doesn't have a death wish. He'd be a complete idiot to come anywhere near me after his spat with Dan. Placing my palms flat against his chest, I push away with all the strength I can muster, but I don't get far. I'm held tight in his grip.

'Just leave it with me. No arguments,' he warns. 'It's going to happen whether you like it or not.'

The determination etched across his face tells me everything. I'd better change the subject.

'So, where's my phone?' I ask.

'In the cupboard.'

Nuzzling his mouth against my neck, he kisses a spot just below my ear lobe.

'Which cupboard?' I gasp, fighting off an attack of quivers.

'That one.' He nods towards a cupboard next to the fridge. 'Just behind the muesli.' He grins. 'I figured toast woman would never go anywhere near a healthy breakfast cereal.'

After a second fruitless attempt to prise myself free, I give up on the struggle.

'You don't need it.' He lowers his face to mine, studying my lips.

'You're a complete ....' I get nowhere near the end of my complaint. Before I know it, his mouth is on mine and I'm absent without leave. A hand comes to the back of my head, holding me tight while he kisses me, pressing his hard-on against my crotch.

At last, he pulls away.

'Fucking hell. You turn me on constantly.'

I'm about to tell him that he has exactly the same effect on me when a loud growling sound interrupts us. Releasing me, he takes a step back and glances down at my stomach.

'Somebody's hungry. I think we'd better get some food into you.'

'Food can wait.'

'No, it can't. Once I get started again, I won't be able to stop. And besides, the pasta's ready.' He holds up his hands, as if in surrender. 'I'm not touching you again until we've eaten.'

Leaving me disappointed, he saunters off to the hob and lifts the lid on a pan. Whatever it is, it smells divine.

'Five minutes,' he calls, lifting the lid on a second pan.

More than enough time to check my mobile. I head straight for the cupboard, push aside the muesli, and there it is. Grabbing my phone and leaving the cupboard door open, I settle onto a stool and check for messages. Three from my mum, along with a handful of missed calls. And a text from Sara. I open it up.

Are you OK? x

With a sigh, I look up, catching a momentary glimpse of life with Daniel Foster. Quietly humming to himself, he's busy stirring the contents of a pan. Places have already been set at the granite bar: plates, cutlery, two empty glasses and a bottle of red wine, uncorked and breathing. Another plate sits at the centre of the counter, complete with a focaccia loaf. I'm smiling now because I really could get used to this. Tearing myself out of idiot mode, I text back.

I'm fine. Back with Dan. Tell Mum for me. See you soon. x

'Anything interesting?' he asks.

'Just my sister.'

He still has his back to me, but there's an instant change in his stance: his shoulders tighten and his back stiffens, just a little. I watch in silence as he takes the first pan and drains it over the sink, releasing a cloud of steam. When he's finished, he transfers the contents to a bowl.

'You two are going to have to talk at some point.' I slide my mobile onto the counter.

I'm pretty sure he shakes his head at that. Moving to one side, he takes the second pan, adds the contents to the bowl and then he sets about stirring it all up with a huge wooden spoon. I'm half tempted to just enjoy the sight of a sex god making me dinner, but I've got work to do.

'I know it's not easy for you.'

He turns, bowl in hands.

'Puttanesca.'

'Pardon?'

'Spaghetti alla Puttanesca.' Joining me at the counter, he slides the bowl onto the top and kisses the end of his fingers, Italian style. 'Just for you.'

'You're not going to distract me with food.'

'If I wanted to distract you, I wouldn't use food.' He takes a seat on a stool opposite me.

'You've got to talk to her.'

'And I will.' Picking up a pair of huge silver spoons, he dishes out a serving for me, tears off a piece of bread and places it onto my side plate. 'Eat.'

He watches me, and I watch him right back, incapable of working out what's going on behind that perfect face of his. At last, his features soften.

'I'll do it, Maya. I promise. But let's not talk about it tonight. Let's just eat.' He pushes the plate further towards me. 'And then let's fuck.'

I'm not entirely sure if it's his words that cause it, or the way he's looking at me right now, his eyes dancing with promise, lips curled up into a knowing smile, but suddenly, for some reason, something seems to be pulsating between my legs.

'How romantic,' I comment.

'Eat.'

This time, I do exactly as I'm told. Picking up a fork, I twirl it through the spaghetti, silently triumphant when I finally manage to catch a single strand. Before it can escape, I shovel it into my mouth, savouring the taste.

'This is gorgeous,' I mutter, going in for more with a spoon. 'What's in it?'

'Tomatoes, anchovies, capers, garlic, chili peppers.' Dishing out his own serving, he reels off the list as if it's nothing.

I gobble up another mouthful, this time managing to collect spaghetti and sauce. God, I'm so hungry. A single fish finger sandwich in over twenty-four hours just doesn't cut it, especially when you're halfway through a shag fest with Mr Foster.

'So, you can cook?'

'A bit.'

'How come?'

'Betty taught me the basics.' He takes a mouthful of pasta and chews. 'And I went from there.'

'Mmm,' I muse. 'I've landed on my feet.'

'Of course you have.'

While we settle into a comfortable silence, devouring the piles of spaghetti, I take every opportunity to admire the man in my life. At last, I just can't hold it in any longer. Egged on by a contented stomach, my heart brims over with happiness and I'm suddenly consumed by a need to let Dan know how bloody wonderful he is.

'I've got the perfect man,' I muse.

He looks up from his plate. 'How come?'

'Well, for a start, he's good in bed.'

'Excellent in bed,' he corrects me.

'And he's fucking gorgeous.'

'If you say so.'

'With a perfect backside.'

'Is it?' He shifts to one side, pretending to inspect his bottom.

'God, yes. Those receptionists in the lobby eye it up whenever they can.'

'Remind me to sack them.'

He levels his gaze at me.

'And he can cook. He's the real deal.'

'Of course he is.' He points his fork at me. 'And you should move in with him.'

I should have seen myself walking straight into that one.

'Are we heading towards a yes?' he asks, expertly gathering up strands of spaghetti.

'No.'

Pausing mid-chew, he rolls his eyes. 'Che la dura.'

'What?'

He chews some more, swallows and then explains. 'Persistence pays off.'

I lay down my cutlery. Somewhere in the depths of my brain, a light flickers. He's at it again, speaking Italian as if it rolls of his tongue. And here I am, seriously considering the prospect of moving in with a man I barely know.

'Italian,' I state simply.

'What about it?'

'You speak Italian.'

A frown appears. 'Just a smattering.'

A smattering? Oh come off it, Mr Foster. Rifling back through the last few days, my thoughts land on our visit to Gabriel's Wharf and his little chat with the Italian barista.

'It's more than that. When did you learn? It wasn't at university …'

'No, it wasn't.' He rests an elbow on the table. 'It was after I left.'

'After you got thrown out.'

He eyes me suspiciously. Shit. I shouldn't have spewed that one out. Not yet.

'Lily told me,' I explain sheepishly.

'Of course she did.' He picks up the wine bottle, pouring a half glass for each of us. 'So exactly what is this? Small talk or big talk?'

'It all depends on what you tell me. What happened after you left university?'

'Not a lot.'

'Lily told me …'

'Lily's got a big mouth.'

I pick up my glass. Suddenly, I seem to be in need of some Dutch courage. 'If you want me to move in,' I take a sip, 'then you've got to give me a bit more than that.'

He leans back, sucks in a deep breath and stares at me. It takes a few seconds for him to make his decision.

'Okay.' He cocks his head to one side. 'I travelled. I took off for a couple of years and I just travelled. I was a mess. I needed to sort my head out.'

'And you did?'

'Yes.' He picks up his own glass and gulps down a mouthful of wine.

'But Lily said …'

While I trail off into silence, wondering if I'm going too far too soon, he stares at me some more, waiting, holding the glass in mid-air. And then he lifts an eyebrow, as if to say 'go on.' Gathering my resolve, and a whole pack of words along with it, I push it all out at once.

'She said you were different when you came back. Did something happen?'

His lips tighten. Putting down the glass, he picks up his fork and jabs at his pasta. 'People just change.'

'Maybe ...'

'Maybe what?'

'Maybe losing your parents changed you? Your adoptive parents.'

'Maybe.'

Deep in thought, he stares at his plate, absent-mindedly shoving food around. Within the space of a minute, I've transformed him from playful to deadly serious and I really should leave it now, but intrigue has elbowed its way into my head, barging right past common sense and knocking it to the floor.

'So, you went to Italy?' I ask.

'Eventually.'

'And that's where you ...'

'That's where I learned to speak Italian.' He sighs. 'It's a good place to learn it because that's where they speak it. In Italy.' He puts down his fork, rubs his forehead and finally makes eye contact. 'I lived in Rome for about a year.'

'On your own?'

'No. I lodged with someone.' His bottom lip twitches, a cagey twitch, an I'm-not-telling-you-everything kind of a twitch. He bites it into submission: a sure sign that there's something more. And I think I might just know what it is.

'With a woman?'

He stares at me, his face inscrutable.

'Yes,' he says at last.

And memory kicks into action. That's not what he's told me before. In fact, it's the exact opposite of what he's told me before: *No serious relationships. No non-serious relationships. I've never been married. Never had any children.*

'But I thought you'd never lived with a woman.'

'I lodged with her. There's a difference.'

He folds his arms, unfolds them, reaches out and tears off another chunk of bread. Examining it for a moment, he drops it onto his plate.

'And you fucked her?' I ask, nervous of the reply, because unless she was a huge Italian mama, I can't imagine he kept his hands off her.

'Yes.' He leans back again, resigned.

53

'Great. So I'm here for what, three hours, and I've already had another Dan bombshell.'

'It's not a bombshell. It's nothing. It wasn't exclusive.' With a scowl, he takes another sip of wine. 'And just for the record, I also fucked half of Rome.'

Suddenly, my face seems to have a life of its own. My nose scrunches, my eyes narrow and my lips curl up in disgust.

'Any European capital cities you haven't shagged your way through?' I demand.

'Berlin, Madrid, Lisbon. Do you want me to keep going?'

'You've been a serious man-slag.'

He smiles at that.

'This isn't news. You know I used to sleep around. And now I'm a serious monogamist. Don't read anything into the arrangement I had in Rome.'

'Arrangement?'

He leans forwards. 'Yes. Arrangement,' he breathes. 'It was an arrangement.'

Oh Lordy, arrangement. He's mentioned that word before, on more than one occasion: an arrangement with Claudine, arrangements with other women.

'So, it was a kinky thing?'

'Yes. It was the first kinky thing. She's the one who got me into it.'

I must be pulling an almighty I'm-disgusted-by-this sort of expression now because he's inspecting my face. And before I can say anything else, he's putting me firmly in my place.

'If you want to do the big talk thing with me, Maya, you're going to hear some things you don't like. You asked for this.'

Yes, I did. And now that I'm getting it, I'm not so sure I want it at all. Perhaps I should just do what Dan wants me to do and brush the past under the carpet. But no, I remind myself, that's not the way ahead. If I'm going to spend the rest of my life with this man, then I need to know everything about him. I need to hear it all, digest it, process it, and at least try to understand.

'How?' I demand.

'How what?'

'How did she get you into it?'

He sucks at his top lip.

'She picked me up in a bar and took me home. It went from there. She introduced me to the BDSM scene in Rome.'

'Rome? They do it in Rome?'

His eyes flash.

'You get kinky weirdos all over the world, not just in London,' he explains, evidently amused by my innocence.

While he busies himself with another mouthful of wine, I remind myself that I shouldn't be so surprised by all of this. After all, just because Italians are super stylish and uber cool, it doesn't mean that they're averse to a bit of heavy duty slap and tickle.

'So ... you'd never done it before Rome?'

'No.' His expression clouds. 'But I took to it and it suited me, and that's that.' He touches his forehead. 'When I came back to London, I just carried on.'

Silence washes over us. As we gaze at each other, I ponder over the fact that he 'just carried on' for fifteen years, and then I worry over the distinct possibility that when you just carry on with anything for fifteen years, you're going to have withdrawal symptoms.

'So what we have?' I venture. 'Does that suit you?'

'Of course.'

'But the things you used to do ...'

'Are in the past. You know that. I quit way before I met you.'

Because he went too far, I remind myself. Because of a mysterious visitor who sent him over the edge: the twisted Roman landlady, perhaps.

'But do you miss it?'

He runs a hand through his hair and seems to wince. It's obvious that I'm pushing him too far, right into the realms of exasperation. Any minute now and I'll drop the interrogation ... just as soon as he's answered my question.

'Do I miss what?' he demands curtly.

'You know ... the hard core stuff.'

'Do you even know what the hard core stuff is?'

'No. Would you like to tell me?'

'No. Look it up on the internet.'

'I don't have a laptop.'

He stares at me, as if I'm some sort of anomaly.

'We'll have to put that right.' Tapping an index finger against the counter, he watches me, clearly waiting for the next question to arrive. When it doesn't show up, his face softens into a smile. 'Listen,' he says, his voice gentle now. 'What we have is enough. I still get my kink, you enjoy the kink and we don't go too far. What I did in the past and how I behaved, it's all irrelevant. You need to understand that. What suited me back then doesn't suit me now. I'm not that man any more.'

55

'So what sort of man are you?'

'I have no idea.' The smile broadens. 'I'm a work in progress.' He pushes his plate away. 'But I'll tell you one thing.'

'What's that?'

'I'm the sort of man who needs to nip upstairs for a few minutes.' He shrugs, apologetically. 'After all, I'm only human.'

He gives me a cheeky grin, and I just can't help myself: I giggle.

'You'd better go then.'

Rising from the stool, he collects his mobile and takes to the stairs. Although I'm sorely tempted to sneak up after him and indulge in a spot of snooping, a little trust is in order. Instead of spying I'll get all domestic on his backside: I'll clear away the aftermath of dinner.

Gathering up the plates, I dump them onto the draining board and set about locating the bin, opening one sleek grey cupboard door after another until I finally find it, right next to the fridge. Grabbing a plate and flipping open the lid, I'm about the scrape the remnants of the puttanesca into the rubbish when I catch sight of a piece of card. I come to a halt, registering the fact that it's torn, that there's writing on it: the words 'I hope' in a distinctly female hand.

With my heart thudding against my ribs, I glance back at the staircase, leave the plate on the counter top and reach into the rubbish. I shove aside a handful of onion peel, pick out the fragment, and notice that there's another beneath it … and then another … and another …

Moving quickly, I collect them all and lay them on the granite top. I check the staircase again, move the pieces and realise that I'm re-constructing a birthday card. I catch a name. Layla. An address. My heart thuds again. My thoughts begin to race. Who the hell is Layla? Some ex sub? Another woman from another arrangement? In a fluster, and with no idea what I'm planning to do, I scoop the pieces together and hide them away in the side pocket of my handbag.

And now I need to cover my tracks.

Noticing a silver panel in the wall, I make the quick decision that it has to be a rubbish chute. After all, what sort of millionaire in his right mind is going to lug his rubbish bags down the stairs? After scraping the last of the dinner into the bin, I heave out the bag, tie it together at the top and with a breath of relief, send it down the chute.

The slam of a door heralds his return. Listening to the soft padding of footsteps on the stairs, I will myself to calm down, go back to the sink and switch on a tap.

'You're cleaning up?'

'I'm a domestic goddess.'

'I very much doubt that,' he laughs. 'I have got a dishwasher, you know.'

'Oh.'

I feel a hand on my shoulder. He swivels me round to face him full on.

'I didn't see it.' I feign a smile. 'But I did manage to find the bin. I emptied it.'

The laughter stops.

'It was nearly full. I used the chute. Did I do right?'

'Yes. You did.'

And now the mask descends.

Mr Mean and Hot and Moody is back.

Chapter Seven

In silence, I watch as he takes the bottle of wine and glasses over to the living area, settles himself onto a sofa and pats the space next to him. Rooted to the spot by doubt and confusion, I stay exactly where I am. All I know is this: he's not about to get a quick cuddle and a dash of sweet talk, not while my brain's still beating itself up over an Italian landlady and a ripped-up birthday card. When all's said and done, there are just too many shadows in the room.

I need him to open up. I just have no idea how to do it. Silently resolving not to let him touch me until I'm done, I pick up my mobile and wander over to the sofa. I may not get to the bottom of things tonight, but at least I can make a start. When I'm right in front of him, I stop and survey the room, taking in the seascapes and the landscapes, and finally my own painting.

'I'm sorry I dragged you to Limmingham. It can't have been easy.'

'You weren't to know.'

'Was it the first time you'd been back?'

He shakes his head, making no eye contact. 'One other time. A few years ago.'

To do what? To see who? I land on the obvious answer.

'Are you in touch with your sisters?'

'No.'

He's deep in thought now, gazing at the wine bottle, scratching his right palm over and over again. While raindrops patter gently against the windows and the shadows shift around me, a strange atmosphere settles over the apartment. There's a charge in the air, an edge of awkwardness between us. At last, he rouses himself. Reaching out, he fills the glasses and takes a sip of wine.

'Dan?'

He looks up.

'I want you to tell me more.' I falter, noting the gloom in his eyes, wondering if I'm taking this too far too quickly. 'About Limmingham.'

The gloom deepens.

'You've already had the basics.'

'And now I need more.'

He shakes his head again. 'Not tonight.'

'But you wanted to fast-track.'

'Not this.'

'Yes, this.'

Raising my mobile, I open up the contact list and begin to scroll through it, launching into an elaborate ruse of my own. I can only hope it works.

'What are you doing?'

'Wondering who to call. I can get out of here now.'

He watches me, obviously weighing up the situation.

'You really want to go?'

No, I don't. Even now, Skinny Lily's words are playing on my mind, reminding me of the twelve-year-old boy who fetched up in her life: *very sweet, very kind ... a little lost.* So, in spite of all my reservations, I'm going to see this through: twenty-three years might have transformed the boy into the man, but maybe at heart he's not so far removed from where he began. Doing my best to keep up the mask, I fix him with a long, hard stare. I'm not about to let him know the truth.

'Is it because of what I told you?' he asks.

'No.' Strangely enough, I think I can deal with the fact that he went on a grand shag tour of Europe and shacked up with a spaghetti-loving submissive. I shake my head, reminding myself that I really shouldn't be judgemental about these people. After all, I'm slowly turning into one myself. 'It's because you hold things back.'

He raises a hand, palm upwards.

'What am I holding back?'

'How should I know? You've got a pretty strange idea of what I should be privy to.'

He lets out a sigh, drops the hand.

'Don't go,' he whispers. Suddenly, he sounds exhausted, desperate. 'Please don't go.'

'Then talk to me.'

Occasionally blinking away a ruffle of darkness, he holds my gaze. Clearly, he's not in the mood for my agenda, and perhaps it's time to give him a little nudge.

'I'm not too good with trust,' I begin, my voice trembling. 'There are things that have happened to me ...'

'You don't need to explain. I understand.'

'Do you?' While the silence spreads around us, he gives no answer. 'You've already tested my trust to the limit. You need to let me in.' I pause, wondering if this is making any sense. 'I need to know everything about you, Dan. I don't want you holding anything back.' I take in a breath. 'And I want you to start with your childhood.'

Without a word, he leans forwards. Resting his elbows on his knees, he interlocks his fingers, fixing his attention on his hands. This isn't going to be easy. Short of tying him to a chair, I'm not entirely sure how I'm going to drag anything out of him tonight. Desperate for a way ahead, I scan the room, catching sight of a chess set on a shelf by the fireplace. And suddenly, I have an idea, a full-on bonkers idea ...

Laying the mobile on the coffee table, I make my way over to the shelf and touch the pieces, one by one, rotating them, inspecting the faces. They're carved in wood, obviously expensive. And while the pawns seem to be nothing more than gravestones, embellished with knot work, the other wide-eyed figures are all miserable, or anxious, or both.

'You play chess then?' I ask.

'I haven't played for years.'

'Me neither.' I run my finger over a queen. Sitting on her throne with a palm clasped to her cheek, she seems to be thoroughly fed up. 'My dad taught me to play.'

'So did mine,' he explains. 'My adoptive dad. That's the set I learned on.' He leans back. 'It's a replica of the Lewis Chessmen. Medieval. I love the faces.'

A miserable chess set. Perfect for a miserable conversation. Carefully, I lift the board from the shelf and carry it over to the coffee table, discovering that it's a damn sight heavier that it looks. Repositioning the board near the corner of the table, I take a seat on the floor, crossing my legs and rearranging the shirt to cover my crotch. And then I motion for him to join me.

'What going on?' he asks.

'I want to play.'

'Now?'

'Yes, now. Come on.'

He eyes me suspiciously, forces out a lungful of air and slides onto the floor, crossing his own legs and staring at the set.

60

'This is mad.'

'Then it should be right up your alley.' I smile sweetly. 'Here's the deal. If you can beat me at chess, I'll move in.'

He looks up from the board to my face. 'I don't understand.'

'It's simple. If you beat me, I'll move in with immediate effect. If I beat you, I'm going back to Camden.'

His forehead wrinkles.

'Tonight,' I add for good measure.

'Don't be ridiculous.'

'Don't call me ridiculous. You're the man who lured a woman to his flat and locked her in.'

'Touché,' he mutters, inspecting the pieces. 'So, I'm guessing there's something more to this.'

'Of course there is. Every time you move, you have to tell me something about yourself.'

'Such as?'

'I'll prompt you.'

He rolls his eyes, lets his head fall back and stares at the ceiling. 'So, the challenge is to beat you as quickly as possible?'

'Exactly.'

He fixes his eyes on me. 'And if I don't take it on, you're going home anyway?'

'Yep.' I flash him a look of pure determination. 'And I mean it.'

'I bet you do.' Running a finger across his chin, he slips into thought, weighing up the challenge perhaps, calculating the risks, assessing his capabilities. 'Okay,' he says at last. 'I'll go along with it. Just don't renege on the deal. I beat you, you move in.'

'I'm a woman of my word.' I tidy up the pieces. When I'm finished, I find him smiling at me. 'I'm serious about this, Dan. You need to talk. If you don't play by the rules, I *will* leave.'

'Fair enough,' he counters. 'But I think you ought to know something.' He pauses for effect. 'I was the school chess champion.'

And I'm thoroughly buggered.

But at least I'll get something out of him before he beats me into a cocked hat. Picking up two opposing pawns, I put my hands behind my back, shuffling the pieces before presenting him with closed fists, a pawn hidden in each. He taps my left wrist. Unfurling my fingers, I reveal a brown pawn. Knowing that I've got the upper hand, I punch the air, turn the board and manoeuvre the brown pieces towards Dan. I rub my hands together and make my first move, my usual move, shoving a pawn forwards, two spaces, opening up my queen.

'So,' I venture, suddenly all too conscious that I'm about to force him into talking about things he'd much rather forget. 'The first prompt. Tell me about your real dad.'

His shoulders tense. He stares at the board, and I have no idea whether he's rifling through memories or simply thinking about the next move. I'm expecting him to put a premature end to the game when he finally begins to speak ... slowly, quietly, his voice almost a whisper.

'I never knew him. He left before I was born.' He reaches out, eyes still fixed on the pieces, and mirrors my action, moving his pawn out to meet mine. And then, without any further prompting, he carries on. 'I know his name. That's it. I have no wish to meet him. Your go.'

Resting his right elbow on his knee, his chin against his hand, he presses his lips against his knuckles. I can hear his breathing now: a little faster than normal, each breath catching on itself, faltering slightly.

'Maybe this isn't such a good idea.'

He pins me down with the swirls of blue.

'It's a fine idea,' he says. 'I'm about to beat you at chess, and you're about to move in. Take your turn.'

Half aware that I'm no longer in control, I scan the board. And then, with no idea what I'm doing, I pick up a knight, bringing it out to threaten his pawn.

Registering the move, he settles his eyes on me and waits for the next prompt. I give it to him.

'Your sisters.'

He studies the pieces before he begins to talk again.

'Layla was born when I was two. Sophie a couple of years later.'

Barely registering the second name, I stare at him open-mouthed, but he doesn't seem to notice: he's mulling over the next move. Layla. So, that's who the card was from: not some ex-submissive, but his sister. With one mystery solved, I should begin to relax, but I can't. A new set of questions are already jostling their way into my head. Why would he rip up a birthday card from his sister, and why would he exclude her from his life?

'Is that it?' I ask.

'There's not much to know. I didn't have a lot to do with them. I wasn't allowed.' He squints at the chessboard. 'Layla was ...' He drifts into silence. Reaching out to move a knight, he changes his mind and retreats. 'She was more sympathetic. Sophie didn't give a shit. She was a daddy's girl.'

'Don't you want them in your life?'

He opens his mouth, closes it again.

'But they're your family.'

'It's not ...' He hesitates. 'It's not that I don't want anything to do with them. It just can't happen.'

'Why not?'

Making a decision, he leans forwards, bringing out one of his own knights, ready to take mine if I capture his pawn.

'It's complicated. Your move.'

And now I'd really like to finish with the game. My brain's all over the place and I can barely concentrate on the miserable Medieval chess pieces. I'd rather focus on the miserable man right next to me. But this was my stupid idea and I just need to get on with it. As shadows dance in the corners of the room, I pick up a bishop and take him diagonally across the board until he's level with my pawn.

'Your step-father.'

He forces out a quiet breath.

'A drunk and a thug.' He reaches out again, his fingers unsteady, retreats again, balling his hand into a fist.

I'm not about to push him further and, as it happens, I don't have to. Still focussed on the board, he carries on, speaking quickly, his tone flat and lifeless.

'I don't remember a time when he wasn't around. I irritated him because I wasn't his. I was a nuisance. Baggage. He was always shouting at me, smacking me, reminding me what a useless piece of shit I was, that sort of thing. The older I got, the worse it got, especially when he'd been down the pub.'

He shifts a pawn, opening up his king, and I watch him silently as he works at his bottom lip with a thumb, staring resolutely at the board. Come what may, he's clearly determined to meet the challenge. Playing by my silly rules, he's going to make absolutely sure that I don't leave. I pick up my second knight and move it into play.

'But he wasn't like that with your sisters?' I ask uncertainly.

'No.' He runs a hand through his hair. 'I was the handy target. Every last bit of frustration he had, he took it out on me.' He brings out a bishop, sweeping across the board and moving it into position next to my knight. He'll take it if I don't defend myself. 'Your turn.'

'But what about your mum?' I move the knight out of the way, using it to capture a pawn in the process. I'm one up, but that was a seriously bad decision. I've just cleared the way for him to take my queen. 'Why didn't she try to stop it?'

'Because she was weak. Because she was afraid of him, or afraid of losing him. I don't know. All I know is that she turned a blind eye.' Finally, he looks up. 'She drank a lot. She was worse than useless. She didn't care. I have no feelings for her.'

Although the words are flowing now, his eyes seem to have darkened with memory. I can practically see the pain.

'We should stop.'

He shakes his head. 'I want to finish.'

'But ...'

'You need this, Maya. And I'll give you anything you need.' He picks up his bishop and takes my queen. 'Now ask a question.'

I fumble through my head, searching for something to ask, but it's impossible. His words have set my heart into overdrive, and suddenly I'm overwhelmed by what he's doing for me.

'I can't think of one.'

'Then allow me. How did I cope with all this shit? That's what you want to know, isn't it?'

I nod.

'I spent a lot of time at the beach, hung out in the woods. When I had to be at home, I stayed in my bedroom ... when I had a bedroom.'

'And when you didn't?' I slide my bishop across the board, taking a second pawn and much to my surprise, putting his king into check.

'I was eight. He gave my bedroom to Sophie. I had a mattress in the outhouse, a duvet, a pile of clothes.'

'Check.'

He pushes his king forwards.

'I didn't have many clothes and I grew out of them quickly. They weren't washed that often.'

I stare at him, in awe of the fact that he's talking freely now, no prompts needed. His shoulders seem to have relaxed, as if he's unburdening himself little by little.

'Your move, Maya.'

I try to focus on the game. Sensing an opportunity, I move a knight, forcing him back into check.

'Check.'

He studies the board, silent again. Perhaps I should try another prompt.

'You said they didn't feed you.'

'At first they did. And then it was some of the time. Eventually, I suppose they just saw it as a waste of money. So I took things from packed lunches at school, stole from the local shop. I got quite good at that.' Suddenly, he seems to have divorced himself from his own words. Fully focussed on the board, he's working through scenarios, only half conscious of what he's saying. 'Layla used to slip me something every now and then.'

'Is she the one who found you?'

'Yes.'

So, why rip up her card? Why shut her out? Those are the questions I'd really like to ask, but it's not the right time. I'll have to go with something else.

'I can't understand why the school never picked up on this.'

'They did. A couple of times. A letter, a warning about my appearance. My mother made an effort for a few weeks and then it all tailed off again. She did just enough to keep Social Services off her back. And in the meantime, he took it out on me.'

He surveys the board.

'School,' I whisper.

'What about it?'

'You said it was a nightmare.'

'It was, but kids are kids. They make fun of anyone who's different.'

'But my sister made it worse.'

'She didn't know what she was doing. She didn't know the truth. She was just a part of it.' His voice is breaking now, cracking at the edges. 'There were a whole load of things that drove me to ...'

He comes to an abrupt halt, glancing up at me. He doesn't need to say any more. We both know what he's talking about now: how he lay down with a razor blade and waited for the pain to stop. I reach out, noticing that my own hands are shaking, and take a hand in mine. Turning his palm upwards, I gently run my fingers over his wrist.

'No scars.'

With a sigh, he offers the other hand. I take it, examine it, but in the gloom, it's difficult to see anything.

'You wouldn't know it's there, but it is.' He straightens his lips and stares at me. 'You've beaten me.'

'What?'

He nods at the board. 'Check mate. You get to go home.'

'How the hell did that happen?' Letting go of his hand, I scrutinize the board. Yes, he's totally right. There's nothing he can do. I've backed him into a corner. When I look at him again, I catch a hint of despair in his eyes, and I'm not having that, not after what he's just done. Reaching out, I topple my king.

'You can't do that,' he complains. 'You know the rules. You've won.'

He reaches out to topple his own king. I grab his hand just in time.

'I'm not playing by the rules tonight.' I smile at him. 'I'm staying.'

Chapter Eight

I open my eyes and blink at the skylight, surprised to find that I'm being greeted by the sun. For a handful of seconds, I wonder where I am, and then confusion gives way to contentment: I can already smell him, feel his arm behind my neck, hear the deep, regular rhythm of his breathing.

Careful not to wake him, I roll over to find him on his back with his head turned towards me, not a trace of tension in his features. Reaching up, I trail a finger down his face, wondering if last night's revelations have left him feeling this way, but the truth is I have no idea. After we showered in silence, holding each other under the streams of water for an age, he took me back to bed and made love to me until we finally drifted off to sleep on the cusp of dawn. And through it all, hardly saying a word, there was a new reverence in his eyes, a new tenderness in his touch ... a deeper connection between us.

I move the finger downwards, opening my palm, running it gently over his chest, across the smattering of hair and up to his shoulders, enjoying the firmness of his muscles, the softness of his skin. I've obviously been too preoccupied with his physique to notice the change in his breathing. When my eyes return to his face, a small smile has crept into the corners of his lips.

'Feeling me up?' he asks, eyes still closed. 'You're a pervert.'

'You created the monster,' I remind him, snuggling up against his chest. His arms close around me and we spend a minute or two in silence, enjoying the simple experience of being together. It's interrupted by a ring tone.

I give a start. His arms tighten.

'That's your phone.' While he brought his mobile to bed with him, I left mine downstairs on the coffee table. 'Aren't you going to answer it?'

'No.' Slowly, he reaches over to the bedside cabinet, picks up the mobile and focuses on the screen. 'Norman.' Silencing the call, he drops the mobile and looks at me.

My stomach lurches and my heart begins to thud, and I'm hardly surprised. His hair's a glorious mess and he's still half-asleep, and my God, I could eat him.

'It might be important.'

'It's never important. Not with Norman. He can wait. Come here.'

He pulls me in, bringing my face right next to his and without any persuasion at all, I move further. Determined to be on top this morning, I straddle him, placing a hand to either side of his head and letting my hair tumble over his face. With a broad smile, he cups my right breast, kneading gently, pulling the nipple between his thumb and forefinger, causing a ball of warmth to fizzle into life between my thighs.

I lower my lips to his, kissing him lightly, teasing him, moving to the edges of his mouth, along his chin, across his cheek. Impatient for the endgame, he reaches to the back of my head and draws me closer. The kiss deepens, tongues intertwine, and I sense his other hand against the small of my back, pushing me in to his morning erection.

'You're wet already,' he murmurs into my mouth.

'It's a nice way to start the day.'

'And now that you're moving in,' he smiles, 'you can start every day like this.'

'What makes you think I'm moving in?'

'Oh I don't know. A little game of chess.'

I try to sit up straight, but I don't get very far. I'm clamped into place by his hands.

'Hang on a minute,' I protest. 'We made a deal. I beat you.'

'And then, rather strangely, you conceded defeat.'

'I said I'd move in if you beat me. You didn't.'

He screws up his nose. 'You're being pedantic.'

'And you're being pushy.'

'So, that's a no then?'

'Of course it's a no. There's plenty more talking to do yet.'

The grip on my hair relaxes. I sit up. He grimaces.

'No more big talk, Maya. Please.'

I gaze down at his face and begin to crumble. There's something so innocent, so child-like about his plea that I just can't refuse. And besides, after last night, I'm not entirely sure that I'm ready for any more heavy-duty conversation. Perhaps we should lighten things up a little.

'Not today,' I reassure him. 'We did enough of that last night. I think we can move on to the small talk today.'

He rolls his eyes.

'All the little things.' I take his chin in my hand. 'The window dressing.'

As if I've just asked him to drink straight out of an unflushed toilet, a frown takes hold of his face.

'If we must.'

Before I know what's going on, I'm flipped onto my back, my hands pinned into place above my head, and now he's straddling me. Jesus, this man can move at the speed of light.

'I suppose it had to happen sooner or later.' His lips skim across mine and then, without warning, he pushes himself up from the bed.

'What are you doing?' I demand, flummoxed by the move.

'Wouldn't you like to know?' With a wink, he makes his way over to the wardrobes. Sliding open the door, he pulls out a drawer, rummages around and retrieves the leather cuffs. 'Kink.' He sidles back over to the bed, holding the cuffs in the air.

Oh shit, my brain gurgles, you're in for it, lady.

'You're not going to torture me into moving in.'

He climbs onto the bed and kneels next to me. 'Give me your hands.'

'I mean it, Dan.'

'So do I. Hands.'

Within seconds, I cave in. While every last part of my body lights up with excitement, I offer him my wrists. With a smile of satisfaction, he wraps a cuff around my left wrist, concentrating intently as he buckles it up, moving on to my right wrist when he's satisfied. Finally, he motions towards the headboard and knowing exactly what I have to do, I lie on my back and raise my arms, watching as he manoeuvres himself above me, tugging out the straps and fixing the cuffs in place.

'Seriously,' I breathe, my pulse quickening. 'You're not forcing me into it.'

'That's not my intention.' He checks the bindings and looks down at me, his eyes hooded.

Starting at my clitoris, a tremor of lust passes right through me.

'So, what is your intention?' I ask, my voice uneven.

He traces a finger across my cheek.

'Small talk is eminently dull.' The finger moves further, down the side of my neck, causing me to close my eyes and groan. He pauses at my sternum. 'Legs apart.'

Immediately, I follow his order, watching as he repositions himself. Lying next to me and watching out for every single reaction, he runs the same finger from my chest downwards, stopping to circle my belly button, slowly, lazily. 'However, I clearly need to discover the tiny, irrelevant facts about you.' The finger travels further down, across my left thigh. 'And you need to discover the tiny, irrelevant facts about me.' While he gazes into my eyes, he brushes the finger across my pubic hair. 'So, I might as well have some fun while we're at it.' Lightly, he traces a path around my labia, pausing to press against my clitoris, sending a flutter of want deep into my loins.

'What?' I gasp. 'You're going to ask about my favourite sandwich while you're ...'

'Doing this?' he grins, sliding the finger into my vagina.

'Oh.'

'Oh, Miss Scotton, you're so wet.' He bites his lip. 'Now, what is your favourite sandwich?'

I almost laugh. Almost. But it's pretty much impossible with Dan's finger causing all sorts of havoc inside. Waiting for an answer, he begins to massage me, but not for long. Removing the finger, he replaces it with two, gently thrumming them against the inside of my clitoris while his thumb squeezes rhythmically at the outside. I take in a deep breath, fighting the need to moan again.

'Ah ... I don't know.' I can barely think already. A knot of warmth has formed deep inside.

'Cheese or ham?'

'Oh shit. Prawns. Prawn salad.'

'Duly noted.' He picks up the pace, pushing a little further inwards, knowing exactly which spots to hit. 'Mine's a BLT, by the way. Favourite drink?'

Assuming a serious face, he waits for an answer, but I just can't give him one. The knot has doubled in size, and now it's pulsating outwards. Suddenly, I seem to be close to hyperventilating.

He helps me out. 'Oh, that's a no-brainer. Dry white wine, preferably in a pint glass. And mine's a decent whisky.'

'Stop.'

'No.'

Lowering his mouth to mine, he kisses me deeply, and while he's otherwise engaged, I take advantage of the situation, moving my legs together, just a little. I need to come, and it needs to be soon, and closing the gap can only help matters. Breaking the kiss, he shakes his head. Oh bugger. He's noticed. And I have no choice: obediently, I part my legs again.

'Favourite meal.'

'This ...' The fingers probe further. In an instant, my brain turns to mush. It's a miracle I manage to finish the sentence. 'This is ... childish.'

Ignoring my complaint, he leans down, taking my right nipple between his lips and sucking slowly, gently at times, harder at others. Tingles of pleasure cascade throughout my breast, and I'm lost. I hear a long, low moan and I know that it's mine. Finally, after what seems like an age, he lets go.

'This is small talk,' he reminds me. 'You asked for it. Favourite meal.'

'Spaghetti,' I gulp. 'Puttanesca.'

'What a coincidence.' He smiles brightly. 'Now, let's see.' He lowers his mouth to my left nipple. Sealing his lips around it, he repeats the process while the fingers continue to work me into a frenzy down below. I'm barely conscious when he raises his head again.

'Tell me something. Where's your favourite place for a holiday?'

'No,' I cry.

'Oh come on, Maya.' The fingers begin to circle now, exploring the depths of my muscles.

'I don't know.' My voice jumps through the air. 'Cornwall,' I splurt.

'Cornwall?' The fingers move deeper still, rubbing against my g-spot. 'Nowhere a little more exotic?'

I catch my breath and force out the words, one by one. 'I've ... never ... been ... abroad.' I gasp, and then I pant. He presses his thumb against my clit, sending a super-charged bolt of energy through my nerves.

'Never?' He eyes me, quizzically.

'Never. I've got a passport. Lucy ... Lucy made me get it. Never used it.'

'Then we shall have to rectify that situation. I'm going to take you away, Miss Scotton.'

Oh, bloody hell. That's not good news. A stinking rich man wants to whisk me away to an exotic location and that can only mean one thing … because stinking rich men just don't do ferries. I might be teetering on the edge of sexual oblivion, but I really do need to sort this one out.

'Not on a plane.'

'Yes, on a plane.'

'I … I can't do planes,' I stammer. 'Big scary things. Shouldn't fly. Witchcraft.'

'You and your fears.' He chuckles. 'You're going to conquer them all. I'll take you to *my* favourite holiday destination. Bermuda. In fact, I'll take you next week.'

Fighting back a floodtide of spasms, I raise my head.

'What?'

He removes the fingers and gets onto his knees.

'Find your passport. Favourite song.'

My head flops back.

'I don't know. I like Elbow.' While my crotch takes a break, I wrestle my lungs back under control.

'I like arse.'

'Dan, that's not funny.'

Manoeuvring himself between my legs, he turns his attention to my labia, parting the folds gently. Oh good God, I know what this means: he's about to go in again, only this time with his tongue.

'Woman,' he says quietly, running his thumb across my flesh.

'What?'

'Woman. John Lennon.' He slides the fingers back into me and I let out a breath. 'I love that song. You should listen to it.' He lowers his head to my crotch and while his fingers continue to work their magic, his tongue begins to swirl against the bundle of nerves at my clit. The warmth begins to rise again, pulsating, radiating, consuming every muscle, every nerve, every last bit of me.

'Holy fucking fuck,' I groan, digging my head back into the pillow and closing my eyes.

I hear him laugh. 'I like this small talk thing. It's not so bad after all. Film.' His tongue goes back to torturing me. My insides crackle. My muscles tense.

'*Jane Eyre*,' I pant. '*Jane Eyre*. Orson Welles.'

'Romance?' He looks up, his hair a tangled mess.

'Yes. Oh, romance.'

Slowly, he withdraws the fingers. Slowly, he pushes them back in again.

'The rich, powerful, domineering man.' He watches me closely as I writhe under his touch. 'Unexpectedly tamed. The happy ending. I think that might be my favourite too.'

He swirls the fingers some more, slowly, patiently. He's in no hurry. Again, he pushes deeper, and I convulse. Taking hold of my thigh with his free hand, he presses a reminder into my flesh. I have to stay still.

'Favourite colour,' he demands.

And while muscles quiver, threatening to collapse in on themselves, I rummage through the chaos of my brain. I know the bloody answer. Where is it?

'Burnt Sienna.'

His free hand travels round from my thigh to my stomach. While he continues to work me up into a storm inside, he begins to trail a finger across my stomach, setting off a whole new wealth of sensations.

'White,' he murmurs. 'Mine's white.'

I lift my head again, let it drop back against the pillow, wondering why the hell he's staring at me now as if the colour white has some sort of massive significance.

'Why are you ...' This time, I'm incapable of getting to the end of my sentence. Instead, I decide to tug pointlessly at my bindings. I'm close now. So bloody close.

Removing the fingers, he places a hand to either side of my body, arching himself above me, and for a few precious seconds I get to ogle the perfect torso. Good God, why did I ever contemplate turning my back on this? In one easy movement, he's inside me.

'And now we know each other inside out,' he whispers, sliding further, 'you can agree to move in.'

And so, in the blink of an eye, the small talk thing has transformed into a big talk thing. I'd give him a damn good glare, but my eyes seem to have lost the ability to focus. A shimmering heat is rippling through my muscles and I strain at the cuffs.

'No,' I groan.

He fills me completely, staying buried deep inside for a few seconds before he draws out again, right to the tip.

'Why ever not?' he demands, pushing inwards, quickly now.

'Because ...' My lungs contract and I gasp. 'Because you've got to say the words.'

'I've already said them.' He pulls out. 'Move in with me.'

'Not those words.' I do my best to stare resolutely into his eyes. It's not easy. My vagina is twitching, quivering. 'The other words.'

Three words, to be exact, my brain complains, and you know exactly which words I'm referring to, you bastard. With a wry smile, he adjusts his angle and pounds back into me, as far as he can go, with all his might. A free kick to lust and pleasure. My brain spins off into the distance and I'm nudged away from reason, dragged into a glorious wonderland of mindless fucking. His lips cover mine, delivering a kiss that seems to go on forever. It's demanding, raw, possessive. And all the time he plunges into me, driving me to the edge of insanity. Tightening his grip on my body, he ratchets up the tempo, thrusting hard and ramming me further up the bed while the pressure builds inside, reaching almost unbearable levels. I'm about to implode when he slows once more, releasing my mouth.

'Say yes.'

Gulping for breath, I shake my head. 'You said you wouldn't ...'

'Torture you?' He grins. 'I lied.' He begins to move again.

'You won't last,' I cry out. 'You're shit at tantric sex.'

'This isn't tantric sex.' He withdraws to the hilt. 'This is me controlling you.' He takes a breath, pushing into me again. 'This is me withholding your orgasm. Come on, Maya. It's inevitable. You know it.' Another lunge. 'I'll keep this going until I get my answer.'

Manoeuvring a hand under my buttocks, he urges me up against him and slips into a steady rhythm. And I see nothing but pure determination in his eyes. I don't doubt him at all. He's trapped me and tormented me with ecstasy, and right now I'll say anything to get what I need.

'Okay, okay, okay,' I practically shout. 'I'll do it. Now finish me off.'

'Good decision.'

He picks up the pace again, keeping it going this time, and while my muscles tense around him, I watch as his pupils dilate and his lips part. Finally, his breathing begins to unravel. His grip tightens against my buttocks and I can barely hold it any longer. As his thrusts reach their peak, he empties himself inside me, and a pin prick of heat at my core explodes. My vagina contracts, clenching at his cock as he pumps into me. I'm shaking now, crying out incoherently while he slows the movement, shuddering his way down from his orgasm. Quaking in his grasp, I'm silenced with a kiss. When I'm finally released, I struggle to control my lungs.

'You're a devious pig,' I gasp.

Saying nothing, he bites back a grin as he pulls out of me.

And I'm in a stupor. Closing my eyes, I melt into the sheet, thoroughly contented and utterly exhausted. He's reaching over me now and I already know what he's doing, and I just don't care. I hear the beeps as he calls up a contact on his mobile.

'Carla, I need you to do something for me.' He's silent for a few seconds, listening to the voice at the other end of the line. 'Never mind about that. I want everything of Maya's moved to my apartment ... as soon as possible. Arrange for a removal company. Invoice it to me personally. Call Clive for her friend's number and liaise.'

He ends the call and I open my eyes, watching as he slides the phone back onto the bedside table.

'Done.'

He leans across me, unfastens the cuffs and lies back, opening his arms in a silent invitation. Loving the smell of his sweat, the warmth of his body wrapped around mine, I shuffle into his embrace. I'm in heaven, and it may well be perfect, but I've still got a point to make.

'I'm not having total strangers going through my stuff,' I grumble.

'Lucy's going through your stuff. She's not a total stranger.'

'I want to go home and sort it out. And I need clean knickers.'

He lands another gentle kiss on my nose.

'Take the ones you've got, turn them inside out and wear them for another day.'

'God.'

'Besides, you don't need knickers at the minute.' He grins mischievously and slides a hand underneath the sheet. 'See how easy it is living with me?'

The smell of something mouth-watering wafts through the apartment, snaking its way up into the bedroom. I can barely concentrate on trying to tug a brush through my hair, I'm so hungry. Half an hour ago he left me with orders to shower and dress appropriately for breakfast. And now, with those orders duly followed, I've donned yet another of his white shirts and I'm ravenous. Finally satisfied that my hair's in some sort of order, I make my way downstairs. Passing through the living area, I cast a quick look at the chess set, recalling the shadows of last night, thankful that they've been pushed aside by the morning's shenanigans. And then I come to a halt, stopped in my tracks by the sight of Dan. Dressed in grey joggers and a T-shirt, he's busy at the hob. I take a moment to admire his backside before sidling over to him and slipping an arm around his waist.

'Smells good.'

On tip-toes, I peck him on the cheek. He's not shaved yet and there's a smattering of stubble on his chin. Suddenly, I'm not quite so hungry. In fact, suddenly, thanks to the rough and ready look, I'm feeling quite horny.

'Stop staring.' He turns off the gas. 'You're making me all self-conscious.'

'I can't help it. My boyfriend's a fucking gorgeous sex god.'

'Just for the record, I'm not your boyfriend, I'm the man you live with.'

'Yada, yada, yada.'

'Go and sit down.'

Releasing him, I take my place on a stool and push his mobile to one side. Almost as soon as I move it, it begins to vibrate. Norman's name appears on the front screen.

'He's ringing you again. Norman. Is he always this persistent?'

'Just lately, yes.' He brings the frying pan over to the breakfast bar. 'The closure at Tyneside. Don't get me wrong, I admire the man, but bloody hell he can flap.'

'Why doesn't he just text?'

Dan shakes his head. 'I've showed him how to do it more than once. It's like trying to teach a fish to tap dance.'

With a giggle, I think of Norman: a kindly man, nothing more or less than a colossal teddy bear. He doesn't deserve to be ignored.

'You should call him back.'

'I'm on holiday.' He points a spatula at the phone. 'And he knows that.'

'Then it must be important.'

'I'll call him later.'

Tipping a pancake onto each of the plates, he nods at the bottle of maple syrup. I pick up a fork and glance at the window, noticing that it's open. Outside, it's begun to rain again.

'Hang on a minute,' I remark. 'Those doors are open.' I don't know why I'm so surprised.

'Uh huh.' He's back at the sink now, dumping the pan in a bowl of water. 'Eat it while it's hot.'

'But why are they open?'

'Because I like the sound of the rain.'

Okay, so maybe that was the wrong question.

'How are they open? I thought Clive had all the keys.'

'Oh, about that ...' He shrugs. 'Turns out I was wrong. Tea or coffee?'

'I drink tea in the morning. A fact you should know.'

'And now I do.' He flicks on the kettle, takes a mug and a teabag out of the cupboard and sets about making me a drink. 'So, what do you want to do today?'

Leaving the kettle to boil, he comes back to the counter.

'Seeing as you've locked us in, we haven't got that much choice.'

'Oh ... about that.' Reaching into his jogger pockets, he produces a set of keys.

'You bastard.'

He throws the keys onto the counter and gives me a smile, one of his lop-sided specials.

'Are we good?'

I glare at him for as long as I can, and then the glare disintegrates. I just can't be angry with him, and he knows it.

'We're very good.' I take a mouthful of food.

Sitting down beside me, he sets about drizzling syrup onto his pancake and devouring it. I'm just about half way through my breakfast when I'm suddenly distracted by his iPad. There it is, sitting in plain sight, right next to the fruit bowl.

'And what's that doing there?'

'I had a bit of work to do. Turns out it wasn't in the car at all.'

Without batting an eyelid, he leans over, cuts off a slice of my pancake, drizzles it in syrup and brings it to my lips. As soon as I open my mouth, he slides the pancake in, grinning mischievously, moving the fork about so that syrup dribbles down my chin.

'Oh, oh,' he murmurs. 'I'd better clear that up.'

Dropping the fork, he brings an arm around my back, pulling me in while he licks away the syrup. And then he moves upwards. It's a good job I've chewed furiously and swallowed because before I know it, he's homing in for a kiss. As soon as our lips make contact, his mobile begins to ring again.

'Oh, for fuck's sake.' Swiping up the phone, he checks the screen and answers. 'Norman. What is it?' He listens intently for a minute or two, his expression clouding. 'When?' Turning away, he listens some more. When he finally speaks again, his voice has softened. 'And where is she now?'

My brain begins to tumble. I have no idea what's going on, but I'm suddenly wondering if it's something to do with Betty.

'I'm on my way.' His shoulders slump. 'Don't worry. I'll deal with it. Leave her where she is.'

He ends the call. Still facing away, he stares out of the window. I touch his arm and when he turns back to me, I'm shocked by the sadness in his eyes.

'What's the matter?' I ask.
He shakes his head.
'Dan?'
'It's Molly.'
'Your dog?'
He nods. And then he takes a breath.
'She's dead.'

Chapter Nine

It's a relief when we leave the M25. After spending the best part of an hour in Dan's Mercedes, gripping the seat and staring out of the windscreen at a mess of spray and tail lights, I can finally relax. As we begin to wind our way through the Surrey countryside, I peel my hands away from the leather. My attention shifts from the road in front of us to the man I love.

Delectable in faded jeans and a white shirt, open at the collar, he's fully focussed on driving, checking his rear view mirror more frequently than necessary, but now that we're off the motorway, he's clearly beginning to relax a little too. Taking his left hand away from the steering wheel, he rests it on my thigh, setting off a flurry of lust right at my core. He's probably not in the mood for a bit of filth right now, but it's hardly my fault I've been transformed into a shameless floozy. I'm about to hitch up Lucy's dress and guide his hand further towards my crotch when he breaks the silence.

'Listen ... I've organised a bodyguard for you.'

Oh, for God's sake. I thought he'd forgotten about that. The last thing I need is a burly piece of meat shadowing me.

'A bodyguard?'

'Don't act so surprised.' He checks the mirrors again. 'I told you I'd do this.'

I scowl at him, pointlessly, because he doesn't look my way.

'I need to go back to work tomorrow,' he explains. 'When I'm not around, you'll need protection.'

'From what?'

I catch a glance.

'Boyd.'

I tut, roll my eyes. 'You scared him away. I don't need a bodyguard.'

'Don't play this down, Maya. It's just for the time being. He starts tomorrow morning.'

The hand leaves my thigh, and I miss it immediately. Changing down a gear, he flicks the indicators and takes a right onto the driveway of the house. We creep through the canopy of trees, rattling further along the gravel until the trees give way to the lawn and the house slides into view. Drawing to a halt, he silences the engine and squints up at the three storeys of Georgian splendour.

'This wasn't what I had in mind for today. I'm sorry.'

I touch him on the cheek.

'It can't be helped.'

With a smile, he unfastens his seatbelt and gets out. Quickly circling the car, he opens the passenger door and offers me a hand. I lap up the gentlemanly gesture, allowing him to help me to my feet before I take a moment to straighten out the dress, only too conscious that where underwear's concerned, I've decided to ignore Dan's advice and go commando.

'Right,' he sighs. 'Let's get this sorted.'

Taking my hand in his, he leads me round to the back of the house. We've almost made it to the door when he pauses, suddenly distracted by something. I follow his line of vision and spot a small mound in the distance, shrouded with a sheet. He hesitates for a few seconds.

'I let her out first thing this morning.' Norman's voice jolts him back to life. Standing at the door with his hands in his pockets, the big teddy bear takes a step forwards. 'She was totally fine. I went to get ready for work, and then ...'

Dan places a hand on Norman's back. 'Are you okay?'

'It's just a dog.' The old man forces an embarrassed laugh. 'But you know how it is.' He waves a big hand through the air. 'I'm fine.'

But I can tell he isn't. His eyes are red.

'Betty's in the kitchen. I'd better ....'

While Norman disappears back inside the house, Dan surveys the orchard, the fields, the woodland beyond.

'She was only six,' he says, his voice barely a whisper. 'No age at all. Always healthy.' He shakes his head, and suddenly I realise that he's just as upset as Norman. 'We always had a dog. Family tradition. We used to go for walks in those woods over there.' He nods towards a copse, his eyes glimmering in a shaft of sunlight. 'I'd never done anything like that before ...'

Suddenly, I'm overwhelmed by the need to comfort him, but no words come to mind. All I can do is touch his arm and give him a smile.

'Go on in,' he says at last. 'I'll go and see to her.'

I watch as he walks away, towards the kitchen garden, deciding that he wants a few minutes on his own to say goodbye, and there's no way I'm about to intrude. Instead, I take myself into the kitchen where I find Norman fiddling around with tea cups and Betty slumped at the table.

'Oh, Maya,' she groans. 'Isn't it awful? Who am I going to talk to now?'

I'd like to offer up Norman's name, but I have the distinct feeling it might be a ridiculous suggestion. Instead, I give her my condolences and take a seat at the table. Before long, we're joined by Norman and a pot of tea. As the silence lengthens, I'm not entirely sure what else to say. Occasionally shaking his head, Norman sips at his tea while Betty pulls a handkerchief out of her apron pocket, wipes her eyes, blows her nose, and then tucks it away again. The process has been repeated at least five times when Norman eventually leaves us and joins Dan outside.

'Will you be having dinner here?' Betty asks.

'I'm not sure.'

'I expect you will.' Shoving the tissue into her pocket, she rises from her chair and busies herself with moving things about: saucepans, cups, a bag of potatoes. 'Cottage pie. Do you eat cottage pie?'

'I eat just about anything, Betty.' I get up. Making straight for the window, I spot the two men immediately. They're standing beneath an apple tree, deep in conversation.

'Oh, I'm glad to hear it,' Betty says. 'I can't be doing with those fussy eaters.'

I turn from the window just in time to see her pick up an envelope. 'Don't let me forget to show this to Dan.'

'What is it?'

'A quote for the decorating.' She slaps the envelope back down. 'Has he told you about it?'

I shake my head. Grabbing a tea towel, she flaps it in the general direction of the door. 'It's since he's met you. He's been on about redecorating the bedrooms. He wants you to choose the colours.'

'Me? Why me?'

'It's your house now.'

My house? Has Betty taken leave of her senses?

'Betty, I'm just moving into the flat in London, that's all. This isn't my house.'

'And it's not mine either.' She flaps the tea towel again. 'It's Dan's. And it's going to be yours too when you get married.'

I swallow hard and blink.

'Married?'

'Oh, it's going to happen.' She wafts the tea towel at my frown. 'I can feel it in my water. I expect he's thinking about the future. You know, the pitter-patter of tiny feet.'

Excuse me? What? With the full intention of hiding an incoming blush, I look out of the window again. Dan's talking on his mobile now while Norman listens intently, occasionally scowling at a hedgerow. Finally ending the call, Dan slides the phone back into his pocket and the two men talk some more. At last, when they seem to have finished, Dan leads the way back to the house. Dodging away from the window, I sit back at the table.

'Did you bury her?' Betty asks as soon as they enter the kitchen.

'No.' Dan makes for the sink, washes his hands and grabs a towel. 'I've put her in my car. I'm taking her to the vets later.'

'Why?'

'She must have eaten something. I want to know.' He flings the towel onto a worktop.

Suddenly bristling, Betty folds her arms. 'It can't be anything in the garden. Norman's never used anything that could harm her.'

'I know. That's not what I'm saying.'

'And she never wandered off. And there's nothing in the house.'

'I'm not trying to blame anyone. She might have picked up something while she was out on a walk, down in the woods. It could be anything. I just need to know.'

Placated by Dan's words, Betty finally seems to relax a little.

'What happened to her name tag?' he asks.

Norman's eyebrows lurch upwards. 'Nothing.'

'It's gone.'

'I don't know ...' Norman shrugs.

'Never mind. It probably came off a while ago.' Moving closer to the table, Dan holds out a hand to me. 'Let's go for a walk.'

'What?' I glance from Norman to Betty and back again. 'Now?'

'Yes, now.'

'But the vets?'

'Busy this morning. They can't deal with this until later.'

I stand up, anxiously smoothing down the dress before I slip my hand into his. I'm led through the flag-stoned hallway, out of the back door and across the lawn. In silence, we stroll past the orchard, this time skirting the wall of the kitchen garden and emerging into a section of the grounds that I've never seen before. I'm guided forwards until we're about twenty feet away from the wall. And then we stop. I'm left to take in the view, to wonder at the beauty of it all. We're at the top of an incline now. To the left, acres of woodland stretch out into the distance while to the right, I can see nothing but fields, divided by plush hedgerows that dip and rise as far as the eye can see. Ahead of us, there's a fence, and beyond that a meadow sweeps down towards a copse. Right on cue, the sun comes out. Shafts of light glint across the wet grass.

'What do you think?' he asks, watching my face.

A breeze sweeps up the hill, catching hold of my dress. I grab it quickly and push it down.

'It's beautiful.'

'And it's all ours, right down to the woods at the bottom.' He slips his arms around me, pulling me into his warmth. 'What do you think of the light here?'

'The light?'

'That stuff that comes from the sun.' He smiles indulgently.

Confused by the sudden change of topic, I look round. In the blink of an eye, he's gone from dealing with the dog to talking about light. I have no idea what's going on inside his head, but I'll hear him out.

'It's good.' Actually it's not just good. It's much better than that. We're totally clear of the trees and there's no shadow in sight. 'It's great.'

'Perfect. Do you like the view?'

I gaze out over the copse, puzzled by the train of questions.

'Yes, it's amazing. Why?'

A hand comes to the back of my head.

'I'm having some plans drawn up.'

He leans in for a kiss, his lips gentle against mine, sending a thrill right through me. I could lose myself in the sudden rush of sensations, but my brain is currently yelling out for an answer.

'For what? Plans for what?'

'A studio.'

Everything slams to a halt.

'Here?'

'You really can be a bit slow sometimes, Maya. Of course here. It's away from the house. The views are amazing and the light's perfect.' He lets go of me.

In a complete daze, I wander round, occasionally catching hold of the dress, mulling over his latest idea. Decorating six bedrooms is one thing, but sorting out a purpose-built studio is on an entirely different level. This is commitment on a grand scale, and I just can't let him do it.

'You … you can't,' I stammer. 'It's going to cost a bomb.'

'I can afford it.' Shrugging off my concerns, he becomes business-like. 'I'm thinking glass doors on this side.' Pacing out the shape of the building project, he swipes his hand through the air, as if he can already see it. 'You'll be able to open them out in the summer. But you'll want total climate control: under-floor heating, air conditioning. The temperature needs to be perfect. And you'll need a bathroom, of course.' And then he stops, glancing at me, maybe realising that he's going too far. 'I can get the architect to come and talk to you. You'll need to tell him what you need. I think we can get this up by Christmas.'

Muted by shock, I watch as he approaches me. Dipping his head, he looks into my eyes.

'Say something, Maya.'

The wind catches at the dress, and I catch hold of the hem … just in time. The movement seems to jolt my mouth into action.

'I've only just agreed to move in with you.'

'And?'

'And?' Another gust of wind skitters up the hill. The dress billows and rises. 'Oh for fuck's sake.' I push it back down. I'm not sure whether it's the wind/dress/lack of knickers situation or the bulldozer of a man I'm dealing with, but suddenly I seem to be teetering on the edge of full-blown irritation. 'We've hardly known each other for five minutes and you want to build me a studio? It's mad. And so is the decorating, for that matter.' Risking a few seconds of one-handed dress control, I wave a hand towards the house.

'I'm having the bedrooms decorated. What's mad about that?'

At this point, I'd very much like to bring up the pitter-patter of tiny feet, making it perfectly clear that even though it's a nice idea – and I've certainly thought about it before now – I'm nowhere near ready for taking the plunge. But then again, it's probably best to keep schtum for now. After all, Betty might just be talking bollocks, and I could end up looking like a prat. I settle for something a little less problematic.

'This is too quick.'

'We're moving at our own speed.'

'As far as I can see, we're moving at your speed. This is the maddest sodding roller-coaster ride I've ever been on. It's like standing in front of a freight train. It's like you've only got one gear.'

He grins again.

'Are we finished with the clichés?'

'Yes, thank you.'

'Good.' He moves a strand of hair behind my ear. 'Then, I'll slow down. Or at least, I'll try.'

'And you'll hang fire on the studio?'

'Of course.'

There's a flash of something in his eyes, and I wouldn't be at all surprised to find his fingers crossed. I'm on the verge of checking when he tugs me in for another kiss, more demanding than before, as if he's reminding me of who's in charge. When I'm finally released, I gasp for breath.

'Don't be mad at me, Maya. I'm on a learning curve.'

He slips a hand under my dress and cups my clitoris, setting off a spasm of warmth in my vagina.

'Are we about to have al-fresco sex?' I ask, battling off the impulse to drag him down onto the wet grass before he's had a chance to reply.

'Certainly not. You get ramblers in those woods. I'm not performing for some sicko in walking boots.' He pauses, brushing his lips against mine. 'Can we stay here tonight?'

'Of course.'

He fixes me with a good long gaze.

'You and me are for keeps. I just want you to feel like this is your home. That's why I want you to choose the colours. That's why I want a studio here.'

I smile, defeated by his kisses, his touch, his words.

'All I need right now is a few pairs of knickers.'

'Then I'll pick some up in town.' Taking my hand, he begins to lead me back towards the house.

'I'm not coming with you?'

'No. I need to do this on my own.'

I struggle against his grip, annoyed by his pronouncement and deciding that if he's determined to go around making executive decisions, I'm going to make him pay for it in the worst way known to a man.

'Well then, you're going to have to go to the chemists as well.'

He comes to a halt, turns and cocks his head to one side.

'Chemists?'

85

'I need some tampons. I took my last pill yesterday and I'm due on.'

He winces. And oh yes, my weapon of choice has hit the mark, head on.

'Fair enough.' He mutters, managing to suppress a grimace. 'Women's things. I forgot I'd have to deal with all that.'

When we get back to the house, I'm halted in my tracks by the sight of an accountant at the kitchen table.

'What are you doing here?' I demand.

'I heard about the dog.' Leaning back in his chair, Clive rests a hand on the newspaper spread out in front of him, and smiles at me. 'I just wanted to see if Norman and Betty are alright.'

If that really was the intention, he's making a pretty bad job of it, seeing as Norman and Betty are nowhere to be seen.

'Where are they?' Dan asks.

'Gone back to the cottage. Betty got a bit emotional. Norman's taking the day off.'

'So he should. Right, I'm off then.' I'm ushered to a chair and pressed down onto it. 'I won't be long. Clive can keep you company.'

'But ...'

He kisses the top of my head, straightens up and points a finger at me.

'No arguments. And don't give him grief.'

I could try complaining, but I'm pretty sure it wouldn't get me very far. I'm just going to have to go along with Dan's agenda. And besides, while the boyfriend's dealing with the vets and getting thoroughly embarrassed in a chemists, I can drill the side-kick for information.

'Why would I do that?' I ask, smiling innocently. 'Go and do what you need to do. I'll be perfectly nice to Clive.'

With a last glance, he picks up the car keys and leaves us. As soon as the door closes, Clive goes back to reading the newspaper, or at least pretending to, and I wait until the crunch of tyres against gravel fades into the distance before I make a start. I'm about to give Clive a good dollop of grief.

'How was the party at the Tate?'

He flicks over a page of the newspaper. His top lip twitches, ever so slightly. 'Fine.'

'Are you sure?'

Turning another page, he takes in a deep breath, blows it out and looks up.

'Okay.' He scratches the edge of his mouth. 'There wasn't a party at the Tate. We made it up.'

'You lied to me.'

'I know.' He smiles triumphantly. 'It worked though.'

'Of course it did. Just don't make a habit of it.'

The smile mutates slightly, an edge of discomfort creeping into his eyes.

'So, why are you really here, Clive?' I ask.

Looking down at the paper, he sucks at his bottom lip. 'Like I said, I was worried about Norman and Betty.' He's being shifty now and I know it. He flips to another page and takes a pen out of his jacket pocket. 'Sudoku,' he mutters. Avoiding all eye contact, he leans forwards and inspects the puzzle. 'I should be better at these things, but ...' He clicks the pen, holds the nib above the page, and finally fills in the first number.

'Cup of tea?' I ask.

'Super.'

I'm not exactly sure why I'm making a cup of tea. Maybe it's just the process of making the bloody stuff that I need. After all, it's what I seem to do whenever I'm in a flap. Getting up, I locate the kettle, turn it round and try to find a switch.

'It's not electric,' Clive explains. 'It works on the Aga. Left hand plate. Mind yourself. It's hot.'

With a sigh, I fill up the kettle and slam it down onto the hot plate. Good God, if this is going to be my new home, then Mr Foster can rectify this little situation. I'm just not prepared to live in the nineteenth century. An electric kettle is a necessity.

'So, how's it going with you and Lucy?' I lean back against the counter.

'Very well.' He eyes me, warily. 'I like her. She's a bit scatty but a lot of fun.'

Deciding that I really don't want to know about the fun aspect of their relationship, I open a cupboard door. Sugar. Flour. Baking soda. A cake-making cupboard. And what the hell are you supposed to do with one of those? Knowing that I'm never going to venture into it again, I open another. Salt. Pepper. Herbs and spices. A variety of sauces, but no ketchup. I'm about to go for a third door when Clive puts me right.

'The cupboard to the left of the sink.'

Tugging open the correct door, I'm relieved to find a packet of teabags and a jar of instant coffee. Pulling out a couple of teabags, I retrieve two mugs from a mug tree and set about tapping Clive for information.

'Clive?'

'Uh huh?'

'Can I ask you a question?'

'Of course.'

'When's Dan's birthday?' Keeping my back to him, I chuck the teabags into the mugs.

'Why do you ask?'

'Just wondering.' The kettle's beginning to simmer now. 'Shouldn't you know when it's your boyfriend's birthday?'

'I suppose so.' I turn to find him eyeing me suspiciously. 'It's this Friday. But he doesn't celebrate it. I wouldn't mention it if I were you. And I certainly wouldn't get him a card.'

So that's why there was a ripped up card in the bin? Simply because he doesn't celebrate his birthday? Not because of some huge rift with his sister? A screeching whistle jolts me out of my thoughts. Bloody hell, that Aga's quick. Making the tea, I take it over to the table and seat myself opposite Clive. I'm going to have to tackle this head-on, and while I'm at it, I'll need to feign a little ignorance.

'Does he ever see his sisters?'

Clive takes hold of his mug. 'Not that I know of.'

'Does he ever talk about them?'

He shakes his head and takes a sip.

'But he's talked to you about his childhood?'

'I know the bare bones, and it's taken me twenty years to get that far. You probably know more about him than I do by now.'

I stew on matters a little.

'I just can't understand why he wouldn't be in touch with them.'

'Neither can I, but I wouldn't push him on it.'

'But what if we ever ...'

I stumble to a halt, realising that I'm about to take a step too far, and look up to find Clive's mouth open. He's trying his damnedest to suppress a laugh.

'Get married?' he asks. 'Have children?'

I pull an I-know-I'm-talking-crap kind of face, except I'm not talking crap at all. I know damn well why Dan told me his favourite colour's white, just like I know why he's having the bedrooms redecorated. He's planning for the end-game. And when all's said and done, as long as he takes his time, I'll be quite happy to play along.

'If we do get married and have kids … at some point … they might think, you know, it's a bit strange … if they never saw their relatives.' I let out a groan, wondering why on Earth I'm spilling this out to Clive. 'Jesus, don't tell him I said that.'

Clive chuckles.

'Mum's the word.' He lays down the pen and rests his arms on the table. 'He doesn't like to think about where he came from: that's my take on matters. But if you and Dan ever did … you know … then you should probably talk to him about it.'

I stew some more. My mission to dig for information seems to be falling flat on its face. I'm not satisfied with Clive's answers. Which reminds me, there's something else I'm having difficulty believing.

'Why are you really here?'

'I've told you twice.' His lip gives another twitch.

And I've had enough. I'll ask him straight.

'Third time lucky then. Are you here to protect me?'

'Protect you? I couldn't protect a fly.'

'Seriously? You hit Dan the other week. And you managed to drag Boyd out of Slaters.'

And that's it. At the mention of Boyd's name, the lip gives one almighty twitch.

'You know what?' I inform him. 'It's a ruddy miracle you managed to dupe me yesterday.'

Before he speaks again, he spends a few seconds tracing his finger in a small circle across the puzzles page.

'If you say anything to Dan, I'll end up with another black eye. And the last one's only just gone.'

I've got him. Another prompt, and I'll have confirmation of what I think I already know.

'So, what's going on?'

'He didn't want to leave you alone.'

'I'm not alone. Norman's here. And Betty.'

'Norman might be built like a brick shithouse but he's got a heart condition. And as for Betty, she's hardly a black belt.'

Fending off an image of Betty in a karate outfit, high kicking some unseen opponent, I move on to the obvious point.

'Is this about Boyd?'

He groans quietly, shifts about on the chair and scratches his ear lobe.

'Just spill the beans, Clive.'

He shakes his head.

'Now.'

'Okay.' He screws up his face and then blurts it all out in one go. 'It is about Boyd. Dan wanted your bodyguard down here but it couldn't be arranged in time. He called me. I'm a stop gap. Don't say anything.'

'Mum's the word.' It's my turn to smile triumphantly. 'But if he's that worried, why couldn't I just go with him to the bloody vets?'

'I don't know.'

My brain sparks into life. 'He doesn't think … He doesn't actually think Boyd poisoned his dog?'

Clive's mouth twitches again. He raises a hand and points at his face.

'Black eye.'

'Spit it out.'

He sighs heavily. 'He just wants to know for sure.'

'God, he's a piece of work.'

'He's just playing it safe.'

'And I'm obviously in love with a paranoid idiot. Bloody hell.'

Pushing the mug of tea to one side, Clive leans forwards.

'He's doesn't want to worry you. That's all. Promise you won't say anything to him.'

Staring at Clive's anxious features, I tap an index finger against the table, dragging out the wait before I finally give him an answer.

'I promise.' I stand up.

'Where are you going?'

To get some peace. That's what I'd like to say. To clear my head and think things through.

'Upstairs,' I mutter.

He leans back again, a wide grin playing across his face.

'Planning the colours?' he asks mischievously.

And I grimace.

'Oh, shut up.'

Chapter Ten

Leaving Clive to struggle with the Sudoku, I go in search of peace and quiet, but as soon as I reach the top of the staircase, I'm distracted by other matters. Intrigued by what I've been informed is my new home, I begin to wander through the bedrooms, four on the first floor, two more up in the eaves, all decked out with antique furniture, cleaned to within an inch of their life and definitely in need of a little make-over. At last, I come to the master bedroom, our bedroom. When I open the first of the two mahogany wardrobes, I discover that it's full of Dan's things: a range of suits, shirts and casual wear. When I open the second, I find it empty, waiting for a new set of clothes, evidently mine. Finally, I lie down on the bed and gaze up at the ceiling, wondering if I'll ever feel at home in a place like this, because at the moment I feel like nothing more than a guest in some posh country hotel.

Closing my eyes, I try to clear my mind. I'm nowhere near thinking things through when I hear a door slam downstairs. With a jolt, I sit up, knowing that Dan's returned. I rouse myself, make my way back downstairs, and falter at the bottom of the staircase, listening to the sound of muffled voices coming from the kitchen. I can't make out the words, but it's perfectly clear that Dan's agitated about something. As soon as I open the door, the conversation slams to a halt. While Clive's still seated at the table, Dan's by the window, leaning back against the counter, arms folded, shoulders hunched.

'What's wrong?' I edge forwards.

'Nothing.' Dan shakes his head.

'So, what happened?'

'Tests. They're sending off samples to the lab. It's going to take a couple of days.'

91

'And Mr Rush-it here can't wait that long,' Clive interrupts. 'I've got to get back to London.' Closing the newspaper, he gets to his feet, shrugs on his suit jacket and touches Dan on the shoulder. 'Relax, for fuck's sake. It'll be sorted tonight.' He casts a glance in my direction. 'See you later, Maya.'

While Dan sees him out, I stay rooted to the spot, feeling distinctly unsettled by the tension in the air. Somehow, in the middle of it all, I manage to note the plastic bag on the table, and smile at the fact that he's fulfilled his shopping mission. But the smile dissolves quickly. Hearing him lock the back door, listening to the footsteps that bring him back into the kitchen, my heart begins to pound.

He moves forwards, coming to stand right in front of me.

'Are you okay?' I ask.

'Fine.'

But it's obvious he's not. His lips have tightened into a straight line, his eyes hardened.

'So what was that about? What'll be sorted tonight?'

He shrugs dismissively. 'Nothing. Work.'

'If you're so bothered by it, why don't you just go in?'

'No. Today's for you and me. That fucking place isn't going to make me feel any better.'

'Then what is?'

He grabs hold of my hand.

'You.'

Without another word, he guides me out of the kitchen, through the shadowy servants' hallway and further into the main part of the house. In silence, I'm led back up the staircase, into the bedroom and left to stand in the middle of the room while he closes the door and draws the curtains. Finally, he's in front of me again, a couple of feet away, his eyes fixed on my face. There's no humour in them now, just a hard edge of determination.

'Take off your dress,' he murmurs.

I should really get him to talk, to explain this strange transformation, but logic and sense have been scattered to the wind. For some reason, Mr Mean and Hot and Moody seems to have reared his sexy head, and he's totally in control.

I simply do as I'm told ... and wait.

I have no idea how long he spends just standing there, taking me in, every last bit of me, as if he's surveying his property. All I know is that my skin is beginning to tingle under his gaze, and there's a throbbing sensation at the apex of my thighs, and my heart and lungs are floundering in a mire of lust.

Finally, without the slightest hint of emotion, he takes a step forwards, reaches up and lightly traces his fingers across my lips, down the side of my neck. The tingles multiply exponentially. Like leaves blown in the wind, they skitter and gather and whirlwind their way across my body. I close my eyes and let out a moan. And then I feel him closer, his breath against my mouth, his arms around me as he unfastens my bra and drops it to the floor. Sliding his right hand across my buttocks, he draws me in to his erection while he traces the ridges of my backbone with the fingertips of his left hand, taking them all the way down to the base of my spine. Flattening out his palm between my shoulder blades, he pulls me in tight, nuzzling his face into my neck.

'This is my sanctuary,' he whispers. 'Being with you.'

Tipping my head back, I drink in the sheer bliss of it all.

'I'm never going to lose you again.'

I'd like to reassure him that he won't, but I can't because he's kissing my neck, patiently working his lips from beneath my ear, down to my shoulder and back. I'm about to slide into a chasm of bliss when he nips at my ear lobe, causing me to jolt at the change of tactic. A spark of excitement erupts at the nape of my neck, travelling the length of my spine and balling to a halt in my groin. I gasp in surprise and the grip tightens. He nips again. Another gasp. Another spark. A hand comes to the back of my head, grabbing at my hair and holding me in place while his mouth moves to a spot further down my neck. Sealing his lips against my skin, he sucks hard ... and then he bites. I jolt for a second time, sensing a burgeoning warmth in my groin.

'Do you want this?' he demands.

'Yes,' I breathe, knowing exactly what he means. He wants it rough, and judging by the fact that I'm already wet down below, so do I. Sense and reason have already taken a hike. It's my full intention to be reckless.

'Your decision.'

Tugging my head to one side, he traces his mouth across my throat, sucking hard in places, grazing his teeth against my skin in others, sending me wild with anticipation. I need more, and I need it now. And there's only one way to get it. While my left arm is still pinned against my side, my right arm is free. In a growing frenzy, I reach up and take hold of the back of his neck, driving my fingernails into his skin, instantly achieving the desired effect. He stiffens, digging his fingers into my buttocks, causing me to cry out. And then he brings his lips to mine, silencing me with a ferocious kiss.

Suddenly, we're teetering on the edge of wild. And I want us to topple right over.

When he finally pulls away, his pupils are dilated, his breathing sharp.

'Remember your safeword.'

I nod.

'Use it if you need to.'

Without warning, he spins me round, holding me tight against his chest. While one hand comes to my left breast, cupping it firmly, the other is thrust between my legs, forcing them apart. His fingers slide over my clitoris, probing roughly. Overwhelmed by the attack, I lean my head back against his chest, giving in to a myriad of sensations, aware that he's pulling at my nipple now. Suddenly, he pinches hard. My knees buckle at the sensation and I let out a groan.

'We like pain, don't we?' he whispers into my ear.

'Yes.'

'Do we want more?'

'Yes.'

He pinches again, holding my nipple tight, prolonging the agony. 'Yes, what?'

'Yes, please.'

Immediately, the hands are removed and I'm guided towards the bed. Crawling onto it, I lie on my back, watching as he tugs off his shirt, ruffling his hair in the process. When he looks up, I half expect a cheeky smile or a joke, but I get neither. With his eyes fixed on mine, he unfastens his jeans and shrugs them off, pants and socks following quickly. He straightens up, a powerhouse of muscles, perfectly formed, his expression utterly determined, completely focussed on the moment. He stares down at me, his eyes emptied of all emotion, and my heart thuds with a sudden realisation. This is the man I saw at the club: the cold, hard dominant who surfaced briefly with Claudine. And Jesus, it's hot.

Climbing onto the bed, he nudges my legs apart and positions himself between my thighs. Without taking his eyes from mine, he anchors himself on his right elbow and lowers himself on top of me, grasping my hair at the forehead and forcing my head back. I take a deep breath, waiting for the next attack, and it's not long before it arrives: his lips are on mine again, hard and demanding, while his tongue probes my mouth, lashing out against my own. Fired up by a strange mixture of fear and excitement, I return the ferocity of the kiss, keeping up with his momentum for an age until, at last, he draws away.

Immediately, he begins to work his way down my neck, sucking, biting, licking, every little action growing in force and pressure and before long, I'm on edge, wondering what he'll do next, how far he's planning to go. My pulse is at top speed now. My heart's pounding, and my brain seems to have launched into riot mode, sending out an order to reach up and grab a handful of his hair. Tugging at it with a violence I never thought I could muster, I force him away from me, but it only fires him up more.

He brings his face up to mine, yanks my head back and I reply immediately by digging my nails into his back with all the force I can manage. He lets go of my hair, grabs my wrist and forces my arm above my head, holding it in place. And then he adjusts his position. In a heartbeat, he's propping himself up on his left elbow, grabbing hold of my free hand and pushing it above my head, pinning both of my wrists together with his right hand.

Satisfied that I'm restrained, he moves again, back onto his right elbow. Wrapping his left palm around my waist, he squeezes hard. I buckle at his touch, my lungs contracting involuntarily, and I cry out.

'Use your word, Maya.'

Clamping my lips together, I shake my head. If he thinks I'm going to throw in the towel, he can think again. I'm enjoying this far too much.

His mouth is on me again now, working its way down my neck and across my sternum. At last, he reaches my right breast. Pausing there, he licks at my nipple, setting off a horde of vibrations. I brace myself, my brain on high alert, knowing exactly what I'm in for next. He licks again, dragging out the seconds while he sends me wild with anticipation. I'm writhing under his grip when he finally latches on to my nipple and bites. A shockwave of agony surges right through me, blowing every other sensation clean out of the way. I hear a scream, and I know it's mine. I struggle under the weight of his body, but I'm fixed into place. At last, he releases my nipple. Struggling for breath, I close my eyes, mentally tracking the retreat of the pain, noting the curious sense of calm that arrives in its place.

Raising his head, he searches my eyes for something.

'Use your word.'

It's not an order. It's a plea, and one that I'm going to ignore because when all's said and done, I want to be at his mercy, I want him to control me utterly and completely, and I want this rush.

'No,' I manage to groan.

His eyes flash with understanding. Forcing my legs further apart, he presses his cock against my opening and pushes inwards, quickly.

Moving his left hand to my hip, he digs in his fingertips to the point of pain. And then he lets go of my wrists, moving his right hand to the back of my neck, wrapping his fingers around my flesh and gripping tight. With my hands freed, I scratch and dig at his skin, amazed at how I've been transformed into some violent, near demonic creature.

My actions fire him up again. In one hard movement, he thrusts inwards, hitting the back of my vagina with a force that knocks the air out of my lungs. I've just about recovered, when he thrusts again. And I scream. Picking up the pace now and holding me fast, he pounds into me with quick, vicious movements. And I'm drowning, drifting away in a fog of pleasure and pain, vaguely aware that my fingernails are gouging into his back, punishing him for the onslaught.

As the familiar pressure rises in my core, his eyes remain locked onto mine, unforgiving and demanding. At last he lowers his head, biting at my bottom lip, harder than he's ever done before, before moving down to my nipple and biting again. I let out another scream. In response, he ratchets up the speed again, covering my mouth with his and kissing me fervently. After a few more seconds of pure, unadulterated, animalistic fucking, I feel his body tense beneath my grip, his breath falter against my mouth, and I let go. Muscles contract around him as my orgasm takes hold: an implosion, a rush of warmth travelling from my clitoris inwards.

His lips leave mine, parting as he unravels.

'Fuck,' he rasps. 'Fuck.'

Filling me with his cum, he slows the pace, shivering in my arms as he works himself down from the high. He collapses on top of me, wrestles his body back under control and withdraws, manoeuvring himself into a sitting position. Leaning back against the headboard, he beckons me to curl into his arms and as soon as I'm in position, he checks my wrists, turning them slowly in his hands before he moves his attention to my neck.

'I hurt you. You should have used your word.'

I look up to find him watching me anxiously.

'I hurt you too. And I didn't need to use my word. I liked it.'

I'd be lying if I said anything else. I've just had a good dose of the dominant, and it turned me on big time.

'What's wrong?' I ask, sensing the slightest of tremors in his body.

He shakes his head, brushing off the question with a shrug and propping his head back against the headboard.

'The last few days haven't been easy,' I offer.

'Meaning?'

'You're upset. I get it. At least I think I do. This is your way of dealing with things.'

He runs a finger down my cheek, and although he's looking at me now, I know he's drifting away. He shakes his head.

'This isn't dealing with anything.'

***

I don't know where I am but wherever it is, I don't like it. He's standing in front of me, holding a glass, his dark eyes glimmering with want. He smiles at me, an empty, soulless smile. A hand reaches out, but I don't want it to touch me. It's touched me before, and the thought of it makes me want to tear my skin away from my body. But I can do nothing. I'm frozen, imprisoned in my own body, waiting for that poisonous contact. He lifts the glass, opens his hand and lets it fall to the ground. The glass smashes, sending a thousand shards skittering across the ground.

***

I wake with a start, taking short, sharp, rasping breaths. I'm sweating.

'Maya?'

At last, I manage to focus. Already dressed, Dan's sitting next to me on the edge of the bed. He cups my cheek in his palm. 'Are you okay?'

'Just a dream.' I shiver. The curtains have been opened, the sash window raised slightly.

He feels my forehead. 'You're clammy. What were you dreaming about?'

It's a bad idea to let him know that Boyd's managed to invade my dreams. A little white lie is in order.

'I don't know. I can't remember.'

He frowns, as if he doesn't quite believe me, and then his expression lightens.

'Time to get dressed. Dinner in ten minutes.'

'But I need a bath.'

And I certainly do, seeing as I spent the better part of the afternoon in a sweat. After the mad bout of rough sex, he made love to me twice more before I finally drifted off into a troubled sleep.

'Later. Cottage pie waits for no man. And if we're late, we won't get pudding.'

He taps me on the shoulder, a silent command to get moving, before he collects his mobile from the bedside table and goes to stand by the window. With a yawn, I push myself out of bed and make my way into the bathroom. As soon as I'm on the toilet, I know

I've started. Glancing round, I notice the tampons. They've been left for me on the unit, right next to yet another selection of toiletries. I smile to myself. True to form, while I've been sleeping, he's clearly been busy organising my life for me. After sorting myself out, I make my way back into the bedroom to find a packet of knickers lying on the bed. I pick them up and examine them.

'Did I do well?' he asks. 'Size twelve.'

Opening the packet, I take out a pair and let them dangle in front of me. They unfurl like a sail.

'Lovely.'

'There wasn't much choice in town. They'll have to do for now.'

'Firmly constructed,' I muse. 'Totally unrippable. And thank God for that.' Bending over, I step into the granny pants and pull them up. 'I'd like to hang on to some of my underwear.'

'Mmm.' He licks his lips. 'Sexy.'

'You can forget about sex. I'm on my period.'

A wave of alarm washes across his face.

'For about four days,' I add.

A second wave.

He falters. 'We can work around it.'

I'm not at all sure what he means by that and right now, I really don't want to know. He watches as I collect my bra and dress, put them on and tidy my hair. By the time I'm ready, he's looking out of the window again, his phone still clasped in his hands.

'What's the matter?'

Slipping an arm round his waist, I join him.

'Just thinking about Molly.'

I catch the flit of a shadow amongst the trees.

'There's someone out there.'

He manoeuvres me into his arms.

'No.'

'But I saw ...'

'There was nobody.'

The dream filters back to my waking brain, echoes of Boyd's face in the darkness, and I begin to panic. Is that Boyd out there? Is he really still stalking me? Would he go this far? I turn back to the window. Yes, I saw it that time. There was definitely a movement.

'There *is* someone out there.'

He blinks, suppressing a scowl as he struggles with the next words. 'It's security.'

'What? You have guards here?'

'I do now.' He draws in a breath. 'Look, Norman knows about it. Don't say anything to Betty. She'll only flip.'

My mind's in a spin and somehow, through the muddle, Clive's words come back to me: *It'll be sorted tonight.*

'Why couldn't you just tell me this was happening?'

'I didn't want you to think I was going over the top.'

'You are going over the top.' I try my best to wriggle out of his arms, but I'm held tight. 'Jesus. What's come over you?'

'Don't be annoyed.'

'You're paranoid.'

'No, Maya. I'm not.'

'If that's the case, then there's something you're not telling me. I don't like being left in the dark.'

His mouth opens as if he's about to speak, and then he thinks better of it.

'You said I could trust you, Dan. You said you'd never let me down.'

'I won't.'

'But you've kept this from me. I'm not some weak, pathetic woman who needs protecting. Tell me why you've done this.'

He's not about to admit the truth. I can tell. Maybe I should help him along a little. After all, he doesn't need to know the source of my information.

'Boyd. You think he poisoned Molly.'

He stares at me, saying nothing.

'Just because he's obsessed with me, it doesn't mean he killed your dog.'

'I know that.'

'Then there *is* something else, something you're not telling me, some reason why you've reacted like this.'

He shakes his head.

'It's just me, that's all.' He closes his eyes, lost in thought. When he opens them again, I catch a hint of fear. 'I'm not taking any chances.'

Chapter Eleven

The next morning, we're back in London. As we ride the lift up to his apartment, I take the opportunity to admire the man in my life. While I'm still in yesterday's dress, albeit with a pair of fresh, clean knickers, he's ready for work in a grey suit, complete with waistcoat and a pink silk tie. I'm silently wondering how I can delay his departure for a quick grope when the doors slide open prematurely. We seem to be stopping off at the lobby.

'What's going on?'

Without a word, he leads me out by the hand. The first thing I catch sight of is the reception desk and the slick-headed concierge lurking behind a computer screen. And then I catch sight of the second thing: a burly-looking man-monster who's apparently been stuffed into an armchair. As soon as he sees us, he rises to his feet, doubling in width and tripling in height.

'You must be Mr Anderson.' Moving forwards, Dan extends a hand.

'Beefy,' the creature announces, his voice deep and rough, as if he's been gargling on gravel. 'You can call me Beefy.'

In disbelief, I watch as a chunky hand is extended in return, as Dan shakes it, and I try to take it all in, but I can barely believe what I'm seeing. Good God, this man is huge. A vast bundle of muscles. Everything seems to be bulging: arms, legs, torso, neck. But, as if he's been hastily thrown together, nothing seems to go with anything else. While the legs are too short for his body, the arms are way too thick. And as for the head, that's practically rectangular, almost like a brick. And it's topped with a carpet of close-cropped blond hair, adorned on either side by a miniature cauliflower ear.

'Don't stare,' Dan whispers, giving me a squeeze. 'It's rude.' He shifts his attention back to Beefy. 'This is Maya.' Putting a hand to the small of my back, he nudges me forwards. If he's as disturbed as I am, he certainly doesn't show it. He's as cool, calm and collected as ever.

'Pleased to meet you,' Beefy grates. His tiny, bird-like eyes flit from Dan to me.

'And this is your bodyguard.' Dan looks down at me. 'Shall we go?'

***

If I was in a state of shock at the sight of Beefy, then it's quadrupled when I find myself standing in the apartment, confronted by a scene of chaos. There's a suitcase by the fridge, a messy selection of plastic bags strewn across the sofas, a crate in the middle of the kitchen, canvases lined up against the bottom of the staircase and a pile of cardboard boxes balanced precariously by the breakfast bar. Bewildered by it all, I shuffle forwards and rummage through the plastic bags, dragging out a clump of T-shirts. Suddenly, confusion morphs into something else, and I think it might be anger.

'What the ...' I come to a halt, gazing at the mess.

'Well done, Carla.' Laying his keys on the counter top, Dan motions for Beefy to come through the front door. 'And Lucy too.'

'Jeez, that was quick.' I sling the T-shirts back into the bag and fix Dan with an affronted glare. 'This is ...' I point at the suitcase. I have no idea why I'm flapping. After all, I heard him make the call. I suppose I just didn't expect it to happen so quickly. 'What's ...'

Slipping a hand behind my back, he pulls me in close. 'We move at our own speed, remember? I cleared space in the wardrobes and drawers.'

'When?'

'Sunday.' He smiles brightly.

Stifling an urge to scream, I stare up into those bright blue eyes. I'd like to let him know his arrogance knows no bounds, and I have no idea what our own speed is exactly, but I'm pretty sure it's a bit too fast for me. Get yourself together, my brain grumbles. Say something. You can't just let him steamroller you into everything.

'Is there a problem?' he asks.

'I don't like other people going through my stuff. And I don't like you trying to take over my life.'

'I'm not trying to take over your life.'

'You could have fooled me.' I extract myself from his grasp. 'Hiring big, bloody bodyguards.' I wave a hand at Beefy. 'And all that stuff at the house.' A general wave in no particular direction. 'And now this. I thought you were going to slow down.'

'I am slowing down.' He shrugs. 'I told you about the bodyguard, we've discussed the house and you knew about your stuff being brought over. Chill your beans, Maya.'

'Chill my beans?' I cast another glance at the clutter and push out a sigh. 'Am I going to have a say in anything?'

'You agreed to move in. I'd call that having a say.' He studies my face. 'Don't misread the situation.'

I have no idea what to say to that. It's just as well I'm distracted by a deep, gargling cough. Tracing the direction of the noise, I find Beefy loitering in the open doorway.

'Come in, Beefy.' Releasing me, Dan takes a step back. 'Let's give you the lie of the land.'

While I clear a space on a sofa, flop down onto it and stare at my belongings, Dan gives Beefy a quick tour of the apartment, taking him upstairs. And judging by the fact that my bodyguard doesn't seem to be blushing on his way back down, I can only assume that they've given a wide berth to the room of kink.

'You've got our numbers?' Dan asks, sliding a laptop onto the breakfast counter.

The beef monster does its best to nod.

'How has he got my number?' I demand.

With a shrug, Dan brushes off my question. 'I'd like you positioned outside the door. If Maya decides to go out, you accompany her at all times. Is that clear?'

'Yes, sir.'

'And if you notice anything out of the ordinary, contact me immediately.'

'Yes, sir.'

I curl up my legs and grab my knees. 'Bloody hell.'

'And you.' Dan aims a finger at me.

'What?'

'Spare laptop.' He taps the computer. 'Username and password.' He makes a show of writing something onto a piece of paper and lays it on the laptop. When he's finished, he reaches into his jacket pocket and takes out a set of keys.

'Catch.' He throws the keys onto the sofa. 'House, apartment, car.'

'Car?'

'Car. It's back from the pound. And you're booked in with a personal shopper at Harrods this afternoon.' He checks his watch. 'Three o'clock. First floor.'

'What?'

Where the hell did that come from? I'm definitely not happy about the way things are going now. If I'm not very much mistaken, deciding that my clothes aren't good enough for my new, lavish lifestyle is the very epitome of controlling behaviour.

'Why would I want a personal shopper at Harrods?'

'Clothes.'

'What?'

'Those things that stop you being naked. You can't live the rest of your life in jeans and combats.'

'I think you'll find I can.'

He marches over, pulls me up from the sofa and lays a finger on my mouth. 'Presents,' he announces, giving me a boyish grin. 'It's romantic. Fill your boots.' He plants a quick, chaste kiss on my lips. 'Oh, and get something formal. You're coming to a charity event with me on Friday night.'

'Am I now?' I bristle at that. Now this is really bossy and seeing as he's not my boss any more, I'm determined to put an end to it.

'Of course.'

And that's it. I've had enough.

'Stop it,' I shout. 'Just bloody stop it! I don't want to go to a sodding charity event.'

Without taking his eyes from mine, he addresses the muscle monster. 'Beefy, could you wait outside please?'

'Certainly, sir.'

While Beefy slopes back out into the lobby, Dan raises an eyebrow.

'Problem?' I ask.

'I'd say so.'

'Why?'

'Well, for a start, I'd be seriously pissed off if you didn't want to attend this particular charity event with me, seeing as it's for a charity that supports children's homes.'

'Oh.' My stomach swirls. Gazing into the eyes of a man who spent two years of his life in a children's home, I suddenly feel like a complete idiot.

'And then Lily would be seriously pissed off, seeing as she runs it.'

'Oh.'

'Oh,' he mimics.

But then again, I remind myself, the bloody man could have told me that up front. He's up to his same old tricks, withholding information.

'You could try asking, you know. That's the usual way.'

'Is it?' He feigns confusion. 'Fair enough. Would you be so kind as to accompany me to a charity dinner at the Savoy on Friday night, Miss Scotton?'

And now his expression is so earnest, I know I can't refuse.

'I would love to, Mr Foster.'

He smiles at that, a full-on, no holds barred, wide-open smile, the kind of smile that's always going to melt me.

'Sorted. Wear a dress.'

I flump into his chest. A hand snakes its way around my back.

'A black dress,' he whispers into my ear, drawing me in tight. 'Long, with a plunging neckline so that I can ogle those beautiful breasts all evening.'

I pull my head out of his chest, trying my best to look repulsed. But in reality, it's impossible. I love it when he's crass.

'And preferably with a slit up the side,' he goes on, 'so that I can poke my fingers into your knickers.'

'You're a disgusting, filthy pig.'

'And you love it.'

'So, what will you be wearing? A dirty rain mac?'

His lips curl into a grin.

'With nothing underneath.'

With a second swift kiss, he releases me and makes his way out into the lobby. Struggling to believe that within the space of a few minutes, he's managed to transform me from righteous fury to full-on, doe-eyed lust, I follow, taking the opportunity to admire his magnificent backside as he saunters towards the lift. He steps inside, punches a button and pivots round just as the door slides to a close.

'See you later, sweet pea.' He smiles … and he's gone.

I stare at the door, grinning for England, repeating his words over and over again in my head. Sweet pea. He just called me sweet pea … and that's a pet name, a lovey-dovey name, the sort of name you use when you're in love. And he used it with me. Shit, he's got me again. I'm beaten.

'Are you alright, miss?'

Still grinning, I look at Beefy. His muscly face contorts itself into something that might just pass for fear. The poor man clearly thinks he's landed himself a job with a pair of nutcases.

'Never better.' I grin some more.

Obviously touched by nerves, the bird-like eyes blink and suddenly, out of nowhere, I seem to be softening towards my bodyguard. There's no way he can spend all day standing in a bland, expensive lobby. And besides, I could do with a strong pair of hands.

'Beefy.' I wave at the doorway. 'You're coming inside with me. A nice cup of tea, and then you can help me get my life in order.'

I spend the best part of an hour stuffing clothes into empty spaces. Bras, knickers, jeans, combats and T-shirts: I shove them randomly into any drawer I can find, vowing to sort it all out later. With Beefy roped in to carrying the junk upstairs, we make quick work of it. Finally, every last bit of chaos is concealed and I take myself into the studio, pleased to discover that my bodyguard has emptied out the contents of the crate and arranged them for me on the sideboard. Not only that, but he's also displayed my latest painting on the easel.

Slumping onto the sofa, I stare at the stormy depiction of Southwark, relieved that I actually managed to finish the picture before those feelings of anger dissipated. And now there's a new blank canvas is waiting for me. I'd love nothing more than to make a start on it, but I'm not in the right frame of mind. Out of nowhere, my thoughts are consumed by images of the man who surfaced yesterday, and the fact that it turned me on. Shifting uneasily on the seat, I remind myself that he's left me with a laptop and an open invitation. He's researched my life, and now it's time to return the compliment.

Minutes later, I'm in position on the bed, staring at the search bar of the laptop and wondering what on Earth to begin with. Prompting my brain into action, I type in BDSM, and immediately I'm bombarded by images of men and women bound and restrained in a whole variety of ways – with straps, tape, rope, manacles – and they're all either blindfolded or gagged, or both. I scroll further, click onto suggested websites, working my way through more pictures and videos. Women suspended from the ceiling, fixed to walls, manacled to tables, even the floor. Women being fucked viciously, aroused with vibrators, spanked, whipped, or flogged.

Involuntarily, I suck in a lungful of air, conscious of the familiarity of some of those scenes, knowing that others bother me deeply because while some of those women are undeniably in pleasure, there are plenty of others who are definitely in abject pain. I have no idea what's staged and what's not, but I have a vague understanding of why they'd willingly put themselves into these situations. After all, I've already experienced the rush, the arousal of being at a man's mercy. But why does that turn me on? In spite of my little research session, I still have no idea.

I close the laptop. For now, I've had my fill of Dan's past and, anyway, time's marching on. Faced with a hideous trip to Harrods, I decide that I'm going to need some decent back-up. And there's only one person who's capable of taking on that job. Changing into combats and a T-shirt, I shrug on a denim jacket and head back downstairs where I find Beefy settled at the breakfast bar. I collect my handbag, the new set of keys, and breeze towards the door. In a sudden panic, Beefy shoots up from his stool, latching on like a limpet.

'Where are we off to?' he asks in the lift, taking his mobile out of his jacket pocket.

'Why do you want to know?'

He looks up. His heavy forehead furrows a little.

'I like to think ahead.'

Even though I know exactly where we're headed, I shrug my shoulders.

'I'm not sure yet. Let's just treat it as a walk for now.'

As the lift door opens onto the lobby, he's still tapping out a message, probably informing my control freak of a boyfriend that his woman is on the move. Shooting out of the lift and giving a brisk wave to the concierge, I head for the revolving doors. Beefy's still with me as I come to a halt, waiting for a gap in the traffic before I sprint across the road and begin the now familiar walk eastwards along the embankment. Staying a good ten feet behind me, he maintains exactly the same speed, whether I slow down or quicken up. I cross the Golden Jubilee Bridge and track my way northwards, past The National Gallery and Nelson's Column, aiming for Leicester Square. At some point, I hang a left, hoping to stumble over the beginnings of Soho, but it's evidently the wrong left. Coming to a halt outside a deli and dodging a delivery van, I glance up and down an unfamiliar side street, realising that I'm completely lost, yet again. I'd better sort this out pretty quickly. The sky's darkened and rain's beginning to spot. We're going to have another downpour soon.

'Are we still just having a walk, miss?' Beefy asks, turning up the collar of his jacket, as if that's going to stop him getting wet.

'No ...' I squint at a sign. 'Actually, we're going to Frith Street. I think I might be lost.'

He produces his mobile.

'Shall we use the sat nav?'

'I think so,' I mutter, feeling like a total idiot.

He enters the details and finally points in the direction of the receding van.

'This way, miss. It's not far. I'm afraid I'll have to walk next to you.'

'That's not a problem.'

With an embarrassed smile, I set off again, strangely reassured by Beefy's presence by my side. Along the way, I decide to find out more about my new companion but he's giving very little away. By the time that we make it onto Frith Street, I know that he used to be in the army, that he's been working in Germany and that he flew in especially for this job. And by the time that I push open the door to Slaters, I've managed to glean one little snippet of personal information: he has a wife and a three-month old son.

'Darling.' Reclined on a sofa with a catalogue on his lap, Little Steve beckons me over. 'What are you doing here?'

I lean down, allowing him to plant a soggy kiss on my cheek.

'I've just come to see Luce.' I straighten up. 'Is she around?'

'Downstairs, sorting through business from Friday. She'll be up in a minute. We've got a cheque for you ...'

As soon as I move to one side and sink onto the opposite sofa, Little Steve's attention is gripped by something near the door. Clearly, I've just revealed the presence of Mr Beefcake.

'Oh my Lord,' Little Steve gasps. 'Who's this delectable creature?'

'Beefy.'

Little Steve's eyes flip back to me.

'But I thought you were with Dan.'

'I am with Dan. Beefy's my ...' I falter. This is going to sound distinctly strange. 'He's my bodyguard.'

'Oh, dear God. A bodyguard?' Little Steve clasps a palm to his chest and purses his lips. 'He can guard my body any time.'

'Behave,' Big Steve calls, emerging at the top of the stairs. 'Nice to see you, Maya.' He inspects Beefy as he prowls past. 'Is this because of those shenanigans last Friday?'

'Yes.' I grit my teeth. 'Dan's insisting on it.'

I ought to invite Beefy to sit with us, but he quickly takes himself off to the far end of the room, positioning himself on a red velvet bench.

'Who was that man?' Big Steve enquires, emphasising each word with a grimace. 'He was an awful Scottish prick.'

'An ex-boyfriend.' I look out of the window. 'I really could do without talking about Boyd.

'With a severe personality disorder,' Lucy intervenes, joining us from the basement. 'He's been stalking Maya.' She plonks herself next to me, gawping across the room at Beefy. 'And Dan's come over all protective by the look of things.' She nudges my arm. 'Is that actually Hulk Hogan over there?'

107

I shrug her off.

'Don't stare,' I whisper. 'It's rude.'

'We ought to celebrate your first sale, Maya,' Big Steve announces. 'I'll fetch the vino.' With a flirty glance in Beefy's direction, he lumbers off to the kitchen.

'I don't know why we're bothering,' I grumble. 'It was Dan who bought it.'

'There was plenty of other interest.' Little Steve throws the brochure onto the coffee table. 'The sex god just made sure he outbid the others.' He folds his arms. 'So, how's the painting coming along, my love?'

'I've finished another canvas.'

'Ooh, what is it?' He claps his hands together. 'Do tell!'

'The South Bank. Southwark Cathedral. Around there.'

He studies me quizzically.

'It's a personal thing,' I explain. 'I probably won't put it up for sale.'

'I'd still like to see it.'

I nod, although I'm pretty sure I'm never going to sell. Before he can push me any further on the matter, Big Steve returns with the wine, glasses are poured and we drink a toast to me.

'So,' Big Steve begins. 'Lucy's told us all about the big dramatic thing at your parents' house.'

I choke on a mouthful of wine. 'Pardon? Why?' I watch as Lucy drowns in shame.

'I'm sorry,' she mutters.

'And she told us about the intervention.' Big Steve grins over the rim of his glass.

'Is anything private around here?' I demand. 'And I don't know what that look's for.' Suddenly, Lucy seems incredibly proud of herself. 'You lied to me.'

'Well ...' She shrugs. 'You should be thanking me. It did the job.'

And she's right, of course. Deciding to drop the 'affronted cow' act, I slip her a smile.

'Thank you for being a sneaky bitch.'

She raises her glass.

'Turns out I'm good at it. Anyway, I'm sorry I lied to you, but it had to be done. You love him and he loves you. Anyone can see that.'

So why can't he say the words, I wonder. I have no idea why he's holding off, but every time I say them to him, he seems to change the subject. And maybe it's time for me to change the subject too.

'You packed my stuff.'

'Yup.' Lucy takes a gulp of wine. 'Dan's secretary called me yesterday. Me and Clivey packed it all up last night.'

'Clive?'

'Don't worry, I dealt with your rancid underwear. Your drawers were a complete bloody mess. I hope you're sorting things out the other end.'

I think of all those expensive, built-in drawers that are now overflowing with randomly-placed items of clothing, and I scowl.

'Ooh, what's that face for?' Little Steve asks, pouting at me.

'What face?'

'Bulldog sucking a wasp, darling. You've just moved in with him. Is he cheesing you off already?'

'No.' I blow out a lungful of air. Instead of brooding over the drawers, my brain has decided to brood over Dan. 'Well, yes.' Another lungful. 'Oh, I don't know. It's all a bit quick. I just wish he'd slow down.'

I hear a snort.

'It's like the tortoise and the hare.' Lucy waves her glass at me. 'And she's the tortoise.'

'Is she?' Big Steve's eyebrows shift upwards. 'What's the problem then? If I remember rightly, the tortoise won in the end.'

A few moments of silence pass between us.

'So, when's the sale going through?' I ask, desperate to shift the conversation away from my love life.

'Probably next week.' Big Steve eyes me carefully.

'And who's the new owner?'

'Nobody interesting. Some American chap. He likes what we've built up and wants to keep it going. He's buying the top floors too.' He points at the ceiling. 'He wants to expand, but he's not going to be a hands-on owner. He's giving Lucy more of a say in the general running of things, day-to-day ... and a rise.'

While Big Steve snakes an arm around the back of Little Steve's head, Lucy rubs her thumb and forefinger together.

'Now, honey buns ...' With a squeeze of his partner's shoulder, Big Steve stands up. 'Let's get back to work. We've got a camper van to buy.'

The two men set about hanging a landscape in the gallery, roping in Beefy to hold the canvas up against a wall while they bicker over its exact placing. And I take my opportunity.

'I've got something to show you.'

Lucy's face lights up with excitement.

'Shuffle round a bit. Put your back to them. I don't want thunder thighs seeing this.'

Once Lucy's in place, I reach into the side pocket of my handbag and lay out the pieces of card between us on the sofa.

'What's this?'

'I found it in his bin,' I whisper, making sure that Beefy's still fully engaged by the faffing Steves. 'It's Dan's birthday on Friday.' Rearranging the pieces, I slot them into place, revealing the message.

'This is a birthday card from one of his sisters.'

Lucy's eyes widen. 'He tore up a birthday card from his sister?'

She stares in amazement at the mess on the sofa. I read the message out loud.

'Happy birthday, Dan. This is my new address. Hoping we can be friends some day.'

'Ooh.'

'She wants to get back in touch, but he's having none of it.' I tap a piece of card and continue quickly. 'Layla. She's the one who found him, the one who saved his life, and he doesn't want anything to do with her.'

Thinking deeply, Lucy chews at her lip. 'Why not?'

'He says it's complicated.'

'What does that mean?'

'I have no idea. He won't talk about it.'

'Maybe it's his childhood. Maybe he just doesn't want to think about it.' She sucks in a breath. 'Emotional constipation. And that's not good.'

I move a piece, just slightly.

'So what should I do?'

Lucy shrugs.

'You could always go and see her.'

'What?'

'Go and see her. You've got an address. Limmingham. Clive says you've got a car. If he won't talk, you can always talk to her. Maybe you can ... I don't know ... help him sort it out.'

As if she can't quite believe what she's just said, she stares at me, wide-eyed.

'That's dicing with danger,' I murmur.

'I know,' she murmurs back.

We don't get the chance to discuss the matter any further. At the sound of approaching footsteps, I gather together the fragments and stuff them back into my handbag. Within seconds, the Steves flop down onto the sofa, helping themselves to more wine while Beefy goes back to propping himself up on a fancy stool.

'He's a nice bloke,' Little Steve remarks. 'You'll have to bring him again.'

Big Steve lays a warning hand on Little Steve's lap.

'You're mine, little man. Don't you forget it.'

'Oh, he's so possessive,' Little Steve chuckles. 'So, what are you doing with the rest of the day, Maya?'

'Oh shit.' I pick up my glass and slug back the rest of my wine. It's absolutely necessary. 'I've got to go shopping.'

'You? Shopping?' Lucy snorts.

'He's making me go to Harrods. No limits. A personal shopper.' And I'm scared, I'd like to add. In fact, I'm terrified.

'Is Dan going with you?'

I shake my head.

'Oh God.' Lucy's giving me a concerned special now, and I know exactly why. 'This is an emergency.'

'I've got to get an evening dress for Friday night. Are you and Clive coming to the Savoy?'

Lucy shakes her head. 'Clive's got some family do. I'm going with him.'

'Shit.'

'You're on your own, matey, but at least I can help with the shopping crisis.' She turns to Big Steve. 'I need the afternoon off, boss. You know what Maya's like. She can't do that sort of thing on her own. Remember the jumper she bought last Christmas?'

While the Steves set about laughing, and Lucy joins in, I fold my arms and slide into a grump.

'Of course you must have the afternoon off,' Little Steve chuckles at last. 'She needs all the help she can get.'

Chapter Twelve

While Lucy studies a sign to the right of the doorway, oblivious to the fact that it's simply a list of cafés and restaurants, I stand in a stupor, gazing up at a green canopy, reminding myself over and over again that this really doesn't have to be painful. Swivelling round in search of Beefy, I'm relieved to find him standing right by my side, oozing sympathy from every pore.

'Are you alright, miss?'

'No,' I manage to gulp. 'Stay with me.'

Suddenly realising the error of her ways, Lucy springs into action. Grabbing me by the arm, she tugs me through the doorway, and into the depths of Hell.

'This way,' she growls, guiding me straight ahead as if she knows exactly where we're going.

Besieged by perfume and handbags and meandering bodies, I stagger forwards, my pulse in overdrive. I've already broken into a sweat.

'First floor,' I wail. 'He said it's on the first floor. We need an escalator.'

I'm yanked to the left. More handbags flash past and then they disappear, only to be replaced by some sort of mad, multi-coloured chocolate fantasy world.

'Chocolate,' I gurgle, my eyes dilating.

'Not now. You can treat yourself later if you're good. Up here.'

I'm hauled to the right and met by a winding Victorian staircase, complete with ornate tiles and oak panelling. Following in Lucy's wake, I grab hold of the handrails, and begin to climb. A few steps later, I'm launched back into modernity. A wall of bright light hits me and my stomach lurches, and then my heart beat does a manic dance. I'm surrounded by women's clothing.

'We've made it,' Lucy exclaims, shooting a look right, then left. 'We'll find the personal shopping bit, no problem.'

With Lucy in the lead and Beefy bringing up the rear, we begin to wander aimlessly through a labyrinth of cream walkways, past endless rails of designer clothes. Here and there, I notice a name – Donna Karan, Versace, Stella McCartney, Escada – and I wonder what on Earth I'm doing here. I've never worn a designer label in my life.

'Evening wear,' Lucy squeals.

Without warning, she veers off to the right, into a separate section that's guarded by a ball gown in a glass case. And I follow, my mouth lolling open at the rails of long dresses: some tight and sleek, some huge and billowy. I daren't even breathe on them, let alone touch one of these things. I'm half way round the room when I catch sight of a simple black gown displayed on a stand. Slowly, I circle it, taking in the fact that it's silk, that there's a lace-up bodice and yes, a split down the side. With nervous fingers, I reach up and inspect the price tag, and my lungs seem to shrink. Eight thousand, eight hundred pounds. This just won't do. No way am I letting Dan blow that kind of money on a frock. I let go of the tag and resolve to leave.

'You're not getting out of this,' Lucy snarls, grabbing hold of my forearm. 'Come on.'

At top speed, she drags me back out of the evening wear section.

'But have you seen the prices?' I come to a halt right next to a fluffy orange jacket. 'Look at this.' Grabbing the tag, I glance at it and nearly pass out. 'Two grand.'

'Shush,' Lucy hisses into my face. 'You'll give yourself away.' She fingers the price tag of a thin white jacket. 'Shit!' she exclaims. 'Nine hundred and five pounds! Where did the five come from?'

'We need to go.'

'No.' Pausing to feel the quality of a pashmina, she shrugs. 'No limit,' she reminds me. 'He wants to treat you. So just get on with it.'

I've never heard such a ridiculous statement. How the hell am I supposed to just get on with it? For a start, I've no idea what's in fashion. And worse than that, I've absolutely no idea what suits me. I'm a ticking time bomb of clueless anxiety. This is bound to end in disaster. I've pretty much made up my mind that we're leaving when we stumble into a collection of bikinis.

'Personal shopping,' Lucy whispers, pointing into a corner. 'This is where it's at.'

I follow the direction of her finger and spot a set of frosted black doors emblazoned with a simple sign: 'By Appointment. Harrods.' I swallow hard. So, this is it. We've made it. No turning back. A bolt of something shoots straight through me, and I'm pretty sure it's terror.

'Let's just go down the pub,' I mutter, tugging at Lucy's jacket.

'No,' Lucy mutters back.

'But it's too posh.'

'And it's too late. Quick. Look like you're rich.'

Keeping hold of me, she opens the doors and drags me into a reception area. I come to a halt, staring aimlessly at a perfectly-primped woman behind a perfectly-polished desk. It's Lucy who makes the first move.

'This is Maya Scotton,' she announces, in an unusual sort-of upper class accent. 'She has an appointment with a personal shopper.'

'Good morning,' the receptionist replies. 'We're all ready for you.'

She motions towards a luxurious seating area from where an impossibly slim, supremely elegant creature is currently eyeing us up as if we're her prey. She doesn't look like a personal shopper at all. In fact, with her jet black bob and her tight grey dress, she looks more like a ruthless assassin straight out of a James Bond film. Glancing down at her stilettos and silently wondering if they come complete with retractable daggers, I shuffle uneasily from one foot to the other.

'I don't like it, Maya,' Lucy hisses. 'That woman's looking at me funny.'

'I'm not surprised.'

The assassin glides forwards, effortlessly. Her lips rise into an I-could-kill-you-with-my-bare-hands type of smile and suddenly, I'm half expecting her to wrestle me to the floor and crack my skull between her thighs. Gathering every last atom of self-control, I do my absolute best to seem sober.

'My name is Tatiana,' she announces. Jesus, such precise consonants, such curly vowels, all wrapped up in something that sounds vaguely Russian. 'I'll be accompanying you this morning, Miss Scotton. I'm sure that we'll manage to find everything you're looking for. Where would you like to begin?'

I stare at Tatiana and she stares right back at me, all dark-eyed and intimidating.

'Can't we just sit down?' I ask, detecting a wobble in my voice. 'It's just that I'm a bit tired and ... Can't you just show me things?'

Tatiana's eyebrows straighten out, like cheese wire.

'Of course, madam. Follow me.'

I do exactly as I'm told. Accompanied by Lucy and trailed by a nervous-looking bodyguard, I'm led into a private room. Once inside,

I head straight for the sofa, collapsing onto it and bouncing into the air when Lucy lands next to me. While Beefy stations himself in a corner, I survey my surroundings: a coffee table in front of us, a door to the left which probably leads to a fitting room, a huge mirror, an imposing pot plant or two, a bank of windows giving out over Knightsbridge.

'Can we offer you some refreshments?' Tatiana purrs, almost menacingly.

I'm about to suggest a cup of tea when I hear Lucy's voice sidling its way into the conversation. 'What have you got?'

'We can get you anything you like, madam.'

'Champagne?'

I check out my idiot friend. Jesus, after the session in Slaters, we're already half-cut. A couple of glasses of bubbly and I won't be able to tell a skirt from a hat. But then again, it can only make this entire, hideous experience a fraction less hideous.

'Bollinger La Grande Année?' Tatiana folds her arms in front of her taut stomach.

'That will do nicely, thank you,' Lucy replies.

While Tatiana disappears in search of alcohol, I remain silent. Angst is bubbling up, threatening to spill right over the brim.

'This is awful,' I complain.

'No it's not.' Lucy scowls at me. 'How often do you get to do this?' She wafts a hand about at nothing in particular. 'Any normal woman would give her right arm for this. But you?' She squints at me. 'You're not normal.'

Returning with a tray laden with two champagne flutes, a bucket and a bottle of something fizzy, Tatiana sets down the offerings in front of us and pours out two glasses.

'Thank God for that.' Lucy's eyeballs swivel a couple of times before locking onto the glasses. In one fell swoop, she leans forwards, grabs a glass and knocks back her drink. 'Now, that's better. Have you got any more of this stuff, Tatiana?'

'Of course, madam.'

'Excellent, we're going to need at least three bottles.'

The Russian hit-woman doesn't seem to be the slightest bit fazed by Lucy's announcement. She simply nods, gracefully. Finally, my breathing is back under control. Deciding that if I'm going to be strong-armed into a shopping trip, I'm going to bloody well enjoy it, I pick up my own glass and finish it off.

'What are you looking for today, Miss Scotton?' Tatiana asks.

I rummage around in my head for an idea. What am I looking for today? I have no idea. I'd like to say 'combats and T-shirts', but I'm pretty certain that Mr Foster has other ideas. At last, stifling a burp, I say the only thing that comes to mind.

'Clothes.'

Slapping my lips, I fix my attention on the champagne bottle.

'Any sort of clothes in particular?'

'Oh, I don't know.' I hiccough. 'Can't you just choose some for me? I don't know what I'm doing.'

I catch the hint of a smile on Tatiana's mouth. 'Size twelve?'

'Yes, but ... how ...'

'Let's call it experience. Mr Foster has stipulated that you need a black dress for formal wear.'

I bridle.

'Has he now?'

'Yes.' If she's noticed my annoyance, she certainly doesn't show it. Instead, she simply carries on regardless. Jeez, this woman knows no fear. 'And a range of other feminine attire.'

'Really?' I demand. 'He stipulated that?'

'Yes.'

'Mr Foster can stick his stipulations right up his backside.' I smile an agreeable sort of a smile, slightly suspicious now that I'm behaving like a spoilt cow. I'd put an end to it if I could, but my mouth seems to have been hijacked by a lethal combination of panic and alcohol.

And now it's Lucy's turn to wade in.

'Maya.' She lays a hand on my lap. 'You've got enough combats and jeans and bloody T-shirts to last you a lifetime. Just go with it. You look lovely in dresses.'

'But ...'

'No bloody complaints.' She helps herself to another glass of champagne, refilling my glass while she's at it. 'Tatiana, trust me on this one. We need a two-pronged attack here. Bring us more Bolly. Lots of it. I'll get Maya pissed and you fetch all the feminine stuff you can find.'

'Certainly, madam.'

The dark Russian eyes spend a few seconds assessing me, and I don't really blame them. After all, they must see me as an alien species: a woman who hates shopping for clothes; a woman who hates shopping, full stop; a woman with less fashion sense than your average tree. I wouldn't have been surprised to find a sneer spread across that perfect assassin's face by now. But instead, I note a

116

glimmer of sympathy. Leaving us to slump back on the sofa and down even more champagne, she makes an elegant exit from the room while another perfectly presented assistant enters, surveying us as if we're a pair of unexploded bombs and setting two more bottles of bubbly onto the coffee table. We're half way through the second bottle when Tatiana reappears with a rack full of short dresses: flowery, plain, billowy, tight. A rainbow of colours dances in front of my eyes.

'So, this is a range of summer dresses.' Without making eye contact, she waves a hand at the rail. 'Perhaps madam would like to choose from these … and then try them on.'

Try them on? Why would I want to try them on? No, no, no. I couldn't possibly do that because trying them on would involve getting up which, in all likelihood, would entail falling over. And worse than that, there'd be decisions to be made. Fashion decisions. I look to Lucy for help, quickly realising that there's none to be had: her head's currently resting against the back of the sofa, the champagne flute tilting precariously to one side in her hand. She's nodded off. I nudge her, get no response, and swallow hard.

'Okay,' I whisper like a frightened child. 'Show me what you've got.'

And she does. One by one, the dresses are plucked from the rail and held up in front of me. One by one, I dismiss them with a screwed up nose, a shake of the head and yet another giant gulp of champagne.

'Have you got anything a little less summery?' I slur. 'And a little less dressy?'

The Russian eyebrows launch themselves into a perfect gymnastic crab. 'I am not following you.'

'They're a bit too … feminine.'

'But Mr Foster …'

'Is a control freak.'

The crab tightens a little.

'And he needs putting in his place,' I add.

'I am not sure …'

'More booze!' Suddenly roused and reinvigorated, Lucy thrusts out her glass and belches. 'Don't take it personally, Tats. It's just that clothes shopping brings out the worst in my friend. Why don't you have a drinkie?'

'I am at work,' Tatiana growls. 'Did you see anything you like?'

117

I do my best to focus on her face, but it's not easy. Suddenly, the room seems to be moving of its own accord. At last, I shake my head and place the glass unsteadily onto the table.

'They're lovely, Tats,' Lucy drawls. 'She'll take them all.'

'But madam would like to try them on?'

'No,' I cry. 'Don't make me do it.'

'Tops,' Lucy interrupts, knowing that if I'm pushed any further in the direction of trying things on, there's likely to be a total meltdown. 'Loads of tops and skirts. That's what we should look at now.'

I lean to one side. 'When the hell am I going to wear skirts?'

Lucy shrugs. 'You never know. Mr Mean and Hot and Moody might want easy access.'

'He can want all he likes.' I laugh. And then I wave a hand in the air. And then I laugh again.

While Tatiana withdraws, dragging the rail behind her, Lucy takes off her shoes and curls up her legs on the sofa.

'Oh, I could get used to this.' She lifts her glass. 'Beef!' she shouts. 'Do you want a drink, geezer?'

Beefy seems to shrink into the corner. 'No thank you, miss. Not while I'm on duty.'

'God they're no fun. They're no fun, are they, Maya?' Lucy pokes me, a little too hard, and then she slips into some sort of demented reverie. Her eyes glaze over. 'This is just like those films,' she breathes. 'You're like Whitney Houston, and he's like Kevin Costner.' She points a finger at Beefy, and then she seems to vibrate. 'No!' she shouts. 'It's like *Pretty Woman*. And Dan's Richard Gere, and you're ...'

She's lost in fuddled thought now and clearly her brain can't quite keep up with her mouth. I help her out.

'A prostitute?'

'A prostitute? She's not a prostitute, is she, Beefy?'

In unison, we look to my bodyguard for an answer, but he's on his mobile now, tapping out a message. I have no time to ask him if he's texting Mr Foster because as soon as I open my mouth, Tatiana reappears, pushing a rack stuffed with skirts and blouses. As each garment is presented to me, I sigh deeply, reaching out to feel the material, as I'm sure you're supposed to. And then I shrug my shoulders, apologetically, and quaff more champagne.

'All of them,' Lucy exclaims. 'She'll take all of them. Now, show us some big dresses!'

'Big dresses?' Tatiana asks.

'You know, the ones that go all the way down your legs,' Lucy explains as best as she can. 'The ones you wear at night when you go to posh places. She's going to a posh place on Friday and she needs a big dress.'

'Evening wear.' Tatiana sounds quite world-weary.

Taking the rail of skirts and blouses with her, she disappears for a few minutes, during which time I close my eyes. I'd like nothing more than a quick nap. I'm nearly there when the rattle of tiny wheels stirs me. Forcing my eyelids open, I'm confronted by a selection of evening dresses in a range of colours.

'Can you just find me a black one,' I yawn. 'That's all I need. A long, black dress with a slit down the side.'

'A slit?' Lucy demands. 'Why does it need a slit?'

'Because ...' I hiccough, and then I let out a belch. Jesus, this fizzy stuff has filled me with wind. 'Because he wants to poke his finger in it.' While I waggle a finger about in the air, vaguely aware that Tatiana's bottom lip has taken a dive, I suddenly realise that my filter's malfunctioned. I really shouldn't have said that, but my mouth's pushing on regardless. 'And it needs a low, what do you call those things?'

'Neckline?' Tatiana suggests.

I nod profusely. 'Yes. One of those because he wants to see my boobies.'

She gives me a thoroughly professional smile and disappears again. I'm about to help myself to another glass of champers when I hear a ping. Forgetting about the drink, I lean down, dig my mobile out of my handbag and open up a message from Dan.

Stop being a difficult arse, Maya. Buy some dresses. X

So, I was right after all. Shooting a scowl in Beefy's general direction, I realise that I'm being spied on by Mr Control Freak ... and I'm seriously not having that. I type in my response, stare at the kiss, and decide to take it off again before firing off my reply.

I'll buy what I like if you don't mind.

By the time the next text arrives, I've already downed another glass of champagne.

Of course I don't mind, as long as you buy some dresses. And where's my kiss? X

My mouth smiles and my brain complains. This whole buying-a-load-of-clothes process is bad enough. I just don't need Dan wading into the picture. Without sending a reply, I sling the mobile back into my bag and decide that I should bring Lucy into the loop, only she's not sitting next to me any more. In fact, she's currently staggering around the room, swerving from side to side and pausing to admire a huge pot plant before she finally homes in on the rack of dresses. While Lucy begins to rifle her way through the selection of evening gowns, Tatiana returns, wielding a strapless number with a lace-up back and a slit down the side. My heart beat triples in pace. I know this dress. I've already taken a good look at it, and decided that eight thousand eight hundred pounds is a ridiculous price to pay.

'Not that one. It's too expensive.'

'Actually, madam, this is quite reasonable. We have dresses that are far more expensive. Would you care to try it on?'

I shake my head.

'It would be a good idea.'

I shake my head again.

'Do it,' Lucy growls. 'You've got to. It's fun.'

'Is it?' I don't know why, but suddenly she's making me think of a bulldog on heat. Her eyes darken with determination. Maybe it's time to placate her. 'Fine. Okay.' I stumble to my feet and follow Tatiana into the fitting room. In a drunken flurry, I take off my clothes and stand immobile in my underwear.

'This would be best worn without a bra, madam.' Tatiana gestures towards my chest.

I take off my bra.

'Arms up please.'

I comply and immediately, I'm plunged into darkness. When I finally re-emerge from the top end of the gown, I steady myself against the mirror while Tatiana adjusts the fit and sets about lacing me in with sharp, vicious movements. When she's finished, I can barely breathe.

'There.' She examines my reflection. 'The perfect fit. You must show your friend.'

Again, I simply obey.

I'm staggering out of the changing room when I slam straight into a chest. My nerves suddenly on fire, I raise my line of vision from the grey waistcoat and the pink tie, up to that disgustingly wonderful face of his. Taking hold of my arms, Dan gazes back down at me.

'Shit,' I gasp. 'You're here.'

'Shit.' He frowns. 'I am.'

'And you're pissed off.'

'And you're pissed.'

'Pffff.' I stagger slightly, half conscious that there's a giggle erupting at the base of my wind pipe. 'Whatever.'

'Good work, Lucy.' He scowls at the wretched mess that's now sprawled out across the sofa, watching the scene unfold before her. 'You've managed this situation particularly well.'

Suddenly, she looks cowed. Why does she look cowed? He's not the boss of her.

'We were just having fun,' she pouts. 'Maya can't stand shopping.'

'A fact that you should know.' Releasing the giggle into the wild, I prod him in the chest. 'Seeing as we live together and all that.'

He loosens his grip.

'I think you two should get married,' Lucy announces loudly. 'Don't you think so, Tatiana?'

Tatiana smiles coyly.

'I wouldn't marry him,' I shout, prodding his chest one more time for good measure. The giggle mutates into a full-blown laugh, and it seems to go on forever. When I eventually get my act together, I glance around the room. Bar none, every single mouth seems to have dropped open ... even Beefy's.

'Why not?' Lucy demands.

'I'm not going to marry a man who doesn't even know I can't stand shopping.' I sway. The grip tightens again. 'And more than that, he doesn't even know what my ... oh ... what my favourite sandwidge is.'

'Prawn salad.' He wraps his arms around me.

'And I'm not having loads of children,' I splurt. 'It'll play havoc with my pel ...' I'm interrupted mid-flow by a hiccough. 'Pelvic floor.'

Oh dear, I really don't think I should have said that. I mean, I've put two and two together, and come up with something completely mad here. I'm half expecting him to release me completely and make for the exit. Instead, his eyes seem to narrow and his lips curl up into a smile.

'And what on Earth's made you think about children, sweet pea?' he asks, dipping his face towards mine.

'Bedrooms,' I grimace. 'Redecorating bloody bedrooms. The pitter-patter of tiny ... ooh ... feet.'

His eyes narrow some more. His lips part. He's about to tell me I'm a complete idiot but he doesn't get the chance. Lucy wades back into the whole sorry, drunken mess.

'She should bloody marry him, shouldn't she?' she cries out. 'I mean, he's just called her sweet pea, and he's gorgeous and rich and he ties her up and everything. And he's got a big willy.'

'I think that might be enough,' he says quietly. 'Has she chosen anything?'

'No,' Lucy replies. 'But there's a couple of rails of lovely stuff out there. Tats chose it.'

He turns to Tatiana.

'Then we'll take it all. Charge it to my account, please, and have it delivered. Include the dress she's wearing.'

'And shoes,' Lucy slurs, sliding her glass onto the coffee table. 'Size five. A shed load of shoes. And knickers ... and bras.'

'And stockings and suspenders,' Dan adds, his face inscrutable.

'And handbags,' Lucy slurs some more. 'This woman needs handbags!'

'Do what she says.' And now he grimaces. 'Beefy, would you be so kind as to escort Lucy home – if she can remember where she lives? And then get back to the apartment. I'll deal with Maya.'

Before I can complain, he guides me back into the fitting room. Positioning me in front of the mirror, he stands behind me, inspecting the lacework.

'What are you doing?'

'Getting you out of this.'

'It's got a slit.'

'And you look wonderful in it.' His arms slide around me, holding me tight against him. 'Even if you are three sheets to the wind.'

'We look like the people in those perfume adverts.' I snigger.

'Do we now?'

'Are you angry with me?'

His face breaks into a smile.

'Of course I am.' Releasing me from his embrace and taking a step backwards, he sets about undoing the laces, tugging at them every now and then, concentrating fully on the task in hand. 'I give you carte blanche at Harrods and all you can do is get wazzocked and cause mayhem.'

'I don't like shopping.'

'Trust me. I'm well aware of that now.'

A wave of shame washes right through me.

'I'm sorry.'

'Are you always this unreasonable when it's your time of the month?'

I shake my head.

'I'm just totally unreasonable when I'm forced to go shopping.'

'A woman who doesn't like shopping. I've landed on my feet.' He tugs again.

'How did you know I was being naughty?' I already know the answer, but I'd quite like his confirmation, and he gives it to me.

'I asked Beefy for an update.' Another tug. 'I had an idea this might happen.'

'I don't like you spying on me.'

'I'm not spying. I'm making sure that you're safe.'

'You're spying. You're a control freak and you're using the whole big bad Boyd thing as an excuse to have me followed and ... er ... spied on.' He looks up, fixing me with an uber serious stare. If he's trying to intimidate me, it's not going to work. 'I'm very sorry for being a naughty girl.' I wiggle a finger in front of my eyes. I can barely focus on it. 'I mean a naughty woman, because I'm a woman. But I don't like being spied on. I value my freedom, Mr Foster. I don't like being controlled ... apart from in bed. That's quite nice.' I send him a huge grin. 'Oh, and wherever else you decide to fuck me senseless.'

I bite my lip, realising that I've just pressed the randy button. Something's throbbing right between my thighs, and now my brain's scrambled by lust as well as alcohol. Without taking his eyes away from mine, he tugs again, easing the top of the dress away from me.

'Are you finished yet?' he demands.

'I think so.'

Lowering the gown, he kneels and helps me out of it. I watch in the mirror as he stands again and lays the dress onto a chair. Slipping one hand around my stomach and the other across my chest, he cups my left breast and stares at me some more. With a zing of excitement, I feel his erection against my backside.

'Are you going to fuck me?'

'Here?' He doesn't move.

I pout. I'm on fire at his touch and I need some action, but all I get is the shake of a head.

'Oh,' I whinge. 'Why not? I feel horny.'

He moves his left hand from my stomach, down between my legs and presses against my clit.

'I'm sure you do. But I'm not going to take advantage of it.'

'You wouldn't be taking advan ... advanchidge.'

'I'm not about to fuck a woman who's so pissed she can't even get her words out straight. Besides, you're on your period. I'm going to take you home. You can sleep it off.'

Releasing me, he bends down to retrieve my T-shirt from the floor. Turning me round to face him, he pulls it over my head, guiding my arms through the sleeves.

'Are you going to punish me for this?'

'We don't do punishment any more, sweet pea.' He bends down again, stuffing my bra into his jacket pocket and rescuing my combats. 'You don't like it.'

'Ppphhh … I might like it.'

'Really?' He kneels in front of me. While I hold onto his shoulders, he helps my feet into the trousers.

'I like spanking. I mean, the first time was a bit of a shock, but I do like it, and I want you to do it some more, especially on that spanking bench thing.'

'That can be arranged.'

While he draws up the combats, I sense a fluttering, a clenching of muscles deep inside.

'And you can do that thing when you bite my nipples.'

'You like that, don't you?' He gets to his feet and fastens the buttons.

'Yes,' I grin. I know I'm going too far, but the champagne's talking now and it really has no idea where to stop. 'I want you to do it again … but harder. And I want you to use those nipple things.' Suddenly, I seem to be tapping my index fingers and thumbs together in front of my face. I take in a deep breath, and I really don't know where the next words come from, but I'm pretty sure it's got something to do with a dodgy search on the internet. 'And maybe you should whip me. I think I want to know what it's like. And I want you to be all cold and hard with me, like you were with Claudine. I want you to demean me.'

His arms close around me again, manoeuvring me back to face my own reflection.

'Why?' he demands. 'Why do you want me to do that?'

'I don't know.' I falter. 'Maybe I just want to know everything about you. Maybe I want to see that side of you. Maybe it's turning me on.'

'You're drunk.'

'Damn right there. But I know what I want.'

'Be careful what you wish for.' He tightens his grip. His eyes seem to have hardened. They're cold and steely, just like the first time I ever saw them. 'You might just get it.'

Chapter Thirteen

Water cascades over me, enveloping my body and coaxing me back to consciousness. While memories flash through the darkness, illuminating the gaps between then and now, I stand with my head down, eyes closed, palms against the granite tiles ... and I cringe for England. Suddenly, I'm back in Harrods, demanding a visit to the mad chocolate department, refusing point blank to leave until I've had my treat. And now I'm in the passenger seat of his Mercedes with my feet up on the dashboard, digging into a box of truffles and spilling half of them into the foot well. And now I'm on the sofa, drifting away into a fuddled sleep on his lap. At some point, he must have ushered me upstairs, or carried me, because I was in bed this morning when he set off for work, leaving me with the vague memory of a touch of his lips, his breath against mine, half-registered words.

Once the shower marathon's over and done with, I dry myself off, rummage through the wardrobe and put on a fresh pair of combats and a T-shirt. With my hair tamed, I slope downstairs only to be greeted by a bunch of Harrods bags lounging on the sofas. Ignoring the unwanted guests, I head straight for the kitchen and set about making a plate of toast and a mug of tea. It's only when I settle onto a stool at the counter that I notice a packet of pain killers waiting for me alongside a hand-written note on a scrap of paper: *Somebody's going to need these. D. X.*

Resolving never to drink again, I swallow back a couple of pills, gulp down a few mouthfuls of tea, sift through my handbag and rescue my mobile. It's just after eight and he's already sent me a text. *How's the head? Xx*

My shoulders slump in relief. Two kisses. And although I have a sneaking suspicion that I've already been forgiven, an apology is still in order. With unsteady fingers, I text back.

Pretty bad. I'm sorry. X

Resting the mobile in front of me, I take a bite of toast and wait anxiously for the reply. It's not long in coming and when I open it up, I almost choke.

Get yourself sorted for two o'clock. I'm sending a car. Wear a dress. No bra. Xx

In an instant, my thoughts tangle themselves up in knots. Where the hell has that come from? And why is he sending a car? Another memory launches itself out of the chaos, hitting me right between the temples. My stupid, drunken mouth has landed me right in it, yet again, and I've only got myself to blame. I asked him to demean me, and now he's planning on giving me exactly what I wished for. 'Oh well,' I muse. 'You can always chicken out.' But I won't, and I know it. Come two o'clock this afternoon, I'll be getting in that car wearing a dress and no bra, because I'm far too intrigued by his latest game.

But for the next six hours I need to distract myself, and there's only one way to do that. After a second mug of tea, I stagger up to the studio and begin the job of sorting through the collection of blank canvases, moving the smaller ones to the side and picking out a larger panel from the back. Rectangular in shape, it's about six feet in height and three feet wide, and there are two more just like it. Leaning all three against the wall, side by side, I sit cross-legged on the floor and gaze at them ... waiting.

It doesn't take long for inspiration to arrive. Stunned by the images that invade my mind, I grab a pencil and begin to sketch out a basic form on the left hand canvas: a woman lying on crumpled sheets, head turned to the right, an arm draped across her eyes, her face contorted with pain. I pause and take a step back, mired in confusion. Why on Earth am I doing this? I look at the other two canvases, suddenly aware that I'm about to create a triptych: three images that just can't be separated. Almost on automatic pilot, I move to the right hand section, sketching out the same woman: only this time she's on her back with her arms above her head, her face aimed to the left, semi-obscured by shadow. As I draw out the lines, it becomes obvious to me: she's experiencing pleasure like never before.

When I'm finally satisfied with the basic outlines, I shift my attention to the centre panel, and come to a halt. I know that it's reserved for a man, but although I can see the angles, the colours, the way the bodies interconnect between the two outside sections, as yet I have no idea how he bridges the gap.

There's a knock at the door. I turn the canvases round before I call out.

'Come in.'

Beefy pokes his head into the room.

'I'm to tell you, miss, it's one o'clock.'

'One?' I stare at my bodyguard, unable to believe that I've been sketching for so long. 'Right.' I smile unsteadily. 'I'll get ready.'

Beefy leaves me to it. With a building sense of trepidation, I clean up, take a shower and change into a dress. Leaving my bra on the bedroom floor and plumping for a pair of granny pants from Dan's shopping trip, I go back downstairs, collecting my handbag along the way.

Beefy's waiting for me outside the front door.

'Any idea where we're going?' I ask him as we step into the lift.

He shakes his big head, but the flash of guilt in his beady, bird-like eyes tells me that he's lying. Breezing through the lobby, I toss a brisk 'Good morning' in the direction of the concierge and push through the doors. It's sunny outside and I'd love nothing more than a walk down the south embankment, but there's a black limousine waiting for me on the forecourt, a driver standing by the open passenger door.

'Miss Scotton.' He waves towards the back seat.

I slide in, looking back at Beefy, surprised that he doesn't join me. The door's closed, the driver installs himself and we pull away. Suddenly I feel bereft without the Beef monster by my side. I have no idea where I'm going, or what's about to happen, but I've got the distinct feeling that I might need a bodyguard.

It's a short ride down the back streets, the quickest route to Southwark, and it soon becomes apparent that I'm going nowhere special at all. We're simply on our way to Fosters Construction. Arriving at the rear entrance, I'm greeted by Dave from security and ushered into the building. Before long, still accompanied by Dave, I'm riding the lift to the fifteenth floor. Gazing at my reflection and musing a little more over Mr Foster's plans for the afternoon, his words rattle around in my brain: 'Be careful what you wish for.' By the time the door opens onto the swanky reception area, my stomach is in knots. Leaving Dave behind, I make my way over to Carla's desk, feeling distinctly unsteady on my feet.

'Good afternoon, Miss Scotton.' Looking up from her computer, she smiles a knowing kind of smile, and I'm hardly surprised. After all, she must have seen my scribbles in Dan's diary. She must know exactly what we get up to in his office. 'Mr Foster's waiting for you. Please go straight in.'

Sucking in an almighty gulp of air, I begin to edge my way into the big kahuna's lair.

I catch sight of him immediately. Sitting at his desk, he's busy leafing through a file, so busy that he doesn't seem to notice me. I cough quietly. He glances up, takes in my dress, shows no sign of emotion and goes back to his document.

Keeping my position by the door, I wait.

'Close it please, Miss Scotton,' he murmurs.

Typical. Totally vague.

'Close what?'

'The first thing that comes to mind.' He turns a page.

I look down at my handbag. Yes. That'll do. Clicking the catches together at the top, I continue to wait.

'And now, perhaps you might close the door,' he adds, his voice suddenly laced with impatience.

I push the door shut, and wait some more. If he's after another game of silly buggers, I'm more than up for it. After what seems like an age, he puts the document to one side, leans back in his chair and examines me. There's a tiny quiver, right between my thighs. It's followed quickly by a fluttering sensation.

'So?' I venture.

'So.'

'Is there a reason for you hauling me over to your office?'

'Yes.'

He stares at me some more, the edges of his lips curving up, ever so slightly.

'Would you like to fill me in?'

'Absolutely.' He stands. 'I have a gap in my schedule.' Straightening his jacket, he circles round to my side of the desk. 'And we have some matters to discuss.'

'Oh.'

'Oh,' he mimics, leaning against the desk.

'So ... what matters are we discussing?'

His eyes glimmer. 'Your astonishingly poor behaviour, for a start.'

'I said I'm sorry. And just for the record, you didn't have to buy the whole of Harrods.'

'And just for the record, you didn't have to down a vat's worth of champagne and make no decisions.'

'So, that's it then?'

128

'No, that's not it.' His face is unreadable now. No trace of a smile. 'Come here.'

Nervously, I inch forwards. And the closer I get, the more I fizz with anticipation. I come to a halt a couple of paces away from him.

'We also need to discuss the terms of our relationship.'

'Do we?'

'Of course. If I'm not very much mistaken, you tabled a new set of demands yesterday.'

'I did?' The blood rushes to my cheeks.

'You don't remember what you said in the fitting room?'

Another surge of blood. I decide to plead ignorance.

'Not really ...'

'Then allow me to remind you.' Moving away from the desk, he takes a step forwards. 'You said you wanted me to be cold and hard with you, just like I was with Claudine.'

'Did I?'

He nods, taking another step so that he's right in front of me now. He prises the handbag out of my grasp, places it on the floor and straightens up, running a finger down my arm. A shimmer passes through my spine.

'I'm not prepared to go there.'

'Why not?'

'You don't need to know.'

'But you were like that ...'

While I trail off into silence, pondering over what I was about to say, his eyes flash with understanding. He knows exactly what I'm referring to: those few minutes when he caved in to something dark, when I caught a glimpse of the old Dan.

'It won't happen again.'

I frown at his declaration. Somehow, I need to make him realise that he's given me a taste of something I seem to like, and now I want more.

'What harm could it do?'

'Plenty.'

'But it's just role play, a bit of fun.'

'Not for me.'

'Why not?'

'I'd rather not go into that.'

'Oh come on ...'

And that does it. In a nanosecond, his expression hardens. I'm seized by the shoulders and tugged in close.

129

'Enough, Maya.' Irritation crackles in his voice. 'You have no idea what you're asking for.' A hand comes to the back of my head, holding me tight. Trailing his lips across my cheek and setting off a swarm of tingling sensations, he stops at my mouth, barely touching me now. 'And now onto your second demand,' he breathes. 'You said you wanted me to demean you.'

Oh shitty shit, shit, shit. Why, for the love of God, did I have to go and say that? 'The bloody internet, that's why,' a voice complains from the back of my head. 'A handful of dirty pictures and you're a slut on heat! What's wrong with you?'

'I was drunk,' I explain, my voice sounding worse than pathetic.

'And speaking the truth.'

His lips close around mine. Probing my mouth with his tongue, he kisses me slowly, deeply. I'm under attack ... yet again. And there's no way I'm ever going to come out on top, not now that he's started the whole 'let's mesmerise her knickers off' thing.

'All I ever want is to make you feel good about yourself, and now you're asking me to undo it.' Taking my chin in his hand, he nips at my bottom lip.

I jolt, sensing a rush of warmth between my thighs.

'Why do you want me to do that?' he demands. Letting go of my chin, he traces the outline of my nipple with an index finger.

'Because ...'

He wheels me round, clamping me tight against his chest and squeezing the nipple hard, sending shock waves of electricity right through me. I gasp, trying to control my heart beat, my pulse, everything.

'Because what?' he demands. 'A few days ago, you couldn't understand why a woman would let a man demean her.'

He slips a hand between my thighs, running his index finger over my g-spot. I lean my head back against his chest and close my eyes, drinking in the sensations while my brain battles to stick with the conversation.

'Everything I've done ...' He begins to massage me. 'It's been for your pleasure. I've never gone too far. I've never treated you like an object.'

'I know.' My breath falters. 'But let's just try ...'

'Let's just try what?' He waits for my answer, but it doesn't come. The truth is I have no idea what I'm asking for. 'Whatever we do, we'll do it my way.' I feel his mouth against my neck, skimming from just below the ear, further down. 'Which brings me to your third demand.' He presses a finger hard against my clit. 'Pain.'

130

'I don't remember ...'

'Of course you do.' He presses again, then circles his finger firmly, stirring me up into a storm of lust. 'Now let's get something straight here. I have my limits. And one of those is using a whip on you. Never ask me to do that again.'

Suddenly, he puts an end to the torment. I'm released from his grip, left in a fuddle of disappointment.

'Okay.' Wrestling my breath back under control, I turn back to face him. 'No whipping. Fine. But I like the nipple stuff.' I point at my breasts, as if I really need to remind him where my nipples are. 'And I sincerely hope you're not going to stop the spanking thing.' I glance up at a corner of his office, suddenly washed through with embarrassment. I can barely believe what I'm saying here. It sounded ridiculous enough when I was three sheets to the wind, but now I'm sober ... 'Because I'm good with spanking,' I witter on like an idiot. 'So you can spank me.' I swallow hard and shrug. 'If you want to, that is.'

'Of course I want to.' I risk a look at him now, only to find that he's grinning from ear to ear. 'In fact, I'd love to spank you right now.'

'You would?'

'Oh yes. So long as we're clear about the small print. If I do spank you, you don't go running for the hills.'

'I won't,' I confirm.

'Glad to hear it.' Suddenly brusque and business-like, he straightens his jacket and tie. 'Lean over the desk.'

I open my mouth to speak. I'm silenced immediately by a raised finger.

'Ten,' he says firmly. 'Good and hard.'

Oh, bloody hell. A lunchtime spanking. I wasn't expecting that. My heart judders like an old boiler and my legs threaten to give way beneath me. I can barely believe it when I do as I'm told, steadying myself against the edge of the glass. Immediately a warm hand comes to the small of my back, pinning me into position. He urges my legs apart, pulls up the dress and arranges the material around my waist. Leaving the massive knickers in place, he smooths a palm across my buttocks before moving his attention to my crotch. His finger travels slowly, further down, across the ridge of the tampon string. My mouth dries up. My brain empties itself out. I'm in total limbo as I wait.

'Keep this quiet,' he murmurs.

And then he begins.

The first smack lands on my right buttock, searing straight through me. I choke back the urge to cry out.

'This is for your terrible behaviour yesterday.' The second slap lands on my left buttock, hard and unforgiving. 'And by that, I don't mean downing enough champagne to floor a rugby team, or tormenting a personal shopper.' I close my eyes, whimpering quietly, enjoying every moment of it. The third slap follows quickly. 'I mean your drunken attempt at sexual negotiation.' He smooths his hand across my buttocks, slowly, before landing the next slap. 'You gave me your submission, Maya.' Another slap. 'In everything to do with sex.' Another slap. 'Who's in control here?'

'You,' I mutter.

Another slap. 'I can't hear you, woman.'

'You,' I shout.

'Correct.'

The next slaps come quickly. Before I know it, he's finished. He tugs me up against his chest. 'Lesson learned?'

'Yes,' I breathe.

'Good.' He releases me. 'Now take off your dress.'

'What?'

I swivel round to find him making his way to a sofa. He pauses, beckoning me with a finger and pointing to a spot on the floor. And then he settles himself down. Crossing his legs and snaking his arms across the back, he watches as I sidle over to him. Doing exactly as I'm told, I stand on the designated spot, lift the dress over my head and drop it to the floor. He shakes his head.

'That's an expensive item of clothing. You should treat your possessions with respect.'

'Is that what you do?'

'Always.' He smiles for a second or two, and then he issues the next command. 'Get rid of the knickers.'

Excuse me, what?

'But I'm on my period.'

Suddenly serious, he tips his head to one side.

'Would you like another spanking, Miss Scotton? Or are you simply going to take off those hideous pants?'

I stare at him, silenced by an expression that's telling me he's not going to take no for an answer. Shivering with nerves, I slip my fingers into the top of the knickers and draw them down my legs. Stepping out of them, I kick them to one side.

'Legs apart.'

Suddenly flushed with embarrassment, I lower my head.

'Do as you're told, Maya.'

Biting back the urge to ask what the ruddy hell's going on, I move my feet but not too far. Slowly, his gaze moves from my face to my crotch, taking in everything in between. I could shrink into a ball. The tampon string must be in full view.

'So, at this point,' he says, 'the dominant usually informs the submissive that she's a good girl.'

My head flips up and suddenly, I understand: he's giving me a dose of what I asked for ... his way.

'However, I wouldn't dare call you a girl, because you're a woman, which you've made perfectly clear to me on more than one occasion.'

I smile back at him, coyly.

'Now touch yourself.'

'What?'

He raises an index finger. A warning not to speak.

'I said touch yourself. I'm going to watch you.' He pauses, his eyes darkening. His own smile has disappeared now behind the mask. 'And you're going to make yourself come.'

Oh, Lord above. He wants me to put on a show for him. And bugger it. I've never done anything like this before. Glancing down at my dress, I wonder if I should just make a run for it, but seeing as I've agreed to put an end to the running, that really wouldn't be cricket.

'I'm off to Whitehall in an hour.' He checks his watch. 'A meeting with the Housing Minister. So, if you wouldn't mind ...' He waves at my crotch.

Closing my eyes, I reach down and begin, slowly circling my left index finger over my clitoris. It doesn't take long for the warmth to spark into life between my legs.

'Look at me, Maya.'

Obeying his instruction, I stare at him, noting the smile that plays across his mouth as he watches me intently, sometimes focussing on the movement of my finger, sometimes on my face. I'm a quivering wreck now, breaths faltering, growing ever more shallow by the second, but I'm determined to see this through. Summoning every last bit of willpower, I carry on, circling slowly, and the warmth grows.

'Now this is beautiful,' he says quietly. 'Play with your nipples.'

It's fruitless to complain. Raising my free hand, I touch my left nipple, running a finger across the areola, groaning at the sensations that shimmer through me. And then I take the nipple between my thumb and forefinger, working at it gently, elongating it, suddenly aware that the warmth in my vagina has transformed into a full-on heat. There's a ball of pressure right between my thighs, waiting to implode at any minute. But through it all, I keep up the circling motion, keep my eyes secured on his. Lips parted, he watches me closely as I take myself to the hilt. Finally, after what seems like an age, I'm there. Without an order, I squeeze my nipple, pushing myself over the edge. Muscles contract. The ball of heat scatters through my flesh.

'Oh God.' Closing my eyes, I groan as an orgasm ripples right through me. And then I shake, judder, fold in on myself. I'm half way to collapsing in a heap on the floor when I sense a movement. His arms embrace me, propping me up.

'Nicely done,'

I open my eyes to find his face next to mine. And he's smiling proudly.

'You're an excellent executive toy. Much better than a stress ball.'

'Glad to hear it.'

A hand trails its way from the nape of my neck to my spine, and I'm on fire again. Just fuck me now, I want to scream. Just do it. And I don't care if I am on my period. Get your old fella out and crack on! I'm slightly suspicious that he will when he moves back, takes off his jacket and lays it on the floor.

'I thought you looked after your possessions,' I remark tartly.

'I do.' He points at the jacket. 'Down.'

Suddenly I get it. He's looking after me, making sure that I'm comfortable.

'I'm not your possession.'

'Just do as you're told.'

With a huff, I sink to my knees, watching as he unfastens his trousers, eases down his pants and reveals his cock. And good God, he's aroused, fully erect, ready to go. With one swift movement, he slides a hand round to the back of my head, and grabs hold of his cock with the other.

'I'd love to blindfold you.' His eyes gleam. 'Maybe tie your hands behind your back. But we haven't got time.' He rubs the end of his cock against my lips. 'I seriously want to fuck your mouth, Miss Scotton. In fact, that's what I'm going to do.' He pauses, smiles. 'And when I come, you're going to swallow the whole lot.'

Still breathing heavily from my orgasm, I gaze up at him. My heart seems to have launched into a quickstep, and I'd seriously like to inform the big kahuna that I'm not entirely sure about the whole swallowing thing, seeing as I've never done it before. But, as ever, he's far too quick. As soon as I open my mouth to complain, it's filled by his cock.

Taking it half way into my mouth, I raise my right hand, grip the shaft and begin to ease the skin slowly, backwards and forwards, looking up throughout, watching for every reaction. Raising my left hand, I caress his balls, amazed at how full and hard they are, and my tactics seem to have the desired effect. He tips his head back, closing his eyes and letting out a groan as he begins to sway, gently probing my mouth, edging further each time until he's sliding his cock right to the back of my throat. And then the hand tightens on my hair. I clamp my lips around the shaft, sucking harder now. And the rhythm picks up.

Before long, his thrusts become urgent. Plunging all the way in, again and again, he keeps it going while I take him completely. Breathing through my nose, I massage his balls with greater force, waiting nervously for the moment when I get my first proper taste of him. And it's not long in coming. With a judder, he ejaculates into my mouth, releasing a violent flood against the back of my throat. And in a moment of panic, I swallow quickly, eager to avoid choking or gagging ... pleasantly surprised to find that it tastes just fine. Still twitching his way down from the orgasm, he withdraws his cock, leaving sperm to dribble from the side of my mouth. With a grin, he wipes it away with a forefinger, and treats himself to an amuse bouche.

'Salty.' He slaps his lips. 'Fancy a shower?' Unfastening his tie, he throws it onto the sofa.

'Now?'

'Why not?' He unbuttons his shirt and drops it to the floor.

'But what about your meeting?'

'What about it?'

'You're going to be creased.'

'You worry too much.' He shrugs off his shoes, removes his trousers, pants and socks. 'I've got a spare outfit. Chill out.'

Still on my knees, I gaze up at the man I love. Standing right in front of me, in all his perfect, naked glory, he holds out a hand to me.

'Jesus,' I breathe. 'The first time I ever came into this office, I never thought I'd see you like this.'

I put my hand in his and he helps me to my feet.

'You're covered in spunk,' he remarks.

'You say the nicest things.'

'Stick around, kid. There's plenty more where that came from.'

135

Without another word, he leads me into the bathroom. Leaving me to stand by the counter, he steps into the shower, turns it on and tests the water for the right temperature. When he's finally satisfied, he motions towards my crotch.

'You can take that thing out. I take it you've got more in your handbag?'

'Yes, but ...'

'I told you we'd work around it, Maya. Just because you're on your period, it doesn't mean I'm living like a monk. You might as well ask me to stop breathing.'

'But ...'

He shakes his head, and I do as I'm told, silently mortified as he watches me pull out the tampon and drop it in the bin.

'This is ...'

Whatever I'd been about to say flies straight out of my head. It all happens in a flash. I'm grabbed by an arm, dragged into the shower and pushed back against the tiles. Sealing his lips around mine, he sweeps his tongue into my mouth, launching into a furious kiss while he nudges my legs apart, presses his cock against me, and moves inside. Taking his time, he holds me firmly under the buttocks, sliding my body up against the tiles and letting me fall back down into his grip. I clasp my hands around his back, enjoying those now-familiar contours, the firmness of his muscles, the smoothness of his skin. At last, when he finally breaks the kiss, his eyes meet mine as he thrusts inwards, withdrawing to the edge, over and over again. Running right across my spot, he's working me up into another mindless fuddle.

'Feel it,' he murmurs, water streaming down his face. 'This thing between us ... it makes everything different.'

I groan incoherently.

'I had no feelings for Claudine, not for any of those women.' His eyes search mine for understanding. 'And what I did with them is in the past.'

Chapter Fourteen

I'm sitting at the kitchen counter, downing the first tea of the morning when his text arrives.

I enjoyed last night. Missing you. Xxx

With a smile, I gaze at the screen, picking over the words. He's missing me already, even though he only left for work half an hour ago. And the man who could fuck us both to death actually enjoyed our first sex-free evening together. The smile broadens into a full-on grin while I rake back through the details of a fairly normal kind of evening. Dan coming home late from his meeting, fuming that the Housing Minister was a 'bloody twat'. An hour spent lugging Harrods bags upstairs and storing clothes away, him carefully folding and hanging, me stuffing anything anywhere. A Chinese takeaway ordered in, a film, a cuddle and bed. A mutual decision to simply fall asleep in each other's arms. Yes. A fairly normal evening in the grand scheme of things: a much-needed confirmation, in amongst all the sex and the madness, that we can live together like fairly normal people.

I text him back.

Me too. We'll do more of that. X

As soon as I tap the send icon, I find myself staring at my handbag, suddenly reminded of the bits of card stowed away in its depths. My heart slumps and the smile slips from my face. Normal? Who the hell am I trying to fool? Underneath the veneer of the perfect couple, we're anything but normal. And we're anything but perfect too. Try as I might, there are just too many things I can't understand ... or ignore. I haven't had the full story about Italy, he refuses point blank to discuss his sexual history, and as for his sisters, they're just the biggest puzzle of all. Pulling the new set of keys out of my handbag, I hold them in my hand, knowing that there's something at the back of

137

my mind now, a half-formed notion seeded by Lucy's words: 'You could always go and see her.'

I shake my head. What a ridiculous idea. It's just not my place to meddle in Dan's affairs. But then again, if I leave him to sort things out for himself, he'll never get round to it. And if I'm ever going to trust him completely, I need all the pieces in place. I drop the keys, shocked by where I seem to be going with this train of thought. And then, almost on auto-pilot, I take the pieces of card out of my bag and rearrange them on the worktop. Rummaging through the drawers, I find a pen, a scrap of paper and scribble out the address.

My pulse rages. My heart pummels at my rib cage.

Am I really going to do this?

'Yes, you are,' a voice whispers from the back of my head. 'It's the only way you're ever going to get an answer, and you bloody know it.'

And that's it. Abandoning my mobile on the counter top, I grab the keys and make my escape ... only it's no escape at all. As soon as I'm out of the front door, Beefy latches onto me, squeezing himself into the lift and shadowing me down to the basement. When the lift door slides open, I make a beeline for the Jaguar: a big, black, sleek monster of a thing that's currently sleeping in the corner of the garage. Nervously running a hand over the bonnet, I can't help but remember the spanking session at Fosters. But I can't dwell on that. Instead, I open the driver's door, sink into the leather seat and rearrange its position. Almost immediately, the passenger door opens. Beefy settles himself into the seat next to me and shuts the door.

'What are you doing?' I ask.

'Coming with you.'

'But I'm not going anywhere. I'm just trying it out for size. You can get out again.'

'I'll get out if you get out.'

I take in a few, deep breaths. Okay, so that's not going to work. I'll try another tack.

'And what if I do go for a little drive? Who's going to get me?'

He shrugs his shoulders.

'I have my orders.'

'And this is a free country. I've got a right to be left alone.'

'And I'm paid to follow you, miss. If I don't do my job properly, I'll get sacked. I've got a wife and baby to support. I can't afford to be out of work.'

For a split second, I stare at Beefy's massive, brick-like head and wonder exactly what a baby Beefy could possibly look like. And then, shaking myself out of my reverie, I get on with the job in hand. Okay, so he's determined to come with me which means that I'll just have to cook up a devious plan to lose him along the way.

'Leather and oak.' He runs a chunky finger across the dashboard. 'You've got a nice car here.'

'It's not mine,' I murmur absently, taking in the luxury that I barely noticed last time. 'At least it doesn't feel like it is.'

'A Jaguar XF. Top-of-the-range. This thing's got a top speed of 155mph.'

I detect a touch of terror in his eyes.

'We won't be doing that. Trust me.' Wondering where on Earth to begin, I scan the dashboard, instantly confounded by all manner of knobs and buttons. 'Check the glove compartment. There must be some sort of manual.'

He opens and closes the compartment, and shakes his head.

'You're just going to have to work it out.'

'Work it out?'

Silently panicking, I scour the dashboard again. Working out this little lot could take the best part of a day, and I just don't have the time. At least I know where the key should go. Turning it in the ignition, I listen to the engine as it purrs into life, watch in amazement as displays light up in front of me. Trying out one knob after another, I locate the windscreen wipers, indicators, the horn and the lights.

'Has it got one of those satellite tracking thingies?' I virtually whimper.

'Probably.'

'Can we switch it off?'

'Why would you want to switch it off?'

'I don't know.'

He frowns at me – at least I think it's a frown – and then he shrugs. Okay, so I'll just have to deal with the tracking situation. One thing at a time.

'Where's the sat nav?' I ask, fighting off a sharp stab of anxiety. 'I'd just like to work the sat nav. I'd like to go and see my parents at some point. I'll need it.'

Beefy nods. Leaning forwards, he prods at a screen for at least five minutes before he finds what he's looking for.

'There we are. Just go to the main menu and press this.'

He runs through the process again. I watch carefully. And then it's my turn. Finally, after I've accidentally programmed the sat nav to give me instructions in German and Beefy's reprogrammed it to English, I manage to enter my parents' postcode.

'We're not going there today, are we?' Beefy asks.

'Good God, no.' I smile innocently. 'Just practising. No. Today we're just going for a little run-around.' I grip the steering wheel and realise that my mouth's dried up.

'When did you last go for a drive, miss?'

'About three years ago.'

I glance at my bodyguard, just in time to see his thick lips form an 'o', and inside that square skull of his, I'm pretty sure there's a voice screaming out 'Oh fuck.'

'May I suggest reverse?'

'Yes, reverse.'

Jittering with nerves, I press the clutch, move the gear stick into reverse and take off the handbrake. My heart's pounding as I set the car into motion. Checking over my shoulder, I bring the Jaguar out of its parking space, missing Dan's motorbike by a whisker. We come to a halt. With a shaking hand, I slide the stick into first and we crawl towards the garage doors. As if by magic, they begin to open.

'What? How did that happen?'

'A sensor.' Beefy points to a small black box just above the rear view mirror.

'Oh God, it's like a space ship.'

While my bodyguard gives out a throaty chuckle, I do my best to calm down. Right now I can't imagine that I'll ever get used to this bloody car, but I'm going to have to give it a try. After all, there's no other way of executing the mad, half-baked plan to sort out Dan's life for him. Throwing every last scrap of caution to the wind, I take my right foot off the brake, ease up on the clutch and depress the accelerator. We practically shoot out onto the forecourt. Coming to a second halt, I give myself a silent talking to. Go easy on the pedals, you idiot! And then, without the slightest clue where we're going, I pull out onto the embankment.

I'm a bundle of nerves, super-vigilant, overly slow, keeping an eye out for anything that moves: cars, buses, cyclists, pedestrians. We practically crawl down the road, making for Vauxhall, jerking to a stop at the slightest thing.

'Are you sure about this?' Beefy asks.

'Of course,' I lie, keeping my eyes fixed on the road.

Adrenalin's pumping right through me now, sending my heart beat to the verge of tachycardia. It's a good half an hour before I even begin to think straight. Turning into a side road, I stop the car outside a pub. We sit for a minute or two, saying nothing, accompanied by the soft hum of the engine, the sweep of the wind screen wipers, the tapping of raindrops on the roof. And while Beefy concentrates on controlling his breathing and probably thanking the Lord Almighty that he's still alive, I muse over the sense of what I'm about to do.

'Bollocks,' I scowl, realising that there's absolutely no sense in it at all. I'm about to be the queen of reckless, and I just can't stop myself. Somewhere deep in the lobes of my brain, the amygdalae must have decided to put their feet up and have a quiet cuppa.

'What's the matter?' Beefy asks.

I swallow, blink, and then I just get on with it.

'People keep waving at me.'

'Who?' He leans forwards, squinting into the side mirror. 'I haven't noticed anything.'

'I have.' I try out a concerned expression. 'I think it might be the lights.'

'But this is a new car.'

'I've got my side lights on, but people are waving. Someone flashed me earlier. I don't think they're working.'

'I'm sure you're imagining things.'

'I'm not. Can't you just get out and have a look?'

'In this?' He gesticulates at the windscreen.

The rain's pelting down now. And yes, I do feel like a complete bitch, but I also need to seize the day, even if we are currently in the midst of a downpour of Biblical proportions.

'Please, Beefy. I need to know.'

He watches me, and then he shrugs. Finally, with another squint into the side mirror, he grabs the handle. Getting out of the car, he shuts the door and walks round to the back, and I waste no time at all. Slamming my foot on the accelerator, I'm off, haring up the road like a demon, weaving my way from one street to another. Central London in the rain is no place to get used to a new car, but I don't slow down until I'm convinced I'm out of Beefy's reach. Eventually, I come to a halt at the kerb and fiddle with the sat nav, keying in my parents' postcode and lurching back in surprise when a disembodied, super-cool voice begins to speak.

'In twenty metres, turn right.'

'Yes!'

I punch the air, satisfied that I've managed to conquer technology. Now all I need to do is conquer this bloody car. I have no idea how long it takes before I'm out in the suburbs. As the traffic thins and the outskirts of London give way to countryside, I opt for a quiet life, tucking myself into the inside lane of an A road and refusing to overtake. It's going to take forever like this, but I don't care. Hardly daring to take my eyes off the road for a second, I drive on in silence, listening to the sat nav's occasional instructions and thinking about Dan. By now, he'll know that I'm absent without leave. And if he hasn't already chartered a helicopter to come and find me, the very least he'll be doing is plotting my comeuppance.

At last, the countryside flattens. Fenland skies stretch out above me, swathes of blue and grey arching across a landscape of soulless fields and ruler-straight roads. As I push further northwards, the earth slowly comes to life again with hills and hollows, the roads lined now by pine trees rather than ditches. And after what seems like an age, the squat church of Limmingham comes into view, its tower like a chunky hand acknowledging my arrival. The sat nav continues to dish out instructions, but I'm no longer listening. From here, I know the way. Navigating the dip into town, I take a left along the sea front and head for the housing estate where I grew up.

When I finally park in front of Mum and Dad's home, I rest my head on the steering wheel and try to compose myself. It's a good few minutes before I get out of the car and look down the road, catching sight of the nondescript house where Dan spent the first ten years of his life. There's a sudden chill in my blood. I shrug it off quickly and make for my parents' back door.

I find no one in the kitchen and no one in the living room. They're both out in the garden, fussing over the rockery. Stepping through the open French windows, I call to them.

'Mum! Dad!'

The look up in unison.

'Maya,' Mum calls back, dropping a trowel. 'What a nice surprise. Have you brought Daniel with you?'

'No. He's at work.'

'We're so glad you're back together.' She plants a kiss on my forehead. 'Sara told us. We felt awful about what happened. Was he alright? Tell me he was alright.'

'Don't worry about it,' I reassure her. 'You didn't do anything wrong. And he's fine.'

'Come here!' Dad leans his spade against the fence. 'Come and give us a kiss.'

142

I step out over the lawn, into his arms.

'It's been piddling down all morning.' Releasing me, he squints up at the sky. At just the right moment, a crack in the clouds lets through a thin shaft of sunlight. 'But you've brought the weather with you.'

As quickly as it arrived, the sun disappears.

'How did you get here?' Mum demands.

'I drove.'

She stares at me as if I'm mad.

'And I can't stay long,' I add.

'Oh, why not?'

'I've got to go somewhere.'

'But you've got time for a cup of tea?'

'No, Mum. I'm sorry.'

'Next time you come, you can stay longer ... and you can bring Daniel with you. We'd love to see him again, wouldn't we, Roger?'

'Oh yes.'

'I mean, we don't mind about all that stuff. He's a lovely lad.'

'I'm not sure.'

'What do you mean you're not sure?' Her eyes widen.

'I don't know if he wants to come back.'

She stares at me again, and suddenly I'm wondering how much she actually knows.

'I've been thinking about that family,' she muses. 'You never saw much of them. I mean the girls used to come out and play in the street, but not Daniel.' She glances at me, her eyes awkward. 'His mum kept herself to herself. And I never liked his dad.'

'Step-dad,' I correct her.

She barely seems to register my words. 'He was always down the pub, wasn't he, Roger?'

Dad nods. 'One of those nasty types. He'd fight you over a bag of crisps. No one liked him. Remember that time he got beaten up?'

'Oooh yes.' Mum shakes her head. 'And then he dropped dead not long after.'

'Dead?' The word flies out of my mouth and I stare at my mum, amazed by her little afterthought. 'When did he die?'

'A long time ago. You were about eleven or twelve. Died in his sleep.' She points a finger at her head. 'A brain whatsit.'

'Haemorrhage,' Dad mutters.

I blink and blink again, dislodging a vague recollection of it all. I remember a death on the road, and that's about it. I suppose I was too caught up in my own little world to pay much attention to what went on around me.

'You were at school when they took him away,' Mum goes on. 'And then they moved out, her and the two girls. They didn't go far though. Other side of town.'

I don't want to hear any more.

'Why don't you two come down to London?' I suggest quickly. 'We'll put you up in a nice hotel.'

'A nice hotel!' She claps her hands together. 'Hear that, Roger? We haven't been to London since we went to see *Cats*. When was that?'

'Oh, I don't know.' Dad rolls his eyes. 'It was my first and last musical, Maya. Singing cats. I can't bloody well stand cats, and she drags me to see that. We get enough of the bloody things in the garden.'

Mum fires off a quick scowl in Dad's direction.

'So, why *are* you here?' she demands.

'I'm meeting an old friend.' God, I wish I'd come up with a decent back story. 'And I don't want Dan to know about it,' I add quickly.

Mum's gawping at me now, as if I'm totally deluded. I never really had any friends until art college, and she knows that.

'Oh God, Maya, it's not a man, is it?' she gasps. 'You're not turning into a trollop?'

'Of course it's not a man. I'm ...' I trail off into silence, desperately fumbling through my brain for something half-way decent. Out of nowhere, an idea shuffles into view and seeing as it's all I've got, I'll just have to go with it. 'She's an artist. I'm fixing up a surprise for Dan's birthday and I don't want him to know. It's a portrait ... of me. And I need you to do me a favour. If he ever asks, tell him I've been here all afternoon.'

And now, my mother looks positively affronted.

'You've just got to trust me on this one,' I insist. 'I've got my first sitting in ten minutes.'

She folds her arms and pouts. Okay, so maybe I should make a quick concession.

'I'll come back for a cup of tea afterwards. How about that?'

At last, her face breaks into a smile.

'Don't you forget,' she warns me.

'Of course not.'

With another kiss, I make a hasty exit.

Just in case Mr Foster can track my movements in the Jag, I decide to leave the car where it is and walk. After all, Dan's sister didn't move far away from the original family home. In fact, she's only three streets away and less than five minutes later, I'm standing on her road, feeling like I'm about to throw up. I have no idea what I'm playing at, meddling in things that are none of my business, but I'm incapable of stopping. Drawn on by a need to fill in those missing pieces of the puzzle, I know I'm going to see it through. For a few brief seconds, sunlight appears again, scudding its way across the road and guiding me towards my target: a modern house, much like the one I grew up in, complete with a neat front lawn and a tarmac drive. I'm in a daze, conscious that my legs are moving again and before I know it, I'm right in front of the door, watching helplessly as my hand reaches up to press the bell.

'Shit!' my brain cries out. 'You've done it now!'

As the seconds draw themselves out, I swallow hard, realising that my mouth has dried up. I glance along the road, seriously considering making a run for it, but it's already too late. Before I can act, the door swings open, revealing a flustered-looking woman.

'Hello?' Drying her hands on a tea towel, she tilts her head to one side. 'Can I help you?'

'I ...'

Struggling to find the right words, I take her in. Maybe in her mid-thirties and about my height, she's dressed in a pair of jeans and a strappy T-shirt. And then I notice her eyes: bright blue, just like Dan's. But that's where the similarity ends. Her hair is darker than his, a deep brown. And her features aren't quite the same. She has thinner lips, a slightly more oval shape to the face. There are traces of the man I love, but differences too.

'Can I help you?' she repeats.

'I'm ... I'm sorry.' I falter.

'For what?'

'For just turning up like this ... out of the blue.'

'Are you selling something?'

'No.' I manage to conjure up a smile. 'No, no. I'm ...' I swallow again before I land her with the news. 'I'm Dan's girlfriend.'

Her forehead dips. Her lips part. Somewhere behind her, I catch a movement. A voice calls out.

'Mummy! Cameron did a wee in my bucket!'

'I'll be there in a minute. Go and play.' She waves a hand. 'Dan's girlfriend?' she asks. And then, as if she needs absolute confirmation: 'My brother's girlfriend?'

145

'Yes.'

I watch the shadows flit through her eyes: first shock, then disbelief. Understanding that I need to explain myself a little, I reach inside my handbag, my fingers shaking, and grapple for the pieces of card.

'I found these.' I thrust a handful at her. She looks down at them. 'I found these in the bin … your birthday card. It had your address on it and I wanted to meet you and …' Oh God, I'm gabbling now. She really must think I'm a lunatic, but I've started so I might as well finish. 'I thought I could get him to meet you.'

Her mouth opens further. She leans out of the door, taking a quick look up and down the road, a flicker of excitement in her eyes, a touch of nerves. And suddenly I realise what she's doing: she's searching for him.

'He's not here,' I explain. 'He doesn't know.'

My admission plants a frown back on her face.

'You've done this in secret?'

'Yes.' Shoving the pieces of card into the handbag, I realise that I need to introduce myself properly. 'I'm Maya. Maya Scotton.'

She raises a hand as if she's about to point at me, and then seems to think better of it.

'Maya Scotton? Sara's sister?'

I nod. Her face tightens. And I think I've just met another of my sister's victims.

'But you lived over the road from us.'

'I did.'

'And now you're seeing Dan?'

Jesus, this must be weird for her. She's shaking her head now, ever so slightly, and it's clear that she's struggling to take it all in.

'It's kind of … kind of complicated …' I stammer. 'How we got together.'

'And he knows you're from here? He knows you're from Limmingham?'

'Yes.'

She stares at me, wide-eyed with confusion. I'm pretty sure I'm about to be told to sling my hook when she steps back, waving the tea towel in the direction of the back of the house. 'You'd better come in.'

Stepping over the threshold, I'm ushered through a gloomy hallway into a kitchen-diner where a set of French windows give out onto a modest garden. Outside, the sun has come out again and two young boys are whirling about on the lawn, circling a paddling pool and shrieking with delight.

'Take a seat.'

She motions to a table. It's littered with pencils, colouring books and mangled Plasticine figures. I sit down just as the boys skitter into the kitchen and come to a halt in front of me.

'Who's that?' Clutching an Action Man in one hand, the smaller boy gazes up in awe.

'A friend,' Layla explains, eyeing me suspiciously. 'And this is Cameron.' She places a palm on the back of his head. 'He's my youngest. How old are you, Cameron?'

'Three!' he squeals.

'Hi, Cameron.' I smile.

'Did you wee in Ben's bucket?' Layla asks with mock sternness.

'Yes!' He runs back out into the garden.

'And this is Ben.' The taller boy comes forwards, watching me cautiously. 'He's five.'

'Hi, Ben.' I smile again.

'We've got a paddling pool,' he announces proudly.

'Go and play in it,' Layla encourages him.

I watch as Ben runs back out into the garden to join his brother. Picking up the offending seaside bucket, he slings it across the lawn before jumping into the paddling pool and disappearing from view.

'We had it out last week when it was hot.' Layla throws the tea towel onto the counter. 'I can't get them out of it. I filled it again this morning and it's already clogged up with grass. Who'd have kids, eh?'

I grin like an idiot, recalling my little day dream in Dan's garden. Shaking it quickly out of my mind, I drag myself back to the task in hand.

'Cup of tea?'

'Please.'

I don't want a cup of tea at all, but I know the deal: we're about to have a difficult conversation, something that's always easier to bear with a touch of caffeine. In silence, she flicks on the kettle, makes two mugs of tea and brings them over to the table.

'So ...' She pauses, settling herself onto a chair. 'Dan's girlfriend, eh?'

I nod.

'And you're Layla.'

'That's me.' She raises her mug as if making a toast, and takes a sip of tea. 'He definitely doesn't know you're here?'

'No.'

'Good.' Placing her mug on the table, she runs a finger round the rim, watching its slow progress while she speaks. 'I don't think he'd be too pleased about it. You know he doesn't want anything to do with me?'

I nod again.

'So, what made you come?'

Oh God, how do I explain that? Trying desperately to put the chain of events into order, I run through it all in my head, every last detail that's brought me to this point. And then I simply give up, open my mouth and let anything spill out.

'Because I love him, and I want to spend the rest of my life with him ... because I need to understand him and trust him.' The words begin to catch in my throat. I must sound ridiculous. 'I just can't work out why he's so determined to cut you out of his life. He says it's complicated, but it doesn't make any sense to me. And I don't think he's happy about it, not really. I want him to work it out. I want him to get back in touch with you.'

She seems to wince. 'I'm not sure that's possible.'

'But why not? Why won't he see you?'

'I don't know for sure.'

Her eyes shift from my face to the garden. She watches her boys, clearly thinking things through. I have no idea how long we spend in silence before she finally speaks again.

'I'd love to see him again, Maya. I'd love nothing more. After all, he's my brother ... and their uncle.'

I take a sip of tea, listening to the sound of splashing and squealing.

'Do they know about him?'

'I tell them he works abroad. He's a very busy man, but they might meet him one day.' She picks up a lump of Plasticine and rolls it between her thumb and forefinger. 'Has he told you anything about when we were kids?'

'Not a lot. Just the basics. It's pretty difficult to get much out of him.'

'That's not surprising.' She takes in a deep breath. 'He had a hard time. I don't blame him for wanting to forget.'

While she drifts away into memory, staring at the Plasticine and squeezing it over and over again, I begin to wonder exactly how I'm going to keep her in this conversation.

'He told me you saved his life,' I venture.

The fingers come to a halt. Convinced I'm about to be told to mind my own business, I'm on the verge of apologising when she looks up, smiles and leans forwards.

'I wasn't that old,' she explains, her voice lowered. 'Eight, I think. He was sleeping in the outhouse.' She checks the garden, making sure the boys are still otherwise engaged. 'You know about that?'

I nod.

She nods back.

'It was freezing cold out there.' Dropping the lump of Plasticine, she begins to move an index finger about on the table top, as if tracing the outline of the rooms. 'There was a door from the kitchen. Dad locked it at night, but I knew where he left the key. Every now and then, usually when he was pissed, I'd sneak a bit of food out to Dan.'

She pauses, waiting for my reaction.

'I know they didn't feed him. He told me.'

Her eyes widen slightly and she smiles again. Evidently satisfied that I've been allowed a handful of confidences, she presses on with the story.

'He used to pretend to be asleep, so I just left the food next to him. A bit of bread. A biscuit. Anything I could find. He never said thank you but I didn't care. He didn't need to.' She checks the garden again. 'But that one time, I just knew there was something wrong. He was on top of the covers and there was this weird smell ... like metal.' She pauses. 'I tried to wake him up ... and then I saw what he'd done ...' Her voice wavers. She's deep in the past now, her eyes unfocussed.

'You don't have to tell me.' I lay a hand on her arm.

She shakes her head.

'I want to.'

'But I'm a stranger.'

'For now.' She watches me for a moment or two, her bottom lip trembling. 'I've never talked about this before, not even with my husband.'

Watching me some more, she waits for a sign that she can unburden herself. With a slight nod, I give it to her.

'I called the ambulance. I had to get it done before Dad woke up. God knows what he would have done if he knew ... And then I got a cloth and tried to make it stop, but it wouldn't stop. I thought he was going to die.' She stares at something on the table top. 'They took him away. That was the last time I saw him, for years. He never came back and we never got to visit.'

149

She checks the boys again, the ghost of a smile playing across her face. It doesn't reach her eyes.

'So what happened to you?'

Pulling her arm out of my touch, she leans back. 'Me?'

'Your dad? Was he the same with you?'

'Nothing quite so bad. With Dan out of the picture, I was his next target. He was always more careful, but it didn't stop him.' She levels her gaze at me. 'I felt the back of his hand.'

'And Sophie?'

She laughs quietly.

'Sophie was the apple of his eye. The special one. He never touched her. To this day, she won't accept what he was really like. I didn't even go to his funeral. She didn't talk to me for years.'

'But you're talking now?'

'A little. But we don't talk about ... that.' She chews at her lip. 'Sophie's not well. She wanted to get back in touch. We've kind of turned a blind eye to all the crap.'

She frowns, and I decide not to ask any more. After all, I've done the same with my own sister.

'I heard he'd died.'

'In his sleep. Too quick. Too easy.' She's deadly serious now. 'He should have suffered more.'

Trailing into silence, she flicks a pencil across the table.

'Does Dan know that he's dead?' I ask.

'Yes. And he knows about Mum.'

My forehead furrows. 'His mother died?'

'Liver cirrhosis. Last summer. After Dad went, she drank more than ever. Maybe it was grief. Maybe it was guilt. Anyway, she drank herself to death.'

My mouth opens but nothing comes out. My brain's far too busy stumbling through the facts and tripping over connections. Last summer. When he was miserable. When a visit from someone sent him over the edge. When he walked away from his old life forever.

'It was you,' I gasp. 'You went to see him.'

Her eyes meet mine.

'I did. When I knew Mum was on the way out, I traced him. Somebody contacted him for me, just to see if he was interested, and he said yes.'

'He agreed to it?'

She nods. 'I shouldn't have left it so long really. We organised to meet at his office.'

'So, what went wrong?'

'I have no idea. He was on edge right from the start. It felt like ... like he changed his mind as soon as he saw me. I told him that Dad had died, but he already seemed to know about that. And then I told him about Mum, and he just flipped, completely lost it, told me to get out.'

'Why would he do that?'

Turning her mug on the table, she shrugs.

'I don't know. Maybe I reminded him of someone he'd rather forget. People always say I look like my dad. That's my best guess.'

'Maybe you should try again.'

'What difference would it make?' She nods towards my handbag, her eyes clouding with tears. 'He ripped up my birthday card.' She falters, suddenly perplexed. 'How did you know I was his sister?'

I hide behind a sip of tea, wondering just how much I can explain, how much I can offer.

'He's talked about you. I think he wants to get back in touch, deep down.'

Her eyes glimmer.

'He does?'

'We just need to give him time.'

'Time?' She laughs. 'It's already been over twenty-five years. How much longer is it going to take?'

'You can't rush him,' I interrupt, suddenly panicking.

'And you never know what's round the corner,' she smiles. 'Life's taught me that. I've got my sister back now, and maybe there's another chance with Dan.' She drifts away for a few seconds, gazing down at her mug. When she finally looks up again, she's suddenly excited. 'If I could see him again, if I could just talk to him, maybe I could win him round.'

'I don't know.'

I shift about on my chair, uncomfortably aware that the conversation has taken a new, unexpected turn. I came here to do nothing more than rebuild a bridge, but now that I've given her hope, Layla seems determined to push right across it.

'You could help me,' she suggests. 'You could fix this up.'

Before the next words creep into the open, my heart gives a leap and the sickness returns. I shouldn't get involved. I really shouldn't. But I just can't resist this woman's pleas, or the desperation in her eyes.

'I suppose I could,' I murmur. 'Leave it with me. I'll see what I can do.'

Chapter Fifteen

It's almost eight o'clock by the time the sat nav brings me back to Lambeth House. Lunch with Layla and the boys, followed by tea and chat with my parents, followed by rush hour snarl-ups on the way back into London haven't helped at all. I glance up at the penthouse, wondering what on Earth's waiting for me up there. One seriously pissed off boyfriend is my best guess. But never mind, I'm just going to have to face the music. And whatever type of music that turns out to be, it's all going to be worth it in the end.

The garage doors slide open automatically and I drive into the gloom, only to find a stranger waiting for me: a giant, suited goliath of a man, standing impassively next to the lift door. Edging the car back into its space, I kill the engine. As soon as I get out, the goliath approaches me, holding out a huge spade of a hand, palm upwards. I examine him closely, noting the shaved head, the iron-like eyes, a straight, humourless mouth.

'Who are you?' I ask, my voice quivering.

'Security, miss. May I have your keys?'

'What?' Instinctively, my fingers tighten around the fob. 'But this is my car.'

'And Mr Foster would like me to look after the keys.'

So, that's it then. The start of the retribution for today's wilfulness. He sends in some sort of Terminator creature to confiscate my freedom. I should have seen that coming.

'Where's Beefy?' I ask with feigned innocence.

'He's been replaced.'

And I should have seen that coming too.

'So, what's your name?'

'You can call me Spencer.'

'As in your first name?'

'As in my surname. I'll be your bodyguard from now on. I'll need those keys.'

As if to make a point, he thrusts the hand forwards. I take another peek at his eyes and immediately, I know I'm about to get nowhere in this particular stand-off. With jittering fingers, I give him the fob.

'This is bloody ridiculous,' I complain. 'I'm a grown woman.'

Without responding, he opens the back door of the Jag.

'What's going on?'

'Mr Foster's waiting for you. I'm to drive.'

'But where?'

'A restaurant, just round the corner. It won't take a minute.'

And from the look on his face, I'd say this is a second stand-off I'm not going to win. Reluctantly, I slide onto the back seat, watching as the door closes and the Terminator takes his place behind the wheel. The car pulls back out of the garage, taking a left down the embankment and veering into a side street. Before I can even begin to calm down, we draw to a halt outside a restaurant: nothing swish or posh, just a cosy little local establishment, and Italian judging by the green, white and red flag fluttering above the front door. Before Spencer can do anything, I'm out of the car and staring in through the window at a clutter of plain wooden tables, all candlelit, some of them taken. On any other day, this would be the perfect location for a romantic dinner, but right now my stomach is threatening to turn somersaults, especially as there's no sign of Dan.

'Miss?'

My bodyguard holds open the door. With a grimace, I shuffle past him. As soon as I cross the threshold, I'm met by a small, round, black-haired waiter.

'Miss Scotton?' he asks, his Italian accent playing havoc with my name.

'Yes.'

'Mr Foster's waiting at the back.'

He guides me through the restaurant, round the edge of a bar and into a back room where there are no tables, only booths: four of them in all, and all of them empty apart for the one at the end where I find Dan studying his mobile, a glass of water in front of him. Suddenly aware of me, he looks up, puts the phone into his jacket pocket and stands. Curling an arm around my waist, he smiles with an unnatural warmth and kisses me on the cheek. Instead of the normal reaction, my body seems to freeze. It's clearly all for show.

'Glad you could join me.'

He signals to a leather bench and I sink onto it.

153

'What would you like to drink?' he asks.

'Same as you.'

He turns to the waiter. 'Acqua.'

With a nod, the waiter scurries off, leaving me alone with Mr Mean and Hot and Moody. Seating himself opposite me, he stretches an arm across the back of the bench and says nothing. Instead, he simply rests his gaze on my face, his irises dark and inscrutable. In a split second, my heart rate seems to triple. Willing it back into submission, I watch as the waiter returns, leaving a glass of water on the table. With a shaking hand, I take a sip, place the glass down and look back at Dan. As if he can see right into the depths of my soul, he examines me, and I shiver, reminding myself that there's no way he can know where I've been, or what I've been up to.

'What's going on?' I ask. Somebody needs to break the silence, and it might as well be me.

'We're having dinner,' he replies without a smile, just a cold edge of irritation in his voice.

'Why here?'

'Why not?'

'You're mad at me.'

'Fucking furious.'

'So that's why we're here then? Because you don't trust yourself at home?'

I search his face for a reaction. All I get is the slightest hint of a frown.

'Is that what you really think of me?' he asks.

'I don't know what I think of you.'

He tilts his head back and takes in a breath.

'We're here because I booked a table. And for your information, I arranged this meal before you went off on your little jaunt. It was supposed to be a romantic gesture but it's obviously been ruined. I've been out of my mind with worry all day.'

'What was there to worry about?' I swallow back a lump of nerves. I hate this deception, but it's all for the best. 'I went to see my parents.'

'Really?'

He watches me some more. Instructing my face to behave, I send up a silent prayer that he'll be satisfied with my answer.

'Really. But you probably already know that.'

'Of course I do. Satellite tracking systems are wonderful. Why couldn't you just tell me you were going to Limmingham?'

Quick. Come up with an excuse, woman, and make it good.

154

'I didn't want to mention the place.' Shit. That'll have to do. 'I didn't want to upset you.'

'And that's all you did?'

'Yes.' I should leave it at that, but I don't. 'You can call them if you like.' Bugger. That really is giving the game away.

'Why would I need to call them?'

'You might not believe me.'

'Of course I believe you.'

I'm not so sure about that. Maybe a little more explanation is in order.

'I went to apologise, to sort things out after what happened.'

His eyes examine mine, probing for the slightest tell.

'You left your mobile at home.'

'I forgot it.'

'And you left your bodyguard in a side street. Did you forget him too?'

'He was annoying me.'

'He won't annoy you any more. Thanks to your actions, he's no longer employed.'

We're interrupted by the waiter's arrival. He speaks to Dan, in Italian of course, and Dan replies. I simply let him get on with it. I have no idea what's going on, and even less interest. Suddenly, I'm seething. As soon as the waiter leaves us, I launch my attack.

'You got him sacked?' I scowl.

'He didn't do his job properly.' With a slip of the mask, he scowls right back at me.

'He's got a kid. He needs the money.'

'You should have thought of that before you blew him out.'

'If I'm going to be shadowed by a piece of meat, I want Beefy. I don't like the new man.'

'And I want you protected properly. Beefy made a mistake.'

'We all make mistakes.'

'Yes, we do.'

I grind to a halt. I'm not exactly sure he's talking about Beefy any more. I definitely need to waft the conversation in another direction. I'll make damn sure I get Beefy back some other time.

'So, are you going to punish me for this?'

'Punishment only extends to sexual matters.'

'No spanking then?'

'Oh, I'd love to give you a spanking.' He half-smiles. 'A proper spanking ... on the bench.'

A flutter of want is quickly followed by shot of panic. As appealing as it is, if he spanks me tonight, then I'll only end up in some weird sort of trance, spilling the beans left, right and centre. And there's no way that's going to happen.

'Not tonight.'

'Why not?' He cocks his head. 'Scared you might say something?'

We're interrupted again, this time by a waiter carrying two plates of ravioli. He places the dishes in front of us, takes a bow and scurries away.

'That was quick.'

'I'd already ordered. He just asked if we're ready for our food. This is the best ravioli in London. I thought you'd enjoy it.' He gives me a small, evidently sarcastic smile.

Grabbing the salt, I liberally sprinkle it over my dinner before slamming the cellar back down and picking up a fork.

Dan eyes me with disapproval.

'You don't need salt on it. You'll spoil the taste.'

'It's already spoilt by you being an arse.'

I stab at a square of ravioli, raise it in front of my mouth and inspect it before taking the plunge. And oh dear God, it's amazing. If I wasn't currently locked into a battle of wits with a man who's clearly ready to explode, then I'd be groaning in food ecstasy.

'I'm not being an arse.' He spears a square of his own and begins to eat.

'I'd say you are. A big, fat controlling arse.'

And that does it. The façade crumbles. Confusion and disbelief battle for prime position on his face and when they're done with jostling, they simply give way to anger.

'How?' he demands.

'You've taken my keys. I'd call that controlling.'

'I gave you a car,' he growls. 'I gave you freedom. I also gave you protection. You don't get to use one without the other, not at the minute.'

'Freedom? How can you call it freedom when you're spying on me every step of the way?'

He slams down his fork, sits back and glares at the bar. 'For fuck's sake. Okay, so maybe I've started off a little heavy-handed.'

'Heavy-handed?' I laugh. 'I'd say so. Normal boyfriends don't spy on their girlfriends.'

'I told you. It's not spying.'

'Why can't you just be normal?'

'I wouldn't know where to begin.'

We glare at each other. I have no idea what's going through his mind, but I soften a little, reminding myself that he's anything but normal, and in the grand scheme of things, it's hardly his fault.

'Besides,' he goes on. 'Normal boyfriends don't have the likes of Ian Boyd to worry about.'

Seriously wishing that Ian Boyd would simply vanish from the face of the Earth, I push out a massive sigh.

'And I'm not paranoid, so you needn't start on that. Let's stick to the real issue here.'

'Which is?' I demand tartly.

'Trust.'

I just can't help it. That's a rich statement, coming from the king of secrets. I burst out laughing.

'Shush.' He casts me a warning glance.

'No, I will not shush. You're talking to me about trust?'

He picks up his fork and points it at me. 'I trusted you, and you threw it straight back in my face. Now, I don't know what you've been up to ...'

Seeing as I'm not prepared to be lectured, I cut him off in mid-flow.

'I've already told you where I went, cloth ears.'

He spears a slice of pasta. 'And it doesn't add up.'

'There are plenty of things about you that don't add up.'

'Such as?'

Oh, where to start?

'Italy.'

His eyebrows squeeze together. 'I told you the truth.'

'Not all of it.'

'And what makes you say that?'

'Women's intuition.'

'Good old women's intuition,' he sneers.

And that gets me going. No man on Earth has the right to sneer at women's intuition. He's dicing with death.

'I tell you what, it's taken me a while but I'm finally learning to use it. And I can see it in your eyes when you're keeping things back.'

He pauses, for just a little too long, his lips straightening. And then he repeats his words: 'I told you the truth.'

'Of course you did ... to a point. You tell the truth, but you just don't tell all of it. This happened before, Dan. I ignored the clues and you were hiding one big fuck-off secret from me. Well, guess what? I'm not ignoring the clues any more.'

His eyes widen. He shakes his head. And then he shifts his attention to the fork, turning it over, again and again, watching it glint in the light.

'So, what else is bothering you?' he asks.

I'm going to need all my resolve now.

'Why are you so cagey about the way you used to be? The whole BDSM thing?'

'I'm not cagey. It's in the past, that's all.'

'Is it?'

He narrows his eyes.

'I saw that change in you. When we got rough the other day, I saw it. You were exactly like you were with Claudine. It was like you were someone else.'

'It was a slip. A mistake.'

'The cold, hard dominant. The man you used to be.'

'A role I used to play,' he corrects me. 'And I don't want to play it any more. I don't want to be that man. I don't want to hide behind him.'

'But you spent a fifteen years hiding behind him. What were you hiding from?'

Dropping the fork, he sits back and stares at a glass. His eyes flicker. At last, he says one word.

'Hurt.'

So, that's it then? He behaved the way he did to avoid being hurt? I'm about to ask for a little clarification when he flips my thoughts upside-down.

'If you never get close to anyone, you never hurt them.' Still staring at the glass, he avoids all eye contact.

'Who have you hurt?' I demand.

Suddenly, I'm beginning to suffer from a serious attack of the heebie-jeebies, and as if he's trying to push straight past it, the answer comes immediately.

'Too many people.'

Moving quickly, he picks up the glass, takes a sip of water and places it back down, but I've seen enough: his hands are shaking.

'Who have you hurt?' I repeat, raising my voice.

'There's a time and a place for everything. This isn't it.'

And if you think you're dictating every single one of our conversations, you're very much mistaken.

'Your sisters?'

'Drop it,' he snarls.

'And who's to say you won't hurt me?'

158

'That's never going to happen. I'm different now.'

'Really? Do I just have to trust you on that one?'

He levels his gaze at me, breathing quickly.

'Yes.'

'It works both ways,' I remind him. 'Trust. And I can't trust you until I know everything.'

His jaw tightens. Suddenly, he's like a coiled spring. I should back off a little, take my time, tread warily. But now I'm thinking about Boyd and Tom and every single lie I've ever been told, every single deception that's ever screwed me over. It's all there at the back of my mind, urging me on.

'Tell me something,' he grumbles. 'How did we get from the subject of where you've been to the subject of me?'

'I don't know,' I grumble back. 'And why don't *you* tell me something while we're at it?'

'What?'

Fuelled by anger, I steel myself. I'm going to get to the bottom of this if it kills me.

'Why won't you see your sisters?'

The colour rises in his face.

'I told you. It's complicated.'

And maybe it's not. Maybe he's worrying over nothing. After all, even if he did behave like a complete bastard with Layla, she's ready to forgive and forget.

'What harm could it do?'

A vein throbs in his neck. His shoulders seem to tense.

'All you need to do is meet them and talk. You might even find out ...'

'What?' he snaps.

My entire body gives a jolt. 'Don't push him,' the sensible half of my brain warns me. 'He's about to blow.' And as usual, I ignore it. I'm just not prepared to give in.

'They might have suffered too,' I offer. 'After you left.'

He shakes his head.

'Have you ever thought about that? Who your stepfather turned on next?'

He stares into space. 'No one,' he mutters. 'I'd gone. He must have had a fucking party.'

'Dan ...'

It comes out of nowhere. In one swift movement, he swipes his plate onto the floor. The smash of crockery echoes round the room, leaving absolute silence in its wake. A waiter appears, hovers for a few seconds, and then he's gone again. In a panic, I stare at the mess on the floor, and then at the man in front of me. Barely able to breathe, he's holding on to the edge of the table, glowering at nothing in particular. I have no idea what he's about to do or say. All I know is I don't want to be around to witness it. I need to get out of here.

As I get to my feet, he looks up, suddenly alarmed.

'Don't go.'

He's moving now, and I don't have time to hesitate. Breaking into action, I bluster out through the front of the restaurant, yanking open the door and flinging myself into the night. I register the car, the bodyguard standing ready on the pavement, the fact that it's raining. And then I begin to run.

I hear Dan's voice calling.

'Maya!'

I don't stop. With my pulse in top gear, I make for the lights of the embankment. If I can get to the river, I'll be able to find my way back to Camden, and sanity. But I don't get very far. It's all over in seconds. I feel a hand on my wrist, an arm around my stomach. I'm grabbed from behind and hauled into the shadows of a side street.

Swinging me round, he presses me against a wall, pinning me into place with his chest and holding my arms against my sides.

'Let me go,' I growl.

'Never.' Tightening his hold, he brings his face to mine. 'We agreed. No more running.'

'And maybe I've changed my mind,' I shout. 'Maybe I can't deal with this. I need answers and you ... you ...'

The sentence can't find an end. My throat constricts. And damn it, I'm sobbing.

'Listen to me ...'

I hear the voice, but I don't want to acknowledge it. Closing my eyes, I lower my head.

'Listen.'

I feel his fingers under my chin, gently urging my face upwards.

'Open your eyes, Maya,' he whispers. 'Open them. Please.'

With the full intention of telling him to piss off, I simply do as he wishes. But I'm stunned by what I see. His face is half in shadow, half illuminated by a street lamp, but it's clear that he's struggling to control himself. And those aren't just raindrops on his cheeks.

'You're crying.'

'No shit.' He half-laughs. 'Look what you've done to me. Happy now?'

'Why are you crying?'

160

Fighting back my own tears, I reach up and touch his face.

'Because I can't lose you.' He swallows, blinking into the rain. 'I need to make this right.'

'I shouldn't have pushed.'

I feel his chest rise and fall.

'You have every right to push.' He gives me a weak smile. 'You need answers. I understand.'

'Then give them to me,' I beg.

We're silent for a while, gazing at each other. At last, he begins to speak, slowly, in the quiet tones of a confession.

'I'll see my sisters, I promise. One day, I'll get back in contact.' He tips his head forwards. 'But I can't rush it. Okay?'

I nod.

'And as for Italy ... I was a mess back then. It wasn't a good time. I'd just rather forget.'

I look into his eyes, picking up on silent desperation, and resolve to leave the subject of Rome behind. He lived with a woman. It was an arrangement. Nothing more. I just need to take his word for it.

'But Lily was right,' he goes on. 'When I came back, I closed myself off. The club served a purpose. Every time I visited, I played a role. I wasn't Daniel Foster and I wasn't Daniel Taylor. I was someone else. No baggage. No past. No connection. No hurt.'

I trace a finger down his cheek.

'It's an addiction for me, Maya. You need to understand that. The more I played the role, the more I needed it, the further I went. Claudine was the wake-up call. After that, I thought I was done with it. But I slipped the other day, just like any addict can slip ... and it freaked me out. I didn't think I needed it any more. I don't want to need it any more. This is all I want.'

He kisses me gently. And suddenly, I find myself panicking. Jesus, if he wants to leave all that behind, then we might have to go vanilla.

'No more kink then?' I ask.

I catch the hint of a smile in the shadows.

'That's not what I'm saying. Plenty more kink.' His voice is warmer now. 'More kink than you can shake a stick at.'

I giggle and he touches my lips.

'But always with this.'

'With what?'

'Smiling, laughing, talking. Feeling like I'm a part of you, and you're a part of me.' He takes my hand and lays it over his heart. 'With this.'

Chapter Sixteen

He's out on the terrace. Dressed in grey sweat pants and a white T-shirt, he's leaning against the parapet, coffee in hand, watching the morning unfold over the Thames. Conscious that he doesn't know I'm here, I observe him for a minute or two, wondering what he's thinking about. His past, perhaps? I wouldn't be surprised, especially as today's his birthday. Clive's words come back to me: I wouldn't mention it if I were you. And I won't. I've already stirred up too many memories and now it's time to calm things down. As soon as I move forwards, he's conscious of me. Putting down the mug, he motions me into his arms.

'Morning, sweet pea.'

He kisses the top of my head and I grin. Realising I should have some sort of lovey-dovey nick name for him by now, I say the first thing that comes to mind.

'Morning, shit head.'

'Shit head?'

I wince, shrug apologetically. 'It was all I could think of.'

'I'm sure it'll grow on me.' He squeezes my arm. 'Are we good?'

'We're very good. In spite of the fact that you fucked me to death last night.'

And he did ... for at least three hours. After Wednesday night's row, we simply called a truce, swept the problems back under the rug and slept in each other's arms. But last night was an entirely different matter. With my period almost over, it was open season, time to make up for lost sex. And we did it with a vengeance.

'I fucked us both to death.' He smiles knowingly, brushing his lips across mine and sending a rush of warmth to my core. 'I'm knackered.'

162

'So take a day off.' I may be totally spent, but I'm also totally up for a day of solid sex.

His eyes glint in the early morning sunlight. 'I'd love to.' He touches the pendant. 'But I can't. Too much on at work.'

While we gaze at each other, lost in our own private bubble, the seconds seem to stretch out into an eternity. Finally, he speaks.

'It's the Savoy tonight. The car's picking us up at seven. I'll be home by six.'

And then, without warning, he swings me round to take in the scene. Sunlight glistens across the water, glowing against the limestone of the Houses of Parliament, catching on the ironwork of Lambeth Bridge. And I'm thinking about a time when we can both face the past and move on into the future, without any shadows.

'The colour's back,' I murmur. 'Every day's a new beginning.'

'It is.' I hear him breathing slowly, calmly. 'Food,' he says at last. I feel his hands on my hip bones. 'I'm not having my woman turning scrawny on me. Come on.'

While Dan sets about making me tea and popping bread into the toaster, I rummage through my handbag and find my mobile. I've got Layla's number now, but I've been careful, storing it under the name of 'Fiona', an acquaintance from university I never kept in touch with. As yet, there's no communication from her, and I'm relieved. As far as I can see, he's just not ready to meet her yet. But there is a text from Sara. I groan.

'What's the matter?'

'My sister. She wants to meet up.'

He shrugs. 'Does she know we're back together?'

'Yes.' I watch as he leans against the counter, fixing me with the pools of blue. 'It's going to be complicated,' I warn him. 'You can't just carry on as if nothing ever happened.' I slide the phone back onto the counter.

'Why not?'

I stare at him, perplexed.

'Dan, she made your life a misery. She's got a lot of explaining to do.'

'Not to me.' With a shrug, he makes his way over to the fridge, opens the door and takes out the milk. 'It's all in the open now. I'm not interested in what made her behave that way. If there's anyone she needs to explain herself to, it's you.'

The kettle flicks off and while I try to work out what on Earth he's going on about, he makes the tea and brings it over to the counter.

'Why would she need to do that?' I demand.

He nudges the mug towards me.

'Because you doubt yourself.'

My mouth opens.

'Don't kid yourself, Maya. It's obvious. You have no idea how wonderful you are. I want to see you confident, afraid of nothing. I want to see you to blossom.'

He straightens up and I throw him a smile.

'That's very thoughtful of you, Mr Foster. Thank you so much, but we've already sorted it.'

'Have you?' He cocks his head. 'Does she really know what she's done to you?'

I twist the mug around on the top, resolving not to get annoyed with him for bringing this up. After all, I've forced him to confront a thing or two about his own life in recent days. And anyway, he's pushing in exactly the right direction. I've never really discussed anything with Sara. She has no idea what she's done to me. Finally, I shake my head.

'Then I'd say you need to talk.' He stares at me, utterly determined.

'Fair enough.'

With a satisfied nod, he sets about preparing my breakfast. He's just sliding a plate of toast under my nose when the doorbell chimes. I watch as he answers the door. I don't get to see who's on the other side, but I recognise Spencer's voice.

'This was delivered for you.'

Without a word, Dan closes the door and returns to the breakfast bar, clutching a small black box in his hands. He opens the box and immediately snaps it shut again.

'What's that?' I ask.

'Cufflinks,' he answers with a quick smile. 'I need to get going.' Suddenly distant, he gives me a quick peck on the lips before taking himself upstairs with the box and his mobile.

Sipping at my tea, I wonder what he's hiding from me now, because those certainly weren't cufflinks in that box. A gift, perhaps? A little trinket? Resisting the temptation to follow him and indulge in a touch of snooping while he's in the shower, I finish off my breakfast and wait until he reappears, looking ridiculously delectable in a tailored grey suit. He slips his briefcase onto the counter and sets about rearranging his tie.

'I'm going to take you away next week,' he announces, completely out of the blue.

'What?'

'I told you I would.'

'But next week?'

'Next week. I'll get Carla onto it today. Bermuda.' He gives me a flash of his eyes. 'You need to find your passport.'

I prod at the remnants of my toast.

'I don't really fancy it.'

'You don't really fancy finding your passport?'

'I don't really fancy Bermuda.' I tut. 'I don't even know where it is.'

'In the Atlantic.'

'Can't we just go to Cornwall? That's in the Atlantic.'

'No.'

My nerves are getting the better of me now, and he seems to notice.

'The flying thing?' he asks.

'It's dangerous,' I explain solemnly.

'Statistically speaking, it's less dangerous than driving to Cornwall. You'll be perfectly safe. Find your passport.'

'Oh for God's sake.' Just thinking about all those messy drawers is putting me into a grump, let alone worrying about a huge, airborne lump of metal.

'First thing, Maya. I'll get Carla to call you for details. I want this booked.' Eyeing me for a moment, he seems to melt a little. He leans down and kisses me. 'Let's not argue. I want to treat you.'

'I know that. But I'm not just going to accept everything your way.'

'And I know that.' His mobile vibrates. Taking it out of his jacket pocket, he checks the caller identity. 'Passport.'

I watch the door close behind him, and silently resolve to get my own way. If he wants to whisk me away, then he'll have to be content with Cornish rain and cream teas. Instead of hunting for my passport, I'll simply get on with my day.

After taking a shower when I'd rather have a bath, I pull open the walk-in wardrobe and survey a mound of clothes that were chosen for me by someone else. Ignoring them all, I tug on a pair of trusty combats and one of my favourite tatty T-shirts, noting with delight that at least my drawers are still an unholy mess. And then I come to a halt, looking round at a bedroom that just doesn't feel like mine. For a start, in spite of all my best efforts, it's far too tidy. Ever since I moved in I've been busily dumping my clothes on the floor, only for Dan to pick them up again and store them neatly away. Suddenly missing my tiny, chaotic bedroom back in Camden, I wonder how the hell I've managed to end up in a super-tidy, ultra-posh penthouse world. I may well be in love with Daniel Foster, but this just isn't me. And however long I spend here, I can't imagine it ever will be. There's only one way to avoid the strangeness of it all. With a quiet sigh, I take refuge in the studio and bury myself in the triptych.

I choose my colours, squeezing a good amount of each onto the palette, thinning them with linseed and blending until I'm satisfied. And then I start on the left-hand panel. Using charcoal browns, deep reds, hints of gold and bronze, I add definition to the woman's body, breathing life into her flesh and watching in amazement as her pain becomes ever more apparent. It's everywhere: in the tension of her muscles, the position of her head, the closed eyes, the bared teeth. But even more evident is the fact that she wants it. I have no idea how long I've been painting for when I'm interrupted by a knock at the door.

'Come in,' I call, half expecting the Terminator to show his face.

But it's not the Terminator at all. As the door's eased open, I'm presented with a grey-haired woman, in her fifties maybe. Dressed in jeans and a pink blouse, she's clutching a mobile.

'I'm sorry to bother you.' Clearly embarrassed, she wafts the mobile in front of her face. 'I'm Geena.'

'Geena?'

'Dan's housekeeper.'

I drop my brush onto the palette and stride over to greet the poor woman.

'And I'm Maya.'

'I know.' She smiles warmly. 'Dan's warned me about you.'

'Has he now?' I grin. 'Look, I'm sorry. I'm a bit of a walking disaster when it comes to keeping things tidy, but I promise I'll do my best.'

'Oh, you just carry on being yourself.' She glances past me at the canvases. Her eyes widen. 'He's increased my pay. He says it's danger money.'

I laugh. 'As long as you're happy with that.' Suddenly, an idea occurs to me. 'Oh, I'm sorry. Do you want to clean in here?'

'No, not just now. I just thought you should know. Your phone. Well, I think it's yours.' She holds it out.

'Yes, it's mine.'

'It's been pinging and buzzing like mad for the last half an hour.'

'Oh, bugger.'

Taking the mobile out of Geena's hands, I open up the screen: three missed calls from an unknown number, probably Carla, and two from Dan, followed by a text.

Answer your phone, sweet pea. Carla needs your passport details. Xxxx

And then another.

We're going to Bermuda whether you like it or not. Details. Now. Xxxx

And finally.

Don't make me come home and spank you. Xxxx

Grinning at the fact that I'm getting four kisses today, I text him back.

You wouldn't. X

The reply comes immediately.

I would. Xxxx

And that does it. In spite of the fluttering sensation between my thighs, I can't let the man get me anywhere near the spanking bench until he's sorted things out with Layla. I'll sing like a canary. And that means I'll just have to humour him with the whole Bermuda thing. But never mind. As soon as he gets me anywhere near a plane, he'll be regretting his control freak tendencies. Without bothering to tidy up, I hurry back to the bedroom and rummage through the boxes at the bottom of the wardrobe, searching for my passport. I find it eventually, shoved into a shoebox, and take a moment to gaze at my passport photo: taken five years ago when Lucy finally convinced me to take a holiday abroad ... shortly before I chickened out.

My phone pings. Another message.

You've got one more chance, sweet pea. Carla's about to phone you. Xxxx

I type in my reply and fire it off.

Back off, shit head. I'm onto it. X

'Just not in the way you think I am,' I muse out loud.

Suddenly, alongside feeling utterly flustered, I'm also feeling utterly determined to give the big kahuna a piece of my mind. Ignoring the calls from my mobile, I clean up in the bathroom and return to the wardrobe for a change of clothes. My T-shirt's already spattered with paint and I'd like to look half-way respectable for what I'm about to do. Opening up one drawer after another, I gasp and growl and curse. Somehow, within the space of the last couple of hours, every last scrap of my messiness seems to have been eradicated. In its place, T-shirts are neatly folded in one drawer, knickers rolled up in a second, bras arranged in third. Swapping the ruined T-shirt for a clean one and shoving my mobile into my pocket, I skitter downstairs to find Geena busy in the kitchen, cleaning out cupboards that already seem to be perfectly clean. She turns and smiles.

'Off out?' she asks.

'Yes.' I pause, grabbing my keys, not entirely sure how I'm going to broach the subject. 'Did you ... Did you tidy my wardrobe?'

The smile widens.

'Yes. Mr Foster told me to do it.'

'He did?'

She nods and I sense the first stirrings of anger in my gut, but I'm not going to take it out on Geena. My target is a mile or so down the south bank. He's gone too far again ... and I'm going to tell him, right to his face.

'I didn't do the boxes. But he said I should sort out your clothes.'

And he should have consulted me, I'd like to add.

'Thank you.' I force the most natural-looking smile I can muster. 'I appreciate it. I'll see you later, Geena.'

Passport in hand, I slam the front door behind me, and come to a sudden halt. Rising to his feet like a Titan, I'm greeted by Spencer.

'I'm going for a walk. I suppose you'll be accompanying me?'

'Of course.'

He follows me into the lift, out of the lift, through the lobby and onto the forecourt. I cross the road and begin to make my way down the south embankment. Picking up the pace past Lambeth Palace, I'm half running as I take the walkway under Westminster Bridge, threading a path through the crowds at the aquarium and the Eye. By the time I get to the Jubilee Gardens, I slow down again, checking to see if my bodyguard's still behind me ... and of course he is. After all, he's an unstoppable machine. When I finally come to Gabriel's Wharf, I pause, leaning against the wall and taking in the view across the Thames.

And then I feel my mobile vibrate. Taking it out, I'm greeted by yet another message from Dan.

Nice walk? Xxxx

The hairs on the back of my neck prickle. Thrusting the mobile back into my pocket, I beckon the Terminator to join me. It's a foregone conclusion that he's been texting Dan, and I'm going to make sure it doesn't happen again.

'Can I use your phone?' I ask. 'Mine's out of battery.'

His mouth opens.

'It's just that I really need to make a call.'

He eyes me suspiciously, before fishing out a mobile and handing it to me.

'This is nice,' I remark. 'Is it your own?'

'It's a work phone.'

'And it's the phone you're using to contact Mr Foster?'

Guilt sweeps across his face. Ah ha! Gotcha! In a flash, I reach out and drop the phone into the river.

'What the ...'

'Whoops.' I smile. 'Butter fingers. Sorry about that. I'll make sure Mr Foster reimburses the company.'

'But ...'

I continue to walk, and if the Terminator wants to follow me, that's fine. At least, he won't be able to forewarn the control freak of my imminent ambush. It doesn't take long for me to reach the headquarters of Fosters Construction. As soon as I'm through the main door, I stride purposefully towards the lifts, determined that nobody's going to stop me.

'I'll be five minutes,' I tell Spencer. 'Up and down. Wait here.'

He shakes his head.

'Five minutes. Where on Earth am I going to go?'

He shakes his head again and I make my decision. I really don't want to be a complete shit, but considering the current situation, it seems to be the only option.

'If you don't stay here,' I hiss, 'I'll have you sacked.'

His chin tightens.

'Five minutes,' I repeat, thoroughly surprised when he finally agrees.

Leaving him to sweat it out in the lobby, I step into the next car, impatiently tapping the passport against my thigh as the lift stops at one floor after another, swallowing up employees and then coughing them out again. Deciding that I don't have time to visit Norman, I give the fourteenth floor a miss, waiting until the doors slide open onto the fifteenth floor reception area. With a deep breath, I stride forwards across the marble floor, stopping at the glass desk where Carla's busy staring at her computer monitor. As soon as she sees me, she stands.

'Miss Scotton.' She smiles.

I slide the passport onto the desk.

'There you go.' I smile back.

Enough said. Before she can stop me, I'm on the move again, pushing open the oak door and barging straight into Dan's office.

Standing by his desk, he's talking on the phone, and I waver for a moment, thrown off course by how ruddy fuckable he looks. He's jacketless now, and that waistcoat really accentuates his trim hips. 'No, no, no!' a voice screeches from the back of my head. 'Don't get waylaid by all that sex stuff.'

Putting down the receiver, he opens his mouth to speak but I get in there first.

'I've had enough!' I announce.

'Enough of what?'

'Enough of you, you controlling twat!'

He casts an anxious glance at something behind me.

'I've had enough of you organising my bloody life for me,' I go on, determined to get it all out. 'If I want messy drawers, then I'll have messy drawers. And I've handed over my bloody passport, so you can stop nagging me about that. And just for the record, I don't want to go on a bloody plane. Let's just make that perfectly bloody clear. And while I'm about it, I've had enough of you snooping on me and you *are* snooping on me.' I point at him for good measure. 'And I've had enough of that big bastard following me around everywhere I go.' I gesticulate at the open doorway, noticing that Carla's standing in it now, looking distinctly worried. 'If I've got to have a bloody bodyguard, I want Beefy back! At least he's human.'

Hearing a cough, I stop mid-flow. That was a man's cough, and it certainly didn't come out of Dan's mouth. He's staring straight past me again, his lips set into a half-smile … almost apologetic. With a building sense of dread, I pivot slowly, following the direction of his gaze, only to find several suited types sitting around the table, including Clive and at least four Chinese men. The blood runs cold in my veins. A wave of nausea bubbles through my stomach. I feel a hand at the small of my back.

'I'm so sorry, Mr Sun,' Dan says.

The eldest of the Chinese men rises to his feet.

'This is Mr Sun, Maya. He's an important client. We're just putting the finishing touches to a three point two billion pound deal.'

I hear the words slip out of my mouth. 'Oh shit.'

Mr Sun approaches me.

'And you are?' he asks in a perfect English accent.

'Maya Scotton,' Dan interrupts. 'My fiancée.'

Suddenly forgetting the fact that I've just stormed right into the middle of a meeting, I swivel round to face Dan.

'I beg your pardon?'

'The future Mrs Foster,' he continues. Smiling fondly, he slides a hand around my waist and touches me gently on the end of my nose. I shake my head away. 'She's a little irritated with me right now – for various reasons – but on a good day I can assure you that she's the most delightful young woman you're ever likely to meet. She's an artist.'

'Is she now?' Mr Sun asks. A wrinkled hand is thrust towards me. 'Pleased to meet you, Maya Scotton.' His eyes crease into a smile. 'And congratulations. When is the happy day?'

'There isn't one,' I answer quickly.

I'm about to ask Dan what the hell he thinks he's playing at when he intervenes again.

'What she means is that we haven't set the date yet, but I'd say before Christmas.'

'What?' My mouth is wide open now. 'What are you going on about?'

He doesn't answer. Instead, he begins to manoeuvre me towards the door.

'I'll just escort her out.'

'Excuse me? Marriage?' I turn back to Mr Sun, deciding that this is the moment to put a spanner in the works. 'He hasn't even told me he loves me yet.'

I spot a hint of surprise in Mr Sun's eyes.

'Oh no. That is a bloody bad show,' he laughs. 'That's simply not cricket.'

And now it's Dan's turn to stare open-mouthed at Mr Sun.

'They're a basic requirement of a good marriage, Dan.' Mr Sun crosses his arms. 'Those three little words. I tell my wife I love her every day.' Uncrossing his arms, Mr Sun presses on. 'If I were you, I'd tell her now. Go on. We've covered the basics. I can talk to Clive a little more about the details.'

Clearing his throat, Dan looks at me, and if I'm not very much mistaken there's a hint of a threat in that look. 'If you don't mind, I'll be a few minutes.'

'Of course I don't mind.' Mr Sun smiles. 'You must keep your fiancée happy.'

'I'm not his ...'

I catch a glimpse of Clive. He's grinning from ear to ear. Before I can squeeze out the final word, my hand is grasped and I'm dragged out of the office.

'More coffee in there, Carla,' Dan barks, hauling me to the lift and punching the call button. He tugs me in, letting go of my hand as the doors slide to a close.

'Fiancée?' I spit. 'Where did that come from?'

He hits another button. The lift judders to a halt.

'Oh, I don't know. A mad fiancée seemed to be slightly less embarrassing than a mad girlfriend.'

'What are you doing?'

He says nothing. Instead, he simply takes out his mobile and calls up a contact. I hear a muffled voice at the other end of the line.

'Dave, lift number two is out of action. Leave it that way.'

He ends the call, immediately making another. Glaring at me, he listens to the dialling tone.

'Where's your bodyguard?' he demands. 'He's not answering his phone.'

'That's because I threw it in the river.'

He frowns.

'To stop you snooping on me,' I explain.

He opens his mouth.

'But don't worry. He's down in the lobby.'

'You are a fucking piece of work, Maya.'

'Thank you.'

He drops the mobile back into his pocket and glares at me some more.

'You're angry with me again,' I venture.

'No shit.'

Taking a step forwards, he rams me against the wall, grabs my hands and pins them back.

'Now let's get a few things straight here.'

I'm expecting a good talking to, but that's not what I get. Instead, he covers my lips with his, and kisses me for an age.

'You have a bodyguard for a reason,' he growls when he's done. 'I'm not going over that again.'

'I feel trapped.'

'It's a temporary measure. I want you protected until I've dealt with Boyd.'

Dealt with? What the hell's he going on about now?

'You wouldn't ...'

He picks up on my train of thought and derails it.

'Relax. I'm not the Godfather. I'm the CEO of a fucking building company. I don't go around cementing my enemies into the foundations, but I don't let them walk all over me either, especially when it comes to the things I value in my life. I know you hate feeling hemmed in. What we need is a few days away from this shit. I need it. You need it. A taste of things to come.' His eyes soften. He reaches down and unbuttons my combats. They drop to the floor. 'Talking of which ...'

Slipping his fingers into the top of my knickers, he tears them away.

'Not again,' I groan. 'I'll have no underwear left.'

'I'll buy you plenty more.'

He presses a hand against my clit, sending a pulse of warmth right through my vagina.

'You're not winning me round with a good fuck.'

'That's not my intention. Legs apart.'

I groan, kick off my combats and simply do as I'm told. Immediately, a single finger slides further between my legs and enters me, pushing deep, finding my g-spot and massaging it. I bang my head back against the lift wall and draw in a breath. I'm done for now.

'You've given me the mother of all stonkers, woman. I can't go back into the meeting like this.'

Withdrawing the finger and releasing me, he unzips his trousers and reveals his cock. True to his word, he's completely ready, fully erect.

'I don't need to win you round.' Grabbing hold of my right thigh, he urges my leg up to his waist and guides himself into me, readjusting his position until he's happy. Holding my leg in place, he snakes his free arm round my back. 'You're mine already. And that's the way it's going to stay ... for good.'

'For good?' I gasp, fighting against the flood of warmth in my core.

'Oh yes. Now, hold tight.'

I have just enough time to wrap my arms around his shoulders when he begins to thrust, drawing out to the hilt and pounding back into me, knocking the air out of my lungs.

I'm determined to get at least one thing my own way. 'If it's for good, you'd better tell me you love me. Mr Sun says you've got to.'

'He's not the boss of me.'

Again, he pulls back and rams inwards, setting my insides on fire. At this rate I'll be a brainless, groaning wreck within a minute. I'm going to have to work fast.

'No, I'm the boss of you.' I reach up and grab a handful of hair. 'Say it.'

'Well ...' His eyes sparkling, his fingers tightening around my thigh, he drives into me again. 'I love your skin.'

I let out a tiny, involuntary yelp of delight before gathering enough wits to battle on.

'That's not enough.'

'And your tight little cunt.'

'Filth.'

'And your tits.' With a grin, he drives again. 'I love every last bit of your body. I love tasting it. I love fucking it.'

'How romantic.'

'Not enough?'

'No.'

Digging his head into my neck, he picks up the pace, increasingly breathless, pushing out his next statements between thrusts.

'I love spanking your backside ... I love making you come ... I love fucking your arse.'

My muscles clench. I'm already teetering on the edge, and so is he. Putting a temporary stop on the list of things he loves about me, he tightens his grip again and pounds into me relentlessly.

'Fucking hell,' he rasps at last.

Sensing the moment, I let go, digging my fingers into his broad shoulders and groaning in pure ecstasy as I contract around him. A flood of warmth pulsates through my crotch, and I'm spent. I've had it. I'm done. In a state of pure bliss, I relax into his arms.

'I love that.' He slows the pace, wrestling his breath back under control and leaning his forehead against mine. 'I love the fact that we come together.'

At last, he withdraws, tucks away his cock and zips up his trousers. Taking a handkerchief out of his pocket, he sets about cleaning me up.

'I love wiping my cum from you.'

I lean down, scooping up my combats and the latest pair of ruined knickers.

'I love the fact that you love all this stuff,' I inform him, pulling on the combats and stuffing the knickers into my pocket. 'But it's still not enough.'

'Okay,' he sighs. 'I love the fact that you leave the top off the toothpaste, that you can't cook to save your life, that you leave your clothes all over the bedroom floor. Still not enough?'

'No,' I smile.

He takes his phone from his pocket and taps in a contact.

'I love your eyes.' He raises the mobile to his ear. 'They're so green. What colour eyes do you think our kids are going to have?'

'Stop it.'

A muffled voice interrupts the conversation.

He replies. 'Dave. Fix the lift.'

Almost immediately, we begin to move. Depositing the phone back in his pocket, he folds his arms, leans against the opposite wall and studies me.

'So that's it?' I ask. The lift doors open at the twelfth floor. Mrs Kavanagh enters, stops in her tracks and backs out again. The doors close and we continue downwards.

'I love the fact that you're incredibly talented.'

'And?'

'I love your spirit.'

The doors open again. He shakes his head at a man. The doors close.

'Just fucking say it, Dan.'

'I love your potty mouth. You swear like a navvy.'

'Still not enough.'

He smiles and shakes his head.

'Okay. I love your intelligence, your wit, your sense of humour.'

This time, the lift continues uninterrupted. He watches as the numbers count down.

'I love the fact that you love me, in spite of everything I've done.' As if he's wafting away everything he's done, he waves a hand. 'And now I think about it, I love the idea of you being my wife.'

'I beg your pardon?'

'Yes, that's definitely the way ahead.'

'But ...'

The lift judders to a halt. We're at the ground floor. The doors slide open. Before I know it, I'm tugged away from the wall and propelled out into the lobby while Dan stays put.

'Oh, and Maya!' he calls. 'One last thing!'

I stagger to a halt and turn, just as the doors begin to close.

'I love *you*.'

Chapter Seventeen

Fiddling with the dress, I rearrange it for the umpteenth time. Eight thousand eight hundred pounds' worth of black silk, very badly laced up at the back. But what am I supposed to do? Arriving home nearly half an hour late, Dan greeted me with a quick kiss, apologised and jumped straight into the shower, leaving me to struggle into the dress by myself, nearly dislocating both arms in the process. I stare at myself in the mirror. The low neckline reveals far too much of my cleavage, and the whole thing is threatening to come away at any minute. At least I've managed to tweak my hair into an up-do and apply the usual smattering of make-up. And then there's the Tiffany necklace, resting against my chest.

I don't hear the en-suite door open. He slips into view behind me, stunning in his black dinner jacket, his hair still a little damp, his bow tie undone. He curls his hands around my waist, drawing me in tight and I drink in his scent.

'You look amazing,' he murmurs against my neck.

'It's too loose,' I murmur back. 'I can't reach the laces.'

Releasing me, he steps back and inspects my handiwork.

'Mmm,' he muses. 'It does look like it's been done up by a two-year-old.'

He sets about tightening the bodice.

'Did you paint today?' he asks.

'A bit.'

In fact, in between my trip to Fosters and getting ready for the big night out, I managed another four hours, concentrating on the right hand panel, adding colour and depth and definition, choosing from a range of blues: Prussian, cerulean, cobalt. After Dan's admission, it was the obvious way to go. I spent the afternoon in the company of sheer pleasure.

'So, did you have a good day at work?' I ask casually.

'Fine.' He shrugs, re-threading a lace. 'The usual. Sealed a big deal with a Chinese billionaire. Fucked a beautiful woman in the lift.'

And told her you love her, I'd like to add. Those three little words have been hanging around in my brain all afternoon, teasing me and causing my stomach to trip over itself. And I want to hear them again. I can only hope he's forgotten the weird marriage proposal bit. No way am I ready for that.

'You love me then?' I venture.

'Looks like it.' Still focussed on the lacework, his blue eyes dance.

'Since when?'

'Oh, I don't know. Monday the twentieth of June. About two o'clock in the afternoon. There, that should do it.' He pats the dress and slides his arms back around my waist, smiling at me in the mirror while I process this new information. That was the first day I showed up at Fosters.

'Love at first sight?'

'If you like.'

I grin like a prize idiot.

'Say it again.'

He leans in, his mouth next to my ear. 'I love you,' he whispers. 'I'm in love. With you.'

I'm reeling again. It was one thing having those words fired at me from behind a closing lift door, but now he's standing behind me, his blue eyes flashing with delight, I'm in Wonderland. That's the second time I've heard those words from his disgustingly wonderful mouth. It makes my heart trip, and I'm pretty sure it always will.

'Aren't you supposed to ...' He straightens up. 'Say it back?'

I gather my senses. 'Oh that. Yes. I love you too.'

'So, we're in love?'

'Yup.'

'It's a nice feeling. I've never felt it before and I'll never feel it again. Not with anyone else. You're definitely the one.'

'I am?'

'Oh yes.'

'That's nice.'

'It is. In fact, I love you so much, I'd do anything for you.'

'Flash your cock at Mrs Kavanagh.'

'First thing Monday morning.' He grins. 'And you should do anything for me. It's only right.'

'Okay ...'

He stares at me. Don't say it, I will him silently. Don't go there. Not yet. It's madness.

'Marry me.'

And oh, he's done it. Bugger. He hasn't forgotten the weird marriage proposal bit at all. I'd better knock this on the head, and quickly too.

'No.'

'Why not?'

'Because you're going too fast. Again.'

'Oh come on, Maya. It's the next logical step.'

'And it can wait.'

'Why?' he demands. 'I've done the small talk thing. I've done the big talk thing. I've given you stuff. I've told you I love you. What more do I have to do?'

Sort your shit out. That's what I'd really like to say. If you want me to face my demons, then you can face your own while we're at it. But this isn't the right moment to open up yet another can of worms. It's his birthday, we're off to a party and he's in a good mood. And I'm not about to ruin any of that. Instead, I go for an easy answer.

'Be patient and wait.'

He rolls his eyes.

'It's going to happen.' He smiles, one of his slow languid specials. 'I'll drag a yes out of you soon enough.'

'Try your best.'

'I will.' He gives me a mischievous grin. 'And now I've got a little present for you.' Reaching into his jacket pocket, he pulls out a little black box. It must be the same box he took delivery of this morning. My stomach lurches. Good God, no. Don't let that be an engagement ring.

'What is it?'

'The general idea, as I understand things, is that you open it and find out for yourself.'

With a nervous smile, I turn, take the box and open it, letting out a sigh of relief when I catch sight of a pair of earrings: two silver pendants, each one fashioned into the shape of a sweat pea and centred with a pearl.

'They're beautiful.'

'I had them made.'

'But when did you find the time?'

'Where you're concerned, I always find the time. Lily put me in touch with a jeweller. I sent him a photo of the necklace and told him I wanted something to match.'

'When?'

'A couple of weeks ago. Not long after I met you.'

'I bloody love you, Dan.'

'And I bloody love you too. I'm going to make you the happiest woman on the planet. And I mean that.' He touches me on the cheek. 'Come here.'

Taking the box from my hand, he places it on a shelf in the wardrobe and picks out an earring. Coming back to me, he sets about threading the silver hook into my ear, glancing at me every now and then, clearly anxious not to hurt me. When he's finished with the left ear, the repeats the process with the right. And I watch, smiling at the intense concentration on his face, my heart flooding with warmth, my brain casually waving goodbye to any scrap of logic and sense. I've been charmed right to the verge of giving him a 'yes.' I'm about to open my mouth and agree to the maddest thing I've ever heard, when he finally straightens up.

'There.' He moves me round to face the mirror. 'We look like the people in those perfume adverts.'

I burst into a fit of giggles.

'And we need to go,' he adds. 'Our carriage awaits.'

***

A Rolls-Royce! I'm only sitting in a bloody Rolls-Royce! Ignoring the views as we glide across Lambeth Bridge and down the North Embankment, I stare at my surroundings, taking in the solid teak dashboard and the hand-sewn leather trims. When I'm finally done with staring, I play with the silver panel in my door, amazed when it opens gracefully at my touch, revealing a cigarette lighter and an ashtray. I close it again, switching my attention to the two rectangular units built into the leather roof lining, a control unit between them. Tempted beyond belief, I'm about to reach up and press one of the buttons above my head when I catch sight of Dan watching me, an amused grin on his face.

'Is this yours?'

He laughs. 'Don't be ridiculous. It's hired. I thought you deserved something a little special tonight.'

And shit, this is something a little special.

'You haven't done up your tie,' I remark.

He looks down.

'I hate these things.'

While he fiddles with the bow tie, I decide to ask for a little more detail about the function.

'This thing at the Savoy? Is this because of ... you know ... your past.'

He nods curtly, flipping one end of the tie over the other and letting out an exasperated sigh.

'Lily got involved with the foundation,' he mutters, 'and I've supported her with it for years.'

I watch in awe as he performs some sort of complicated folding and threading operation. As if by magic, a bow tie appears.

'Whatever else you think of her, she's got a good heart.' He straightens out the bow, runs an index finger across it, scowls and begins all over again. 'She hasn't worked a day in her life ... but the Foundation keeps her busy, gives her something to do ... and I suppose she does it because of me.'

An idea scratches at the inside of my head.

'Do you think she's in love with you?'

He breaks into a laugh, completes the bow, unravels it and starts again.

'Not likely. She's more like a sister.'

Eugh. Now, come on, considering what I know, that's a disgusting idea. I can't help it. I have to let him know.

'She told me she popped your cherry.'

'That woman needs a filter.' He grimaces. 'It was a long time ago. A drunken mistake. Neither of us want it to happen again.' Finally satisfied, he pats the bow. 'What do you think?'

'It looks like it's been done up by a two-year-old.'

'Touché, Miss Scotton.' His lips curl into a smile. 'We're here.'

The car takes a left, circling the end of a park and drawing to a halt outside the rear entrance to the Savoy. I've never been here before. I've never considered myself posh enough. And even now, dressed in an expensive gown and sitting in the back of a Rolls-Royce, I still don't.

A doorman steps forwards and opens the door on Dan's side.

'Stay where you are. Let's do this properly.'

While he gets out, I do as I'm told, waiting patiently for him to circle the car and open my door. A hand appears in front of my face. I slip my fingers into his, allowing him to help me out, but in spite of my best efforts, it's not exactly the most graceful of exits from a car. Grappling with the slit, I totter from side to side on the high heels.

'Steady now.' Wrapping an arm around my waist, Dan comes to my rescue. 'You're being papped. You don't want to show off your knickers.'

'What?'

Squinting into the flash of a camera, I'm temporarily blinded. With a few blinks, the scene finally comes into focus: a group of men standing by the edge of a red carpet, their faces obscured by cameras.

'Paparazzi?'

'They're here for the high society types.'

'Not us then.' I grin at a photographer. He eyes me up in return. 'Two nobodies from the East Coast.'

'We're not nobodies.' Dan places a hand at the base of my spine, and I tingle at his touch. 'Let's give them a pose.'

I have just enough time to tuck my hair into place and straighten out my dress before I'm tugged in by his side. The cameras flash again.

'Excuse me, mate,' a photographer calls. 'Give us your names, just in case you're anyone worth bothering with.'

I'm surprised when Dan obliges.

'Daniel Foster and Maya Scotton. I own Fosters Construction. Maya's an up-and-coming artist.' He begins to move away, pauses, turns back to the photographer and adds: 'And she's going to be my wife.'

'Dan,' I hiss.

'Come along, darling.'

Taking me by the hand, he leads me through a set of wooden revolving doors, up an incline and straight into a ballroom. We wait by the entrance and while Dan talks to an attendant, I take in the opulence of it all: the duck egg blue panels decorated with intricate stucco flowers; the arched doorways, each one containing a set of mirrored double doors; the swirling blues and golds of the carpet; a vaulted ceiling that curves above my head; six vast chandeliers spilling out a low, comfortable light. To my right, a small stage has been set up with a band's equipment while in front of me, I count about thirty round tables, all covered with a crisp white cloth, set with silver cutlery and an array of crystal glasses. The room's already full, swelling with expensive dresses and tuxedos: all the men dapper in their dinner jackets, the women brimming over with diamonds and self-confidence.

'Jesus,' I breathe, sensing a knot of anxiety in the pit of my stomach.

'You'll be fine,' Dan murmurs into my ear, taking my hand in his. 'Let's find Lily.'

As we push forwards into the room, I realise that we're being watched ... or rather Dan's being watched. He's catching the eye of just about every woman in the place. One by one, they drop their conversations to watch him pass by … and I'm not at all surprised. On any normal day, he's absolute male perfection, but in a tux, he's something else. Every single female pair of eyes takes in the lean frame and the broad shoulders, the bright blue eyes, the tousled blond hair. And I just can't help it. A self-satisfied smile settles across my face because he's mine. One hundred percent mine. Suddenly, I feel giddy, totally giddy at the perfection of my life. But almost as soon as the feeling springs into life, I hear a familiar voice at the back of my head, warning me that it just can't last. It never does.

We've almost made it to the centre of the ballroom when the crowd parts, and we're suddenly standing with Lily.

'I'm so pleased to see you here, Maya.'

Taking me by the arms, she kisses me on both cheeks. And even though it's completely alien to me, I do the same in return.

'I'm pleased to be here.'

'You look absolutely stunning in that dress. What is it?'

I shrug. 'A dress?'

'Which designer?'

I shake my head. 'No idea.'

With a knowing smile, she takes a step back and holds out her arms. 'Daniel.'

He moves in for a quick embrace and pecks her on the cheek.

'How are you doing?' she asks.

'Never better.'

'Glad to hear it.'

'So what's the plan for tonight?'

'The usual. Dinner. Auction. Dancing.' She glances round the room, waves at somebody. 'I need you to do a bit of networking.'

He frowns. 'What, now?'

'Yes, now.' Ignoring Dan's grimace, she continues. 'For a start, you can get your backside over there and sweet talk Wallace.'

She motions towards a corpulent, red-faced man. In his mid-fifties perhaps, he's holding court at the centre of a group of women.

'In a bit.'

'No, now. For me. Please.' She runs a hand down his arm. 'You know you always charm him into making the biggest donation. And besides, I need a little word with Maya.'

Dan narrows his eyes at Lily.

'Why?' he demands. 'What little nugget of information are you going to pass on this time?'

'I'm going to fill her in on all the details of when we were young.' She smiles archly. 'Your obsession with *Star Wars*, your collection of *Care Bears* stickers, that sort of thing.'

'She's talking bollocks,' Dan warns me.

'Wallace. Now.'

Swivelling him round, Lily sends him in the general direction of the gathering. While the women hastily rearrange their cleavages, Wallace thrusts out a hand in greeting.

'Wallace Ashford,' Lily explains. 'He owns half of Belgravia. Dan's done some work for him in the past, cut him some good deals. He's had Wallace in his pocket ever since. You haven't met rich until you've met Wallace.' She grabs two flutes of champagne from a passing tray, handing one to me. 'I'm so glad to see you two back together.' She takes a sip. 'You're good for Dan ... and he's in love with you.'

I take a sip of my own champagne, allowing myself a smug smile.

'I know.'

'He told you?'

'He said the magic words.'

Lily's perfect little lips form a perfect little circle. She glances at Dan. He's leaning in towards Wallace now, apparently listening to something incredibly interesting.

'Excellent,' Lily chirps. 'He obviously took Mr Sun's advice then.'

'You know about that?'

'Clive told me.' She giggles. Taking another dainty mouthful of champagne, she fixes me with her hazel eyes. 'Apparently, you're getting married.'

'No, we're not.'

'Oh, why not? You've moved in with him.'

'Living with a man is one thing. Marrying him is something else. It's all going a bit too fast for me.'

'That's Dan all over, I'm afraid. When he decides he wants something, he goes full speed to get it. If he wants to marry you, I'd say you're in trouble.' She giggles again, and I wonder just how many champagnes she's had so far. Finally, she manages to calm herself. 'You won't regret it,' she adds seriously. 'I promise you, you've got a good one there.'

'How's *your* love life?' I ask, deciding that it's a good idea to change the conversation. 'You were having a little trouble the other week.'

'Oh that.' She screws up her perfect little nose. 'It's all finished. I think I might be leaning back in the male direction.'

'Seriously?'

'Seriously. You know I'm fifty-fifty?'

I nod.

'I've met someone I like. Hot in bed.'

'Tell me more.'

She pouts, licks her lips and touches her nose with an index finger.

'Early days. Let's just see how it goes.' Her eyes widen. 'Ooh, Dan's coming back. Don't mention the new guy. He'll come over all brotherly and protective.'

She winks at me, just as Dan returns.

'Having fun?' Lily asks.

'No.' Clearly riled, he grabs a glass of champagne. 'That man's a fucking bore.'

Putting an arm around his neck, Lily lets off a laugh.

'Daniel, darling, that fucking bore over there donated ten thousand last year.'

'And he's just bought a fucking yacht,' Dan fires back. 'Fifteen million on a fucking yacht. Imagine what you could do with that instead of wafting round the fucking Med.'

'And you don't chuck money around?' Lily demands.

'No, I don't.'

'You just bought yourself a new Jag,' she reminds him.

'The Jag's for Maya. See that twat.' He points his glass in Wallace's direction. 'He's got seven cars. Seven. Who needs seven cars?'

'My God, you're such a scrooge.' She pokes him in the chest. In return, he gives her a good scowl. 'I'm going to mingle, darlings. You ought to do the same.'

While Lily drifts off, glass in hand, Dan curls an arm round my waist and takes in a deep breath.

'You *do* throw money around.' I prod him gently. 'Remember packing me off to Harrods?'

His eyes lock with mine, and my heartbeat quickens.

'You needed clothes, Maya, and I wanted to spoil you. Is that so bad?'

'And you chartered a helicopter.'

'Necessity. There were no seats on any flights. I had to fuck you.'

'And what about the Rolls-Royce? I bet that didn't come cheap.'

'Cheaper than buying one.' He takes a sip of champagne and smiles. 'Okay, so I do have some perks and I can afford them, but there's no need to go buying a fucking yacht.' He waves his glass at

Wallace again. 'He's got a Lear jet as well. Can you believe that? A fucking Lear jet.'

'Will you stop swearing?'

'Fuck it. Sorry.' He shrugs. 'He just annoys me, that's all.'

'So, what do you do with your money?'

He shrugs again. And now he seems embarrassed.

'I leave it in the bank.'

'All of it?'

Refusing to answer, he scans the room.

'Mr Foster, am I right in thinking that you make donations to charities?'

'Drop it,' he growls out of the corner of his mouth.

'Soft centre.'

'I said drop it, Scotton. Now, let's go and sit down before any more of these well-heeled shitheads try to talk to me.'

Without another word, he grabs my hand and guides me through the maze of tables, stopping at one and then another until he finds our names. Pulling out a chair for me, he waits until I'm seated and then settles in to my left, draping an arm around my back and moving in close.

'What are you doing?' I demand.

'Making myself comfortable.'

The dress parts at the slit, falling away from my legs. I'm just trying to rearrange it back into a more modest position when he leans in further. His left hand lands on my thigh and squeezes, a warning to leave the dress alone. In a fluster, I stare at the hand, watching as it creeps in towards my crotch. I look up to find him smiling across the table at a couple.

'Good to see you, Dan,' the man exclaims. 'How are you?'

'Very well, thank you,' he answers, gently coaxing my legs apart.

'No,' I breathe.

'Submission,' he whispers into my ear. 'It's mine. Any time. Anywhere.'

He turns to face me, his nose almost touching mine, and smiles. And oh shit. He wasn't joking about the slit thing at all. In fact, he was deadly serious. And he's about to make his move. The smile broadens as he strokes the nape of my neck.

'Relax, sweet pea.'

'You can't do this here.'

An eyebrow lifts. 'Oh yes I can.' The fingers move further, warm, gentle, probing into the top of my knickers. He leans in to whisper again. 'These things are a bore. I'm in the mood to lighten it up a bit.'

I'm in a complete tizzy now. Straining to see past the side of his head, I survey the table, noting that everyone's engaged in conversation ... apart from us. His fingers brush over my pubic hair.

'Forget this lot.'

Spreading his hand around the back of my neck, he holds me firmly while he brings his face back to mine. His eyes sparkle. Down below, the finger begins to circle against my clit, slowly working me up into a feverish ball of lust.

'Submission,' he reminds me. 'You have no choice.'

Sealing his lips around mine, he coaxes my mouth open with his tongue, matching the slow, unhurried circling motion of the finger. As the pressure rises, I groan into his mouth, but the kiss doesn't end ... and neither does the torment between my thighs. While the noise and chatter of the room seem to drain away, I focus for dear life on the growing warmth in my groin, willing it to ignite quickly, silently hoping that I'll be able to control the rest of my body when it does. Minutes drag by in silence and I slip away into oblivion. I'm right on the edge when his fingers tighten against my neck. And at last, somewhere deep inside, a spark catches hold, sending a wave of delicious ripples right through me. Kept in check by the hand, I tremble in his grip as I come.

'Shit,' I gasp.

Suddenly back in the room, I'm released. And immediately, I survey the other guests, nervously checking that our little liaison has gone unnoticed. Evidently, it hasn't. The lady at the opposite side of the table is smiling at me, knowingly.

'Oh God.'

Rearranging my dress, Dan sits up straight, adjusts his dinner jacket and sucks at his index finger.

'So, tell us, Dan,' the woman begins. 'What's the latest news at Fosters?'

Without a care in the world, he leans forwards, elbows on the table, and begins to explain the ins and outs of work on a shopping mall.

I feel a hand on my shoulder, and find Lily smiling down at me.

'That was a show and a half,' she grins. 'What's got into him, kissing your face off in front of all and sundry?'

Jesus, I hope she didn't get the full extent of what's just happened.

'I'd better buy myself a new hat.' She winks and disappears back into the crowd.

Chapter Eighteen

I take the last mouthful of the starter, a fancy salad that was certainly a few notches up from a prawn cocktail. I'd like to ask Dan if he enjoyed it, but he's busy talking to the woman on his left about the Foundation. I'd like to listen to what he's got to say, but it's almost impossible to hear anything above the general din of the room. Deciding that I'm in need of a little break, I lay down my cutlery and stand up.

'Where are you going?' Dan asks, breaking off his chat.

I lean down and whisper into his ear.

'I need a wee.'

He throws his napkin onto the table. 'I'll come with you.'

'No you won't.'

'But there's no bodyguard.'

'And I'm sure I can make it to the toilet and back without an incident.' I give him my best do-as-you're-bloody-well-told glare. 'Stay here.'

He glances at the main doors.

'Be quick,' he warns me. 'No mucking about.'

Still wondering what sort of mucking about he thinks women get up to in toilets, I meander through a labyrinth of corridors, stumbling over the Ladies by accident. An ornate antechamber comes first, followed by a luxurious washroom, and finally the cubicles. Once I'm locked inside, I set about fiddling with the dress, desperate not to dunk any of the eight thousand eight hundred pounds' worth of material in the toilet. Gathering it together at the front, I bunch it around my waist, knowing full well that it's going to be creased beyond recognition by the time I emerge again. When I've finished, I straighten out the dress as much as possible, open the door, and

187

head for the sinks. I'm reaching for some high-end liquid soap when someone speaks behind me.

'Maya.'

I turn quickly, recognising the voice. I've heard it before. In fact, if I'm not very much mistaken, the last time it spoke to me, it called me 'sewage mouth.' Staring into the pompous face of Claudine Thomas, I wrestle with the urge to tell her to fuck off. But I'm dressed like a lady, and for once I'm determined to behave like one. Which is more than I can say for her. Wearing a ridiculously short, green silk dress and impossibly high heels, she looks every inch an escort.

'How do you know my name?' I seethe.

Her thin lips fake a smile. Her eyes glimmer with threat.

'I've done my research.'

'And what are you doing here?'

Because if Dan sees you, he's going to go ballistic ... and that's putting it mildly.

'I paid for a ticket, silly.' She smiles again. It makes my stomach curdle. 'I'm here with Isaac. You remember Isaac, don't you?'

How could I ever forget him? An overweight, over-the-hill walrus of a man, the owner of a kinky club, and a lecherous pillock to boot.

She sidles forwards. 'Did he make you come?'

'I beg your pardon?'

'Just now.' The lips curl up a little further. 'At your table. You weren't just kissing, were you?'

'You saw?'

Oh bugger, I really shouldn't have said that. I should have feigned innocence.

'I wasn't the only one. Isaac enjoyed it too. And a few other people, I should think.'

My cheeks flood with embarrassment.

'Looks like you're in love.'

'It's no business of yours.'

'Of course not.'

Her cat-like eyes glisten in the light. I need to get away from this woman, and quickly too. But before I leave, I need to put her in her place.

'If you're here to cause more trouble, you can just forget it.'

'I never cause trouble.'

'Oh no?' I smile back, determined to play this coolly. Turning to the sink, I squirt a dollop of soap into my hands and lather them up. 'So spreading rumours that Dan's a whip-cracking sadist isn't causing trouble?' Watching Claudine in the mirror, I run my hands under the water.

'He was a whip-cracking sadist with me.'

'Only because you asked for it.'

'He enjoyed it.'

'He didn't. Believe me.' I shake my hands, switch off the tap and reach for a hand towel.

'You don't know your boyfriend as well as you think you do.'

'I know him better than anyone.'

'He's keeping plenty of things from you.'

She cocks her head to one side and my body stiffens. Right now, I'd love nothing more than to knock the wind out of her sails. I'd love to inform her that she's telling me nothing new, that I'm working on it, slowly encouraging the secrets out of him one by one. And I'd certainly love to tell her I don't need some self-satisfied, red-headed, kinky freak meddling in my business. But that wouldn't be wise. The less said, the better. And besides, I need to ratchet this up a little and while I'm at it, I'll put an inevitable end to the ladylike behaviour.

'Why don't you just fuck off, Claudine?'

Totally unaffected, her face remains impassive.

'And why don't you just ask him about his wife?'

She's staring at me now, like a child torturing a fly, intrigued by its every reaction, and I'm not entirely sure what she's picking up on. All I know is this: I can't move and I can't breathe, and the room seems to have melted.

'Oh, I'm sorry. Did I shock you?' She smiles, a Cheshire cat sort of smile, all teeth and lipstick. 'You didn't know about her, did you?' Tipping her head to one side, she proceeds to drag out the next few words, punctuating them with ridiculously long pauses. 'His rich ... beautiful ... Italian wife?'

Blind-sided, I drop the towel into the sink, steadying myself for a moment against the marble top before I swivel round, lean back and stare straight into Claudine's smug little face.

'What are you talking about?'

'Isn't it obvious?'

'You're lying.'

'I'm sorry, Maya. I'm not.'

'But how do you ...' I falter, choking on my own words.

'How do I know?' She leans in to me. 'Isaac,' she whispers. 'Dan might not be too keen on him now, but when he was younger, he used to tell Isaac all sorts of things, especially after a few whiskies.'

'I don't believe you.'

Her eyes crease. Another fake smile.

'I don't care.'

With a shrug, she turns on her heels, leaving me in chaos, floundering in a quagmire of confusion.

A wife.

A rich, beautiful Italian wife.

His words replay themselves in my head: 'I was a mess back then. It wasn't a good time. I'd just rather forget.'

But why, Mr Foster? Is it because you hurt her? Or did she break *your* heart? Is that real reason why you shut yourself off for years on end? I shake the questions out of my head, wondering why I'm even bothering to sift through the possibilities. After all, if Claudine Thomas is telling the truth, then I'm living with a big, fat, dirty liar because as far as I can remember, he told me categorically that he'd never been married. And if he's lied to me about that, then what else is he holding back? With a resounding crash, confusion gives way to anger. He's reeled me in, and I've made it oh so easy for him.

Well, I'm not going to make it easy any more.

'Hey.' I look up to find Lily standing in front of me. 'Dan sent me to fetch you. He said that's enough mucking about. The main course is being served.'

'Is it?'

At last, I come back to my senses.

'I'm just coming.' Rearranging my hair, I resolve to serve up a main course of my own.

***

I follow Lily back to the ballroom. As soon as I'm through the door, I catch sight of him, chatting and laughing with our fellow table-mates, totally unaware of the drama that's about to erupt in his life. With my heart crashing at my rib cage, I weave my way back through the tables and take my seat.

His arm snakes around my back and I shudder.

'What's the matter?' he asks. The smile disappears. 'Maya? Talk to me.'

Oh, where to start?

'Do you think we're having pizza tonight?' I ask chirpily.

'Pizza? I wouldn't think so. This is the Savoy.'

'How about spaghetti then?'

Withdrawing his arm, he leans back. 'What's come over you?'

I survey the room. And there she is, Claudine Thomas, standing by a table, chatting to Isaac, glancing over in our direction every now and then.

190

'That pair.' I nod towards her.

I feel him tense. He's obviously spotted them.

'What the fuck are they doing here?' His eyes are back on me. 'Did they speak to you?'

'I've just had a lovely chat with Claudine in the toilets ... in between mucking about.'

'What did she say?'

'I don't want to talk about it here.' I rest a hand on his arm. 'I just want to leave.'

'I can't go yet. Lily's doing an auction.'

'I'm sure she'll understand if we say *arrividerci*.'

I smile sweetly.

'Maya, she wants me here to support her.'

'Yes, but if you say *ciao, bella* ...'

Without warning, he slams a fist on the table. The conversation around us grinds to a halt.

'What's with the Italian?' he demands.

'I could ask you the same question.'

'What are you going on about?'

'Your Italian wife.'

He hesitates.

'I have no wife.'

'And are you sure about that?'

'Of course I'm sure. What did she say?'

'I told you, I don't want to talk about it here.'

'And I do. What did she say?'

'Ask her yourself.'

Before I can grab at his tux, he's on his feet, twisting and turning through the tables, making his way towards Isaac and Claudine. I watch as he grabs Claudine by the arm, as Isaac reaches out to stop him. There's about to be a scene, and I don't particularly want to witness it. I need to get away from this place, and I need to get away from Dan. Rising to my feet, I focus on the exit.

And then I run.

Within seconds, I'm out of the ballroom, tottering back down the incline and out through the revolving doors. Removing the high heels, I dodge a passing Ferrari, head to the left and skirt round the edge of the park. I'm quickly onto the embankment, crossing the road and setting off towards the Golden Jubilee Bridge, but it's not that easy making a getaway in a full-length evening gown. Before I'm even half way there, I run out of steam, coming to a halt by Cleopatra's Needle, as good a place as any to hide out for a while.

Stumbling down the steps onto a stone observation deck, I lean against a wall, catching my breath as I look down at the dark, sleek waters of The Thames. After a while, I raise my head and take in the view: Waterloo Bridge to the left; and to the right, a skyline dominated by the Eye. Illuminated now against the night, it's still rotating slowly.

'Beautiful, isn't it?'

I turn quickly, and then I'm frozen to the spot.

Ian Boyd is standing right behind me.

'How did you …'

He takes a step forwards, his face silhouetted against a street light.

'What's the matter? Have we fallen out with Mr Swanky Pants? Where is he?' He makes a theatrical show of looking around, and then he shrugs. 'Oh, he's not here.' He pauses, and I'm pretty sure he's smiling. I catch a flash of teeth in the shadows. 'Nowhere to be seen,' he goes on. 'And where's your Neanderthal of a bodyguard?'

Not here. Neither of them are here. I'm totally alone, totally unprotected. A strange, cold sensation oozes through my veins, like lead.

'Leave me alone.' My voice sounds timid, pathetic.

'There's nobody to rescue you.'

'Oh fuck off, Ian.'

'Still swearing. You know, I never liked that about you. But I suppose a woman can change.'

Not this woman. This woman is never going to change.

'I'm not interested. I never will be. Get that into your head.'

'And get this into your head,' he shoots back. 'I never give up.'

He takes another step. Close now, he reaches out, runs a finger down the side of my face. I flinch.

'There'll be no secrets with me, Maya.'

The sounds of London ebb away. There's nothing now. No traffic. No sirens. No shouts. Apart from Boyd's voice and my own heartbeat raging in my chest, I can hear nothing.

'You can't trust a man like that. A man who keeps secrets.'

My mouth falls open, and he smiles.

'It's easy enough to dig up the dirt, you know. And where Mr Swanky Pants is concerned, I've found it by the shovelful.'

Desperately, I will my brain to kick into gear, my mouth to function. At last, I hear the words come spilling out into the dark.

'Don't waste your breath. I already know it all.'

Boyd smiles. He's clearly about to waste his breath anyway.

'Really? Did you know he grew up in the same town as you?'

'Yes,' I sneer, determined to steal his thunder. 'And I know he was adopted. I know he was thrown out of university. I know he ended up in Rome. I know he lived with a woman.'

'And married her?'

'Yes, I know that,' I snap, and suddenly I'm wondering if Boyd is behind Claudine's meddling.

He reaches up to touch me again. I take a step to the side.

'And, of course, you know about his penchant for kinky clubs.'

'Yes.'

'He's got a reputation, you know. He's into the serious stuff.'

'Not any more.'

'Are you sure about that? Is it just the light version for you? I can offer you kink, if that's your thing.'

'You can't offer me anything.'

'I can offer you plenty.'

I look past him, at the steps, the row of little white lightbulbs strung out between the lamp posts. If I'm quick enough, I could make a run for it, but he'd only follow me. My head's swirling now: a mess of panic and fear. There's a hand on my arm, fingers closing around my flesh ... Boyd's fingers.

'Come with me, Maya. I'm not the man I used to be.'

I shake my head and do my best to glare at him, but it's almost impossible. The world's a blur. And suddenly I realise that I'm crying.

'Back off.'

I jolt at the sound of the voice.

The fingers release my arm and I let out a breath. Moving away, Boyd turns his back to me, revealing a figure on the steps behind. And even though I hate him right now, even though he's destroyed every last remnant of trust in my possession, relief floods through me at the sight of Daniel Foster.

'And so, like a bad penny ...'

'I said back off. If you lay one finger on her, I'll rip your fucking head off.'

'Nice. I'm not here for a fight. Not this time.'

'Then what *are* you here for?'

Boyd laughs: an empty, curious sort of a laugh.

'I need to sort out the Feng Shui. It's all wrong.' He wafts a hand between us. 'You don't go with her ... and she doesn't go with you.'

Moving forwards into the light, Dan holds out a hand to me.

'Come over here, Maya.'

Drowning in confusion, I stare at the hand.

'Maya,' he pleads. 'Just come over here.'

I falter, take a step towards Dan.

'You're going back to him?' Boyd demands. 'With what you know?'

With his eyes firmly fixed on mine, Dan repeats himself, slowly.

'Just come over here, Maya. I'll explain everything. I promise.'

He turns the hand, opening his palm to me, as if he's offering everything. And what choice do I have? I watch as my own hand slides into his and before I know it, I'm standing by his side.

'Just make sure he doesn't lie to you,' Boyd's voice echoes in my ears. 'You never know what else you're going to dig up with this one.'

'There's nothing more to find,' Dan hisses, reaching into his jacket pocket for his mobile. 'So you can keep your nose out of my life.'

'And you can keep your nose out of mine,' Boyd retorts.

The two men glare at each other, and I'm half expecting Dan to release me, to lurch at Boyd and rip him to pieces.

'Oh yes, I know what you've been up to,' Boyd pushes on relentlessly. 'You've had a private dick nosing through my affairs. Are you, by any chance, trying to bury me?'

'I will bury you. There's no doubt about it.' Dismissing Boyd with a glare, Dan taps in a contact on his phone and holds it to his ear. 'We're ready to go home. Get the car down to the embankment now. We're at the Needle.' Fixing his attention back on Boyd, he slips the mobile into his pocket. 'You need to disappear. Stay away from Maya. Don't come anywhere near the apartment, anywhere near the house.'

'And if I don't, what are you going to do about it?'

'I'll think of something.'

'Is that a threat?'

'Could be.'

'Well, Mr Foster, I've got news for you.' Slowly, very slowly, Boyd's lips curl into a smile, but his eyes remain hard. 'Two can play at that game.'

He raises a hand, points a finger at Dan, squints ... and pulls an imaginary trigger.

Chapter Nineteen

While Ian Boyd climbs the steps, Dan follows in his wake, his hand still clasped firmly around mine. Watching as Boyd saunters off into the distance, past a row of trees and a red telephone box, he releases my hand, retrieves his mobile and makes another call.

'He's on the embankment, making for Waterloo Bridge. Be quick.'

'Who's that?' I ask, glancing back along the road. Boyd's already out of sight.

'It doesn't matter.' He shakes his head, drops the mobile back into his pocket and takes me by the arm. 'I'm having him followed. I want to know where he's holed up.'

Struggling out of his grip, I meet his gaze, finding nothing but steely determination in his eyes. And suddenly, with Boyd out of the way and the whirlwind of the last few minutes beginning to calm, I don't know what the hell I'm doing.

'How did you find me?'

'Lily followed you, saw you take off down here and came to get me. You're bloody lucky she did. Your luck's going to run out one day, Maya.'

'Maybe it already has,' I sneer, registering the fact that the Rolls-Royce is pulling up at the kerb.

'How come?'

'How come? I've just fallen in love with a man who's already got a wife.'

He grimaces. 'I told you, I don't have a wife.'

'She was making it all up then? Claudine was lying?'

'No.'

195

The word hits me like a bullet, and there I have it: a confirmation I didn't want to hear. A wave of nausea rolls straight through my stomach. My legs weaken beneath me.

'It was a long time ago,' he states flatly. 'It didn't last and it was nothing to do with love.'

'I need the details.'

'You'll get them later.' Without waiting for the driver, he opens the back door. 'Get in.'

'I don't want to.'

'Just do it, Maya.'

'You told me you'd never been married.'

'I know that.' He shakes his head. 'Okay, I lied to you. One stupid, ridiculous lie. And believe me, I wish I could take it back.'

'And now, you want me to just carry on as if nothing's changed?'

'No.' His face stiffens with resolve. 'I want you to get in this car and hear me out. I want you to remember that I love you. If we can get past this, we have a future together … an entire life.'

'But you lied.'

'Because I was scared.' In an instant, the resolve cracks. While his voice rises in desperation, his eyes plead with me. 'Scared that if I told you the truth, you'd make a run for it.'

'You told me, no more bombshells.'

'I wasn't exactly planning on this.' He holds the door, watching me carefully. 'Just get in the car and let me explain. You might understand.'

'And what if I don't?'

'I don't even want to think about it.'

He holds out an unsteady hand, and I realise that I have very little choice in the matter. After all, I have no handbag, no money, and the last thing I want to do is wander off into the night while Boyd's on the prowl. My body makes the decision for me. One minute I'm standing on the pavement, the next I'm sitting in the back of the car … and Dan is by my side.

'Get on with it then,' I mutter.

'Not now.'

'It's always not now.'

'I'll tell you everything tonight.' He leans across and fastens my seatbelt. 'I just need to organise a few things first.'

'I'm not going back to the apartment.'

'Where else are you going to go?'

'Camden. I need some space.'

I glare at him, knowing full well that Lucy's away for the night. If I want to go back to my old flat, then I'm going to have to pay a visit to Lambeth and dig out my own set of keys. And besides, I could do with changing out of this ridiculous dress.

'It's not going to happen,' he informs me, taking out his mobile.

'Is that what you think?'

'Absolutely.'

While he presses on with his seemingly urgent phone calls, I slump back in the seat, watching the skyline as it slips past and silently resolving not to let this man have his way. Before long, he begins to speak.

'Bill. I'm good, thank you. Listen, I haven't got much time. We're going to be joining you a little earlier than planned. Tonight if I can manage it.' He listens to a voice at the other end of the phone. 'Thank you. I'll explain more when we get there.'

'I'm not going anywhere with you,' I grumble.

He holds up a hand. 'I'll call you with the details when I have them. Yes. Me too.' He slides his thumb over the end-call icon.

'I said I'm not going anywhere with you,' I repeat.

Ignoring me, he makes another call.

'Wallace? Where's your jet at the minute? I need to get somewhere fast. Tonight.' He listens intently. 'Bermuda,' he says crisply. 'Call me back. I need this done quickly.'

'Like everything else in your sodding life,' I complain. And then my brain begins to whirl. He's talking about a jet?

'Tell no one about this, Wallace. And I mean no one. Yes, two people.'

He ends the call, dropping the mobile onto his lap.

'I'm not going on a plane.'

He shrugs and looks out of the window.

'I said I'm not going on a plane,' I repeat, panic surging in my gut. 'Wallace? That's the one with the Lear jet.'

He nods.

'A Lear jet? You think you're taking me on a Lear jet?'

He nods again.

'Wallace owes me a favour. I'm calling it in. We need to get out of London.'

'No ... no,' I stammer. And now the surge has gone. Retreating for a few seconds, it gathers force, returning as a full-blown tidal wave of anxiety, hitting me head-on and knocking everything else clean out of the way. 'I can't. I just can't.'

'And I don't care if I have to drag you onto that jet, kicking and screaming. It's going to happen.'

Wrestling my heart beat under control, I watch as Lambeth bridge flies past, listen as he takes another call from Wallace, apparently confirming a flight that I have no intention of boarding. When we finally draw up outside Lambeth House, he's out of the car in a flash. And so am I, utterly determined to go through with my own plan: within the next hour, I'll be back in my pokey little flat, soaking in a hot bath and making a few important decisions of my own. In silence, I'm guided through the lobby and into the lift, back out of the lift and into the apartment, led straight up the stairs and into the bedroom. Without hesitation, he opens up the wardrobes, pulls out a pair of matching suitcases and slings them onto the floor.

'Pack for a hot climate.'

While he unzips both suitcases, I stand my ground. If he thinks I'm simply going to comply, he's got a surprise in store.

'No.'

He strides over to me, takes me by the arm and tugs me in close.

'We haven't got time to mess about.'

'Then you tell me about your wife.'

'When you're on the plane, I'll tell you everything.'

'When you tell me everything, I might just get on the plane.'

'We need to do this my way.'

'Why? Because you think I'm going to run a mile when you tell me?'

He stares at me, all mean and hot and moody, and I realise I've just hit the nail right on the bloody head. He's not going to tell me anything until he's got me holed up on a Lear jet at thirty thousand feet. And if that's the case, it must be one hell of a story.

'Pack your case. I need to get you away from Boyd.'

'You're over-reacting.'

'Am I?' Releasing me, he sets about packing, tugging out shorts and T-shirts, tossing them into his case.

'Yes.' Determined to dig my heels in, I watch as he rifles through his drawers, adding underpants to the general mess. 'You're dragging me halfway across the world because of Ian Boyd? Come on. He's not that much of a threat.'

He stops again and examines me, obviously mulling over what to say.

'Oh, he's a threat, Maya. You'd better believe it.'

'Would you care to elaborate?'

'He's still obsessed with you. He wants you back.'

'And he can't have me. It's as simple as that.'

He laughs. 'And you think that's the way he sees it?'

'Do you know something I don't?'

Running a hand through his hair, he glances round the room and at last, he seems to make a decision. Slowly, carefully, he begins to pick his way through the details.

'That night at Slaters ... You'd passed out. I had my hands full, carrying you to the car. I left Clive to deal with Boyd. He dragged him outside, but he didn't go easily. He was ranting like a madman ... nobody takes what's his, that sort of shit ... And he made a few threats.'

'Such as?'

He meets my gaze. 'He said he'd make me suffer.'

'You?'

'He's already started.'

'You still think ... You actually still think he poisoned your dog?'

'I know he did. The lab results came back. Strychnine. A massive dose. We don't use it. None of the local farmers use it. There's only one way she could have been poisoned, only one person who'd do it.'

'Oh please.'

'You need proof?' Without waiting for an answer, he marches over to a wardrobe and returns with a little black box in one hand, an envelope in the other. He hands me the box. 'This was delivered here yesterday.'

'It wasn't the earrings?'

He shakes his head. 'Open it.'

I do as I'm told. Inside I find a small silver tag, the name 'Molly' engraved onto one side. I stare at it, horrified.

'A little message.' He says quietly, taking the box from me.

'But why couldn't you just tell me?'

'I didn't want to worry you.'

I shake my head.

'It worries me more when you don't tell me things, Dan. Can't you see that?'

His shoulders slump. Suddenly, he seems exhausted.

'I thought it was for the best.'

'Well, it's not.' I hold his gaze, determined to make my point. 'Don't try to protect me by keeping me in the dark. I'm not weak. I told you that. I can deal with these things. Understand?' I wait for him to nod before I go on. 'You need to call the police.'

'They wouldn't be interested.' He holds up the box. 'This hardly counts as proof in a court of law.'

'But if he delivered it, he'll be on the CCTV.'

'He's not. I've already had it checked. It was some kid in a hoodie. You can't even see his face.'

He presents the envelope to me. Tentatively, I take it, turning it in my hands.

'What he did was a warning shot. He wanted me to know he means business, and he does. The man's screwed up, Maya.'

'What's this?'

'A full report from the private investigators. A few documents they've managed to lay their hands on. Take a look.'

Seating myself on the edge of the bed, I open up the envelope, emptying out a handful of sheets onto the covers. I take the first one: a photocopy with a hospital logo at the top.

'A psychiatric report? How did you get this?'

'Don't ask.' He sits next to me. 'He's suffering from schizophrenia. He's been prescribed drugs to control it but judging by his behaviour, he doesn't take them. On top of that, he drinks heavily, and I mean heavily.' He rubs his forehead. 'And on top of that, he's a regular drug user. Weed and coke, mostly.' Clasping his hands together, he lowers his voice. 'I've had a private investigator up in Scotland. He managed to track down a retired detective. He had Boyd in his sights for years but never got anywhere. He was blocked at every turn.'

'How?'

'It's amazing what money and connections can do for you.' His eyes rest on mine, gentle now. 'There are plenty of stories, too many of them, quiet gossip in certain circles: Boyd's hounded other women, and he's abused them too. But not one of them has ever gone to the police. They've just run, like you ran. He's always got away with it.'

'But if they all pressed charges …'

'They won't. They're terrified.' He pauses, swallows. 'He moved in on you tonight. What happened with Claudine was a distraction. Isaac helped to set it up.'

'How do you know?' I search his face for a clue, and find it in a flash of guilt. 'You hit him?'

'It did the job. Isaac's the only person I ever told about my marriage. I have no idea how Boyd found out about the club, but he visited, trying to sniff out more dirt. And he found it. Claudine's got an axe to grind with me. It wouldn't have taken much to rope her in. And Isaac? Well, he'd do anything for that woman.' He takes my chin in his hand. 'Listen to me, Maya. Ian Boyd banked on you storming out of that place tonight and it worked. You walked right into his hands. If I hadn't found you, what do you think would have happened?'

My mouth dries up.

'I was in a public place. I was fine.'

'Get real. Whatever you think of me right now, I'm taking you away for a few days. To keep you safe. Even if he finds out where we've gone, there's no way he can get into Bermuda without me knowing.'

'Seriously?'

'Seriously. And while we're there, I'll have him tracked down.'

'And then what?'

'Frightened off.' Releasing my chin, he stands up. 'Now get packing.'

I falter, glancing at the empty suitcase.

'I can't go.'

He freezes. His shoulders tense.

'You lied to me,' I remind him.

'I'll explain. On the plane.'

'I should walk out on you ...'

'And you wouldn't get very far,' he interrupts, kicking the empty suitcase towards me. 'I'm not about to let you go.'

***

We ride to the airport in silence. While Dan busies himself on his iPad, I gaze out of the window, no longer impressed by the luxury of the Rolls, watching numbly as the lights of London give way to the suburbs, and finally the motorway. After an hour or so, we reach Gatwick, threading our way through a maze of lanes and drawing to a halt. I'm ushered out of the car, only to find myself standing on the tarmac, the hastily packed luggage on one side, a gleaming white jet on the other. While Dan talks to an official, handing over our passports, my heartbeat stalls and my throat constricts. And this is just the beginning, the opening bars of a symphony of panic. I have no idea how I've let it get this far, why I simply packed up my case like an obedient little woman and let him drag me out here, but it's too late now. There's a plane in front of me. A bloody plane. And my body's telling me loud and clear that I'm not too happy about it. Still dressed in the black evening gown and chilled to the bone, I stand rooted to the spot, mesmerised by its sleekness.

'A plane,' I gasp.

'Well spotted.' Dan's voice reaches me above the low growl of the engines. 'Get on.'

It starts to rain again, only a light drizzle but I'll be soaked through in no time if I don't move. And I don't move. Because I can't move. If I get on this thing, I'll die. I know it. A clutching sensation kicks off in my stomach and my head begins to swirl. I watch as our luggage is carried on board, as Dan shakes hands with the driver and the Rolls-Royce glides away into the night, taking with it my only practical escape route. I'm still debating the sense of making an impractical escape, scarpering off across the runway, when I feel a hand close around mine.

'I can't get on. It's a tin can with wings.'

'We need to get going.'

I shake my head.

'I can't.'

'Oh, for fuck's sake.'

My hand's released and within the blink of an eye, I'm upside down in a fireman's lift, being hauled up the steps. I'd scream but my vocal chords seem to have malfunctioned.

'Keep your head down.'

Grabbing hold of his back, clamping my eyelids shut and digging my nails in for dear life, I do as I'm told. I'm on the verge of hyperventilating when I'm lowered into a leather seat. I sense a movement in front of me, the tightening of straps as I'm fastened in for take-off. Suddenly, I seem to have turned to stone.

I hear a woman's voice.

'Is she alright?'

'She'll be fine,' Dan answers. 'Just tell the pilot to take off before she comes to her senses, and bring us some wine once we're in the air.'

'Yes, sir.'

I hear the roar of engines and grip leather, refusing to open my eyes. This isn't happening, I tell myself. This really isn't happening. But it is. In fact, we're moving now. As the G-force kicks in, I clench just about everything I can. Shit. We're taking off. We're actually taking off. Swimming through the chaos in my brain, I find the only sensible thing I can to cling to: I'm in the woods, back in Limmingham, and that's the distant rumble of the sea. Relax. Relax. Relax.

'Maya.'

'What?'

'Open your eyes.'

'Can't.'

'We're in the air. You can't spend the next six hours like this.'

And yes, I suppose he's got a point. Gradually willing my eyes to open, I take in the curve of the fuselage, the bright lighting, a mahogany table in front of me. I'm in a black leather seat, and Dan's right next to me. He reaches out and takes my hand. Prising it away from the arm rest, he closes his fingers around mine.

'You did it.'

'I did it,' I whimper.

His smile sends a quiver of warmth right through me. I'm pretty sure that's pride in his eyes.

'Planes,' I groan. 'Big scary things.'

'Not this one. This is a little scary thing. Only it's not scary.' He speaks quietly, slowly, as if he's reassuring a child. 'And you're not going to die.'

A super slim, uniformed woman appears from behind a partition. She slips a Kindle onto the table in front of me.

'What's this?'

'Something to keep you occupied.' He reaches over and tucks my hair behind my ear. 'I had Carla send it over. I'm sorry for man-handling you.'

The attendant re-appears with a tray, carrying a bottle of wine and two glasses. With the utmost elegance, she places the glasses down and half fills them.

'Can I get you anything to eat?' she asks.

Dan shakes his head, downs the wine in one go and refills his glass.

'Madam?'

Looking up, I realise that she's speaking to me.

'No thanks. Just more of this stuff.'

With shaking hands, I take a gulp of my own wine. My brain seems to have jolted itself back into life, reminding me that the time has come for Dan to spill the beans. I wait until the attendant disappears into her corner.

'Get on with it then,' I begin. 'I got on this bloody thing, and now you can deliver your part of the deal. Explain yourself. Every last detail.'

He takes another mouthful of wine and looks at me, full on, his blue irises shimmering in the low lighting. The copper flecks seem to dance.

'You promised,' I remind him.

He stares at me, wordless. Is he clamming up? Well, I'm not having that.

'Come on. What's her name?'

'Antonietta,' he whispers, his reply barely audible above the hum of the engines.

'Antonietta Foster. It's got a nice ring to it.'

He shoots me a scowl.

'Maya Foster sounds better.'

'Drop it.' I scowl right back at him. 'Don't even think about side-tracking me.'

He leans his head back against the rest.

'Okay.' He takes a moment or two to ready himself, obviously sorting through the order of the details, the choice of words. 'The woman in Rome.'

'The one you lodged with?'

'Yes.'

'That's a pretty strange definition of lodging.'

He frowns. 'Give me a break, Maya.'

'I've already given you several.'

'One more.' He pleads. 'Just let me explain.' Turning away, he takes another mouthful of wine, puts down the glass and stares at it. 'It was a bar in Rome, some upmarket place. That's where I met her. She took me in and sobered me up. I was twenty-one, she was thirty-three. I lived with her for a year.'

So far, so good. I already know this. What I'm waiting for now is the twist in the tale. He closes his eyes, as if he doesn't want to acknowledge the next part.

'As far as I was concerned, it was an arrangement, nothing more.'

'So what happened?'

I wait for his words to edge their way past the dull roar of the jet engine.

'She fell in love with me.'

At last, he makes eye contact.

'And you fell for her?'

He shakes his head.

'I used her.'

He notices my alarm.

'I've told you, Maya. I'm not the man I used to be.'

'That's exactly what Boyd said.'

'And I'm not Boyd.'

He waits for a sign that I believe him, and I must have given it, maybe with a flicker of the eyes, because before long he's talking again.

'I didn't want to come back to England. She gave me a roof over my head. I got to fuck the way I wanted to. No strings. It was perfect. But when she told me she loved me, I knew it was time to go.'

'Did you ever tell her you loved her?'

'No. Because I didn't. There's only one person I've ever said those words to.' His blue eyes pierce me right to the soul. He picks up his glass and finishes off the wine. 'I told her I didn't feel the same way, I told her I was leaving ... and then she told me she was pregnant.'

My mouth opens. Gathering every last ounce of self-control, I close it again and wait for him to continue. I'm going to say nothing.

'I couldn't understand ... We always used condoms.' He chews at his bottom lip, his eyes distant now. Clearly, he's flipping back through the memories. 'I was on the verge of making a run for it ... and then I had a visit.' He looks directly at me now, a wry smile on his face. 'Three men. They forced their way into the apartment one night and beat me up.' He rubs his forehead. 'And then they made it perfectly clear that if I didn't do the right thing, I'd be dead. They said they'd follow me if I tried to run.'

'Mafia?' I gasp.

He laughs quietly.

'Nothing quite so dramatic. Just a few unsavoury family members. They probably wouldn't have gone through with it, but I was young and scared and stupid, so I did the right thing.' He shrugs. 'I married her.'

'And she had the baby?' I stare at him. 'Oh, my God, you've got a child?'

'No.' He grabs my hand and squeezes it. 'A couple of weeks after we got married, she told me she'd lost it.'

'Oh Jesus. I'm sorry.'

'Don't be. She was never pregnant in the first place.' He takes in a deep breath and holds up an index finger. 'One friend. She had one friend with a conscience. They told me.'

'So you left her? You divorced her?'

He shakes his head.

'I didn't dare leave. But I didn't touch her either. I went nowhere near her. I didn't even speak to her. I hated her, hated the sight of her ...'

'So what happened?'

He pauses, takes in a deep breath and sighs it out.

'You want me to tell you the truth? Well, here's the truth. I was a bastard. I treated her like shit.' He wavers. 'And then she killed herself.'

I stare at him, and he stares right back at me.

At last, his lips part.

'So, what do you think of me now?'

I say nothing.

He nods, clearly understanding that I need space to process this new information. For now, there's nothing more to say. I sit in silence, watching as he leans forwards, moving the Kindle towards me and switching it on. Reading? He actually wants me to read at a time like this? I'm on the verge of telling him to piss off when I notice that he's flicked to the front cover of a book. Leaving it in front of me, he sits back and waits.

I pick up the Kindle and focus on the screen. *Jane Eyre*? Why has he done that?

Isn't it obvious, you dope, a voice cries out at the back of my head. The story of a man tricked into marriage, made miserable by deceit, searching for his one chance of redemption.

'Read it again,' he murmurs. 'All the way through. And remember ... it's got a happy ending.'

Chapter Twenty

I only manage a chapter or two, but that's hardly surprising: I can barely concentrate. Curling up in my seat, I try to sleep, but sleep's impossible in a world that seems to be fraying at the edges. Instead, numbed by exhaustion and the evening's revelations, I simply lower my eyelids, doing my best to ignore the fact that I'm whizzing across the Atlantic at thirty thousand feet, caught up in a limbo while the seconds, minutes and hours all merge into one. It's only when my ears begin to pop that I'm jolted out of it, vaguely aware that the first signs of fear are stirring to life in my brain. I have no idea how long we've been in the air, but we must be coming in to land now.

When I open my eyes, he's watching me, concern ingrained into every square inch of his face. He reaches out, offering me comfort, but I don't want any. I shake my head, grab hold of the arm rests and stare at the cockpit door for the duration. With every single drop in altitude, my stomach tumbles and my lungs flounder, but through it all, even when the engines decide to screech like a pair of deranged cats, I hold on tight, willing myself to stay absolutely still. After all, if I'm about to die, I'd rather do it with a scrap of dignity.

'Well done,' he whispers, when the jet finally comes to a halt.

'Thank you,' I whisper back, silently relieved that I still seem to have a pulse.

Refusing his help, I unbuckle the seat belt and choose to make my own distinctly unsteady exit through the open door. It's dark outside, but a wall of warmth hits me immediately and within seconds, I'm hot and sticky in the evening gown. Careful not to trip over it, I struggle down the steps and sink into the back of a car, waiting while Dan goes through the process of border control. Before long, he joins me, his tuxedo jacket crumpled on his knee. And with the luggage loaded, another silent car journey ensues.

Trying to get my first taste of Bermuda, I spend the entire time peering out of the window, but it's impossible to see anything. Apart from the occasional pin-prick of light, it's a pitch black night.

It doesn't take long for us to reach our destination. A pair of wrought-iron gates swing open and we edge forwards onto a drive, coming to a halt in front of a bungalow. As soon as I get out of the air-conditioned car, the heat hits me again, and my ears are assaulted by a strange tinkling, singing sound.

'Tree frogs,' Dan explains, coming to my side. 'They go on all night every night. You'll get used to it.' He turns to the driver. 'It was good of you to pick us up. I haven't got any dollars yet. I'll have to tip you on the way back.'

Dropping the suitcases by the front door, the driver joins us. An older man, ebony-skinned, maybe in his sixties.

'No need, Danny boy.' He grins. 'You're welcome.'

Danny boy? I'm about to burst into a fit of over-tired laughter when I notice Dan tipping his head to one side, his eyes narrowing a little shortly before he breaks into a wide smile.

'Charles?'

'The one and only.'

'My God.' He steps forwards, clasping the driver by the hand. 'Why didn't you say? I didn't realise it was you. I'm just so tired. How are you?'

'I'm good.'

'And Louis? Kathy?'

'Louis's married with two beautiful children.' For the first time, I notice the curious lilt in Charles' voice, his accent almost American ... but not quite. 'And you'll see my good lady in the morning. She's still working for Bill, just like me.' His smile straightens. His voice lowers. 'I was sorry to hear about your parents, Dan. They were good people.'

'Yes, they were.' He glances into the shadows before he remembers that he's not alone. 'And this is Maya.'

He curls an arm around my waist and I wait for something more ... but nothing comes.

And perhaps that's not so surprising. He looks as shattered as I feel. But more than that, he seems completely lost. Unable to cope, I've simply blanked him, and now the poor man must be convinced that he's about to be dumped on the back of his confession. Out of nowhere, my heart swells, and suddenly I feel the need to let him know that all is not lost.

Far from it.

'I'm Dan's girlfriend,' I announce.

Charles takes me by the hand.

'Hey, that's wonderful.' He plants a kiss on my cheek. 'Welcome to Bermuda, Maya. I hope you like it here.'

'I'm sure I will.'

Still smiling, I turn to Dan. We gaze at each other for a few seconds. It's long enough to reconnect. His eyes spark back to life.

'Now, let's get you settled in,' Charles says, sliding a key into the lock and pushing open the door. 'Maybe you can grab a few hours' sleep.'

***

As soon as we're alone, Dan throws his tux onto a chair and buries his hands into his pockets, obviously waiting for the discussion to resume. But I'm too tired for big talk. It can wait until tomorrow.

'You've been here before?'

'A lot,' he confirms. 'Every summer. My parents were friends with Bill. We stayed here five years running.'

I wander through the hallway into a huge open-plan living area. With a kitchen-diner at one end and a lounge at the other, it's edged by French windows down one side and lit by a handful of lamps. In spite of the fact that it's been modernised, it's clearly an old building, infused with a colonial feeling: the ceilings are high; white shutters adorn the windows; and a dark wooden fireplace, intricately carved with leaves, dominates the room. But it's furnished with a modern touch, everything solid and expensive. Before long, I find myself gazing at the art work on the walls, noting that in amongst a smattering of oils, there's a small collection of watercolours: exotic flowers, gardens, houses – all Bermudian. I recognise the style. I've seen it before, back at the house in Surrey.

'Your mother painted these?'

I find him standing close by.

'She did. She spent a lot of time painting here.'

'And you? What did you get up to?'

'I used to hang around with Charles and his son. Mostly we'd just swim, jump in off the rocks, that sort of thing.'

I smile, trying to imagine a young, carefree Dan.

'It's a lovely house.'

'It's the guest house. Bill's place is up the hill. You'll meet him tomorrow.'

My eyes must be the size of saucers. If this is just the guest house, then God only knows what the main residence is like. Realising that I'm close to collapse, I roll my shoulders.

'I need to go to bed.'

He hesitates. 'Shall I come with you?'

Holding out a hand, he watches me, and I wonder if that's fear in his eyes. I have no idea, but as soon as I put my fingers into his, it melts away. With a smile, he guides me out of the living area, down a corridor and into the master bedroom. Again, everything around me is solid and luxurious: the blinds that hang at the windows, the mahogany furniture; the vast wooden bed that's draped with rich white cotton sheets. At the centre of the ceiling, attached to the main light, a fan circles slowly, and in the background, I can hear the quiet hum of an air conditioning unit.

Without a word, I take myself into the bathroom, brush my teeth, let my hair down and return to the bedroom where I find that Dan's already slipped off his shoes and socks. Staring at another of his mother's water colours, he's currently unbuttoning his shirt.

I stand absolutely still, staring at the bed, sensing him when he comes behind me and begins to unlace the bodice of my dress, slowly, sliding a palm under the material. Soft against my skin, it's warm in contrast to the cooling air. He loosens the dress from my torso, letting it fall from me, and draws me in to him, nuzzling his face against my neck. His arms are around my waist now and I rest my hands over his, melting at his touch. At last, he rouses himself, turns me round to face him and kisses me slowly, tenderly, brushing his lips across mine before he claims my mouth completely.

'Let's sleep,' he whispers.

With a nod, I peel his shirt away from his shoulders and run my hands across his bare flesh. I have no intention of turning him on. All I want is to reassure him. And he seems to understand. I get into bed, loving the fresh smell of the sheets, the rich comfort of the pillows, and wait while he undresses. Climbing into bed next to me, he clicks off the lights. I feel the touch of a finger against my hip, put my hand over his, and guide it further round. He readjusts his position, urging me to move so that my back is against his chest. And then gently, very gently, he strokes my hair, and I close my eyes in a strange land, spiralling quickly into the dark.

***

When I wake up, I remember no dreams. Just a solid wall of sleep separates me from yesterday. Rolling over onto my back and finding an empty space next to me, I spend a minute or two watching the fan rotate above the bed before I gaze at the window. The wooden blinds are still closed, but here and there, a glimmer of sunlight winks through the slats. Feeling distinctly lazy, I'd love to stay here all day, but there's a whole new world to discover outside and at least one person waiting to meet me. With a yawn, I get up, find my suitcase and open it. After the manic, last-minute packing session, everything's creased beyond recognition, but never mind. Putting on a pair of shorts and one of my old strappy T-shirts, I freshen up in the bathroom, fix my hair into something that passes for an up-do and wander out into the day, bare-footed.

The living room is empty, and so is the kitchen, but the French windows are open wide, framing a scene of brilliant sunlight and vibrant colour. Edging my way forwards, allowing my eyes to accustom themselves to the light, I begin to take it all in: the deep green of a lawn edged by flower beds, a slight incline leading down to a clump of trees, an azure blue sea in the background.

'Wow,' I whisper, completely overwhelmed by the view.

The slow murmur of conversation leads me out onto the covered veranda. With his back to me, dressed in dark blue shorts and a white T-shirt, Dan sits at a wooden table, opposite a grey-haired old man. As I approach, the old man notices me. His pale blue eyes twinkle with delight. He takes off a pair of steel-rimmed spectacles, placing them on the table top.

'Here she is,' he announces.

Dan looks up.

'Maya.' He smiles warily. 'Come and meet Bill.'

Both men stand and while I'm clasped on the arms and kissed on the cheek by Bill, Dan pulls out the chair next to him and gestures for me to sit. When I've taken my place, I turn to Bill.

'It's good to meet you.'

'And it's good to meet you.' He nods his approval at Dan. 'You're a lucky man.'

'I know.'

'He told me you're a beauty.'

'Really? What else did he say?'

'Oh.' Bill touches the side of his nose. 'There are some things I can't divulge. Let's just say that I'm certain we're going to be good friends.'

And I know exactly what that means. Mr Rush-it just can't help himself. In spite of everything else that's going on, he's clearly already informed his old friend – in no uncertain terms – that I'm the future ball and chain. Resisting the urge to slap my apparent fiancé around the back of the head for his impatience, I settle for a demure smile and something fairly non-committal.

'I'm sure we will.'

'Tea?'

'Yes, please.'

Bill picks up a silver teapot and pours me a cup. I take the opportunity to examine him in more detail. At least as old as Norman, he's lean and trim and sprightly. On the surface, he's nothing more than a kindly old gent, dressed in a ridiculous pair of Bermuda shorts and a pink polo shirt, but I get the distinct feeling that there's much more to this man. His keen eyes flick between us, his face wrinkling into a smile every now and then, and he has the look of someone who's seen and done it all, someone who knows plenty, but doesn't feel the need to broadcast the fact.

'Maya, I've sorted a little brunch for you. You must be hungry.' He waves a hand at a silver platter, laid out with French toast, crispy bacon, grilled tomatoes and mushrooms. 'Take whatever you want.'

While the two men chat, I help myself to a selection of everything and finish it off. I'm washing it all down with a second cup of tea when my attention is lured back to the sea, casting me away into a world of colour. For the most part, it's glass-like and calm, a giant blend of gemstones: from zircon and aquamarine at the shore, through sapphire where the waters deepen, to lapis lazuli along the horizon. In a trance, I watch as the colours merge and mutate in the light, wishing that I had my oils with me.

'That's impressive,' Bill remarks.

His words jolt me back into the real world. I'm in the middle of a conversation.

'What is?' I ask.

'Flying. Dan was just telling me about your fear of flying.'

'Oh that.'

'It's good that you've faced it head-on.' He laughs. 'And my God, you don't get any more head-on than six hours on a Lear jet. Quite some accomplishment. Are there any other fears we need to know about, Maya?'

'Heights,' Dan answers absently, running his fingertip across the table top. 'And storms.'

'We've all got fears,' I mutter.

The fingertip stops mid-movement. He squints up at me.

'Not Dan.' Bill smiles. 'Dan's afraid of nothing.'

Apart from his own past, I'd like to add. And believe you me, I'd like to see him face that head-on.

'So what are your plans for today?' Reaching forwards, Bill offers to pour me a third cup of tea.

'No plans.' Clearly relieved that the conversation's moving on, Dan leans back, resting an arm across the back of his chair. 'We just need to relax. De-stress a little.'

The old man places the teapot back onto the end of the table. 'So, this is your first time on the island, Maya?'

'Yes.'

'It's a beautiful place. Dan used to visit a lot, but I haven't seen him since he was eighteen. Can you imagine that? All those years and he never bothered.'

Dan looks down, seemingly sheepish.

'I'm teasing him,' Bill laughs. 'We've talked on the phone. I've tried to get him to come back, but he was always too busy. Always.'

And now my apparent fiancé shifts about in his chair. Suddenly, he doesn't seem quite so relaxed. 'Running that company isn't easy, Bill.'

'I know that, but you could have taken a holiday every once in a while. Maya, have you met Norman?'

'Yes.'

'An old friend of mine. He hasn't been out here for a few years now. Too old for the flight, he says. But me and Norman talk. And I know what goes on with this boyfriend of yours. I know he works too hard. Why did you never take a holiday, Dan?'

'I've travelled all over the world with Fosters. There's been no need.'

Bill shakes his head. 'You've been punishing yourself.'

I watch as Dan bites back a scowl, realise that Bill's managed to hit the nail right on the head, and resolve to change the course of the conversation.

'How did you know Mr and Mrs Foster?' I ask.

'John and Lydia? I lived near them. We were good friends. John did some work for me on my house. I was in banking. I had a pretty big house in Surrey, but it was falling to pieces. John helped me put it back together again. I moved out here about twenty-five years ago. They used to come out every summer. And then Dan arrived.' He shoots a questioning look at Dan.

'It's alright,' he says quietly. 'She knows.'

Bill nods. 'I first met him when he was thirteen. Those were good holidays, eh, Dan?'

'They were.' He smiles.

'I know I've said it on the phone, but I'm sorry about what happened. They were taken from us too soon.'

While Dan goes back to trailing his fingertip across the table, Bill watches him carefully.

'Well,' he says at last. 'I'll leave you two alone for now.' Standing up, he touches Dan on the shoulder. 'I want you to come up for dinner tonight. Seven o'clock. Shorts and T-shirts. We don't stand on ceremony here, Maya. Have a relaxing day.' He leans down and kisses me on the cheek. 'And make sure he takes you for a swim.'

'But I don't have a swimming costume.'

'I'll have a quiet word with Kathy. She'll go into Hamilton and pick something up for you and Danny boy.'

I catch a wince from Dan.

'Seven o'clock. Be late if you like.'

With a laugh, Bill makes his way up the path, back to the big house, stopping off here and there to smell a flower or take a look at the ocean. When I turn back to Dan, he's gazing at me.

'So,' he begins.

'So?' I bat the word right back at him.

'I'm sorry. I'm sorry I lied to you. It was stupid and I'm an idiot.'

'You can say that again.'

'I just didn't know how to tell you. I was terrified of losing you. I still am.'

'You're not going to lose me.'

'But now you know what I've done.' He frowns. 'I caused a woman to kill herself.'

'You've got it all wrong,' I inform him. A good night's sleep has clarified matters for me, and with the clouds of shock and exhaustion finally lifted, I'm as clear-headed as they come. 'You've had it wrong for years.'

He's clearly confused now, and I really don't blame him. After all, while he's been busy preparing to ask for my forgiveness and understanding, I've been slowly coming to the conclusion that he's not the guilty party at all.

'You didn't mislead her?' I ask.

'No.'

'Then she's the one who caused the situation. She trapped you. You just reacted the same way anyone else would have done. Whatever decisions she made, that was her business, but you're not responsible for her death.'

He lowers his head.

'It all makes sense now,' I press on quickly. 'Why you closed yourself off. Why you worked yourself half to death. It was because you didn't want to hurt anyone again. It was guilt. You punished yourself for what happened ... only it wasn't your fault.'

He takes in a breath, but says nothing. And he doesn't have to. I can see it in his face: I've finally got to the truth.

'The past is the past. That's your mantra, isn't it? Draw a line under everything, block it all out.'

'It's seen me through.'

'But at what cost?' I pause, already knowing the answer. 'You didn't confront the past. You just buried it ... and you ended up lonely.'

He frowns, disbelieving, as if I've just told him he's grown an extra leg.

'I've always had people around me.'

'But you never let anyone get close. You've already admitted that.'

He's still not convinced. And maybe I should provide a little first-hand evidence of my own.

'I saw you, Dan. That first time I ever stayed over, I saw you in the morning, out on the terrace. You didn't know I was there but I was watching you, and I've never seen anyone look so lonely in my life.'

'I'm not lonely any more.'

'Maybe not. But you still need a new mantra. You've got to deal with the past, not hide from it. You've got to face your demons just like I've got to face mine. We're the king and queen of brushing the crap under the carpet, you and me, and because we've never really faced it, we've never really lived.'

His lips curl up into a smile.

'So, we're both fucked up then?'

'Maybe,' I smile back at him. 'But we can both undo the damage. Together.'

Taking my hand in his, he begins to stroke his thumb across my palm, over and over, watching its slow progress against my skin.

'You've already told me what I need to do. I need to talk to Sara.' I hold my breath for a moment. We're both fully aware of what's coming next. 'And you know what you need to do. You need to get back in touch with your sisters.'

Still stroking my hand, he looks out to sea.

'Whatever you did to hurt them, they'll forgive you for it.'

He turns back to me and gazes into my eyes for an age.

'Does this mean I'm forgiven?' he asks at last.

'For getting married? There's nothing to forgive. For lying to me? I suppose so.' Prising my hand out of his, I take another sip of tea. 'But, just for the record, I'm still bloody angry with you, and I can't deal with any more secrets, and I definitely don't want any more lies.'

With a sigh, he picks up a teaspoon and taps the table.

'There won't be any.'

'You'd better make sure of it, Mr Foster.'

'I certainly will, Miss Scotton.'

I finish off the tea.

'Anyway.' Putting down my cup, I sit back in my chair. 'I've actually had a gutful of big talk. Are we going to get on with the business of relaxing now, or what?'

His face melts into a broad smile and my heart rate accelerates. I'm lost again in the blue of those irises, as bright and complex as the sea in front of me. I'm about to suggest that we go straight back to bed for a good old session when his attention wanders to something behind me.

'Here comes Kathy.'

An older woman approaches the table, maybe in her sixties, dark-skinned, almost as rotund as Betty.

'Danny boy!' she screeches. 'Come here and give your aunty Kathy a big hug!'

With another wince, he gets to his feet and wraps his arms around Kathy. She laughs loudly, her eyes bright with pleasure. 'Oh Lord, you've grown into a big, strapping man. And this is Maya?'

'Hi Kathy. It's good to meet you.'

I stand up and let myself be squeezed half to death.

'You two getting married, eh?'

I shoot a look of almost certain death at Dan. He grins back at me, and I really could give him his comeuppance. But Kathy's appearance seems to have completely banished the serious mood, and I want it to stay that way. After we put in our orders for swimwear and two pairs of sunglasses, Kathy collects up the remnants of the breakfast.

'A couple of hours.' She smiles. 'Hamilton's only down the road, but we're on island time. I'll leave you two love birds alone now. Hey!' She touches Dan on the arm. 'You'd better have your honeymoon right here.'

Chapter Twenty-One

'So ...' He stands up and holds out a hand. 'How about that swim?'

It's an automatic reaction: I slip my fingers into his. And then I glance up the hill at Kathy's receding figure. 'But I need a bikini.'

'Bollocks to that.'

Urging me to my feet, he tightens his grip on my hand and leads me across the lawn. In silence, we thread our way down a path where the trees overhang the walkway, forming a canopy of welcome shade, further down a set of steps, encroached by bushes that seem to be overflowing with flowers in every possible colour. Eventually, the bushes and trees give way to a small, secluded cove. Walking out over the sand, he releases my hand and I come to a halt, turning slowly to take in the view. Joining up with the woodland behind, two banks of grey, volcanic cliffs curl around us like a pair of arms hiding their secret from the world. In front of me, a bed of untouched pink sand glistens in the sunlight, burying itself into a turquoise sea. In between the fingertips of rock, wave after wave rolls gently against the shore and further out, shimmering in the late morning sun, I spot a tiny island, topped with a clump of strange, jagged trees. It's incredible. Just perfect.

I'm about to tell him as much when I realise he's taking off his T-shirt and ruffling his hair. Suddenly, instead of gawping at the scene, I'm gawping at his muscles, wishing that he'd drag me back to the bedroom for another slice of sexual paradise.

'Come on, Maya,' he grins. 'Get your clothes off.'

'We're skinny dipping?'

'Oh yes.' He scans the cove, homing in on a patch of shade beneath a cliff, and a pair of huge sunbeds. 'Actually ...' Obviously having second thoughts about the swim, he leaves his shorts in place. 'We should stay out of the sun for a while. Don't want you to burn

217

up.' Raising an eyebrow, he saunters over to the cliff, settles onto a sunbed, puts up his feet and leans back, making himself completely comfortable.

'You want to lie in the shade?' I ask, coming to stand by his side.

'Of course not.' He smiles lazily. 'I want to fuck in the shade.'

And that does it. A rising heat in my groin, a flutter in my clitoris. I look back at the pathway.

'What? Here?'

'It's the only shade on the beach, Maya.' He snakes an arm behind his head. 'Strip for me.'

'But ...'

'Chill out. This place is completely private.'

'But what about Bill?'

'He never comes down here. Now get on with it. Strip.' Lips parted, eyes hooded, he waves a hand. 'And do it slowly. You know what I like.'

Feeling distinctly nervous, I lift the strappy top over my head and drop it onto the sand. He smiles, taking in my body as if he's savouring a work of art, and I know exactly what he wants next: a good view of my breasts. But he's not getting it, not just yet. I'm going to make him wait. Deciding to leave the bra in place for now, I unfasten my shorts instead and edge them down my legs, taking my time, stepping out of them in slow motion before I straighten up. When I finally take off my bra, I throw it at his face, but he's far too quick. With a grin, he catches it, swirls it round a finger and flings it off towards the second sunbed.

Before I can even make a start on my knickers, he signals for me to get closer. Tucking an index finger into the waistband, he runs it from side to side, smiling to himself in a reverie that doesn't last for long. He tugs at the knickers, forcing me onto the sunbed, his big hands manoeuvring me into position and I'm kneeling now, straddling his crotch, his hard-on totally evident. I feel a hand at the back of my head, and I'm pulled in for a kiss.

'What now?' I breathe.

'This.'

In an instant, he reaches down and tears away the knickers.

'Oh, bloody hell.'

Ignoring my complaint, he takes hold of my thighs and grinds against me. Already pulsating deep inside, I swallow back a groan. He reaches up, eases the band out of my up-do and tosses it away, leaving my hair to tumble onto his bare chest. I get a few seconds to run my hands across his muscles, loving their tautness, before he issues the next order.

'Get these shorts off me.'

Quickly, I raise myself onto my knees and pull at his shorts, realising that he's gone commando today. His cock springs free: hard and ready to go. I draw the shorts down over his feet, discarding them on the sand with the rest of our clothes. Holding out an arm, he motions for me to return to my previous position, and I shuffle back into place, straddling him again. Only this time, skin on skin, I get the full effect of his erection.

'Are you wet?' he asks.

'I believe so.'

He smiles mischievously. 'What am I going to do with you, Miss Scotton?'

Without waiting for the obvious answer, he clasps one hand around my upper arm, urging me upwards, while he guides himself into me with the other.

'Slowly,' he warns me.

Resting my hands on the sunbed, I begin to work, up and down, as slowly as I can, but it isn't easy. Almost as soon as I begin, ripples of warmth flood through my abdomen, causing the walls of my vagina to quiver.

'God, Maya. I fucking love you.'

'And I fucking love you too.'

He lets go of my arm, clamps a palm around my buttocks and begins to thrust. Steadying himself against the sunbed with his free hand, he matches my action with his own and before long, we fall into a perfect, steady rhythm.

'I'm not going to last long,' I warn him, only too aware of the growing tension inside.

'And you think I am?'

He switches up the tempo, punching into me with quick, deep movements that hit the back of my vagina, and even though I'm the one on top, I know he's gradually taking over. With a dishevelled heart rate and a rampaging pulse, I struggle to suck in a decent breath. I'm pretty sure that I'm about to pass out when a fizzling sensation erupts deep inside. The grip tightens on my buttocks. I watch as his pupils dilate and his lips part. Overcome by the moment, he takes a handful of my hair, tugging me in for a ferocious kiss. He jolts and thrusts, one final time, groaning into my mouth as we come together.

'Fucking hell,' he gasps, still twitching inside. 'Paradise just got better.'

Exhausted and contented beyond belief, I crumble into his arms, conscious of the fact that bodily fluids are already beginning to obey the laws of gravity. If we're not careful, we're going to ruin one hell of an expensive sunbed. I'd get up and avoid the impending mess, but I can't move. An arm is locked around my back.

'I'm going to bring you back here every summer and fuck you on this thing,' he breathes into my ear.

'This one? Not the other one?'

With a laugh, he releases me.

'Definitely this one.' He smiles lazily. 'I'll make a notch on it.'

'I'm hot.' I blow a strand of hair out of my eyes.

'Then it's time for that swim.'

Gently prompting me to move, he sits up. I struggle to my feet, face the ocean ... and stall. It's calm, inviting, glorious, but I can't remember the last time I swam in the sea. And anyway, every single time I've ever taken a dip in salt water, it's always been in England. Here, I simply have no idea what's lurking in the depths.

I feel an arm around my waist.

'Tell me you can swim.'

'Yes.' I bristle. Really? Does he think I'm that hopeless? 'But aren't there sharks?'

I look up to find amusement in his eyes.

'Yes.'

'Then I can't ...'

He raises a hand, halting me in my tracks.

'Bermuda's surrounded by a reef. The sharks hardly ever come in. There's never been a shark fatality here. You're perfectly safe.'

'You could have just told me there weren't any.'

'And lie to you?' He clasps my hand. 'Come on. Remember what Bill said. You need to face your fears head on.'

He leads me into the water, one step at a time, keeping hold of my hand, smiling in reassurance. It deepens quickly and before long I'm up to my waist, surprised at how warm the water is, how quickly I get used to it. But still ...

'I could be the first fatality,' I splurt.

'Relax. Sperm's a natural shark repellent.'

'Is it?'

He laughs, urging me further. When I'm up to my breasts, I look back at the deserted shore, hardly aware that his hand has left mine.

Jesus, we could both be eaten now and nobody would know about it for hours. I hear a splash, turn quickly and find him treading water.

'Come on, Maya.' He grins. 'You might as well.'

'Yeah.' I nod frantically.

And that's when it happens. In an act of pure lunacy, my brain flicks a switch and hurls me into reckless mode. Almost panicking, but not quite, I take the plunge, swimming off towards the entrance to the cove.

'Sod the sharks,' I shout. 'Bollocks to the sharks! They're not eating me.'

I swim on, hearing the smash of water by my side as Dan overtakes me, showing off with a front crawl. There's no way I can match that. Instead, I decide to carry on with my lady-like breaststroke, watching as he finally realises that he's left me behind and comes to a halt, treading water until I catch up.

'Further?' he asks.

'Out there?'

I squint and gulp, accidentally swallowing a mouthful of salty water.

'It's perfectly safe. I've swum to it before.'

'Okay.' My heart beat jitters, but I'm determined to meet the challenge. 'Let's do it.'

He stays by my side now, sometimes on his back, sometimes slipping into a sedate breast stroke, watching me constantly and smiling his encouragement as we swim. It doesn't take long to reach the island and when we get there, I'm amazed to find that someone has gone to the trouble of fashioning concrete steps into the water.

'Why are there steps?' I ask. 'There's nothing here but rocks and trees.'

'Bill had it done.' He hauls himself up onto the bottom step, still waist-deep in the water. 'For me and Louis. We used to come out here and pretend we were explorers.'

With a smile, I pull myself onto the step, settling in between his legs. He curves an arm around me, under the water, and rests his chin on my shoulder. For a minute or so, we remain silent, gazing back at the shoreline, and right here, right now, it feels as if there's no one else in the world.

'Listen to that,' he whispers at last.

'I can't hear anything.'

'Precisely. Peace and quiet. Nobody bothering us. How much better can life get?'

'It can't get any better.'

'It can,' he whispers, leaving a good pause before his next words. 'Marry me.'

I turn to look at him. He touches a palm against my cheek, his eyes soft, waiting for an answer. And I'm so close to giving him what he wants. But I can't. Not yet.

'Still too fast,' I inform him.

'Bugger.' He smiles. 'I thought I'd have you this time.'

'Patience.'

He grimaces at the word. 'Just for the record, should I try every day, or every other day? It's just that I'm not too sure.'

'About once a week.'

His eyebrows curve upwards. 'Fair enough. Well, this is Saturday, so every weekend. Is that okay?'

I nod, nonchalantly. His smile widens.

'We should go. We're going to fry in this sun. Are you ready to swim back yet?'

'I think so.'

'Not scared?'

'A little,' I admit. After all, what's the point in trying to deny it? 'But what the hell?' I slide away from him, back into the water. 'It's day for facing fears.'

A shower, a quick session in the bedroom and a light lunch lead us neatly through to the afternoon. With a few hours to kill before dinner, Dan announces that we're going out to explore and before long I find myself in the passenger seat of Bill's BMW, skirting along a coast road and ignoring the scenery. I'm far too distracted by the sight of the man at my side. Wearing a pair of Ray Bans that Kathy bought in town, and back in his shorts and T-shirt, he could easily pass for a movie star. Nobody would ever guess he spends his days discussing the ins and outs of multi-storey car parks and shopping malls.

'We need to go back to the house,' I announce, fiddling with my own pair of sunglasses and slipping them on. 'I want more sex and I want it now.'

He smiles.

'My nymphomaniac girlfriend is going to have to wait. I'm taking you somewhere.'

'Where?' I lean my head back against a leather rest, enjoying the cool rush of the air-conditioning.

'Surprise.'

Flicking the indicator, he flashes me a quick grin, and we head away from the coast, pressing inwards now, passing the occasional field or a smattering of pastel coloured bungalows, all topped with the same white roofs. At last, we leave the main road behind and begin to trundle along a track. Up ahead, perched at the top of a hill, I can see a white lighthouse ... and we seem to be aiming straight for it.

As we come to a halt in the car park, my pulse begins to splutter.

'A lighthouse?' I falter.

He nods. 'Gibb's Lighthouse.'

'You're not ... We're not going up it?'

He nods again. 'It's a day for facing fears. You said so yourself.' Placing a palm on my thigh, he leans in towards me. 'Flying. Swimming in the sea. You're on a roll.'

I take another peek. My lungs threaten to explode out of my ribcage.

'And I'll be with you every step of the way.'

'Seriously, I can't do this.'

'Wrong. You can do anything.'

Unbuckling my seatbelt and then his own, he's out of the car before I can complain any more. Coming quickly round to my side, he opens the door and encourages me out into the heat.

The lighthouse rises above me like a huge white Dalek, and I stare up at it, reminding myself that if I can manage to stay sane on a Lear jet, then I can definitely drag my sorry backside to the top of this thing. It's entirely my choice whether I take those steps or not, but if I am going to do it, then there's definitely going to be some sort of payback.

'Okay,' I murmur at last. 'I'll do it ... on one condition. You've got to give me something in return. You face your own fears.'

'Meaning?'

'Take a guess.'

'Sisters,' he mutters.

I watch silently as he chews at his lip, glances up at the lighthouse, then back to me. My sudden attack of bravery seems to be catching because he holds out a hand, and I interpret it the only way I can. I've thrown down another gauntlet, and I can only suppose he's picking it up.

'One hundred and eighty-five steps,' he says quietly. 'Then we come out onto the observation deck. You get a full three hundred and sixty-degree view of the island. It's worth it.'

'Fine.' I hold out my own hand in return. 'Let's do it.'

223

Without letting go of me, he pays for our tickets and leads me inside.

And so ... we begin to climb.

Taking one step at a time and ignoring the porthole windows, I tell myself that I'm absolutely fine. I'm really not bothered at all. And why would I be? The top floor of Fosters is higher than this. It's just that I've never been on the outside. As we come to each landing, we take a rest, allowing me to get my breath back while Dan gently strokes my arm. Finally, we arrive at the eighth landing. No more steps. No more rests. This is it.

I face an open doorway.

'Why don't you close your eyes for a start?' He places a hand on my back. 'I can hold you, then get you into position.'

'Okay.'

As my breathing grows increasingly shallow, I lower my lids and immediately, his arms are around me, manoeuvring me slowly through the doorway from behind. I know I'm outside now. I can feel the sun on my face.

'Keep them closed,' he whispers into my ear. 'I'm just moving you a little further. Trust me.'

I'm gently urged on and then I come to a halt. With his arms clasped around my stomach, he pulls me back against his chest. His chin comes to rest on my shoulder.

'Maya?'

'Yes?'

'Are your eyes still closed?'

'Yes.'

'I've got you. You're not going to come to any harm. It's perfectly safe up here. Understand?'

I nod.

'There's a railing in front of you. The body of the lighthouse is behind you. I'm here and I'm not letting go. Open your eyes when you're ready.'

For a few seconds more, I cower in the darkness. And then I make the move. At first, I see nothing but my own eyelashes and through them, the glare of the sun.

'Breathe slowly.' His arms tighten around my midriff. 'Deeply. I've got you.'

I do as I'm told, raising my lids a little further. Slowly, my eyes begin to focus. Another breath and I can see it all: the island laid out below me, virtually flat, with only the hint of a hill in places. From up here, we can see right down to the far end.

'What do you think?

'It's beautiful.'

And it is.

To the right, the coast curves around on itself, neatly defined. To the left, it's a ramshackle collection of outcrops, islands and inlets. Everywhere I look, I see the same white roofs – a sprinkling here, a thicker collection there – scattered in amongst patches of grassland and the deep green of tree foliage. I raise my eyes to the dark strip of the horizon. Above it all, the sky's a cobalt blue today, touched by feathers of cloud.

'Feeling okay?'

I swallow, looking down at the lawn below us and the sharp features of cedar trees beyond.

'I might fall.'

'No way. I've got you.' He tucks a strand of hair behind my ear. 'About twenty miles long and two miles wide. Over six hundred miles away from the nearest land mass.'

What's he trying to do now? Distract me from my fear with a few choice facts?

'We're in the middle of nowhere,' I comment, going along with it.

'Pretty much ... And we're on top of a volcano.'

Now, I'm not entirely sure he should have added that bit. As my body stiffens, I hear him chuckle.

'Don't worry. It's extinct.' He points straight ahead. 'To the right, that's the South Shore.' He pauses, suddenly noticing a tiny but distinctly important fact: I'm not breathing. 'Take a breath, Maya.'

One consciously drawn breath follows another until my lungs finally seem to remember what they're supposed to do. Leaving the matter of breathing behind, I'm aware that my legs have turned to jelly. If Dan wasn't holding me up, I'd be flat on the floor by now.

'Nice and slow,' he whispers. 'Keep it going. You're doing brilliantly.'

'I'm shitting myself.' I glance down at my hands. They're shaking.

'I should hope not. Enough?'

'No.' I may be malfunctioning in just about every possible way, but I'm not ready to give up on being brave, not just yet. I can hear the pride in every word he speaks, and I want more.

'Okay,' he goes on. 'Hamilton to the left. The North Shore. That's where we're staying. Spanish Point.' He raises a hand, motioning vaguely. 'No sharks.'

I hear myself laugh. And then the laugh fades. We stand in silence for a few minutes, taking in the view. My heartbeat slows, my breathing settles back into a normal rhythm and all the time his arms remain clamped around me, keeping me safe.

'Take me to the other side,' I say at last.

'Really?'

'Really.' I squeeze his forearm. 'Before I chicken out.'

Slowly, he guides me to the other side of the lighthouse.

'Docklands.' He points. 'Right at the end. There's not so much to see on this side.'

I gaze at the ocean, the smattering of islands, and realise that I've lived with fear for too long. Chained up by its constrictions, it's kept so much hidden from me. But now those chains are slipping away.

'It's stunning.'

'You think?'

'I do.'

He kisses my cheek and we stand in silence for a little longer while I enjoy the view. Held tight in his arms, I'm loving it.

And more than that ... I've stopped shaking.

Chapter Twenty-two

Light dances across the scene, fairy-like, hopping from lily pad to lily pad, and in amongst the swirling mass of water, a clutch of delicate white lilies float just beyond the reach of the shadows. I stand in awe, transfixed by the colours, examining each and every brush stroke. I can barely believe what I'm looking at. If I'm not very much mistaken, this is a Monet.

'Do you like it?'

I turn to face Bill. Looking slightly ridiculous, he's sporting another pair of Bermuda shorts, matched with a white shirt, open at the collar. But it's the socks and sandals that really do it. Biting back the urge to giggle for the umpteenth time, I decide to press on with a conversation.

'It's amazing.' I aim my wine glass at the picture. 'It's real, isn't it?'

'No.' He smiles knowingly. 'I don't believe in keeping beautiful works of art to myself. The real one's in Belgium. This is a very good fake. I'm a sucker for the Impressionists. How about you?'

'I've got broad tastes.'

'The best kind to have.' He takes a sip of wine. 'Dan tells me you're a gifted artist.'

'Oh, I don't know about that.'

'He's pretty insistent. Landscapes?'

'Mostly.' I'll leave it at that. I'm not about to share the fact that I'm currently working on a strange nude triptych, desperately trying to figure out my new-found obsession with kink. 'I'm influenced by the Impressionists.'

'Then I must see your work.' He slips into silence for a few seconds, his eyes shifting with thought. 'He's a good man,' he says at

227

last, gesturing towards the veranda where Dan's reclined on a wicker chair, watching the sunset.

I sense a rush of warmth in my chest.

'Yes, he is.'

'The pair of you seemed on edge this morning. Maybe you'd had a row?'

'A misunderstanding,' I half whisper. 'It's sorted now.'

'Good.' His lips pucker into a satisfied smile. 'You know he had a rough start in life.' It's a statement, not a question. I nod. 'And then there was the blow of John and Lydia.' He checks my reaction. I nod again. 'It hit him hard. All of it. But every single time, he picked himself up and got on with it. Just look at what he's done with Fosters.' He watches me. 'And now he's got you. He'll make you very happy, Maya. I know that.'

'He already does.'

He holds up his glass, raising an index finger at the picture. 'You scrape back the layers on this thing and pretty soon you'll find out it's not authentic.' And then he turns slightly, pointing at Dan. 'The real thing. Whatever misunderstandings you have, promise me now you'll sort them out.'

I give him a smile, wondering why it is that everyone in Dan's life feels the need to argue his corner. It's as if they all know it can't be an easy ride. But they all seem to be utterly determined for us to see it through.

'Good. Now, let's go and sit down. Dinner's about to be served.'

He leads me through the vast living area, out onto a veranda that looks over the sea. All around us, garden torches have been set. Flaring up against the shadows, they cast a magical, dancing light across the table top. And the sun's dipping now, the bright colours of day changing to deep reds, coppers, bronze and gold – soon to disappear altogether.

'It's cooler now, Dan,' Bill remarks, jolting him out of his daydream.

'Wonderful,' he murmurs.

'The cockroaches have been pretty bad this year.' The old man motions for me to sit before he takes his own place. 'Hey, you remember that time you brought Clive over? You must have been fourteen or fifteen.' He bites back a laugh. 'We had an infestation, Maya. Cockroaches everywhere. And those little buggers can fly. We were sitting right here, having a meal, and a big daddy of a cockroach flew straight at Clive's head. It near on knocked him out.'

Dan laughs. 'He ran inside and wouldn't come out again all evening.'

Bill calms himself.

'How's Clive doing?'

'Fine. He's got a new girlfriend. Maya's friend, Lucy.'

'Looks like you're both settling down. You know, Dianna never took to Clive.' He laughs again. 'Always moaning, complaining, scared of cockroaches, funny with his food. He wouldn't eat fish. That's what did it. This is an island, Maya. You've got to like fish.'

'He's alright now,' Dan assures him. 'He'll eat anything.'

'Then you must bring him back out here. And bring his young lady too. And when you have kids, bring them all!'

Dan smiles. 'We will.'

'Who's Dianna?' I ask, quickly brushing aside all mention of children.

'My wife. I came out here for a holiday, fell in love and we married a few weeks later. I lost her five years ago. She was the love of my life. We never had any children, not for lack of trying. Just couldn't. It would have been nice too, seeing the kids, the grandkids. But no. It's just me and my fake Monet.'

While Bill gives out a loud laugh, Dan seems to be lost in thought.

'I'm sorry I didn't come out when it happened,' he says quietly.

Bill's laugh is silenced.

'It's okay. You didn't have time.'

'I could have made time.'

'No need to worry. You had your reasons.' He studies Dan. 'We all go through periods when we forget about our friends, when we obsess over things that do us no good. And most of us manage to snap out of it. I think you have. Perhaps Maya here has made the difference.'

'Maya *has* made the difference.' He runs a finger around the base of his wine glass. 'And from now on, I'm going to find time for all the important things in life.' He looks at me, his eyes glimmering in the torch light.

'Hey!' Bill calls. 'Here comes the food.'

Charles and Kathy appear in the doorway, each carrying a silver platter. Unsure of what to do, I simply watch as Dan and Bill spring to their feet and lend a hand, taking the platters and laying them on the table.

'It's pretty simple,' Kathy explains. 'I didn't have time for no fancy stuff.'

I gaze at the food. It doesn't look that simple to me.

'You got fresh tuna and salad.' Kathy points to the platter in front of me. 'And you got Hoppin' John.' She waves a hand at the second platter which seems to be piled up with rice, mixed in with a selection of black-eyed peas, onion and some sort of meat.

'Aren't you eating with us?' Dan asks.

'Not tonight, Danny boy.' Charles shakes his head. 'There's a storm coming on. We've got to get home and batten down the hatches. Tomorrow maybe.' With a touch on Dan's arm, Charles takes himself back inside the house, and Kathy follows behind.

'A storm?' I turn my face to the sky, my stomach clenching. I haven't noticed the clouds creeping in overhead.

And, for once, Dan doesn't seem to pick up on my unease. Running his thumb across his bottom lip and gazing into the night, he's preoccupied with something else. We're both startled into action by Bill's voice.

'Eat! That storm's not coming yet.'

Half-soothed by Bill's words and suddenly aware that I'm ravenous, I push all thoughts of bad weather to one side. Piling up my plate with fresh fish, salad and Hoppin' John, I finish off the entire lot and dive in for more. This might be Kathy's idea of simple food, but it's incredible. While I clear my plate for the second time, I listen in as the men chat amicably between mouthfuls: Dan sketching out the last few years at Fosters; Bill telling stories of his life on Bermuda. At last, with the meal finished and a comfortable silence descending between us, I sit back, noting that the wind is getting up now, that the torch flames are beginning to veer to one side.

'I need to ask you something,' Dan says at last.

It's not aimed towards me. I wait for Bill's answer.

'Anything.'

'You knew my parents well. You helped them with the business.'

'I did.'

'What would you think ...' He dries up, swallows hard.

'If you sold it?'

I gape at Dan. Suddenly, my pulse seems to be racing and I don't know whether it's because of the sudden charge in the air or the turn in the conversation.

'How old are you now?' Bill asks.

'Thirty-six.'

'And you've been running for Fosters for how long?'

'Fourteen years.'

The old man considers his words for a minute or so before he finally gives his verdict. 'From what Norman tells me, the company consumes you, and that's not good. John and Lydia would have been proud of what you've done, but Fosters is ... a different animal now. And more than anything, they would have wanted to see you happy.'

The two men watch each other, neither giving away anything much. At last, Bill moves things on.

'Are you happy, Dan? Having your energy sapped by this beast of burden?'

I'm thoroughly surprised when Dan shakes his head.

'Then I'd say it's time to think of yourself. You owe nothing to no one. And if you ever thought you did, you've paid your dues.'

I hear a distant rumble, notice that the air has cooled a little more. Sitting bolt upright in my chair, I grip the arms and look up at the sky. It's darkened further.

'The storm, Maya,' Bill smiles. 'It's coming in a little faster than I thought. It'll be cleared by morning. Don't you worry.'

Don't you worry? Tightening my grip, I glance at Dan, relieved to see that he's now fully alert to the situation.

'We have to go back to the guest house,' he says, suddenly rising to his feet. 'I'm sorry, Bill. We'd like to stay longer but ...' He clamps his lips shut and widens his eyes at me.

'Of course,' Bill nods. 'I'm sorry. I forgot. Maya's not too good with storms.'

'And it's best that we go back.' Holding out a hand, Dan beckons for me to move.

With an apologetic smile, I get up.

'I'm sorry, Bill.' I shrug. 'It was a lovely meal.'

'No worries, Maya. I'll see you tomorrow.'

Leaving Bill to clear up the dishes, Dan leads me down the steps, back to the guest house. Within a couple of minutes, we're inside the bungalow. Closing the French windows, Dan takes me straight to the bedroom and draws the shutters.

'Get into bed.'

Struggling out of my clothes, I do as I'm told.

'No tent?' I ask.

He glances round the room, at the over-sized antique furniture. Making a tent in here would take a serious amount of effort and probably cause a hernia. Instead, shaking his head, he strips off and joins me under the sheet. I'm wrapped in his arms, trembling like an idiot when the first real crash of thunder arrives.

'Shit.' I squeeze my eyes shut. Adrenalin begins to pump.

'It's okay,' he whispers, smoothing my hair. 'Thunder can't hurt you.'

'No, but lightning can.'

I hear him chuckle.

'By the time you hear the thunder, the danger's already gone. Light travels faster than sound.'

Another crash resounds through the house. The tremble mutates into a judder.

'I don't need a fucking physics lesson.'

Shit. I'm swearing again.

'But there's no danger anyway.' Ignoring the petulance, he pushes on, still smoothing my hair. 'Lightning hits the highest point. The trees are far more likely to cop it.'

Through the shutters, I catch the flash of a lightning bolt. The crash comes almost immediately. It's deafening. My body convulses.

'Jesus,' Dan breathes, tightening his grip. 'That was close.'

'This isn't working,' I wail.

'I know. I'm moving on to plan B.'

I have no time to ask what plan B involves. I'm manoeuvred onto my back. Moving on top of me, he leaves my hands free, rests on one elbow and coaxes my legs apart, positioning himself between them.

'You're not going to fuck me?'

'No.' He plants a gentle kiss on my lips. 'I'm going to make love to you.'

'That won't distract me.'

He grins.

'It might take the edge off a little.'

Another flash of lightning spills through the shutters. Tensing every muscle, I close my eyes, waiting for the thunder clap. Again, it's almost immediate. Letting out a quiet sob, I feel a finger at my clit. Slowly, he parts the folds of skin, finds my spot and sets about working me up into a mess down below.

'Oh, Jesus,' I groan. 'I'm telling you, it won't work.'

'Open your eyes.'

'I can't.'

'Do as you're told, woman. This is sex. I'm in charge.'

Reluctantly, I comply. Watching me tenderly, he slides the finger inside, easing me open.

'I'm here with you,' he informs me.

'That's pretty fucking obvious,' I cry. 'But you know what it's like.'

'It's a day for conquering fears, Maya. I've got you. You're perfectly safe.'

Slipping an arm beneath me, he nudges my legs further apart and enters me, pushing inwards, filling me completely.

'Feel this, Maya. Concentrate on this. You and me. When we're together, we can get through anything.'

He adjusts his position, sending a spark of electricity right through my abdomen. I see a flash, count the seconds as Dan continues to move. And while the thunder rumbles across the ocean, my insides quake.

I glance at the shutters.

'Hey.' He strokes my hair. 'Don't look at that. Look at me.'

I do as I'm told.

'That's it. Keep it there.' He withdraws slowly, kissing me again. 'Stay with me. Feel this.'

'I can't ...'

'Yes, you can.' Proving the point, he drives back into me and I feel it straight away. A glowing sensation takes hold deep in the pit of my vagina. 'You're doing it now.'

I moan, let out a jittering breath.

'I'm still fucking terrified.'

'Just like our first night together.' Buried deep inside, he comes to a halt and studies my face. 'Shall I tell you a secret?'

'You might as well. What is it? No, don't tell me. You used to be the Pope.'

He laughs.

'You've got me rumbled. No. That first night we spent together, when I made you a little tent ... I was terrified too.'

I hear another laugh, and it's mine.

'Oh come off it.'

Looking straight into me, his shakes his head. 'I wasn't scared of the storm. I was scared of the way you made me feel. It was something I didn't understand. All I knew was you'd walked into my life and I never wanted you to walk out of it again. That's pretty terrifying for a man like me.'

His admission works like a treat. Somewhere outside, thunder echoes through the darkness but all I can think about is what he's just told me. The first time I went back to his apartment, I had him down as an arrogant prick, and all the time he was simply putting up a front, building his own walls.

'I love you,' I murmur. 'I fucking love you.'

'And I fucking love you too. I'll never stop loving you. I'll never stop protecting you. You'll never come to any harm, not while there's breath in my body.'

He begins to move again, driving into me, over and over, with a slow and steady pace. And as the edge of pleasure broadens out, I don't know if it's the storm moving on or the fact that he's managed to distract me, but the thunder seems more distant now, hardly relevant. All I'm seeing is the man who's arched above me, the powerhouse of his body, the reverence in his eyes. Completely focussed on him, I might just have fear on the run.

'Are we ready?' He smiles.

'God, yes.' I smile back.

He picks up the pace, thrusting into me now, taking himself deeper every single time. And as the pressure builds, I slide my hands over his broad shoulders and down his back, bringing them to rest on his backside. Clutching at his taut buttocks, I thrust up against him, struggling to catch a tattered breath while my muscles twitch and tighten and glow.

He watches me constantly, even as he begins to untangle.

'Fuck it,' he growls. 'I'm coming.'

And I let go, completely and utterly, tumbling into oblivion as my insides pulsate.

'See what you did then?' he asks, slowing the pace. 'You rode out a storm.'

He collapses on top of me, digging his face into my neck.

'I sure did.'

Lifting his head, he smiles and kisses me deeply for an age before he pulls out and sets about cleaning me up with the edge of the sheet.

'Yuk.' I scowl.

'No tissues. I'll put it in the wash in the morning. Kathy's never going to know.'

He rolls onto his side and draws me against his chest, face on. Snuggling into his arms and drinking in his scent, I listen to the rain against the window panes. I have no idea how long we stay like this, enjoying the closeness, the quiet, but as the minutes tick by, my new-found bravery seems to grow.

'I want to go and look,' I say at last.

'You do?' His eyebrows dip. 'But there might be more lightning.'

'And if there is, just hold me tight.'

'Seriously?'

'Seriously,' I confirm. 'I'm sick of running away. I'm sick of hiding. Sometimes it feels like that's all I've ever done. I don't want to do it any more.'

He watches me for a moment. His eyes flicker with admiration.

'Fair enough,' he murmurs at last, pecking me on the lips. 'Let's do this thing.'

Out in the lounge, we stand naked in front of the window, Dan behind me, his arms around my waist. Over the sea, a fork of lightning hits the water. I wait for the sound of the thunder and there it is, rumbling across the Atlantic. A small knot of anxiety forms in the pit of my stomach. The arms tighten and I will the knot to disintegrate.

'It's passed,' he whispers.

'Thank God for that.'

Another minute or so slip by in silence before he speaks again.

'I could stay here forever. No problems. No work. Just you and me.'

'So, this is how it's going to be?'

'With Boyd out of the way? Yes.'

I smile to myself, thoroughly contented. I have the man I love and in every possible way, I'm in paradise. Things are perfect, and they're only going to get better. In fact, I remind myself, he's already working on our future together.

'Why didn't you tell me before?' I ask.

'Tell you what?'

'That you're thinking of selling Fosters?'

He takes in a deep breath.

'I only thought of it tonight, Maya. I'm as surprised as you are.'

***

It's a brilliant morning. With the storm over, the air's a little fresher now, the sun as bright as ever. When we finally join Bill at the main house, we find him buried in a newspaper.

'And so.' He smiles, folding up the paper. 'The love birds emerge from their nest.'

'Sorry, Bill,' Dan says. 'We didn't wake up until late.'

He gives me a sneaky wink. In actual fact, we woke early. We just didn't get out of bed until almost eleven.

'You seem to have relaxed, both of you. The tea and coffee are fairly fresh. We'll have to wait for food. I think Kathy's just gone down to your place. She likes to keep it tidy.'

I stare at Dan, knowing for a fact that he didn't put that sheet in the wash. With a shrug, he pulls out a chair and waits for me to sit before he lowers himself next to me. Without asking, he pours me a cup of tea and then helps himself to coffee.

'Any more thoughts on selling?' Bill asks.

Taking a mouthful of coffee, Dan shakes his head.

'You know, there are other building companies that would snap it up. But they'll dismantle it. Take what they want. People *will* lose their jobs.'

'I know.'

'And I know what you're like. More sensitive than you let on.'

With a grimace, he looks up over the edge of his cup. 'It's time to move on, Bill. I've got other fish to fry. I'll do my best for the people there but, like you said, I can't be responsible for all of them. Not any more.'

'So, how will you keep busy?'

'I have Maya.' He pauses. 'And there are other things.'

'Such as?' I ask, suddenly intrigued.

He doesn't get a chance to answer. Huffing and puffing her way up the steps, Kathy comes to a halt by the table.

'Danny boy! You left your phone in the bedroom. It keeps ringing.' She hands it to him.

'Take a seat, Kathy.' Bill waves at a spare chair.

'I haven't got time for no chopsin.' She shakes her head. 'There's linen to sort.'

With a half-disgusted smirk, she waddles back down the steps and disappears inside the bungalow. I take a peek at Dan, wondering if he's feeling as embarrassed as me, but clearly he's not. Instead, he's busy scrolling through his messages.

'Anything interesting?' Bill asks.

Dan shakes his head. His face clouds over. 'Excuse me. I won't be a minute.'

Getting to his feet, he clasps the phone to his ear and walks away across the lawn.

'Clive, what's going on?'

That's all I hear. Coming to a halt in the shade of a tree, he stays there for a minute or two, listening intently. It's not good. I can tell from the way his shoulders have suddenly hunched. At last, he says something, thrusts the phone into his pocket and returns to us.

'We need to go home, Bill. I'm sorry.'

'But why?' I demand, stunned by his announcement. 'What's the matter?'

'Jodie. She's disappeared.' Sitting back at the table, he takes a sip of coffee.

'Jodie?' I'd virtually forgotten about the pink princess. 'But she's a teenager. She's probably just slipped off the rails. She'll be back.'

'She's been gone since Saturday morning and she's not answering her phone. She's never done anything like this before. She's always kept in touch with her mum.'

'Are we talking about Norman's grand-daughter?' Bill interjects, his face suddenly creased with concern.

Dan nods.

'And they've called the police?'

'Yes, but they're not concerned yet. She's not been gone long enough. And besides, she's been a bit of a tearaway in the past.'

But not recently, my brain muses. It might be nothing more than a simple coincidence, but then again ... Even though it must be a hundred degrees in the shade, I shiver. After what happened at the Savoy, there's every chance that this isn't a coincidence at all. I look at Dan, almost certain that our trains of thought are heading in exactly the same direction.

'What about her dad?' I ask. 'Can't he go looking for her?'

Dan shakes his head.

'He walked out on them years ago. He doesn't care.'

'You don't think ...' I falter.

'I do,' he confirms. 'And so does Clive.'

I feel sick. Boyd may well be unbalanced, but surely he wouldn't go that far.

'What's going on, Dan?'

Bill's voice causes him to start. He turns and fixes our host in his sights. And then, without hesitation, he launches into an explanation of everything: right from his first visit to Boyd's flat in Edinburgh through to Jodie's disappearance. And then he fills him in on Boyd's past record. Listening intently to it all, the old man strokes his chin. When Dan's finished, he takes a minute or two to process the information before he speaks. And when he does, he sounds different. There's a hard edge to his voice.

'And you're absolutely sure he's got something to do with this?'

'Yes,' Dan answers crisply. 'I underestimated Boyd, but I won't be doing that again.'

'I don't like the sound of this man. He's got it in for you.' He points at Dan. 'And that makes him my enemy. You know, I still have a few contacts back in London. They'd find him soon enough.'

'You're not talking criminals?' I venture.

From the look on Dan's face, I'm pretty sure I've just said the wrong thing. I'm about to apologise for jumping to a ridiculous conclusion when Bill confirms that I haven't.

'Let's just say I managed a few shady financial deals back in the day. I know people with clout. They can help with finding this bastard ... and then they can scare him off.'

I can't help but think he's planning on a little more than a simple talking to. And while I know the world would be a better place without the likes of Ian Boyd, I'm not entirely comfortable with the possibilities.

'But ...'

Holding up a finger, Bill stops my complaint in its tracks.

'From what Dan's just told me, this man's playing dirty. You need to fight fire with fire.'

Dan gives me an uneasy look. 'Let's leave it to the people I've hired.'

'And they are?' Bill asks.

'A security company.'

'Which one?'

'Foultons. They're good. We've got bodyguards, private investigators. Ex-military, ex-police, that sort of thing.'

Bill considers the information.

'You do what you think is right,' he says at last. 'But the offer's there.' He leans forwards. 'And sometimes you need all the help you can get. Even if you don't like where it's coming from.'

Silence settles over the veranda, each one of us lost in our own thoughts. It's Bill who speaks first, evidently deciding that it's time for action.

'Now, if you give me your passport details, I'll get onto the flights. You can always get a seat in club.'

'Today?' Dan asks.

'If I can't get you a direct flight, there'll be something via New York. And if there isn't, I'll find a private jet.' The old man stands up. 'Go and get yourselves sorted. I'll give Norman a call and tell him you're on your way.'

While Dan embraces Bill, thanking him for his help, I gaze up at the clear blue sky. It's a cloudless morning, completely calm after the storm, and the sea is glass-like once again. I've had my taste of the things to come. No worries. No threats. Just peace, pure and simple.

And my heart slumps.

Because now it's about to end.

Chapter Twenty-Three

I slide onto a stool opposite Clive, grunting a barely conscious greeting in his general direction. Looking pretty dishevelled, he grunts one back in return.

'How was Bermuda?' he asks, opening up with small talk.

'Short and sweet. I love it though ... even with the giant monster cockroaches.'

He smiles a little.

'And the flight back?'

'Flights,' I correct him. 'We had to change in New York. It was bloody awful.'

And that's an understatement. It turns out that conquering a Lear jet is no preparation for the joys of boarding a big scary thing on two separate occasions. While the journey from Bermuda to New York was spent in state of near catatonia, the Atlantic crossing saw me curled up into a ball in a Club class pod, quaking and jittering and letting out the occasional groan. And even though Dan held my hand, or let me sidle over onto his lap whenever the seatbelt sign flicked off, it didn't seem to make the slightest bit of difference.

'Coffee.' Clive pushes a mug towards me, one of three. 'I thought you'd need it.'

I take a sip.

'Do you think Jodie's alright?' I ask.

'She's alive, if that's what you're worried about.'

I sigh in relief. 'Thank God for that.'

'She spoke to a friend this morning.'

'Does Dan know?'

He casts a glance at the open front door. Out in the lobby, Dan's busy talking to a newly-reinstated Beefy.

'Not yet.'

Shoving the suitcases to one side and slamming the door behind him, Dan joins us. He slips his iPad onto the counter, grabs a mug of coffee and takes it over to the window. Looking out over the Thames, he begins to fire off a barrage of questions and although they come thick and fast, Clive manages to catch every single one of them.

'Any more news?'

'A friend managed to contact her. She finally answered her phone. About an hour ago.'

'So, what's going on?'

'She's as high as a kite, holed up in a flat with some bloke, too zonked out to answer her mobile until now.'

'And she knows this man?'

'No.'

'Is it Boyd?'

Clive hesitates.

'No secrets.' Turning away from the window, Dan takes a mouthful of coffee. 'Maya's in on everything now.'

'It's not Boyd. He's too young, about Jodie's age. Apparently, she was out shopping. He chatted her up and invited her back to his flat.'

'Jesus, that girl's got a screw loose. So, any connection to Boyd?'

'I don't know.'

'And where's the flat?'

'The friend asked. Jodie didn't have a clue.'

'That's no help.'

'But she could see a pub from the window. The Tiger.'

There's a silence. While Dan finishes off his coffee, Clive takes a mobile out of his jacket pocket. He seems to be looking up a web page.

'So, where do we go from here?' Dan asks at last. 'There must be plenty of pubs in London called The Tiger.'

'Actually ...' Clive holds up the phone, displaying a map. 'There's only one. And it's in Camberwell.'

Coming over to the counter, Dan puts down his mug, takes the mobile out of Clive's hand and studies the screen. 'We should go down there. Knock on a few doors.'

'Exactly what I was thinking,' Clive smiles.

'So what are we waiting for?'

'What?' I splurt. 'Now? But you're knackered.'

With a shrug, he hands the mobile back to Clive.

'What difference does it make? We need to get her home before Norman has a coronary.'

I'm over-tired and hardly thinking straight after the marathon terror session, and perhaps that's why my brain's suddenly flooded with melodramatic visions of Ian Boyd lurking in the shadows like a spider at the edge of its web. I can hardly believe it when I spring to my feet and grab at Dan's shirt sleeve.

'Don't do anything stupid,' I plead.

With an indulgent smile, he wraps his arms around me and plants a kiss on my forehead.

'Don't worry, sweet pea. It's not in the plan.'

Clive gets to his feet, shrugs on his suit jacket and runs his fingers through his hair.

'You know,' he muses, 'this could be nothing at all to do with Boyd.'

'And if it isn't, that girl's in major trouble.' With another kiss, Dan releases me.

'And if it is, it could be another distraction.' Clive pauses, waiting for Dan's full attention. 'What about Maya?'

'Oh, don't be daft.' I wave a hand dismissively. 'He's not going to break into the Batcave while Dan's out playing the superhero.'

'She's perfectly safe,' Dan confirms. 'We've got Beefy up here. And besides, he wouldn't get past the concierge.' He picks up his iPad and switches it on. 'Give me your phone, Maya.'

I jolt. 'What?'

'Your phone.'

'Why?'

'Because I want to put an app on it. I want to be able to track you if I need to.'

Silently grumbling that this really is going too far, I retrieve the mobile from my handbag where it's been languishing for the past few days, amazed that it's still charged.

He holds out a hand. 'Once Boyd's off the scene, I'll remove it, I promise. But right now, we need to play it safe.'

***

It's early afternoon when they leave. Desperate to distract myself from all thoughts of what might be going on, I haul the suitcases up to the bedroom and unpack. After a shower, I sit in the studio, staring blankly at the canvases for an age. I really should get back to the paintings, but I can't. I'm too consumed with worry over Dan. When my stomach eventually grumbles, I go back downstairs and make sandwiches and tea, inviting Beefy in for lunch. He asks about Bermuda. I gush about its beauty, complain that we couldn't stay longer, and apologise belatedly for abandoning him in a side street.

He thanks me for getting him reinstated. And then exhaustion seeps through every last molecule of my being. While Beefy resumes his position outside, I lie on the sofa, telling myself that I'll just close my eyes for five minutes. When I open them again, I find Clive crouching in front of me, touching me lightly on the arm.

'Maya,' he whispers.

'You're back. What time is it?'

'Nearly six.'

'Jesus, I've been asleep for hours.' And suddenly, I'm panicking. Why isn't Dan waking me up? Something must have happened.

'Where is he?'

'Relax. He's in the shower.'

I sit up.

'Did you find her?'

'Yes.'

'So, what happened?'

Clive blows out a breath and from the look on his face, I'd say that things didn't quite go to plan.

'She was in a flat opposite the pub.' He talks quietly, occasionally looking towards the stairs. 'Smoking dope with some lowlife kid. Dan knocked seven shades of shit out him.'

My face must be a picture of horror.

'It's alright,' Clive reassures me. 'The kid's pretty bruised, but he'll live. And he owned up. He'd been paid to do it.'

'Boyd?'

He shakes his head.

'A third party. The kid couldn't name him ... even after Dan broke his nose.' He winces at the memory. 'But it's Boyd alright.' He nods towards the staircase, lowering his voice and leaning in. 'Look. There's no easy way to say this. I'm worried about Dan. After we dropped Jodie off with her mum, he made me take him back to the club.'

I narrow my eyes, hoping to all that's holy that Clive doesn't mean what I think he means.

'Isaac's place?'

'Yes. He's got it into his head that Isaac's hiding Boyd. He went through that place like a lunatic, caused a total rumpus, had Isaac up against a wall ... again.'

'Again?'

'Like he did at the Savoy. Lily told me about that little episode.' He bites his lip. 'I've never seen him like this before ... I'm scared.'

And so am I. Within the space of a few hours, it seems that my calm and carefree boyfriend has been transformed into a fist-wielding hot head.

'If we don't get this sorted soon,' Clive goes on, 'he's going to end up in big shit. He's lucky Isaac isn't pressing charges.'

'Maybe we should call the police.'

'Are you kidding? If we involve the police, the kid denies being paid and Dan gets done for GBH.'

'That might not happen.'

'I wouldn't bet on it. Besides, Jodie's mum doesn't want any trouble. We just need to find that bastard and deal with him.'

A door bangs upstairs.

'Don't ask him about it,' Clive warns me. 'Just try to calm him down.' He gets to his feet. 'And don't let him come into work tomorrow.'

'He won't. He's on holiday.'

'And like an idiot, I told him what's going on at Fosters. We're having a few issues. He'll want to come in, Maya. Believe you me. And if he does, he'll be biting heads off left, right and centre. Keep him at home.'

'I'll do my best.'

Clive glances at the staircase one last time and stands up.

'I'd better get going. Good luck.'

As soon as he's gone, I make my way upstairs, slowly, warily, as if I'm about to surprise a complete stranger. He's not in the bedroom, but the door to the en-suite is open and I can hear the sound of running water. Entering the bathroom, I find him in the shower, hands resting against the tiles, head dipped under the water, motionless.

'Dan?'

He doesn't respond. Maybe he hasn't heard me.

Unnoticed, I take off my clothes, open the door and slip in behind him, running my hands around his firm waist and noting that his knuckles are bruised. He rolls his head against the tiles, straightens up and turns. Wrapping his arms around me, he kisses me deeply, urgently, and it's obvious that he's wound up tight. Pulling away, I take hold of his hand and inspect the knuckles. I want to tell him that he's gone too far, that he needs to be patient and leave it all to the professionals. But I'm going to act on Clive's advice. Instead, I wait for him to speak.

'It's all out of control,' he whispers, gazing at his hands. 'Everything.'

243

'You'll sort things out. You always do.'

'I can't think straight. I'm making bad decisions.'

'Then tell me what you need.'

He doesn't speak. He doesn't have to. I see it in his eyes as soon as they meet mine. He needs to escape, to hide, call it what you want. It's how he's always dealt with pressure in the past, and it's how he needs to deal with it now. Cupping his face in my hands, I take a deep breath. I'm about to offer him his very own brand of forbidden fruit.

'No baggage. No past. No connection. No hurt.' I can remember his words exactly, and it's all I need to say.

He understands immediately.

'I told you, I'm not going there.'

'And I'm telling you, this is what you need.' He doesn't deny it. 'Do whatever you need to do. Be whoever you need to be. It won't change a thing.'

He shakes his head. 'Maya, don't push me ...'

'Why not?'

'Because I'm really fucking tempted.'

'Then give in to temptation. One last time. With me.'

Exhausted, he leans back against the tiles and stares at the floor. And while he battles his way to a decision, just about every single part of me begins to quake. I have no idea what I'm letting myself in for, but if it's a choice between this – whatever this is – and watching Dan come to pieces, then it's an easy choice to make. Slowly, his shoulders relax, his breathing calms and his fists unclench. When he finally speaks again, his voice is detached, curiously devoid of feeling.

'Go and dry your hair. Wait for me in the bedroom.'

I've had just enough time to sort myself out when I hear the bathroom door open. Completely naked, he enters the room and throws his clothes onto the chaise longue.

'Eyes down,' he orders briskly.

Washed through with nerves and anticipation, I do as I'm told. Taking my hand in his, he leads me out across the hallway, and into our secret room.

I hear the door close behind me. I'm brought to a halt in front of the cross.

'This is it,' he says. 'The moment of no return. Do you want to change your mind?'

I swallow hard, taking in the leather restraints, wondering what on Earth he's going to use on me, how far he's about to go.

'Answer me.'

'No,' I whisper, my voice small.

Instantly, I'm grabbed from behind: an arm across my stomach, a palm across my mouth. His grip tightens. I feel his hard chest against my back, his penis at the top of my buttocks. Forcing my head back against him, he grinds into me and I fizzle at the contact.

'No talking. Understand?'

I nod, my breath quick and ragged against his hand.

'Unless I ask you a question. Then I expect your answer immediately.'

I nod again.

'I need permission to slap you.'

Slapping? My brain fires out. He wants to slap you? For fuck's sake, what the hell are you playing at? Get out of this now.

'All part of the deal, Maya,' he breathes into my ear. 'Control, remember? I'm used to a whip, but we're not going there. That's agreed.'

The hand slides away from my mouth and I'm turned to face him.

'But slapping?' I gasp, careful to keep my eyes trained on the floor.

'Across your thighs,' he explains. 'Only your thighs. And only if necessary.'

'Will it hurt?'

'I thought pain was your thing.'

My breath falters and I take a peek at him, surprised to find that the transformation is already complete. He's gazing at me now from beneath hooded lids, his eyes cold and inquisitive, his entire stance altered. With his shoulders arched and every single muscle tautened, he's clearly primed for attack. Focussed yet unemotional, utterly in control, and with an air of command that expects complete compliance: I'm looking at the dominant, pure and simple.

Locking an arm around my back, he grabs a handful of hair.

'Look at me,' he orders.

I comply, and his blue eyes pierce me to the core.

'You wanted this. You asked for it. I need your permission.'

'Then I give it.'

'Good. And now you'll do as you're told. Is that clear?'

I waver.

'I said is that clear?' he demands harshly, tugging at my hair.

'Yes.' I wince.

'Move backwards. Stand against the cross.'

Hesitantly, I do as I'm told. He moves forwards, slowly, making no eye contact whatsoever, his face expressionless. Concentrating on

245

the job in hand, he takes my left hand and raises my arm, securing the leather strap of a manacle around my wrist and checking for comfort before he does exactly the same with my right arm. And then he kneels, tapping my feet, signalling for me to spread my legs. When he's satisfied with the position, he sets about attaching the lower manacles to my ankles, pinning me firmly into place.

'Comfortable?' he asks, getting to his feet.

'Yes.'

He takes a step back, surveying my body, every last bit of it, and my skin heats up under his gaze. Good God, he's being all mean and hot and moody, and bloody hell, it's turning me on. My pulse is racing now, my heart pounding, my crotch throbbing with need, and I'm struggling to breathe.

Silently, he makes his way over to the wardrobe. Pulling back the door and opening a drawer, he picks out a length of black material, tightening it between his hands as he prowls back over to me. He takes a moment to examine my eyes before he raises the material and I'm plunged into darkness. I feel his breath against my cheek, the warmth of his taut body against my chest as he fastens the blindfold behind my head. When he's finished, he stays exactly where he is, pressing his crotch against me, easing his hands over mine.

'I'd love to gag you,' he murmurs into my ear.

'Then do it.'

The right hand is removed. I'm slapped hard on my left thigh. Hearing the crack of flesh against flesh, I jolt, gritting my teeth against the sting.

'Did I say you could talk?'

'No,' I whimper.

'Then don't.' He pauses, his breath against my mouth now. 'You may need your safe word. What is it?'

'Coffee.'

'Coffee,' he confirms.

And then, as if he's reminding me of our connection, he kisses me, long and hard, demanding full access to my mouth with his tongue. Moving away, he leaves me bereft, suddenly chilled by the air and on high alert. I hear the sound of his footsteps, the soft clink of metal. Knowing exactly what he's got in his hands, I feel his fingers on my right nipple, squeezing, pulling, elongating.

'I'm going to clamp your nipples,' he informs me. 'Tell me now if you've got a problem with that.'

I remain silent. Ever since I first clapped eyes on those things, I've been intrigued.

A hand grabs my chin.

'You asked for this, Maya. You know the way out.'

He waits for a response. I shake my head.

And then I sense the cold edge of metal against my nipple. It closes in on me, tightens, and I cry out at the onrush of pain. Letting my head fall back, I soak it all in: the flood tide of chemicals, the afterglow of adrenalin. Slowly, carefully, he applies the second clamp to my left nipple. It grips me, gently at first, and then with an increasing force.

'Tight enough?'

'Yes,' I moan.

'Well, I'm about to go further.'

The clamps are tightened again. He tugs at the chain between them, sending lightning bolts of agony right through me. For a few seconds, my nerve ends are on fire. My brain empties itself of any thought. My entire body tenses and I scream. And then, as the pain recedes to a dull throb, I groan ... gasp for air ... relax.

'You want more?' he asks, his voice suddenly tender.

'Yes.'

'Why?' He smooths my hair.

My brain scrambles for an answer, finding nothing.

'I don't know.'

'Think.'

Still struggling for breath, I shake my head. Again, he tugs at my hair, pulls at the chain. I brace, fighting to control the sensations, to keep my lungs working. It's clear that he's not giving up any time soon, and I need to say something quickly, before he drives me insane.

'Because it turns me on,' I choke. And that's an understatement. I'm already wet down below. My vagina's pulsing, my clitoris throbbing, and I need him inside me.

'Why does it turn you on?'

Shit. Why? I hesitate. He tugs again. Spinning my way through the cycle of pain, I moan loudly. Come up with something, my brain cries out. And do it now!

'Because I'm at your mercy,' I pant. 'Because I'm totally under your control.'

'You don't need pain for that,' he whispers, drawing his lips down my neck. 'The pain's nothing more than an add-on. What do you get out of it? Tell me, Maya. I want the truth.'

Another tug.

'I don't know,' I groan.

He slaps my thigh. My body jolts again.

'Not good enough, and you know it. I want an honest answer.'

I shiver inside, delving through a tangle of thoughts for something that's going to satisfy him. I have no idea why I'm being interrogated, but there's only one way out of it. There must be an answer somewhere. I just can't put my finger on it.

'I don't know,' I hear my voice quiver. 'I really don't know.'

'Think.'

'I can't.'

He readjusts the clamps, loosening them slightly before he reapplies the pressure. As if a sluice-gate has been opened, a wave of torment floods right through me.

'Oh God,' I cry out.

Another slap on the thigh. Grimacing, I resist the urge to shout, to tell him in no uncertain terms to fuck off.

'I told you to be careful what you wish for.'

'I know, I know, I know.'

Within seconds, his mouth is on my neck, biting and sucking hard, working its way down my throat while the grip on my hair tightens. Forcing my head back, he presses his chest against mine, pushing upwards, moving against the clamps and sending further spasms of pain ricocheting through my nerves. Suddenly, a finger is thrust into me, probing roughly with no intention of causing pleasure. He's simply preparing me for the onslaught to come. Evidently satisfied that I'm ready, he withdraws the finger and pinches at my clit, sending me into a frenzy. I let out a long, low moan as his cock enters me and he begins to thrust.

There's no build-up. Immediately, he begins to slam into me, smashing out a relentless rhythm and causing shockwaves of delicious heat to erupt in the depths of my vagina. And all the time, while the pressure rises inside, he nips at my flesh or grasps at my hair or tugs on the chains between the clamps, inundating me with spasms of agony. It's a full-blown attack, totally ruthless and gaining in frenzy.

'Tell me now,' he growls. 'What do you get out of this?'

'I ... told you,' I manage to cry out between breaths. 'I don't know.'

'Where does this take you?'

I shake my head.

'Think, Maya.'

'I can't,' I shout. And maybe that's it. 'Nowhere.' And suddenly, a sob escapes my throat. 'It takes me nowhere. It blots everything out. Oblivion. It takes me into oblivion.'

'And why do you need oblivion?'

'Because,' I gasp, reeling as he delivers another slap against my thigh.

'I want an answer.'

And I just can't give one. Because another sob has followed on from the first ... and another ... and another. I'm crying now, and it's not because I'm in pain. It's because I want it and crave it. And I don't have the slightest clue why.

'I don't know,' I cry. 'I don't know, I don't know, I don't fucking know.'

Suddenly, he comes to a halt.

'This ends now.' He removes the blindfold.

Head back, I blink at him through half-focussed vision. Still buried deep inside me, his eyes have softened. Completely fixed on mine, they suddenly seem to be filled with concern.

'Dan, what's the matter?'

'This isn't right.' He struggles to catch his breath. 'It's just not right.'

He skims a finger down my cheek, turns his attention from my face to my breasts. Still breathing deeply, he releases the clamps, one at a time, sending fresh waves of agony through my body. Dropping the clamps to the floor, he brushes his thumbs across my nipples.

'Whoever I used to be, he's gone. I don't want to hide and I don't want to blot things out. From now on, we find other ways ... other ways to deal with the shit.' Slipping a hand around the base of my back, he withdraws to the hilt, raising his eyes to mine. 'Never ask me to hurt you, Maya.' And now he presses inwards, sending a shimmer of want right through me. 'Never ask me to be somebody I'm not.' He pulls out again, to the tip.

'I thought it was what you needed.'

'I know,' he whispers, touching his lips against mine, while he drives back in. 'I thought I needed it too, but I don't. Now that I've got you, I don't.'

He picks up the pace, notch by notch, until he's thrusting into me, over and over again. Lips parted, he watches me constantly, one hand on my buttocks, the other at the back of my neck. And while my insides begin to glow, I lose myself in those blue eyes and everything that they're offering me: an ocean of love and reverence and care. Overwhelmed by sensations and emotions, I just can't control myself. I come quickly, convulsing in his arms.

'I'm the man who loves you,' he rasps, ramming into me once, twice, before he comes too. 'That's who I am. Never forget that.'

I listen to his ragged breath as he stays inside me, kissing me slowly, gradually working himself down. With a final peck, he withdraws, releasing my feet before he straightens up and unfastens the straps around my wrists, guiding my arms back down, one at a time. My legs buckle beneath me, and I'm caught. Steadying my body for a moment, he picks a throw out of the wardrobe and wraps me in it, immediately sweeping me up in his arms and carrying me out of the room.

I'm expecting to be taken to the bedroom, but we enter the studio instead. Still holding me in his arms, he lowers himself onto the couch, cradling me gently, and begins to stroke my hair.

'What are we doing in here?'

He nods towards the triptych.

'Pleasure and pain.'

'I didn't think you'd noticed.'

'Of course I've noticed. Pleasure on the left, pain on the right, and I'm assuming that's a space for me right in the middle ... because I give you both.'

I'm suddenly embarrassed. I had no idea he'd even come in here.

'It's just an experiment,' I half-apologise.

'It's more than that. You've been working through it, trying to understand what you get out of the pain, why you crave it.'

I look up at him.

'I should never have introduced you to it.'

'I don't see the problem.'

He smiles wryly.

'I'm no expert, Maya, but I've seen enough over the years. I've met plenty of people who can't get enough of it ... for all sorts of reasons.' He glances out of the window, clearly thinking about how to phrase his explanation. 'There are people who just do it for the rush. It's as simple as that. It turns them on, gets them high.' He looks back at me, eyes glimmering. 'But then there are people who do it because they want to be punished, because they think they deserve to be punished, because their self-esteem is in tatters.'

'And you think that's me?'

'I don't know.' Gazing right into the heart of me, he traces a finger down the side of my cheek. 'But I don't want to take any chances. I don't want to hurt you any more.'

A minute or two pass by in silence before he urges me to my feet. Manoeuvring me over to the window, he pulls the throw away, leaving us faced with our naked reflections, perfectly clear in the darkened glass.

'Look at yourself,' he breathes.

I just want to shrink, but he doesn't let me. Instead, he holds me firmly against his chest, encouraging my chin up so that I'm looking at my own body.

'You're a beautiful woman, Maya Scotton. You need to see that. You need to understand it. You've bewitched me with your intelligence, your humour, your spirit, your talent. Take this all in because it's true. And I know you don't believe it.'

I sense the beginnings of tears.

'Don't cry,' he warns me. 'Don't you dare cry. If you want to know how to finish off that picture, then put me in the middle, but face me away from the pain. I don't want to hurt you any more because you don't deserve to be hurt. Nobody does.' I catch sight of a smile. 'You deserve to be loved.'

Chapter Twenty-Four

I've taken the time to watch him sleeping, happy to see him peaceful, and now I want to send him a message in exactly the way he understands. Organised in strict alphabetical order, my paltry collection of CDs has been added to his, and I know exactly which song I'm looking for. Locating the album, I load it and press random buttons until the display tells me I'm heading in the right direction. I take it to the beginning of the song, ratchet up the volume, open the windows and take my place on the terrace, waiting.

And as I wait, I listen. And as I listen, the song seems to bury itself inside me, the words tugging at every particle of my being. It's Eva Cassidy, singing her version of 'True Colors', and the lyric says everything I want to say. I can see into the heart of him now. I know him, accept him and love him for exactly who he is.

When the song comes to an end, I know he's behind me. I turn slowly and find him standing close by, dressed in a pair of joggers and black T-shirt, his hair still ruffled, his features uncertain. Without hesitation, I step into his arms and feel them close around me. He nuzzles his head into my neck, and says nothing.

'I love you.' Reaching up, I run my fingers through his hair. 'No matter what. I love everything about you.'

'And I love you too.' He pulls back, completely serious, securing his gaze on mine. 'Yesterday was pretty fucked up.'

'For both of us.'

But it seems to have done the trick. This morning, he's calm again. Still tired, but definitely more under control.

'We'll get there,' he whispers with a smile. 'I'll make sure of it.'

'I know you will.'

He closes his eyes. 'What happened last night …'

I lay a finger on his lips. His eyes open.

'It won't happen again,' I inform him. 'From now on, we deal with our shit in different ways.'

I remove the finger and he takes his chance.

'But what I said ... about you.'

'Was right,' I interrupt. 'Don't apologise for making me see the truth.' My bottom lip begins to quiver. I'd better push out my confession quickly, before I crack. 'I wanted pain for all the wrong reasons. You get me.'

He smiles tenderly. 'And you certainly get me.' The smile deepens and I know he's about to try his luck. 'We should get married.'

'Is that a proposal?'

'Could be.'

'But it's not Saturday.'

'Bollocks. What day is it?'

'Tuesday.'

He sighs, and before he can complain, I grab hold of the back of his head and tug him in for a kiss. When I finally release him, he spends a few seconds studying me.

'I need to go into work,' he says at last.

And my brain kicks into life, digging up Clive's words from yesterday: I have a mission.

'You're too tired. Take the day off.'

He sighs again.

'I'd love nothing more, but there are things I need to sort out.'

'But ...'

'But nothing, sweet pea. If I'm going to sell Fosters, it needs to be in a fit state. Trust me, I don't have a choice about this.'

I'm simply not going to win this battle. If he stays at home, he'll only end up an agitated mess. Realising that I've just got to let him go, I cup his face in my hands.

'Then promise you'll be nice to your employees.'

'Of course.' He grins.

'And promise you won't work too late.'

'Promise.' He nods. 'And promise *me* you'll behave with your bodyguard.'

'Promise.' And seeing as I've got Beefy back, that won't be too difficult. 'I'm just going to paint. There'll be no drama today.'

'Thank fuck for that.' He lands a gentle kiss on my lips. 'Get on with that triptych. It's going to be something else.'

***

I've started on the right hand side now, gradually luring the face of pleasure out of the shadows, linking it to the left hand panel with undertones of gold and bronze, the occasional touch of red. Stepping back every now and then to check the overall effect, I'm engrossed in a world of colour and form and angles, determined for the symmetry to flow, the light to reflect across all three canvases. I'm musing over the centre panel when my mobile snaps me out of my trance. Putting down the palette and brush, I pick up the phone, disappointed to find that it's my sister. I'm half tempted to let it ring off, but my old friend, guilt, rears its ugly head. I still haven't spoken to her since she last met Dan.

'Sara.'

'How's things?' she asks, her words slightly slurred, her tone overly-chirpy.

'Fine.' Wishing that I could just dive back into my own little world, I stare at the canvas.

'I'm in London,' she announces.

Oh great. And she's already had one too many by the sounds of things, and that can only mean one thing: she'll be wanting to meet up for a sisterly chat.

'What are you doing down here?'

'The kids are at Mum's for a few days. I needed some space. I'm staying in a hotel. Can we meet up?'

And there we go. Completely as expected. My brain stirs into action, desperate to find an excuse, but it doesn't get far. My better side quickly takes the helm.

'Of course. Where are you?'

'In the hotel bar, getting pissed. Come and join me. We'll have fun.'

I seriously doubt that. I'm just not in the mood for a shed load of wine and a protracted session. The painting's calling to me and if I get no more done today, then I want to be in a decent state to crack on with it tomorrow. A hangover's out of the question.

'Come down to the apartment,' I suggest.

'What apartment?'

'Dan's apartment.' I hesitate. 'Well, it's mine too ... sort of. I mean, I've moved in with him.'

There's a silence.

'Moved in?' she asks, perplexed. 'Isn't that a bit quick?'

'Maybe. But it's what I want. Get a taxi down here.'

Another silence.

'I can't.'

'Why not?

'You know our history.'

Of course I know their history. There's no way of telling what's going to kick off between these two when they get together again. But it's not going to happen. At least not yet. I'll see to that.

'He's at work. He won't be back for ages.'

I listen to the sound of my sister's breathing. It's shallow, uneven.

'I can't,' she mutters at last. 'I just can't. I haven't got enough money. And besides, I'm on my ... er ... second bottle of wine. Come and see me here. Please. I want to talk.'

At this point, I could simply say 'no'. I could put her firmly in her place. 'You can't just turn up out of the blue, get wasted in a hotel bar and demand that I join you.' But then again, I remind myself, this is my sister all over: always wanting her own way, and usually getting it. I'm about to give in to her demands, and I know it. After all, why change the habit of a lifetime?

'Where are you?' I ask.

'Some dive in Bayswater. Seaton's. It's just off the Queensway.'

And by the sound of it, she's more than halfway through the second bottle.

'Stay where you are. I'm on my way.'

With a resigned sigh, I say goodbye to painting for the day. Grabbing a quick shower, I change into a pair of jeans and a Harrods blouse, ruffle my hair, apply a smattering of make-up and I'm ready.

I find Beefy in the lobby.

'Come on.' I wave my handbag as I close the front door.

He rises to his feet, a look of pure terror in his eyes. 'Not another drive?' he asks.

'No, even worse.' I take in a deep breath. 'We're going to meet my sister.'

Deciding that it's best to leave the Jag in the garage, I ask the concierge to call a taxi and before long, we're taking a ride in the back of a black cab. Under a blanket of cloud, we cross the river and thread our way past Whitehall, Trafalgar Square and Hyde Park, eventually slowing to a crawl in a litter-strewn back street and pulling up outside what seems to be nothing more than a dilapidated townhouse.

'Jesus.' I hand over a twenty to the taxi driver. 'She's gone really up-market this time.'

With Beefy following on behind, I get out of the taxi, take the steps, open the front door and find myself in a musty hallway. Straight ahead, there's nothing more than a deserted reception desk, crammed into a space under the stair case, while to the left a set of glass doors lead into the bar.

'Beefy, can you just wait outside?' I ask. 'I'm sure I'll be perfectly safe.'

He glances round and nods. I watch him go before I make my way through the doors into a ramshackle, neglected mess of a place, crammed with a jumble of mismatched stools and tables. It's empty … apart from my sister. Perched on a stool at the end of the room, she's sitting at a table by an unmanned bar. Drawing up another stool, I sit next to her.

She looks up, her hair a tangle, her eyes unfocussed.

'You're here,' she smiles. 'I'm on my third bottle now.'

'So, you can afford wine in a hotel, but you can't afford a taxi?'

'I don't want to go to Dan's place,' she slurs. 'And now I can't walk very far.' She lets off a thick, drunken laugh. 'Have a drink.' She nudges the bottle towards me.

I shake my head.

'No thanks. And you need to slow down.'

While Sara wobbles about on her seat, I move the glass away from her, noting in the process that it's smeared with lipstick that belongs to someone else.

'I can't stay long,' I announce. 'Have you got a room here tonight?'

She nods: a child-like, over-exaggerated nod.

'Maybe you should just go upstairs and sleep it off.'

'Nah, I'm enjoying myself too much.'

'You don't look like you're enjoying yourself.'

'So, what do I look like then?' Narrowing her eyes until they're nothing more than tiny slits, she scowls at me.

'Do you want me to be honest?'

'Yes please, Mrs look-at-me-in-my-posh-clothes.'

'Don't start.'

She leans forwards and tugs at the top. 'Did he buy you that? Mr Money Bags?'

'What's got into you?'

Leaning back again, she almost falls off the stool. Saving herself just in time, she swipes her hand across the table, grabs the glass of wine and takes a huge swig.

'It's alright for some.'

'It's been alright for you for the past ten years,' I sneer.

'And now it isn't,' she sneers back. 'Did you know Geoff's buggered off with another woman?'

'Already?'

'Already. And he's not having anything to do with the kids.'

'Then slam him for maintenance and be done with it.'

She lets off a laugh, and I'm glad there's no one else around because it's a bloody loud one.

'Maintenance?' she cackles. 'He hasn't got any fucking money. His sodding business went down the pan months ago. And did he tell me that?' She taps her chest, swaying again. 'No. And the house? That's being ... what's the word?'

'Repossessed?'

'That's the one.' She laughs again. 'I'm up shit creek without a ...' She looks at the ceiling for inspiration.

'Paddle,' I help her out.

'So, things are crap,' she drawls, 'and I thought I could see my little sister and have a nice chat, and I could tell her all my crap, and she could listen and be all sympathetic and help me out.' She slams to a halt, trying her best to sit up straight. 'And anyway, where have you been? You've not been answering your phone.'

'I've been away for a couple of days. Out of the country.'

'Ooh, anywhere nice?'

'Bermuda.'

Her eyes widen. She leans forwards again, smiling almost benignly.

'Look at little Maya, falling right on her feet with a rich, sexy man.' And now her expression morphs, any hint of kindness banished from the grin. 'It's just a shame he lied to you.'

'Knock it on the head,' I snarl, eyeing up the doorway. I've been here for less than five minutes and I'm already thinking about leaving. 'That's all sorted, so you can drop it. Focus on your own car crash of a life and leave me alone.'

'My life isn't a car crash,' she hisses. 'I've met someone.'

Thoroughly stunned, I sit bolt upright.

'Have you?'

'Yeah.' Self-satisfaction staggers briefly across her face. 'He's lovely.'

'But you've only just split up with Geoff.'

'And?'

'Where did you meet him?'

'In Oxford.' She shrugs, turning the glass on the table, leaving a dribble of wine in its wake. 'Supermarket. Car park. He bumped into my car and asked me out.'

Immediately, I'm on guard. For a start, it's not every day Sara gets chatted up in a supermarket car park. And what with everything else that's happened recently, I'm not about to simply fob it off as coincidence.

'What's he like?' I demand.

'Tall.' Her eyes glaze over. 'Meaty, lovely dark hair. Brown eyes. Really nice brown eyes.' She giggles. 'And he's probably got a massive cock, but I haven't seen it yet.'

I shift about on my seat and glance at the door. Sara's description of her mystery man is far too familiar for comfort.

'What's his name?'

'Name?'

'Name. Tell me.'

Confusion creeps into her eyes. 'James. He's got a lovely voice.'

'Scottish?'

'What?'

'Is he Scottish?' I snap.

'No, silly.' She chortles. 'Why are you asking that? He's English. He lives in Oxford. But ...' She touches the side of her nose. 'He's married. I'm his fancy woman. Or I would have been if he'd turned up.' She waves a hand at the bar.

'Turned up here?'

Suddenly, things just don't seem right. The hairs on the back of my neck bristle with electricity. I scan the empty room.

'Here.' She prods the table with her index finger. 'He was supposed to meet me here. We've got a room together so we can ... you know.' She smiles, a sugary sweet, drunk as a skunk smile. And then the sweetness dissolves. 'But he's chickened out, the bastard. Left me a message.' She goes on in a false upper class accent, drunkenly trying to mimic him. 'Something's come up. Have a drink on me. I'll pay for it all. Why don't you just see your sister?'

I freeze. Now why would he say that? Again, I glance at the door. A shaft of sunlight falls through the glass panes. A pair of flies dance in it.

'How does he know about me?' I demand.

'We talked. That's what you do when you go on a date. I told him about my family. He told me about his.'

No, this isn't right at all. Fishing my mobile out of my handbag, I hold it on my lap.

'I don't like this, Sara.'

'What don't you like?'

'This place. You need to come with me.'

'Where are we going?'

'Back to Dan's flat.'

She shakes her head.

'No. I can't talk to him.'

'You don't have to. I can't leave you here. Just go and pack your things.'

'But I've had ...' She squints at the wine glass.

I lean across the table. Things have gone far enough. It's time to bring out my evil twin.

'I don't care if you can't see straight or string a sentence together or walk in a straight line,' I snarl. 'Now, go and get your stuff. You can crawl up the fucking stairs for all I care. Just do it.'

Stunned by the force of my own voice, I sit back, silently amazed that my little outburst seems to have done the job. With a distinct wobble, she staggers to her feet, pushes back her stool and zig-zags towards the door. As soon as she disappears from view, I call Dan.

He answers on the first ring.

'Maya? Is everything alright?'

I close my eyes. Just hearing his voice makes me feel safe.

'No,' I murmur. 'I'm scared. I think ...'

The phone is snatched right out of my hand. Startled, I open my eyes and look up.

Straight into the face of Ian Boyd.

Chapter Twenty-Five

I hear Dan's voice, faint, shouting my name. Ian Boyd smiles at me and raises the mobile to his ear.

'It's okay, Daniel. I've got her. She's fine.'

He ends the call and places the phone on the table. It begins to ring. I see Dan's name. Boyd hits the ignore call icon.

'That's going to get on my nerves,' he says, his tone light-hearted.

The phone begins to ring again. This time he answers it.

'Listen here, Daniel, old boy. Like I said, I've got her. Maya's fine. Don't worry. And I wouldn't bother with the police if I were you. Things can happen. Know what I mean? Now would you be a good little man and stop bothering me?' He ends the call with a smile and drops the phone back onto the table. 'Now. Where was I? Do you think they've got crisps behind that bar? I'm a bit peckish.'

I can barely believe what's happening. I'm sitting in some tawdry dive of a back street bar with Ian Boyd, and he's chatting away as though we're old friends meeting up for a drink. I'm retreating, withdrawing inside my head. This isn't really happening to me. I'm not here. I stare at the carpet, noticing that it's stained, threadbare in places.

'I've got a bodyguard,' I inform him. But really, what's the point? Boyd's sitting right next to me and unless he came down from a bedroom, it's a sure-fire certainty that Beefy's already out of the picture. I just hope he's okay.

'Have you?' He points towards the door. 'Oh, that big idiot out there? No.' He shakes his head contemptuously. 'He's gone.'

In one fell swoop, my bubble bursts. Denial gives way to fear, and fear to panic. Jesus, I hope he doesn't mean what I think he means.

'What have you done to him?'

'Oh, don't worry.' He picks up the wine bottle and examines it. 'A clonk on the head. My boys won't harm him. They'll just drop him off in an alleyway. He'll wake up with a headache, covered in piss.'

While I battle off a severe case of the shakes, Boyd turns slowly, examining his surroundings.

'I could really do with a snack,' he announces. 'I suppose I'll just have to help myself, seeing as the barman's nipped out for an hour.' He winks at me. 'I asked him to give us a little space. Gave him a few quid to spend. The receptionist was the same.'

My breath catches. My stomach reels. With Beefy out of the way and the hotel staff paid to keep a distance, I've got nothing more than a drunken sister for back-up.

'And what about Sara?'

'Oh, her?' He smirks. 'I'm glad you sent her back up to her room. Nice move, that. Far easier to deal with. She's locked in the bathroom. I'm just glad I never had to fuck her.' He sniggers. 'Not a pleasant prospect.' And now he's serious. 'So, are you going to come with me or not?'

The last thing I should do at this moment is give way to anger, but I just can't help it.

'Why the fuck would I go anywhere with you?' I seethe.

'Do I really have to explain?'

'Yes.'

I look at my phone, reminding myself that I may well be in a state, but I need to string this out for as long as I can. By now, Dan should know exactly where I am, but God only knows how long it's going to take him to get across London.

'Because Mr Swanky Pants needs to be taught a lesson,' Boyd grumbles, rubbing his belly.

'I think you've already done that.'

'And, of course, because you and me are meant to be together.'

'We're not meant to be together. I'm with Dan, and that's the way it's going to stay. So you can stop all this nonsense.'

'Nonsense?' He grins at me, his dark eyes flashing.

'Killing his dog,' I remind him with a scowl.

'Aye, well, he was pissing me off, so I thought I'd piss him off in return. Tit for tat. That sort of thing. Never mind, eh? It was only a dog.'

'Only a dog?'

'Aye. A dog.' He purses his lips in disgust. 'I can't stand the fucking things. Never understood the English obsession with them. I prefer the Chinese attitude.' He raises an eyebrow. 'They eat them in China.'

'You're sick.'

'Maybe. And maybe not. Actually, I could eat a dog right now.' A bright smile crosses his face, collapsing almost immediately. He leans forwards, elbows on the table. 'You know, I really thought you'd leave him when you found out about the Italian Job. But, no.' He shakes his head. 'I let you in on the fact that your boyfriend's full of shit, and what do you do? You jump on a plane with him and scoot off out of the country.' He leans back, holding his hands in the air. 'Go figure.'

'You can't break us up.'

'And then ...' Ignoring me, he presses an index finger against the table top. 'Then I have to go to all the trouble of luring the pair of you back to London.' He shakes his head again. 'I could have done without that.'

'What you did to Jodie was wrong.'

'A teenage pothead. She was an easy target.' He shrugs dismissively. 'So, are you ready to go?'

'I'm not going anywhere with you.'

'I've got a car waiting outside.'

'And I'm not getting into it.'

I glance down at the phone. It's still switched on, and it needs to stay that way. When I look back at Boyd, he's scowling at me.

'Now don't be difficult, Maya. Just get in the car. Let me take you away and remind you what you had with me.'

I'd laugh if I wasn't terrified. What I had with Boyd was nothing less than a nightmare, and I'd remind him of that if I thought it would make a scrap of difference, but arguments and reason seem to bounce off this man like raindrops on glass. I need to stall some more.

'Okay,' I murmur. 'But first I need a drink.'

'Oh, Maya.' He gives me a disapproving look, as if I'm a child. 'You're not still knocking it back are you? It's very un-ladylike, you know. I'll cure you of that.'

Biting back the urge to tell him to get stuffed, I force a smile.

'A drink. For old times' sake.'

He stares at me, perplexed.

'And to steady my nerves,' I add for good measure. 'I wasn't really expecting this.'

He shifts his position on the stool.

'There's wine here … and I paid for it.' He picks up Sara's half-finished bottle. 'Cheap shit. No more than she deserves.'

'I need something stronger.'

'A good malt?'

'If you like.'

He rises to his feet and makes his way behind the bar.

I check the door.

'Don't bother,' he smiles. 'You won't get away.' He examines the optics. 'Jesus, this place is the pits.' At last, he pours two glasses of cheap whisky, takes a sip of one and grimaces. 'How about the South of France? Fancy that?'

'For what?'

'Our little getaway.' He disappears for a moment, rummaging beneath the counter. 'Ah, bingo. Dog flavoured crisps!' With a laugh, he straightens up, shoves a packet of crisps into his pocket and comes back to table, brandishing the drinks.

I shake my head. 'I don't know.'

'Oh come on, Maya. You'd like France. It's all smelly cheese and strong coffee.' He puts the whisky down in front of me. 'Before long, you'll forget Mr Swanky Pants and we'll be happy.' Taking his seat, he opens the crisps. 'You'll remember that you love me.'

'I never loved you.' It's the wrong thing to say, but the words arrive too quickly, shooting out of my mouth before I can stop them. 'I can't force myself to love you. I don't love you and I never will.'

He shoves a handful of crisps into his mouth and chews thoughtfully.

'You're in denial,' he says at last, pointing a finger at me. 'We're made for each other. We're meant to be together. Now, drink up.'

With a shaking hand, I pick up the glass. Taking a small sip of whisky, I wince as it burns my throat.

'Faster than that, lady. We've got to make tracks.'

Realising that I'm running out of time, I stare at the carpet again. Perhaps I should just swap stalling for complete non-compliance.

'I'm not coming with you.'

'Oh, yes you are. Drink up.'

'We're not made for each other. We're not meant to be together. I'll never love you. All I feel for you is contempt. You're a sick man and you need to be locked up.'

He stares at me, wide-eyed.

'That was some pretty nasty stuff. You've hurt my feelings.'

'It's the truth. Just leave me alone.'

'I can't do that.' Taking a slug of whisky, he goes on slowly, as if he's trying to convey a simple idea to a moron. 'I'm going to take you with me, and you're going to learn that you're wrong. I'm going to teach you that you're wrong. And I'm going to teach Mr Foster a lesson.'

'You need help.'

'You think I'm a nutcase.' He finishes off his drink. 'Plenty of people do. But they're wrong. I'm just a little different.'

I look down.

'Why don't you give me the benefit of the doubt, Maya?'

'You don't deserve it.'

'And he does?' He takes a crumpled piece of paper from his pocket and smooths it out on the table top. It's a page from a newspaper. I'm not entirely sure which one.

'One of London's most eligible bachelors,' Boyd reads, 'is officially off the market.' I lean forwards, squinting at a creased up photograph, surprised to find that it's me and Dan outside the Savoy. 'Apparently, you're getting married. Fiancée, it says here. Fiancée?'

Maybe I should tell him it's all a massive mistake. But then again, maybe I shouldn't.

'You will not marry that man, Maya.'

'I'll do what I like.'

He slams his fist on the table, causing me to jump almost clean off the stool.

'I won't have it.'

'You need to see a doctor.'

'Doctors. Ridiculous. I can sort myself out.' Pushing back his stool, Boyd gets to his feet and extends a hand across the table.

'I'm not coming with you.'

'You don't have a choice.'

'I always have a choice. And I'm choosing not to come with you.'

And now I see the anger rising in his face, the real man emerging from beneath the façade of jokes and laughter.

'Maya, I'm through with the game playing and the warnings. Come on.'

I pick up my glass, slowly.

'I'm finishing my drink.' I take another tiny sip.

He turns his attention to the mobile, his face wrinkling into a smile.

'Oh, I get it.' He picks up the phone. 'Mr Foster's tracking you on this and you're giving him the time. Clever girl. So, where's he coming from? The big HQ?' He checks his watch. 'Hmm, not that far. We'd better get moving.'

'No.'

'Get up.'

I shake my head, fix my eyes back on the carpet.

'You always were a wilful madam.'

It all happens so quickly. I feel his fingers close around my upper arm and I'm yanked upwards, off the stool. I let out a scream, hoping that it's loud enough to be heard by a passer-by. Immediately, I'm swung round, my back slammed against his chest. An arm clamps tightly across my stomach while a hand covers my mouth. Fear and panic take hold, flipping me into fight mode. Struggling against his grip, I twist my head from side to side until finally, I manage to bite his fingers.

'Behave,' he shouts.

I kick at his shins, as hard as I can, over and over again. He tightens his grip and drags me backwards, out of the bar, through the main door and onto the street. Still kicking and struggling for all I'm worth, I note a black car waiting for us at the kerbside, the back door open, a faceless man standing next to it. And that does it. Full-blown panic. If he gets me into that car, there's no way anyone is going to rescue me. I've got to rescue myself. Boyd's hand is back over my mouth now, and I take my chance. With one almighty effort, I bite clean into his skin.

'Fucking bitch!' He jerks the hand away.

Swinging round in his loosened grip, I bring my knee up to his crotch and ram it home. He lets go of me and doubles over.

And I run.

I'm at the end of the road when I hear the screech of tyres, stopping just in time to brace my hands on the bonnet of a black Mercedes Benz. I register Clive's surprised face, hear the driver's door open, catch the flash of a suit, and then I'm in Dan's arms.

'Where is he?'

I point back up the road.

'There. He's there.'

Only he's not. The car's already pulled away, disappearing out of the road and taking Ian Boyd with it.

And suddenly, I'm overwhelmed. If I'm not very much mistaken, I've just been almost-kidnapped, and that's ridiculous. Things like that don't happen in the real world. But then again, ever since I walked into Daniel Foster's life, the real world seems to have gone crazy. Digging my head into his chest, I do my best to blot out the madness, without much success. A sob works its way up my throat, and then another. Before long, I'm a jittering, weeping shambles.

'My sister. She's in there.' I force out the words between gulps. 'She's in her room. In the bathroom.'

'Which number?'

'I don't know. And Beefy. They got Beefy. I don't know where he is.'

'Clive, go and sort out the mess in there.' Holding me tight with one arm, he motions towards the hotel. 'I'll call Foultons.'

I'm guided to the car, gently lowered into the passenger seat and left for a moment while he makes the call. And then he crouches next to me.

'Did he hurt you?'

I shake my head. 'I hurt him.' I fight back another sob. 'I bit his hand and kneed him in the bollocks.'

He smiles proudly and smooths my hair.

'I wouldn't mess with you.'

I can barely believe he's so calm, but then it strikes me: no matter how he's feeling now, he's playing down the entire situation, trying to keep me under control. Pushing himself up from his haunches, he reaches across and fastens the seatbelt.

'I thought we were going to have no drama today. What happened?'

He crouches back down and watches me, keeping a hand on my arm. Through more sobs, I tell him everything: from Sara's phone call to Boyd dragging me out to the car. He listens to it all, occasionally glancing up the road.

'Listen.' He says quietly when I've finished. 'I need you stay in the apartment for a few days.'

'What are you going to do?'

'I'm not sure yet.'

I'd like to interrogate him further, but Clive returns, holding an overnight bag in one hand and steadying Sara with the other.

'There's no staff around.' He opens the back door and guides my sister into a seat. I hear a muffled hiccough. 'Should we hang around until they show up?'

'What are they going to tell us?' Dan asks. 'They won't put their jobs on the line for the truth. Let's just get back to Lambeth. I need to think.'

***

I slip into a daze during the journey back, aware of Dan checking on me every now and then, of Clive making calls, confirming that

Beefy's been found with nothing more than a mild concussion. When we finally arrive in the garage, Dan ushers me out of the car and waits with me while Clive does his best to rouse Sara, propping her up as she staggers to the lift. Upstairs, I insist that I'm fine, certainly fit enough to put my sister to bed in the guest room. By the time I leave her, she's snoring like a pig, blissfully unaware of the chaos she's just caused. I console myself with the fact that she'll have one hell of a hangover in the morning. As far as I'm concerned, she deserves it.

Downstairs, I join the men at the breakfast bar.

'Are you okay?' Dan touches me on the back.

'Fine.' I let out a jittery breath.

'We'll call the police.' He turns his mobile in his hands. 'Boyd's gone far enough.' He's about to say something else when the phone begins to buzz. He checks the screen, his expression icing over. From where I'm sitting, I can see it's an unknown number.

'Boyd?' I ask.

'I don't know.'

'Put it on speaker.'

He shakes his head. 'If it's him, you shouldn't have to listen.'

'I'm not an idiot, Dan. I told you not to keep me in the dark. Now answer it.'

With a sigh, he complies. Laying the phone on the counter top, he raises an index finger to his lips, warning me to stay silent before he accepts the call.

At first, there's nothing but the sound of breathing. My stomach knots. At last, I hear a voice. The Scottish lilt is unmistakable.

'I'm not happy.'

'And I don't give a shit,' Dan growls. 'How did you get this number?'

'I have my ways. You won't trace this phone, by the way. A stolen mobile is a wonderful thing. Use it once and chuck it in the river. Is Maya there?'

I cringe at the sound of my name coming from that mouth.

'No.' A hand slides across my thigh. 'Why are you calling?'

'I'd just like to make sure we have no outside involvement.'

'Attempted kidnap is a crime.'

'If you say so, Mr Foster.'

'If I say so? You've gone a step too fucking far.'

'But still ... if you know what's good for you.'

Chewing at his bottom lip, Dan glares at the phone. In silence, I watch as the flecks of copper seem to glow in his eyes.

267

'Are you threatening me?' he demands slowly.

'Just giving you some advice.'

'And I'll give you some back,' he snaps. 'This has gone far enough, Boyd. Maya's not interested. She's with me. Get that into your thick head.'

'Marry in haste, repent at leisure.' Boyd laughs. 'And that's some advice for you, Maya.'

Dan's face floods with confusion. I can only guess he hasn't seen the newspaper yet.

'And anyway,' Boyd goes on. 'It's not just about Maya any more. You've been poking your nose into every part of my life, dragging up my past, and I don't like it. I feel violated, Mr Swanky Pants. You've been playing dirty, trying to destroy me.'

'You need to be destroyed.'

'Do you know what he's been up to now, Maya?'

'She's not here.'

Ignoring him, Boyd pushes on.

'Bribery. He's been bribing women to lie about me.'

I turn to Dan, pinning him down with a good glower, wondering what the hell he's been doing, and when he's had a chance to do it. I can only suppose he made a few calls from Bermuda ... behind my back.

'You abused those women.'

'Really, Daniel. You shouldn't believe everything you're told. An old soak of an ex-copper isn't a trustworthy source, believe you me. And not a single one of those women blabbed. Doesn't that tell you something?'

'That they're terrified of you.'

'Or maybe there's nothing to blab about.' Boyd pauses, his breath coming fast and heavy. He's clearly agitated now. 'You need to stop your witch hunt, Mr Foster. It's going nowhere. And another thing, you need to leave my friends alone.'

'You don't have any friends.'

'Oh, yes I do. And you upset them last night, marauding your way through Isaac's lovely little club. That wasn't very gentlemanly. We've seen your true colours now, haven't we, Daniel? I wonder if Maya knows what you're really like. Does she know what you did to that boy? That you threatened an elderly man?'

Both elbows on the counter, Dan lowers his head.

'They're not innocent.'

'Maybe not. But you can't prove a thing. So, you can go to the police if you like and then we'll see what happens. Isaac's ready to press charges, by the way, and so is the feckless kid with the broken nose.'

'I don't care.'

'Really? So, what do you care about then? Or should I say who?'

Another prolonged silence hangs over us before Boyd begins to work his way through a list of the people in our lives, pausing between each sentence, making it perfectly obvious that he's in the know.

'How about the old farties who live at your house? Or the ditzy teenager and her deadbeat mum? How about Clive and his delicious girlfriend, Lucy?'

Dan's fists tighten into balls.

'And how about you come out of the shadows and deal with this face to face?'

Boyd laughs again.

'And how about Maya's family? Or yours? Your two sisters? Or half-sisters, should I say? They both have children, you know. Think about it, Daniel, old boy. Take your nose out of my business, call off your private detectives ... and leave the police out of it.'

The line goes dead.

It's me who speaks first.

'What have you been up to?'

'You heard him.' Shoving back his stool, Dan paces across the kitchen, leans against a work surface and stares at the floor.

'And I want to hear it from you.'

He runs his fingers through his hair. 'We got a few names. Women he'd ...' He can't bring himself to say any more. 'We thought we could get them to talk. But they won't.'

'Boyd told you to back off,' I remind him.

'I know that. I thought we could nail him.'

'You obviously can't.' My thoughts shift. 'And how *does* he have your phone number?'

'No idea.' He shrugs. 'I can't work it out. The bastard's always one step ahead.' He thinks for a minute. 'Maybe we should just go to the police.'

'No,' Clive interrupts. 'You heard what he said. You'll be the one who ends up in prison, not him. And no amount of money's going to keep everyone safe.'

'It's bluster.' Dan scowls.

'And you're prepared to test that out?' Clive demands. 'Just do what he says, Dan. Back off for a while. And do it properly this time. You've got no choice.'

Chapter Twenty-Six

He slipped out of bed at first light. Vaguely conscious of the movement, I sank back off to sleep, dreaming of shadows and darkness and despair.

When I eventually wake again, I lie on the bed, recalling the events of yesterday, eventually remembering that my semi-comatose idiot of a sister is right next door. And that's enough to rouse me. Getting up, I pull on a pair of shorts and a T-shirt, freshen up in the bathroom and make my way downstairs. I find him sitting at the counter, ploughing through a bowl of muesli. Sitting up straight, he beckons me into his embrace.

'Where have you been?' I ask. I'm sounding pathetic and I don't like it.

'What's the matter? Can't my woman survive without me?'

'Your woman can manage perfectly well, thank you.' I punch him in the stomach, making no impact whatsoever. 'Where have you been?'

'Can't you guess?'

I take a few seconds to examine him. Dressed in jogging bottoms and a T-shirt, he's clearly sweaty and flushed in the face.

'Out for a run.' He skims a finger round the hem of my shorts, catching my bare flesh here and there. I tingle inside. 'Life might be a mess, but I've got to stay fit.'

'I hope you took security with you.'

'No. I left security right here. Outside the door.'

'Dan.'

'What?' He pouts.

'You're a target, just like everybody else.'

'Don't be ridiculous.' With a grimace, he takes a sip of coffee. 'Besides, I can handle myself.'

I dig my face into his neck, drinking in his musky smell.

'Mmm. I actually love your sweat. It's all manly. Is that disgusting?'

'Utterly.' He smiles archly. 'If your sister wasn't in bed upstairs, I'd fuck you right now on this breakfast bar.'

'Why don't you chance it?'

We smile at each other like a pair of teenagers, and I'm sure he's about to rise to the challenge when we're disturbed by a slammed door. Peeling myself out of his grasp, I take a seat by his side.

With her hair unkempt and her make-up smudged, my sister stomps down the wooden staircase. Stopping for a split second, she eyes us warily.

'Good morning, Sara.' Dan slides an arm around my back. 'Sobered up?'

'Sort of.' Unsteady on her feet, she slopes over to join us.

While the seconds crawl past in silence, Dan goes back to his breakfast and Sara settles herself down at the opposite side of the counter. I really ought to offer her a cup of tea, but I'm not sure it's a good idea to turn my back on these two. The air's suddenly charged.

'I'm sorry,' she begins. 'For yesterday.'

'Do you actually remember any of it?' I ask.

'Not really. I was supposed to meet James.' She shakes her head and winces. 'But he bailed, and then I called you ... and then I was in a bathroom.'

Finishing his muesli, Dan places his spoon in the empty bowl and stares at it.

'Priceless,' he mutters. 'You nearly destroyed our lives and you're completely oblivious to it all. But that's you all over, isn't it?'

My sister's eyes flick between us.

'I don't understand.'

He bites back a laugh, stands up and takes the bowl over to the sink.

'You'd better tell her, Maya. I'm going for a shower. I can't deal with this.' Returning to the counter, he takes a last sip of coffee, touches his palm against my back and kisses the top of my head. 'I love you.'

And with that, he saunters through to the lounge.

'Dan,' Sara calls out.

He turns and stares at her, his face impassive.

'I'm sorry.'

He hesitates before he answers. 'I heard you the first time.'

'I don't mean for yesterday.'

271

Oh Jesus. What's she playing at now, dragging up a minefield of unresolved issues over breakfast? I hold my breath, watching his face, catching a flash of disbelief, a hint of disgust. God knows what he's about to throw back at her. My stomach turns a cartwheel as his lips part, but when he finally does speak, I'm astonished at his self-control.

'It's all in the past,' he says quietly.

'But ... the things I did ...'

'Aren't worth talking about.' He's about to leave when he seems to have second thoughts. 'We'll be on friendly terms one day, Sara. We have to be.'

He takes to the stairs, disappearing from view.

My sister turns back to me, eyes agog.

'We have to be?' she asks.

'Because we're a couple and that's the way it's going to stay,' I inform her with a significant dollop of pride. And what the hell, I might as well add on the next bit. 'In fact, he wants to marry me.'

Her mouth opens.

'Bloody hell. He doesn't hang around. Have you said yes?'

I smile.

'Not yet.' And then I realise something pretty important, an absolute truth carved in stone. 'But it's going to happen.' And Jesus, I've finally said it out loud. I really am going to marry the big kahuna. 'So ...' I falter, suddenly tangled up in the realisation. 'You'll be his sister-in-law at some point, and you'll need to work things out.' I wave my hand in the air, as if it's going to make things any less confusing. 'Tea?'

Without waiting for an answer, I set about making a brew.

'When are you going home?' I ask, filling the kettle and switching it on. Seeing as Dan's decided to work from home today, I have no intention of letting Sara hang around.

'I've got a train booked for ten.'

'I'll call a taxi for you.'

She says nothing. With my back to her, I prepare the mugs and watch the kettle as it slowly rumbles its way to the boil.

'I could leave later,' she says at last, her tone uncertain. 'I could change the train time. Maybe we could go for a walk?'

'Not an option. I'm confined to quarters.'

'Why?'

I take in a breath. I need to fill her in on the facts. The kettle clicks. I make the tea and take it over to the counter.

'The man you were supposed to meet yesterday,' I begin.

Heaving up an eyebrow, Sara takes a grateful sip of tea.

'He isn't called James. His real name's Ian Boyd. He used you to get to me.'

My words hit her with the full force of a punch to the jaw. She seems to reel. And then she gapes at me, shakes her head, puts down the mug.

'What are you talking about? He's called James. He shops at Tesco's.'

In spite of everything, I can't help but laugh at her ridiculous comment.

'If only.' I smile. 'His name's Ian and I met him in Edinburgh. And I don't think he's ever been in a supermarket.' I take a sip of tea, deciding that it's high time to veer away from glibness. 'I went out with him for a while, but he turned abusive … and I ran away.'

'Ran away?'

'That was the reason I came down to London. I needed to lie low. And it worked for a while … but now he's found me again. He used you, Sara. I have no idea how he tracked you down, but he used you to get me into that hotel.'

She raises the mug to her mouth, clearly struggling to take it all in. And now for the crunch.

'And while you were locked in the bathroom … he tried to kidnap me.'

I watch in amazement as a spray of tea splatters across the worktop.

'Are you kidding me?' she gasps. 'Kidnap? Nobody gets kidnapped … not really.'

'That's what I thought.' I give her my best sarcastic smile. 'But it turns out they do. Boyd's obsessive, unbalanced – to say the least. He tried to get me into his car. Dan turned up just in time.'

'Shit. What?' She wipes tea away from her chin. 'I hope you called the police.'

'No.'

'Maya! If he tried to drag you off …'

'It's complicated.' Suddenly obsessing over Boyd's threats, my brain shifts into panic mode. Maybe I've revealed too much already. 'We can't get the police involved. And I don't want you to say anything to anybody.'

'But Mum and Dad need to know.'

'No, they don't.' We glare at each other. 'I'm serious about this. Promise me you won't say a word. He's made threats.'

'What sort of threats?'

If ever there was a moment for a little editing, then this is it. After all, if I tell her the complete truth, she'll only freak out.

'Dan could get into serious trouble.'

'But what if Boyd comes back?'

'I've got a bodyguard.'

'And what if he comes back for me?' she demands, her voice rising towards hysteria.

'He won't,' I lie. 'He's had his use out of you.'

Chewing furiously at her bottom lip, she drifts off into thought.

'Maybe I should go and stay with Mum and Dad for a while,' she suggests at last. 'Just to be on the safe side.'

'If it makes you feel any better.' I smile, doing my best to reassure her. 'But it's me and Dan he's after. You're not in any danger.'

'And you are?'

'As long as you stay quiet about this, I'll be fine.'

She stares at me, dumbstruck, swallowing a few times before she finally, and quite inevitably, dips her toes in the pool of self-pity.

'I feel like an idiot. I thought he was interested in me. I believed him.'

'Don't beat yourself up about it. He can put on a good act.'

She hangs her head. Her shoulders sink.

'I'm a mess,' she goes on, clearly happy with the temperature and taking the plunge. 'I can't believe what I did yesterday. My marriage is a wreck. My kids are a nightmare. My sister hates me. Her boyfriend hates me.'

Fantastic. She's gone right in at the deep end, and now I'm going to have to console her.

'We don't hate you.'

'You might not, but he does. And I deserve it. I've been bloody awful to both of you.'

Dan's words echo in my ears. *Tell her. Tell her what she did to you.* Deciding that I'm going no further with the sympathy, I summon up every last scrap of courage. This is the moment for action.

'You're right.'

As soon as I close my mouth, I get the desired reaction. She raises her head, makes eye contact and waits for me to confirm all the things we've tried to forget. And by confirming them, I'll bring them back to life. We'll have to acknowledge them, live with them and deal with them.

'What you did to Dan is between you and him,' I go on. 'But I can tell you what you did to me. You took every opportunity to let me know I was useless, every opportunity to ridicule me and make me look like an idiot. And because of you, I had no self-confidence, no friends. Because of you, I felt worthless.'

And there you have it. Done and dusted.

I'm half expecting her to deny it all, to refute my claims. Instead, she gazes at me and I can practically see the regret in her eyes.

'And now?' she asks. 'Is that how you feel now?'

'A little.' I pause. 'But Dan's undoing the damage. Bit by bit. Because he understands.'

Hands clasped, she lowers her head, slumping towards the counter top. And I give a jolt, surprised to find that Dan's standing right behind her. I'd let my sister know he's here, but he shakes his head. Whatever she's about to say, he wants to hear it too.

At last, a whispered confession trickles out into the quiet. Slow. Punctuated by silences.

'I've thought about it a lot. Why I was like that. Why I did those things. I don't really know why I went so far. All I know is I was fucked up. Spoilt. Before you came along, Mum and Dad gave me everything. I was the centre of attention for nine years. I had them wrapped around my little finger.' She stops for a moment, taking in one jagged breath after another. 'I'm not trying to blame them. I'm just trying to explain. I don't even know if I'm right, but it's the only thing I can think of. I suppose I got used to it. I was Queen Bee at home and Queen Bee at school, right from the start. I got my way. I never stopped to think how I made people feel. It didn't matter to me. And then you came along, and Dad lost his job. I didn't have much to fall back on. I wasn't bright like you. I didn't have any talent. I didn't have anything really.' With a sigh, she finally comes to her conclusion. 'I suppose I made other people miserable to stop myself from feeling small.'

I've heard enough. I lay a hand on her arm.

'You don't have to go on.'

I catch sight of Dan. He shakes his head again.

'Nobody liked me, Maya. I know that. I just manipulated people, scared them.' She looks up with a wry smile. 'I guess I'm like your Mr Boyd.'

'Don't say that. You're nothing like him. He has no conscience.'

'And I do?'

'Well look at you now.' I smile back at her. 'I think you're sorry.'

She nods.

'And you're lucky,' she goes on wistfully. 'You're beautiful and talented. You have the most amazing man in your life. And he loves you. You deserve that. I hope you do marry him. You'd be an idiot not to.'

'And here he is,' I announce breezily. I can't have him listening in to any more of that marriage stuff.

Sara turns. 'How much of that did you hear?'

'Enough.'

Rotating slowly and following his every move, she watches him carefully as he comes to stand by my side.

'You'd better call for that taxi, Maya,' she mutters.

'No need,' Dan interrupts, touching me on the arm. 'I'll take Sara back to the station.'

'What?' she splutters, confused by the sudden change of plan. 'Are you sure?'

'Absolutely.' He gives me a gentle smile. 'Let's get working on those friendly terms.'

'I don't know.' Sara shakes her head.

'I do,' Dan insists. 'It's called fast-tracking.'

***

Almost two hours later, I'm still waiting for his return. Standing in front of the triptych with my mobile in my hand, I'd love to get back to painting ... but I can't. Partly consumed by thoughts of what might be kicking off between Dan and Sara, and partly fretting over the text I've just received, I can barely concentrate on anything. Half wishing I'd never gone back to Limmingham, I read over the text again.

I'd really like to come down and see Dan. It's important. Can you help?

Of course I can help. But should I? I know she's desperate to meet up with her brother, but what with everything else going on in his life, is he really in a position to see Layla? Hearing a movement behind me, I turn to find him seated on the sofa, legs crossed, gazing at me.

'How did it go?' I ask tentatively, shoving the phone into my pocket.

'Fine.' He twiddles the car keys. 'She made it safely onto her train.'

'That's not what I mean. Did you talk?'

'Yes.'

'And?'

'Fine.' He blinks, as if he can't quite believe what he's saying. 'We're fine.'

I'd love to grill him for details, but even I know there are sections of his life he needs to keep to himself.

He stands and stretches. 'I really need to get some work done now, but I'll be finished by six. And then I'm thinking food, film and fuck. How does that sound?'

'Fantastic,' I grin.

'Then it's a plan,' he grins back.

I point at the triptych. 'I'll get on with this.'

I waver, wondering if I really should throw out the next question. But I just can't help it.

'You've forgiven her then?'

The grin fades.

'We've made a start.'

'Well ...' I venture, my voice giving way to nerves. I'm thinking of that text again. 'If you can do it with my sister, I'm sure you can do the same with your own.'

His eyes flicker with thought. He nods slightly.

'I'm sure I can.'

Chapter Twenty-Seven

It's been three days since Boyd's last appearance. Three whole days of relative peace. While Dan's returned to work, leaving me with a clutch of bodyguards, I've busied myself on the paintings. And by night, in between the endless love making, we've settled into the routine of cohabitation, slowly shaping ourselves to each other, fitting together the jigsaw of two separate lives and discovering along the way that the pieces fit just fine. And so, with things settling down, I'm finally seeing more of the world to come, and the more I see, the more I love it. By Friday, if it wasn't for the constant presence of bulky men outside the front door, I could kid myself that life has slid into some sort of normality.

***

I'm in the studio, staring at the image in front of me, satisfied that I've managed to unlock the key to the centre panel, with Dan's help. I'm gazing at the outline of a man, no one in particular to the casual observer ... but not to me. I know his body so well. From memory, I've captured the definition of his neck, the slope of his shoulders, the power of his upper arms. But I've kept his face in the shadows, his features indistinguishable. Turning his back on the pain and angling his head to the left, this is Daniel Foster in all his glory. I let out a quiet breath of satisfaction. Over the last week, I've made good progress with the triptych, tying the three pictures together with light and colour, and now I can move on to the finer details. Picking up a palette knife, I focus in on his face, wondering exactly how I'm going to define his expression.

I'm drifting away in a world of possibilities when a buzzing sound interferes with my concentration. At first, I do my best to ignore it, but it's persistent. Putting down the knife, I make my way downstairs, tracing the source of the noise to the intercom. I press a button on the unit, thankfully the right one, and the concierge's disembodied voice greets me.

'Miss Scotton. There's somebody here to see you.'

I blink at the intercom, confused. I'm certainly not expecting anyone. I check the clock on the oven. It's just after four. So, maybe it's Lucy. Seeing as it's Friday, she's probably left work early, and now she's swinging by on her way to see Clive.

'Who is it?'

'Layla Keene.'

At first, I'm thrown by the surname. It takes me a few seconds to register the fact that Dan's sister is waiting for me downstairs, a few more seconds before tremors of anxiety begin to pass right through me.

'Layla?' And now I gaze at the intercom, totally bewildered.

Since her first text, we've been in touch but no arrangements have been made. Over and over again, I've reassured her that I've been waiting for the right moment to broach the subject of a reunion with Dan, and as yet that moment simply hasn't arrived.

'I'll be down in a minute.'

Collecting my keys, I tug open the front door and find an unexpected surprise outside: stuffed into a chair and staring straight ahead at the lift, it's Beefy.

'You're back!'

'I am.' His big face screws up into a smile, and then he stands, looming over me. I just want to throw my arms around him and give him a hug, but that would be totally inappropriate.

'How are you doing?'

'Good. The head's all better.' He knocks his knuckles against his skull.

'Glad to hear it. I'm sorry about what happened.'

'It's not your fault. There were two of them. Big buggers.'

'So, it's just you today?' I don't even know why I'm asking. Ever since Boyd's last appearance, the bodyguards have been steadily growing in number.

He shakes his head. 'There's another bloke in the lobby. One more outside.'

'Jesus, this must be costing a bomb.'

'It's just prudent, miss.'

'Of course,' I smile, wondering how to word the next bit. 'Listen, Beefy. I've got a visitor, and I really don't want you to tell Dan about her.'

He frowns.

'But I need to fill him in on everything.'

'Not this, you don't. It's his sister.'

'I still have to ...'

'No, you don't,' I cut in, thinking on my feet. 'We're planning a surprise for him and if you let on, it's going to ruin everything.'

His lips pucker.

'And you'd better let the other two know,' I press on. 'They're not to say a word.'

'I'm not sure about that ....'

He digs into his pocket, searching for his mobile, probably with the aim of texting Dan. Keep calm, I tell myself, holding out a hand.

'Seriously, Beefy. What harm can it do?'

'I don't want to get sacked again.'

'You won't.' I nearly choke on my own words. After all, I may well be talking a load of bollocks. The beef monster huffs and puffs. And then he sighs.

'Alright then.'

Relief floods through me.

'Thank you. I'll pay you back. I promise.'

As I ride the lift, the tremors grow in force. Mentally, I skim back through the texts we've exchanged over the last few days: Layla increasingly eager to see her brother; me gently reassuring her that I'm waiting for the right time. But now, from her end at least, the waiting seems to be over. We've reached a crisis point, and if I'd been thinking clearly, I would have seen it coming. The door slides open and I make my way out into the lobby.

Bleary-eyed, Layla rises from her seat and launches straight into an apology.

'I'm sorry, Maya. I should have let you know but I thought you'd put me off, and I needed to come.'

I glance at the bodyguard, the concierge, and then smile at Layla.

'It's okay. Come up to the apartment. We'll talk.'

After delivering a strict warning to the men that Mr Foster is to know nothing about my visitor, we take the lift in silence. On the way back into the apartment, I shake my head at Beefy for good measure.

'Have a seat.' I motion towards the breakfast bar.

Taking off her jacket, Layla positions herself on a stool.

'Wow.' She surveys the lower floor of the apartment. 'This is amazing. He really has made it, hasn't he?'

'He's done alright,' I agree, sitting opposite her.

'I'm proud of him.' She pauses. 'And I'm glad he's got you.'

But for how much longer will he want me when he finds out I've been meddling behind his back? Suddenly, I'm hit by the enormity of it all. If Dan comes home to his sister, I risk losing the best thing I've ever had in my life. And if I'd never gone back to Limmingham, I wouldn't be in this pickle. Jesus, I'm an idiot.

'So, what's brought you here?'

She swallows, fresh tears glistening in her eyes.

'You know what I said about time? I don't know how much we've got.' She gulps in a breath. 'Sophie's been diagnosed with cancer.'

Oh shit.

'I'm so sorry.'

She shakes her head.

'Breast cancer. Early stage. Her odds are good, but it's freaked me out … and it's freaked her out too. She's a single mum. She's got a little girl.'

I fumble for something to say, and find nothing.

'I should have called,' she goes on. 'I only found out this morning, and I just …' The tears tumble down her cheeks.

'It's okay.' I reach out and touch her hand.

'You told me to be patient, but I can't be patient, not any more. I need to see him. I need to tell him. I just left the kids with my husband and got on a train.'

'It's fine. Honestly, it's fine,' I lie, glancing back at the clock. Dan promised he'd be home just after five and it's already half four. It's not fine at all.

'It's at times like this when you just have to put things behind you. Sophie wants him back as much as I do.'

My forehead creases. 'But I thought she didn't believe those things about your dad.'

'Denial's a wonderful thing, isn't it?' She smiles. 'It can be your best friend. It can keep you safe, keep you sane.' She pauses. The smile disappears. 'But it's fragile. All it takes is something like this – a shock, a wake-up call – and it all comes crumbling down. She asked me to contact him. I couldn't refuse.'

'And you want to meet him today?'

She nods.

'Layla, I don't know.' I get up and pace across the kitchen. I can barely believe what's happening. Just when I thought I'd manage to regain some control over my life, it's being snatched away. The tremors evolve, threatening to give way to a full-blown quake. 'If you'd told me, I could have paved the way. I could have talked him into another meeting.'

'Sophie can't wait. She's desperate.'

And so am I.

'A week,' I beg. 'Just give me a week.'

'It wouldn't make any difference,' Layla states flatly, her eyes brimming with despair. 'We both know that. He doesn't really want to see me. You'll never talk him into it.'

'I can,' I insist. 'I've already made progress. I just can't rush him.'

Especially right now, not with Boyd's shadow still hanging over us.

'You're not really making progress, Maya. If you're being honest with yourself, you'll admit that. He'll never agree to meet me. This is the only way. I meet him here. I just need enough time to tell him what's going on, face to face.'

I run a hand over my forehead and stare into space. I understand what she's saying, I really do, but if I go along with this, I'll be dicing with danger.

'You could go to Fosters,' I suggest, knowing it's already too late. 'He's leaving at five. You could catch him there.'

'No,' she says, utterly determined now. 'After last time, I don't think they'd even let me in.'

'But here? You can't see him here.'

'Yes, I can.' Finally, she seems to pick up on my panic. 'He doesn't need to know we've been in touch, Maya. Just make out that I turned up out of the blue. Blame me. I've got nothing left to lose.'

Gazing at the clock, I run through the alternatives in my mind and as far as I can see, there's only one. I could ask her to leave, but that would be pointless. She'd only end up hanging around on the street. And even though she may not be his favourite person, I can't treat Dan's sister like that. There are no two ways about it: I'm up to my neck in shit ... and there's no escape.

'Okay,' I murmur.

She watches me for a moment.

'You've never been on the wrong side of him, have you?'

No, I've not. But now that Layla's here, there's a distinct possibility I'm going to experience it tonight ... and it could change things between us forever. Out of nowhere, nausea grabs hold of my stomach, swinging about the contents with wild abandon.

'If he does kick off, he'll calm down eventually,' I offer, reassuring myself now, or at least trying to. 'And then he'll see sense, and you two can talk. It'll be fine.'

With an uncertain nod, Layla shifts from the stool and wanders through to the living area. Making straight for the windows, she takes in the view of the Thames, and then she turns, catching sight of the paintings that line the room, focussing eventually on the picture above the fireplace

'Limmingham.' Feeling like a condemned woman, I join her. 'I painted it.'

'You?' Her eyes widen. 'It's wonderful.'

'It's the woods. The ones down near the beach. I painted this before I knew about Dan.'

'It's funny you should choose that place.' She doesn't need to say any more. We both know the local legend. The murdered boy. The ghost. 'It's like you're meant for each other.'

We are, and I know that now. We're totally meant for each other. And if we can get through this little episode in one piece, then I'm going to get a ring on his finger before he can blink an eye. I'm never going to risk losing him again.

'I remember you,' Layla smiles. 'I used to see you playing out on the front when you were young. A lovely little thing. You seemed to get more miserable as you got older.'

I feel myself baulk. She's completely right, of course, but I never thought it was that obvious.

'I suppose ...' She hesitates, looks at me and then turns back to the picture, as if she's really not sure whether to go on or not. 'Your sister couldn't have been easy to live with.'

'She wasn't,' I confirm. 'But we're okay now. She's changed.'

'Has Dan met her?'

'Yes.'

She gives me a look of disbelief. 'I know how she treated him,' she explains. 'Everyone knew.'

'And I'm not excusing her, but we're adults now. They've met a few times. At first it didn't go too well, but they're trying. I'm sure they'll get there one day.'

'Well, if he can do that with Sara,' Layla muses, echoing my own thoughts, 'then I'm sure there's hope for me.'

***

I check the clock. Twenty to five. To steady the nerves, I pour us both a glass of wine. To pass the time, we settle down to a few minutes of half-hearted small talk. Layla tells me about her husband and children, a little about Sophie, how she moved to Wales, cutting all ties until her life began to fall apart. And then we move on to me. I take her through a summary of my life, from Limmingham to Dan. And all the time, I keep my eye on that bloody clock, watching as the minutes sneak past.

'You should wait upstairs,' I say at last.

Her forehead creases.

'In my studio. If he sees you as soon as he walks through the door, he'll be off again. I'll get him to take a shower. I'll lock the front door and hide his keys.'

'Hide his keys?'

'A precaution. That way, he can't run.'

'But locking him in?'

'He's done it to me.'

Fuelled by a last minute dose of nerves, she gets up and looks at the door.

'I can't do this.'

I hold out a hand.

'It's too late now. He'll either bump into you in the lift, or see you out on the street.'

'But it's going to be ugly.'

'He's your brother,' I remind her, amazed at my sudden attack of resolve. 'You need him in your life and he needs you too, whether he knows it or not. We're going to sort this out together.'

I lead her up to the studio and leave her on the sofa. As I make my way back downstairs, my heart thuds, my stomach flips over on itself and my legs threaten to collapse. Coming to a halt by the window, I look out at the grey skies and will my body to behave. Big Ben's clock face tells me it's a quarter past five. I ruffle my hair, grab a cushion and lie down on the sofa. I've barely got myself into position when I hear the key in the lock. Holding my breath, I listen as the door opens, clicks to a close, and he places his briefcase and keys on the counter top.

I sit up slowly.

'Hi.'

'Hi back,' he smiles. 'What have you been up to?'

'I've just had a nap. I've been painting most of the day.'

'Shall I take a look?'

He motions to the stairs and I panic.

'No. No. I don't want you to see it yet. I'm not sure about it.'

Pushing myself up from the sofa, I make my way over to him, waiting for him to take off his jacket before I step into his arms. And oh God, I feel like Judas.

'Jesus, what a day,' he grumbles into my neck. 'I need some serious de-stressing.'

'What's been going on?'

'The usual. Negotiations. Problems. I've got a site visit on Monday. There's an issue down the river, one of those complexes.'

'It'll be fine.'

He draws away, smiling broadly. 'At least I'm here with you now. I'm going to forget it all, drink some wine and fuck you good and proper.' And then he frowns, clearly picking up on my unease. 'Are you okay?'

'I'm fine.'

'Are you sure? You're shaking.'

'It's your effect on me,' I lie. 'Go and take a shower. I'll make a start on dinner.'

'Dinner?' He laughs. 'You? No way. We'll order something in.'

He kisses me gently.

'Shower,' I whisper, touching a finger against his chest. 'Now.'

I wait for him to disappear into the bedroom before I set about my preparations. Grabbing the keys, I hide them in a drawer, adding my own set after I've locked the front door. And then I make my way upstairs, silently urging Layla to follow me back down. Within a couple of minutes, we're seated on the sofas: Layla facing the window, me facing the stairs. Eyes locked and imprisoned in a silent mutual panic, we wait.

At last, I hear the slam of a door, his unknowing movements upstairs. And then footsteps. He appears at the top of the staircase. With his hair still wet, he's thrown on a pair of jeans and a black T-shirt. Expecting nothing, he begins to descend and as he moves, he slows, noticing the figure on the sofa. His face clouds. He falters half way down, holding onto the bannister, and then moves again. Slowly, warily, like a cat on the prowl, his body tensing.

Unwilling to wait any longer, Layla gets to her feet and turns.

'Dan?' Her voice wavers.

He doesn't answer. Silence lies heavy in the air. At last, he moves again. Blanking both of us, he simply walks into the kitchen and helps himself to a bottle of water from the fridge. Facing away, his shoulders hunched, he takes a sip.

I get up from the sofa.

Sensing a crackle in the air, a charge of electricity that seems to grow with every faltering step I take, I edge towards him.

'Dan?' Don't touch him, I tell myself. Whatever you do, don't touch him. He's on the brink of lashing out.

He takes another swig of water.

'You can't ignore us.'

'Can't I?' he asks, his voice expressionless. 'What's *she* doing here?'

'I came to see you,' Layla explains quickly. 'I've just arrived. Maya knew nothing about this.'

'Really?' He turns, glances at his sister, and from the look on his face, I'd say it's pretty clear he doesn't believe her.

'Really,' she repeats, visibly shaking now.

'And you feel the need to tell me?' He shifts his attention to my face. 'That says a lot.' He surveys the counter. 'I'm sure I'll get the truth out of the concierge.'

'Okay.' While my brain pauses to consider a spot of damage limitation, my mouth seems to have other ideas. I can barely believe it when the entire truth comes tumbling out. 'I looked her up in Limmingham. I got in touch with her but I didn't organise this. I just wanted to make things better.'

'Well,' he says quietly, his eyes darkening. 'You've just made things a whole lot worse.'

I have no idea what that means, and I'm not about to ask for clarification. All I want is to put back the clock and undo my mistakes because my world is juddering beneath me.

'You've kept things from me,' I remind him. 'You've done things behind my back.'

'I've never done anything stupid.'

'Oh really? What about Boyd?'

'What about him?'

'You didn't back off when he told you to.'

'Because I wanted him out of our lives,' he growls. 'You've poked your nose into things that don't concern you.'

'Don't blame her, Dan,' Layla intervenes. Coming forwards, she holds out a hand. 'Maya didn't know I was coming here today. I need to talk to you. Sophie's not well.'

'And I'm not interested,' he sneers. 'Get out of my home.'

I take a step towards him. 'Dan, she's your sister.'

He turns to me, his eyes burning, and I realise he's doing his level best to reign himself in.

'I don't care. Get her out of here.'

'No,' I say firmly. 'You promised. You said you'd get back in touch. You need to talk to her.'

'I don't need to do anything. I want her gone.'

'She's staying.'

'Then I'm going. Where are my keys?'

'I've taken them.'

'Don't fuck with me, Maya.'

Reeling for a moment, I gather my wits and push on.

'You're not going anywhere. I've locked you in.'

He scowls, takes a step forwards, and I flinch.

'Is this your idea of a fucking joke?'

'I should go,' Layla interrupts.

'No.' Without taking my eyes from Dan, I remind her of our pact. 'I told you we'd see this through. And Dan's going nowhere until he's talked to you.'

'I'm not in the mood. Give me my keys.'

His eyes harden. He thrusts a hand towards me. I stand my ground.

'No.'

'Now, Maya!' He fires out the words. 'Give me the fucking keys.'

I shake my head, look down at the hand and realise it's trembling. My eyes travel upwards, taking in the fact that he's tensed, breathing quickly, ready to erupt.

'No.'

And then it happens. In a split second, the self-restraint snaps.

Frozen to the spot, I watch as he turns, kicking at the door over and over again, lashing out like a madman.

'Calm down,' I yell.

Ignoring me, he carries on.

'Just let him out,' Layla pleads. She's by my side now, white-faced and shaking. 'He's going to do himself some damage. Let him out.'

'Okay,' I shout. 'I'll get them!'

It's enough to stop him. Struggling for breath, he rests his forehead against the door before he turns. His eyes meet mine, cold and resolute, and he holds out a hand. I have no choice. Retrieving the keys from the drawer, I hand them over. Without another word, he leaves, slamming the door in his wake.

'Oh God,' I mutter, gazing into space. 'What have I done?'

'Go after him.' Layla's voice stirs me. 'Go after him and sort it out. I'd better leave.'

With tears gathering in my eyes, I give her an apologetic nod before I open the door and run to the lift. Brushing off Beefy's offer of help, and with my heart pounding in my chest, I push the call button and wait. A couple of minutes later, I'm heading for the basement, staring at a pathetic, tear-stained face in the mirrors and wishing I could blot out the last few minutes. But I can't.

When the door finally slides open, I step out into a brightly lit garage and spot him immediately. Down at the far end, he's next to the motorbike, tugging his leathers out of a store cupboard.

'Dan.'

I take a few faltering steps and come to a halt. Either he hasn't heard my voice or he's simply ignoring me, because he doesn't react. Stony-faced, he slips his legs into the leathers and pulls them up to his waist.

'Please don't go,' I sob. 'I'm sorry.'

Rousing myself into action, I take a few more steps. I'm next to him now, so close I could reach out and touch him, but I daren't.

Shrugging his arms into the top section of the suit, he fastens the zip.

'Don't blank me, please.'

With a shake of the head, he nudges his feet into the boots, leans down and buckles them up. It's not the reaction I want, but at least it's a reaction of sorts. Through blurred vision, I watch as he takes the gloves out of the cupboard and rests them on the bike, his face still inscrutable. Whatever's going on inside that brain of his, he's obviously determined to reveal nothing. The mask is firmly in place.

'She's gone. Please come back upstairs.'

He reaches for the helmet and fiddles with the straps.

'How did you find her?' he asks.

I give a jolt. So, he's finally talking to me.

'A birthday card. You left it in the bin.'

'Snooping.'

'You snooped on me.'

At last, I get some eye contact. He glances at me, dismissively, his eyes steely blue.

'You shouldn't have let her stay.'

'She was desperate. And you've got to face your past.'

He shakes his head.

'You had no right.'

'You block it out and you can't go on blocking it out. It's not healthy. You know that and I know that.'

'I don't need amateur fucking psychology.'

'You need something. What happened between you? She doesn't even know what she's done.'

'She's done nothing.'

'So it's you then? You can't face her because she looks like your step-father. You think you hurt her when she came to see you last year ...'

I'm halted by his laughter. It's hard, mocking, hurtful. And it chills me to the core.

'You have no idea,' he snarls.

I stand there, dumbfounded, watching as he puts on the helmet, and then the gloves. I can think of nothing more to say. Swinging his leg over the bike, he turns the key in the ignition.

'Where are you going?'

He looks at me, and I can barely hear his reply above the rumble of the bike.

'Who knows?'

Flicking down the visor, he revs the engine and pulls away, waiting for the garage door to open before he accelerates out onto the road, and takes a right. I listen to the roar of the engine as he speeds off down the embankment. I watch the door slide to a close ... and then I sink to my knees on the concrete floor.

Chapter Twenty-Eight

It's Beefy who pulls me back to my feet.

'You can't stay here all night.'

I stare at him, touch the sweet pea around my neck, and decide to tell him that I just don't care. I *will* stay here all night. In fact, I'll wait for as long as it takes until that garage door opens again, and Dan comes to back to me. But neither my mouth nor my body seem willing to co-operate with my brain. In silence, I'm guided back to the lift, returned to the apartment and gently placed on a sofa. Before long, I hear the familiar sounds of the tea-making ritual.

'There you go.'

A mug appears under my nose.

'Do you know where he is?' I ask, stirring back to life.

I wait for Beefy's answer, desperately hoping that Dan's been in touch.

'No.'

Disappointment spreads through me.

'What's the time?'

'Just after six.'

My mobile. Perhaps he's texted me. Leaving the mug on the coffee table, I shuffle over to the kitchen and dig the phone out of my handbag. One message. From Layla.

So sorry it didn't work out. I'm on my way home now. Let me know what happens.

I crumple back onto the sofa and gaze out of the window, trying to jolt my brain further into some sort of action. I have no idea how long I spend like this, caught up in limbo, watching the evening shadows as they creep across the Thames. It's only when I turn my attention to the picture of Limmingham that the cogs finally begin to turn. Is that where he's gone? Or has he decided to pay a visit to his old club? I shudder at the thought. No, he wouldn't do that. Surely not. No. In all probability, he's down in Surrey, brooding on his own at the house. I glance at my mobile, wondering if I should text him, and quickly decide to leave it. After all, he's clearly in no mood for communication. In the end, I try the only alternative I can think of. I call Lucy.

She answers immediately.

'Yo!' she chirps, full of the joys of spring, oblivious to the chaos in my life. 'How's it going?'

'Not good.' Out of nowhere, a sob escapes from my throat. 'I've had a massive fall-out with Dan. I've been a complete idiot.'

'What have you done?'

I groan. There's no way I want to go into that. I just need to know where he is.

'Is Clive there?'

'Of course. I'm at his house.'

'Can you put him on?'

'Are you alright?'

'Just put him on.'

I hear the sounds of a muted interchange, then Clive's voice takes over.

'Maya?'

The words stumble out through a torrent of tears. Careful not to mention the reason, I inform him that we've had a row, that Dan's taken his bike and disappeared. I tell him that I just need to know where he is, that he's safe. He agrees to make a few calls, promises to get back to me, and he's gone. Wrapped in a fog of anxiety and clutching the phone, I wait for news, giving a start as soon as the ring tone kicks into life.

'I called Norman,' Clive begins.

'Is he at the house?'

'No.'

'So where the hell is he?'

'No idea. I've tried texting him. No reply. I've called Lily. He's not round her place.' He pauses. 'Maybe he's just gone for a ride. What time did he go?'

'A couple of hours ago.'

A brief silence ensues, and I fuddle my way through the new information.

'That's not too long,' Clive reassures me. 'Listen, he's probably just holed up in some biker café.'

Or he *has* gone to the club, and he's at it right now, getting exactly what he needs from another woman. Awful visions cross my mind. Shit, have I really driven him to that? It's the last thing I want to know, but the first thing I need to find out.

'He could be at Isaac's,' I suggest.

'I doubt it. Not after what happened the other day. Was it really that bad?'

'Yes.'

I listen to the sound of breathing. God knows what's going through his mind.

'It's too soon to do anything,' he decides at last. 'Let's wait another couple of hours. If you haven't heard anything by nine, I'll go over to the club and check.'

'You don't need to.'

'Yes, I do. And if he hasn't turned up, I'll come over to Lambeth. Just stay where you are. I'm onto it.'

I settle in for the wait. Accepting a second mug of tea from Beefy, I suggest it's high time for him to knock off, but even though his overnight replacement is already outside the front door, he refuses, opting instead to sit at the counter and busy himself with his mobile.

Within half an hour, I hear the sound of a key in the lock. Fighting off a sudden flash of nerves, I spring to my feet and hold my breath, bracing myself for yet another confrontation. But as soon as the door opens, I realise it's not about to happen. Instead of Dan, I'm greeted by Clive and Lucy.

Ashen-faced, they enter in silence.

'What's going on?' I demand before either of them can squeeze out a word.

Taking hold of my shoulders, Clive looks me in the eyes. He's preparing me for something. I know it. And from the concern on his face, I'd say it's going to be unpleasant.

'Norman called back,' he says gently. 'The police have been to the house.'

My knees threaten to give way beneath me. Thoughts dissolve into panic. I'm steadied by Clive's grip.

'It's Dan,' he explains. And then the words I'm dreading. 'He's had an accident.'

***

I'm moving, constantly moving, but like a faulty radio, I'm lost in a world of distortion. Every now and then, I tune back in: sometimes to reality, sometimes to a flicker of memory. I'm in a car now, staring into the void of a London evening, registering a flash of light, the turn of a head. And then the air buckles. I'm back in his bed, cast adrift in those bright blue eyes but held safe beneath his body, knowing that this is exactly where I'm meant to be. A wave of static disrupts the flow and I'm walking slowly, flanked by others, making my way through endless corridors. In a stupor, I note the vapid green walls and zone out again, disembodied by interference. And then the movement stops.

Gathering my senses, I look around, taking in a waiting room, a mishmash of chairs, a handful of vacant faces. Betty pulls out a handkerchief and holds it. Norman smiles at me, asks me if I'm okay, but I can't reply. My brain has disengaged, retreated in on itself, and I'm incapable of even the most basic response. Glancing down at my hand, I realise it's being held, look up again to find Lucy next to me ... and pull my fingers out of her grasp.

'Is he alive?' I whisper, surprised that my vocal chords have finally managed to function.

'Yes,' she whispers back. 'Clive's trying to find out what's going on.'

And that's all I can handle. I zone out again. I'm sitting in his arms, half-submerged in the sea, feeling his cheek against mine as I gaze up at an azure sky. And now I'm at the top of the lighthouse, taking in the view, grounded by his presence. The minutes unfold like this. It could be ten. It could be twenty. Immersed in a constant slide-show of memories, I'm only wrenched back to reality by Clive's voice.

'Maya?' Anchoring himself on my chair, he crouches in front of me.

I feel my lips move, hear my own voice ask a question: 'What's going on?'

'He's still in surgery.'

'How bad is it?'

'Pretty serious.'

My brain barely registers the information. As if it means nothing at all, I stare blankly back at him.

'So what happened?' Lucy asks.

Clive shakes his head a little.

'All I know is what Norman told me. He was on the motorway. The traffic slowed. He didn't. He went into the back of a car. The air ambulance brought him here.'

Suddenly, my lungs seem to shrink and my breath quickens.

'Will he die?' I ask.

'No.' Clive touches my hand.

But he doesn't believe it. I can tell from his eyes.

One by one, the blank expressions give way to emotion. Betty raises the handkerchief to her mouth and lets out a sob. Norman bites his lip, wraps a consoling arm around his wife's shoulder. Pushing himself back to his feet, Clive turns to the door and lowers his head, probably wiping away a tear. Even Lucy seems to be on the verge of falling to pieces. But me? Nothing. I'm numb. Gazing round at these normal reactions, I wonder why I can't be normal too. The man I love is in trouble, and I can't even cry.

'He'll be fine.' Norman's voice fills the room, trying to reassure us all, and then me in particular. 'Maya, he'll be fine.'

'He will,' Lucy echoes, brushing my arm.

I stare out of the window, into the darkness. I don't know what else to do. Closing my eyes, I zone out again, and I'm at Seven Sisters, held in an endless embrace. And time expands beyond anything familiar, until it means nothing at all.

***

'Maya?'

My name. Someone's saying my name. I open my eyes, blink into the harsh light.

Lucy frowns at me. 'The doctor's here.'

There's a woman in the opposite seat now, dressed in a pair of grey trousers and a blouse, a lanyard around her neck. I hear her ask for confirmation that there's no family. Dismissing Layla and Sophie's existence, Clive gives it. And then I watch as the doctor smiles uneasily, shifts slightly on her chair, leans forwards and launches into an explanation.

Desperate to make sense of what she's saying, I watch her mouth, but my brain's determined to scramble the information. I catch only words, snatches.

'There's been some internal bleeding. We've managed to stop it ... multiple fractures ... right arm ... both wrists ... both legs ... ribs ... collar bone ... his right leg's pretty badly damaged.'

'But he's going to pull through?' Clive asks.

Finally, I manage to concentrate.

'In some respects, he's been incredibly lucky,' the doctor says. 'No neck or spinal injuries. The internal injuries weren't extensive. But ...' She takes a breath and then she's quiet for a moment.

There's something more.

'But what?' Clive demands.

'We're concerned about a swelling on the brain.'

'He was wearing a helmet.'

'Which made a huge difference. But with a collision at this speed, a helmet can never be one hundred percent effective. It could have been a lot worse.' She pauses, catching each one of us with a reassuring smile. 'He's being moved to intensive care. He'll be put into an artificial coma for a few days. It's standard procedure in cases like these. And then we'll monitor him closely.'

I'm picking back over the details of what I've just been told, recalling what I can, when guilt strong-arms its way into my head. Like a loud-mouthed bully, drowning out everything else in the room, it simply refuses to leave. I glance at the familiar faces, realising that they're suddenly loaded with sympathy … and they're all fixed on me. Moving automatically, I get to my feet. All I know is I need to get out of here, away from these people, because I don't want their sympathy, and I certainly don't deserve it. Leaving the waiting room behind, I make my way down a corridor, passing strangers, aware of shadows, shadows everywhere.

'Maya.' Fingers curl around my arm and I'm halted. 'Where are you going?'

I look up into Clive's face.

'I just need some space,' I lie.

He studies me for a moment, and then he wraps me in his arms. It feels wrong and it smells wrong, but this one act of tenderness opens up the flood gates. Before I know it, I'm sobbing into his shirt, pouring out a guilty confession.

'It's all my fault. I caused this.'

He pulls back and examines my face, frowning in confusion.

'The row,' I explain.

'What about it?'

I blink away the tears.

'His sister. Layla.'

'Layla?' The confusion deepens. 'What's happened?'

I blurt out my story, the whole thing this time. Utterly convinced that I'm making no sense at all, I give him the truth, the whole truth and nothing but the truth.

'I should have asked her to leave,' I round off. 'But I couldn't. She was desperate.'

'It's not your fault.'

'It is. You should have seen him, Clive. He was furious. He wasn't thinking straight. That's why he crashed. It's all because of me.'

'Don't,' he says firmly. 'Don't blame yourself. He's been riding bikes for years. Whatever mood he was in, it wouldn't have caused this.'

I shake my head. He's just trying to make me feel better.

'Seriously,' he insists. 'When he's on his bike, he doesn't think about anything. He's told me that before. He just concentrates on the road. That's probably why he took it in the first place. To clear his head. It wouldn't have affected him, I promise you.'

I sob a little more.

'You had good intentions, Maya. You shouldn't blame yourself. You didn't cause this.'

'Then what did?'

His eyes cloud.

'We don't know anything yet. When Dan wakes up, he'll be able to tell us what happened.' He holds my gaze for a few moments before reaching into his pocket and pulling out a handkerchief. He hands it to me. 'Now, clean yourself up and get back in there.' He motions towards the waiting room. 'You'll be able to see him soon ... and he's going to need you.'

***

When the time finally comes, I'm warned to prepare myself and ushered down yet another bland corridor. Clive holds my hand as we make our way through several sets of doors, eventually coming to a halt next to a desk. At the edge of my consciousness, I register a conversation, and then I'm led further into a world of quiet sterility, past beds, medical equipment, machines, until finally we arrive at our destination.

Taking in a few deep breaths, I steady myself as the scene comes into focus. He's flat on his back, head slightly to one side, eyes closed, mouth obscured by tape keeping a tube in place. And there are wires attached to his chest, more tubes slotted in to a cannula on his left hand. And then I notice the bruises. Bruises everywhere. His arms and legs are in splints, no casts as yet, but his right leg seems to have been pinned with rods. My eyes travel back up his body, past the sheet that lies across his groin, the edge of a dressing protruding from the top, past his chest that rises and falls every few seconds, and back to his face. He seems so peaceful, as if he's simply asleep.

I stand absolutely still. Rigid.

'Maya?'

I jolt. 'Can I touch him?'

'Of course.'

Taking a step forwards, I reach out and brush a finger across his hand, stopping where the cannula's been fitted, afraid to hurt him. And then I hear my own words, quietly uttered.

'I love him.'

'I know.'

'He asked me to marry him.' Tears prick at the corners of my eyes. 'I should have said yes.'

'It doesn't matter,' Clive reassures me. 'You can say yes when he wakes up.'

'If he wakes up.'

'He will.' As if he knows what's going through my mind, Clive brushes my arm. 'He's strong, he's a fighter, and he's got you. Sit with him for a while. I'll be in the waiting room.'

He pulls up a chair, looks at Dan, looks at me, and then leaves.

Staring blankly at the man on the bed, I sit down, unsure of what to do. It must be shock, I tell myself, because right now I seem to be faced with a stranger, nothing more than a body: motionless, empty, sensing nothing. I listen to the murmur of conversation behind me, the beeping and whirring of machines, the quiet, rhythmic rush of air through the ventilator. And at last, I find what I'm searching for: the steady beeping of Dan's heart monitor. It tells me he's alive, that he's still with me. And I hold on to it for dear life, silently willing it to continue from one second to the next.

At last, I rouse myself into action. Reaching out, I gently take his hand in mine, careful not to disturb the cannula. His skin is soft and warm. I stroke his palm, hoping he can feel me now, knowing deep down that he can't. And while time dissolves again, and my vision blurs with tears, I tell him I love him, and I tell him I need him. And I tell him I'm sorry.

***

The days bleed into one. A single mass of emptiness and torpor. As time drags its heels, I'm lost in a nowhere land, like a cartoon character hovering in mid-air, waiting for the fall.

By day, I sit at his side, holding his hand, quietly talking about anything and everything that comes to mind, occasionally weeping, mostly gazing at his sleeping face. And he is just sleeping. I tell myself that, over and over again. Every now and then, a doctor checks on his monitors, administers drugs, or a nurse cleans the dressing, adjusts a tube or a bag. But nothing really seems to change. Sometimes I'm with Clive, sometimes with Norman or Betty, once or twice with Lily. I watch as Norman gently touches his palm against Dan's forehead and whispers into his ear, as Betty berates him for ever buying a motorbike, as Clive simply stares down at his friend, lost in thought, or Lily kisses him on the cheek and rearranges his hair. And never once do I call Layla. Her life's already in turmoil, and I just can't add to that.

Back at the apartment, the evenings are regimented by Clive and Lucy. Staying in the guest bedroom, they present me with food and drinks, make sure I take a shower in the morning, prise me off the sofa and guide me to the bedroom when it's time for sleep. But I hardly sleep. Once the door's shut, I lie alone in our bed, wrapped up in sheets that still smell of him. And I cry.

It's the third day when I finally begin to come back to life. I've spent the morning at the hospital, but on Clive's insistence – along with Beefy who's been a constant shadow – we've returned to the apartment for a rest while the doctors run yet another CT scan.

Only I can't rest. He'll be waking soon. I'm sure of it. And he'll need his things. Like an idiot, I pull a gym bag out of his wardrobe and rummage through the drawers, searching for anything he might need. The first thing I look for is pyjamas, but I find none. Of course, I remind myself, womanising sex gods just don't wear pyjamas, even when they're through with womanising. Instead, I stuff a pair of shorts and a T-shirt into the bag. Several pairs of pants, a toothbrush, toothpaste, a shaver and socks follow suit. I'm reaching for a pair of joggers when Clive appears in the doorway.

'I've just rung in,' he smiles. 'More good news.'

Suddenly super-excited, I drop the joggers.

'The CT scan was fine. They've brought him out of the coma.'

'What?' I stare at him, silently annoyed that he dragged me away. I should have been there when he opened his eyes. 'Already? He's awake?'

Clive nods.

'He woke up without me there?'

'Yes.'

'But ...' I stare at the bag and flap my arms.

'Calm down,' he says sternly. 'And he won't be needing that.' He glances at the mad bag, smiling wryly. 'Not yet. Come on. Let's get moving.'

***

With the streets of Central London throwing everything at us – jams, snarl-ups, red lights, the lot – the journey seems to take forever. It's almost two hours later when we eventually pull to a halt in the hospital car park. I'm out of the car in an instant, ready and raring to go but fully aware that I have no idea how to get to intensive care.

'This way,' Clive smiles, touching me on the shoulder.

Bouncing along in a blur of excitement, I follow in his wake, back through the maze of corridors. It's only when I'm sitting by Dan's side that I finally manage to calm down, helped along by my old friend disappointment. I expected him to be sitting up in bed, bright-eyed and bushy-tailed, but he seems exactly the same as the last time I saw him, only now the tube in his mouth has been replaced by oxygen tubes in his nose.

'I'll leave you to talk to him,' Clive says gently. 'I'll be in the waiting room. I'd better let everyone know what's going on.'

As soon as Clive leaves, a nurse arrives at the bedside.

'I thought he'd woken up,' I mutter.

'He did.' She busies herself with changing a bag. 'He asked for you.'

'Me?'

After days in banishment, a smile creeps out of its hiding place. He asked for me. I was the first thing on his mind. But then again, maybe he just wanted to let me know that all is not forgiven. And oh shit, in the midst of all the excitement, I'd forgotten about that.

'Does he remember what happened?' I ask, terrified of the answer.

She shakes her head and relief courses through me.

'He remembers leaving work. That's it. It's quite common for a few hours to be wiped out.' Checking the connections, she nods to herself, apparently satisfied. 'Anyway, he's been filled in on everything. The accident. His injuries.'

'How did he react?'

'A little shocked.' She folds her arms and gazes at me. 'But the main thing is, he's doing well. He'll probably be moved out of intensive care today. He's sleeping now.' She gives me a sympathetic look. 'Why don't you just hold his hand? Talk to him. He'll wake up again soon.'

Left alone, I take a while to move. Gazing at his face, I reach out and touch his cheek, gently stroking my finger across a three-day growth of beard.

'I love you,' I whisper. 'And I will marry you. I hope you can hear that because it's a yes.'

There's no movement, no reaction. Eyes closed, he continues to breathe, drawing in deep and steady breaths. Unwilling to wake him, I simply do as the nurse suggests. Taking a seat, I hold his hand and rest my forehead on the edge of the bed. It's not long before I feel it: the slightest twitch of a finger. Sitting bolt upright, I stare at his hand, willing the finger to move again.

'Up here,' he whispers hoarsely.

With a jolt, I turn my attention to his face, and my heart nearly explodes with joy. It's what I've been waiting days to see. His blue eyes are open, if a little fuddled, and he's smiling at me. His fingers close weakly around mine and I could punch the air.

'Love you,' he murmurs.

The words I've been craving to hear.

'And I love you too,' I murmur back, rising to my feet and leaning in to plant a kiss on his lips.

'I wouldn't do that,' he grins. 'My breath stinks.'

'And I don't care.' I kiss him gently, run my palm across his forehead and enjoy a few precious seconds lost in those blue eyes. 'How are you feeling?' I ask, sinking back onto the chair and taking his hand.

He seems to think. And then he speaks again, slowly, quietly, pushing out his words on separate breaths.

'Pretty much like … I've crashed a motorbike … at seventy miles an hour … and broken a few bones.'

He raises his eyebrows as if to say 'well, you did ask.' And I'm thoroughly relieved. He's definitely back.

'Sarcastic bastard,' I admonish him. 'Are you in pain?'

'Yes,' he replies archly. 'There's a tube in my penis … and you're giving me a hard-on. It's not good.'

'Seriously? All you can think about is sex?'

'Now that you're here.'

'You haven't been ogling the nurses?'

'Why would I?' His eyes twinkle for a second beneath heavy lids. 'I've got you. Besides, they scare the shit out of me.' He turns his head, carefully. 'That one there? A dominatrix. I'll lay money on it.' When he looks back at me, he's suddenly serious. 'Is Beefy with you?'

Jesus, he's laid up in hospital and he's still worried about that?

'Of course.'

'All the time?'

'All the time,' I assure him. 'And if it's not Beefy, then it's one of the others. Don't worry about me. Just concentrate on getting better.'

Fingers entwined, we stare at each other for an age, cocooned in a quiet bubble of love. My heart beat settles into a steady rhythm, almost matching the beeps from his monitor.

'It's going to take a while,' he says at last.

'I know.'

'I'll be in plaster. Arms and legs. I'll look like the Michelin Man.'

300

'No you won't,' I correct him. 'You'll look like the Stay Puft Marshmallow Man. Much sexier.'

He chuckles a little, and winces.

'Don't make me laugh, Maya. It hurts.'

And we slide back into the bubble. Without breaking eye contact, I reach up and smooth his hair.

'So, what about that leg?' I ask.

He lets out a breath of frustration. 'Another operation. Pins and plates.'

'At least you're not going to lose it.' I run a finger across his upper arm. 'It's just broken bones. They'll heal.'

'I know, but I'm going to be stuck in here for a few weeks.'

'It doesn't matter. We've got years ahead of us. I'm going nowhere. And you'll just have to slow down.'

'I don't do slow.'

'You've got no choice now.'

While his lips curl up at the corners, his eyelids begin to droop. He's clearly worn out, but before he slips away again, there's something I need to tell him.

'You don't remember the accident?' I ask.

He shakes his head.

'I was at work ... and then I was here.'

So I've been given a reprieve. The trouble is, I just don't want it. I can't keep anything from him, not any more. I love this man, and I'm going to be open with him about everything. Starting now.

'Dan, I need to tell you something.'

He lifts an eyebrow.

'When you got home, we had a row. I did something stupid.'

'I don't care,' he cuts in. 'It doesn't matter. I can't remember so it didn't happen. Every day is a new beginning.'

'But ...'

'Stop.'

He winces again.

'Are you in pain?'

'A little.'

'Should I call a doctor?'

'No.' He squeezes my hand. 'Listen. I'm sorry.'

'What for?'

'This.'

'Don't be silly. If anyone's got to be sorry, it's me.'

He shakes his head, grits his teeth.

'There's a rule in here.' He pauses, breathing a little more quickly. 'Patients get their own way.' Another pause. He clamps his lips together. 'I'm the one who's sorry ... and that's that.' He closes his eyes, biting back a grimace.

'You *are* in pain.'

'I'm fine.'

'No, you're not.'

'It's just the leg.'

'Then I'll get a doctor.' I press the call button.

'Wait.' He tries to move his arm, and flinches. 'I need to tell you something.'

He doesn't get a chance. Within seconds, a nurse appears, frowns at a monitor, informs Dan that his blood pressure's on the rise and summons a doctor. A decision comes quickly: an increase in pain relief and sedation. He won't make sense for a while.

'No, wait,' he complains.

But it's too late. Drips are adjusted. His eyelids grow leaden.

'Love you.' The words come out slurred. 'Always.' He struggles to stay with me. 'What you said ...'

'About what?' I have no idea what he's going on about now, and I get no chance for clarification.

'I heard ...'

He smiles dreamily. Drifting away into oblivion, his breathing settles back into a deep and steady rhythm. Within seconds, he's fast asleep.

***

After spending the best part of an hour with Dan, I decide that it's time to move. Leaving him with a kiss on the cheek, I make my way back to the waiting room and find Beefy pacing the corridor outside. He holds out an arm, stopping me in my tracks.

'Give him a minute,' he grumbles. 'He's on the phone.'

I glance through into the room. Clive's standing by the window, his back to the door, his mobile clapped to his ear. He turns, mouth open, eyes serious, and focuses on me.

'I'll do it,' he says emphatically. 'I've got to go.'

Ending the call, he stares at the mobile for a few seconds. Something's obviously riled him.

'Are you alright?' I ask.

'Yeah.' Roused from his trance, he looks up. 'Work. Problems with work. How's Dan?'

'He woke up. He was fine. And then they knocked him out again. His leg was hurting. They said he won't be waking up again, not today. Do you want to go in?'

He shakes his head.

'No point.' He gazes at the phone again, deep in thought. 'I'd better take you home.'

Chapter Twenty-Nine

'Is everything okay?' I ask, fiddling with the hem of the skimpy, flowery dress I've put on especially for Dan.

'Fine.' Clive keeps his eyes fixed on the road.

But it's not, and I know it. Taking a peek at his face, I wonder why on Earth he's so preoccupied. In spite of the fact that his best friend's cheated death, he's slumped into a mood. In fact, since yesterday's visit, he's hardly spoken a word to me, barely made eye contact. And this morning, the bleak atmosphere seems to be catching. Sitting in the back of the BMW and gazing out of the window, Beefy's done nothing but chew at his thick lips ever since we left Lambeth.

Unease prickles at my flesh as the car rolls into the hospital car park. In silence, we get out, scurry through the rain, enter the main building and wind our way through the network of corridors. Arriving at intensive care, we're informed that Dan's already been moved. He's now in the High Dependency Unit, whatever that is. Finally making it to the right ward, Clive leads me through a set of doors and, leaving the noise of a busy hospital behind, we're greeted by a quiet calm. We come to a halt in front of a desk, and a male nurse engrossed in a computer screen. At last, he looks up, questioning.

'We're here to see Dan Foster,' Clive announces.

A smile appears on the nurse's face.

'Are you Mr Watson?'

'Yes.'

'Brilliant. He wants to see you first.'

'What?' The word escapes from my throat before I can grab it. He wants to see Clive before me? It just doesn't make sense.

'He says it's urgent,' the nurse explains. 'He's a lot more alert this morning, but a little agitated.' He turns to me. 'And you must be Maya.'

I nod, mutely.

'There's a waiting room just here.' Rising from his seat, he skirts the edge of the desk and waves towards an open door.

'But why can't I see him?'

I get no answer. Instead, vaguely aware that I'm being side-lined, I'm gently urged towards the room.

'He's pretty insistent. He wants to see Mr Watson first … on his own. You'll be fine in here. Shall I get you a cup of tea?'

A hand comes to my shoulder, encouraging me down onto a chair, and I shake my head. I'm already drinking in a potent cocktail of panic and confusion. The last thing I need is a ruddy cup of tea.

I catch sight of Clive's face in the doorway.

'What's going on?' I demand.

He frowns, shakes his head.

'I don't know. Just wait there. I won't be long.'

'Third door on the right,' the nurse informs him.

As soon as Clive disappears, I pull my mobile out of my handbag and check the time. Just after ten. In the absence of anything else to do, I gaze out of the window, over a clutter of hospital buildings that seem to have been thrown together at random, and then up at the sky, a thick slab of cloud. I stare at the empty chair in front of me, survey the empty room, and check my mobile again. Twenty past. What the hell can they be talking about? Lost in a world of uncertainty, I muddle through the possibilities, but there aren't many: either Dan's checking up on the security situation, or he's remembered something. And if he has … I just don't want to think about it.

I check the time again. Ten forty-three. I'm about to join them when I hear the sound of Clive's voice in the corridor, a grunted reply from Beefy. My heart falters as Clive appears in the doorway.

'Can I go in now?'

He stares at me, enters the room … and shakes his head.

As if a fist grabs at my insides, a clenching sensation takes hold in the pit of my stomach. 'Why not?'

'Let's go for a walk.'

'I don't want to go for a walk. I want to know why I can't go in.'

His eyebrows furrow. Taking a seat next to me, he leans forwards and clasps his hands.

'What's wrong?'

He doesn't reply.

'Clive?'

He swallows a few times, raises his head. 'There's no easy way to say this.' Drifting back into silence, he gazes at the floor.

Beefy's appeared in the doorway now. His sharp eyes flash, watching me closely, and somewhere deep inside, the fist tightens.

'Just say it, Clive,' I prompt him. 'Whatever it is, just say it.'

He sits up, turns to face me, and finally delivers the news.

'He's remembered.'

It's a simple enough statement, easy to process, but nevertheless my brain refuses to take it in. I open my mouth, blink a few times.

'The row you had,' he goes on, his voice catching slightly. 'What you did.' He rubs a hand across his chin. 'Layla. He's remembered it all.'

'And?'

He pauses.

'He doesn't want to see you.'

My heart stops, and suddenly the world recedes.

'No.' I shake my head. 'He wouldn't do that.'

'Maya ...'

'This is a joke, right?'

'Why would I joke about something like this?'

He stares at me, ramming home his point with hardened eyes.

'Okay,' I push warily. 'So he's mad at me. He doesn't want to see me because he's mad at me. But it won't last. He'll calm down. It's just for now ... and then he'll calm down.'

'No,' Clive cuts in, laying a hand over mine.

'Then it's the drugs. He's not thinking straight.'

'It's not the drugs. He's clear-headed.'

'So ...' I've run out of excuses and there's only one remaining option. 'He's breaking up with me?'

He takes in a deep breath and nods. 'Yes.'

And either Clive's misheard or misunderstood, or he's completely lost it, because now he's making absolutely no sense at all. He might as well be telling me that the sky's green and grass is blue.

'Because of that?'

He nods again.

'Just that?'

He says nothing.

'It's over?'

No answer.

I blink again.

'Don't be ridiculous.' There's a smile on my face now, and I have no idea how it got there. All I know is the world's gone mad, and if the accountant side-kick thinks I'm about to give up on Dan, he's got another think coming. I'll never give up. 'I need to speak to him.'

I spring to my feet, but I'm not quick enough. Clive's already standing too. Grabbing my arm, he pulls me back.

'You can't.'

And then I spot Beefy: flexing his muscles, totally ready to do his job.

'I've already told Beefy not to let you in.'

'No,' I breathe, salt water stinging at the corners of my eyes. 'He wouldn't stop me. Beefy, you wouldn't stop me, would you?'

Without a word, he stands his ground, his expression rock-like.

Clive squeezes my arm.

'I know it's a shock, but you've just got to accept it. You've got to go. When Dan makes a decision, that's it'

Oh really? We'll see about that. I'm not prepared to leave without a fight and even if I can't talk him round, the very least I can do is give him a piece of my mind. And I don't care if he *is* laid up in a hospital bed. Through tear-blurred vision, I glance between the two men, wondering if I can dodge them and make a run for it, deciding that if I'm fast enough, I'll be able to reach Dan's room before they can stop me.

'I can talk to him,' I mutter, buying a little time to weigh up my odds. 'It'll be fine. I'll talk to him. He knows I'm sorry. He'll see sense. I can make him see sense.'

'No,' Clive insists. 'He's not fit enough.'

'Fit enough?' I spit. The fury's on the rise now and I'd better keep it under control. 'If he's fit enough to dump me, then he's fit enough to do it to my face.'

Clive shakes his head. 'He doesn't want you in there.'

'Why not? Isn't he man enough?'

'This goes deeper than you know, than either of us know.'

The time for stalling is over. I'm about to make my move. Steadying myself, I pull my arm out of Clive's grip.

'I'd better go then.'

He takes in a breath of relief.

'I'll take you back to Camden.'

'Don't bother. I'll find my own way.'

'Maya, be sensible.'

'Sensible?' I half-laugh, half-sob. 'Nobody else around here's being sensible. Why should I bother?' I pick up my handbag. 'I've had enough. And you can tell him that from me. I've had enough of his secrets and his mysteries and his shit. I'm out of here.'

I glare at Clive, waiting for him to move to one side, and then I glare at Beefy. Still blocking the doorway, he refuses to budge.

'It's alright,' I inform him. 'You can chill your beans. I'm leaving.'

Slowly, hesitantly, the beef monster steps back. And I step forwards. Spotting my moment, I drop the handbag, spilling its contents across the floor. Faltering for a split second, Beefy stoops to gather up the mess, and I'm gone. Hurtling at top speed down the corridor, I head straight for the third door on the right.

'Maya! No!'

Anxious calls follow me, but I dismiss them. Pushing open the door, I stumble into Dan's room and come to a standstill. Propped up on pillows, he seems pretty much the same as yesterday, all the tubes and monitors still in place, and suddenly I'm reminded that less than a week ago, this man was at death's door.

He turns his head and frowns.

'I couldn't stop her,' Clive apologises from the doorway.

He closes his eyes, turns away.

'Maya,' Clive pleads. 'I told you, he's not up to it. You need to go.'

I feel a hand on my arm and shake it off.

'I'm not leaving.' I hesitate, watching Dan, noting the fact that he's beginning to breathe a little faster. If the logical half of my brain was in control, I'd be backing off right now. But the logical half has taken a hike. 'If you think I'm just walking away, then you're very much mistaken.'

'It's over,' he mutters.

'Is it?' I march forwards, lean over him and place my hands on the pillow, one to either side of his head. I'm the one in control now and I'm going to make the most of it.

'Just go.'

'No,' I reply quietly. 'Don't you remember what I said in Bermuda? I'm through with running away and hiding. I'm through with denial and avoiding the sodding issues.'

'Maya ...'

'So, anything you've got to say, you can say it to my face. And while we're at it, you're an idiot. Do you know that? You're the biggest fucking idiot I've ever met in my life. Either that or the biggest liar, or both.' I take in a breath, knowing I should really put a stop to the ranting, but I can't. My mouth seems to have a life of its own. 'Because all that stuff you said – about loving me, about me being the one, about this being for keeps – it was all lies.'

He looks up at me, and I'm halted in my tracks. There's a sheen to his eyes and beneath it, a shadow of desperation.

'None of it was lies,' he whispers.

And I'm flummoxed.

'Then why this?' I demand, straightening up. 'All I did was contact your sister. And now you want to break up with me? After everything you said, you're going to throw it all away because ...'

'No,' he rasps, silencing me mid-flow. He's shaking now, visibly shaking.

'Dan,' Clive interrupts. 'This isn't what we agreed.'

'I don't give a fuck what we agreed.' He grimaces. 'I can't do it. Sit down, Maya.'

Suddenly floundering in confusion, I glance at Clive, watching as a scowl gives way to anxiety.

'I said ... sit down,' Dan repeats.

I falter for a moment. And then, feeling distinctly nervous under his gaze, I draw up a chair and sit by his side.

'Dan,' Clive complains. 'You're in pain. I should get a doctor.'

'Fuck the pain,' he answers quickly. 'And don't let them near me until I'm done.' He winces, taking a few unsteady breaths before he wills his body back under control. 'We haven't got long,' he goes on, talking to me now. 'The police are on their way, so just keep quiet and listen.'

'To more lies?'

'Do me a fucking favour.' He winces again, shifts slightly and gathers his senses. 'I knew what you'd done. As soon as I woke up, I remembered.'

'You did?'

'Yes. But I pretended to forget. It was a lot easier that way.'

'Then why this?'

Clearly exhausted, he turns to Clive for help. 'You tell her.'

'Are you sure?'

'Of course I'm fucking sure.' He closes his eyes.

Hesitating for a moment at the foot of the bed, Clive looks at the door.

'This wasn't an accident,' he begins.

'What?'

'Don't interrupt,' he warns me sternly. 'Like he said, we haven't got long. His brakes had been tampered with. That's why Dan couldn't stop the bike. That's what he remembered this morning. He wanted to tell me ... but I already knew. I took a call from Boyd yesterday, when you were seeing Dan. He just told me straight out:

309

he'd set it all up. One of his lackeys got into the garage, slipped in when the doors were open.'

'So that's why the police are coming?'

He shakes his head.

'Accident investigation. No doubt they've found a fault with the cables. They'll be asking Dan about his enemies ... and he'll be pleading ignorance.'

'But ...' I waver, struggling to keep up with the facts. 'You're not going to tell them?'

Eyes still closed, Dan shakes his head.

'You remember the threats?' Clive asks.

'Of course.'

'Well, they still stand. If we involve the police, he'll stop at nothing. He's made that perfectly clear. He's already shown us what he can do: Jodie, your sister ... and now Dan. The sort of people working for Boyd don't have a conscience. They'll do anything for money. You won't be safe. Nobody's going to be safe. We can't protect everyone, and neither can the police. I've already spoken to Foultons. They agree. No police involvement. Not yet.'

'So why this? Why finish with me? I don't understand.'

Dan's eyelids flicker and rise. Clearly, he's gathered enough energy to talk again. Levelling his gaze on me, he takes over, forcing out a quiet explanation between breaths.

'He wants to split us up, Maya. You know that. Everything he's tried so far hasn't worked. So now he's moved on to something else.'

'Which is?'

He pauses, eyes softening, and swallows. 'He told me to finish with you ... and make it convincing. Layla was the only thing I could think of.'

'And you just went along with it?'

'What choice did I have? It was only going to be temporary. Until we find him.'

'You had the choice to let me know what was going on.'

'Which is what he wanted to do,' Clive intervenes. 'But Foultons advised against it. If you two try to deceive Boyd, at some point, somebody's going to slip up. And look at the state of him, Maya. Can you really keep your distance?'

'She can do it,' Dan says quietly. 'I told you, she can.'

In an instant, every last scrap of anger dissipates, leaving me with nothing but a familiar warmth in my chest, as if my heart's about to catch light. I'm not being dumped at all. In fact, I'm being protected. And more than that, the man I love believes in me, utterly and completely. He trusts me, and I'm not about to let him down. Overwhelmed by it all, I watch as he blinks. Teardrops glisten in his eyes.

'Dan, no.' In a panic, I reach out and smooth his forehead with my palm. 'Don't you dare cry. I hate it when you cry.'

'Touché,' he smiles.

'I'm sorry ... I'm so sorry ... I've been so awful.' My own tears are flowing now, and I can barely get my words out.

'No,' he whispers. 'You just proved how much you love me. The last thing I wanted was to hurt you. I wanted to tell you. I wanted to ...'

'You just did what you thought was right,' I reassure him. 'It's okay. Don't worry.' I look at Clive, catching the warning in his eyes. Time's running out and we need to get down to practicalities.

'So ...' I return my attention to Dan. 'We have to make him think he's won.'

He draws in a breath. 'It could be weeks. Months. I'll have all your things moved back to Camden. You'll be shadowed. Nothing obvious. You'll still be protected, so don't worry about Boyd. I'll be watching you, every day. But you can't contact me.'

My brain fumbles.

'We could phone, text, write to each other.'

'No. No chances. We don't know what he's capable of. He's already got our phone numbers. He might be tapping our calls. And you can't tell anyone. Apart from the security firm, it's you, me and Clive. We're the only people to know.'

'Not Lucy?'

He shakes his head.

'But how can Clive go on seeing her?'

'I can't,' Clive interrupts. 'Our two worlds need to remain separate.'

'But you need to tell her.'

'The fewer people who know, the better.'

'So you're going to end it with her?'

He looks away.

'And this doesn't bother you?'

'Of course it bothers me,' he snaps. 'But she can't know and you can't tell her.' He turns back, his eyes boring into me. 'And don't let her go on the rebound, for fuck's sake.' He points a finger. 'I don't want her seeing anyone else.'

I'm about to tell him he's asking for the moon when the door opens and the nurse appears.

311

'The police are here.' He casts an anxious glance in Dan's direction. 'They want to see you now.'

'I'll stall them for a couple of minutes,' Clive announces. Moving to the doorway, he ushers the nurse away. 'And then we need to get Maya out of here.'

***

I rise to my feet, lean over and kiss him, taking in the softness of his lips. I have no idea when I'll feel it again.

'I love you,' I murmur, nuzzling my cheek against his.

'I know.' A hand comes to the side of my head. 'Be strong. Keep painting. Make sure Lucy stays on the straight and narrow. And put on a good show.' Fighting back a sob, I raise my head and find him looking up at me, deadly serious now. 'You'll need to see other men.'

'What?'

'A few dates. Make it look like you're moving on.' Even though this must be killing him, he gives me a smile. 'But no kissing ... and definitely no shenanigans. I fucking own you, woman.'

'And I fucking own you right back,' I smile through a host of tears. 'So what will you do?'

'I've got enough on my plate for now.' Arching an eyebrow, he nods at the splints, his mess of a leg. 'But when I get out of here, whatever you see, whatever you hear about me, don't believe it.' His blue eyes glimmer. 'And never forget – not for one second – that I love you.'

'How can I ever forget?'

His smile deepens. Eyes locked, we gaze at each other for an age. It's only when I hear voices outside the door that he speaks again.

'We'll sort this out, sweet pea. We'll find Boyd and we'll deal with him. And then you and me ... we'll have a life together.'

I kiss him again, suddenly aware that there's something else I need to do. The nickname's kicked my brain into action. With shaking hands, I unclasp the necklace.

'What are you doing?'

'I can't wear it. If Boyd finds out ...'

He reaches up, closing his fingers around mine, around the pendant.

'Keep it safe,' he breathes. 'Look at it and think of me ... because one day soon, you'll be wearing it again.'

Author's note

Thank you for reading my book! I would love to hear from you. You can contact me on my Facebook page:

www.facebook.com/pages/Mandy-Lee/424286884398779?ref=hl

Or on my website:

http://www.mandy-lee.com

I certainly hope you had as much fun reading my book as I had writing it. If you liked it please tell a friend - or better yet, tell the world by writing a review on Amazon. Even a few short sentences are helpful. As an independently published author, I don't have a marketing department behind me. I have you, the reader. So please spread the word!

Thanks again.

All the best,

Mandy Lee

Printed in Great Britain
by Amazon